THE LADY OF THE
Haven

A Novel by

Betty Thomason Owens

I0544871

Published by

Sign of the Whale Books™

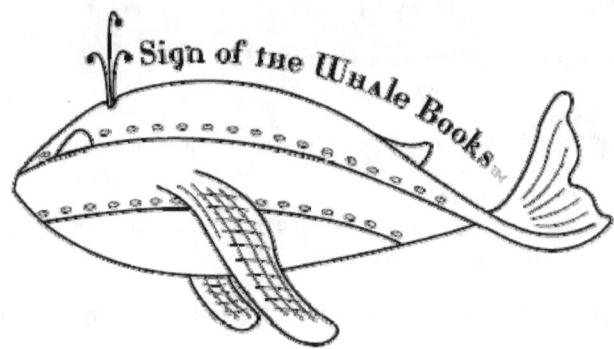

PUBLISHED BY: Sign of the Whale Books™*, an imprint of Olivia Kimbrell Press™, P.O. Box 4393, Winchester, KY 40392-4393
The *Sign of the Whale Books™* colophon and Icthus/spaceship/whale logo are trademarks of Olivia Kimbrell Press™.

Sign of the Whale Books™ is an imprint specializing in Biblical and/or Christian fiction primarily with fantasy, magical, speculative fiction, futuristic, science fiction, and/or other supernatural themes.

Original copyright © 2007. Originally published by AuthorHouse March 28, 2007.

Original Cover Art and Graphics by Debi Warford (www.debiwarford.com)

Library Cataloging Data

Owens, Betty Thomason (Betty Thomason Owens) 1953-
  The Lady of the Haven / Betty Thomason Owens
    274 p. 23cm x 15cm (9in x 6 in.)
Summary: Jael of Rogan, a young woman with a past shrouded in mystery, fights for a future with the Prince who promised to protect her.
  ISBN: 978-1-939603-20-3 (ebook)
  ISBN: 978-1-939603-21-0 (trade perfect) ISBN: 978-1-939603-70-8 (POD)
  ISBN: 978-1-425997-01-4 (trade perfect out of print)

1. Christian fiction 2. Christian fantasy 3. adventure 4. love stories 5. family relationships

[PS3568.O3475 0328 2007]
[Fic.] 813.6 (DDC 23)

The Lady of the Haven

A Novel by

Betty Thomason Owens

Table of Contents

Dedication

In memory of

Thomas Dean Thomason

My Favorite Dad

Verani Haven

𝕯arkness blanketed the haven as Jael, daughter of Jonathan Rogan, stepped through the hedge for the first time in many months. Ears attuned to every noise, her eyes scanned the paddock and its surrounds. Other than the roar of the nearby cascade, all was quiet. No one was about.

Wary as a doe, she crept across the paddock to the stone hut, built on an elevated foundation. Every round rock of the edifice had been excavated from the mighty Verani River's bed.

Swift and sure, she sped across open ground to the stone steps and up to the oaken door. Here she paused. How many months had come and gone since she'd last stood in this place? How many summers since she'd dwelt here? She reached up to touch the lintels where was carved the blessings. She laid a hand on either side and whispered the prayer. "Under thy divine protection come I, blessed going in, blessed coming out."

She lifted the latch, turned it sideways then hooked it to the side and down. The door gapped open with a soft screech. Jael slid inside and stood still again, listening. Nary a sound greeted her. Not even the scratch of a mouse. A quick look around told her the place was empty, except for the occasional spider in its web.

Removing a smooth flint from the pocket of her apron, she knelt on the hearth. But long since, the fire she'd laid ere last she left, had burned. Some brave soul had slept here. Someone unacquainted with the haven's reputation. No one from these parts would pass the night within the hut.

She wouldn't wish it back. She'd never deny a stranger in need of a warm fire, a roof over his head. With a soft sigh, she took up her scoop and broom and cleared away the ashes, emptying those into a basket. She pushed away from the floor, tied her shawl at her waist then let herself out the door and down the steps.

Gray light spread over the horizon in front of the dawn. Eerie shadows danced in the haven as Jael followed the path to a pile of ancient wood. Her mind traveled across the years to the sound of water rushing over the falls. Her da splitting wood while she stacked it.

"Have a care, love," he sang out. "Lest Grandmere must dig splinters from thine hand."

Though so long a time had passed, and both Grandmere and her da lay in the sepulcher, it was as though she could still hear the echo of his voice.

She pulled on her leather gloves and reached for the wood. Her arms loaded down, she crossed to the porch and mounted the steps then pushed the door open with the toe of her boot. Once she had enough wood to build a fire, Jael stepped to the porch. Here, she pulled open the shutters to reveal a wide sill with an inner set of shutters. She piled more wood on the sill, and closed the outside doors.

As flames danced on the aged wood, she turned her thoughts to a meal. There was never a shortage of trout in the basin below the falls. But she must take care, lest anyone see the smoke of her fire, and come to seek her out.

Her heart constricted painfully. How she longed to live here on her own. The place she loved more than any. Her home, passed down by countless generations. But she could never claim ownership, being a woman on her own, for women were not allowed to own land. And that was not the only reason she could never live here.

"Go away from here," Da had said to Grandmere. "Never let them find her." His voice still whispered on the wind.

With a shake of her head, Jael strode to water's edge and dropped onto her knees. Taking up a basket sieve stored beneath the nearby boulders, she lowered it into the water, and pulled it out again, a very pretty trout within.

She made quick work of its cleaning then sat back on her haunches and gazed into the waking light while thick fog billowed over the falls, pulled downstream by the current. A loon called, waking her from her reverie. She rose, the trout in hand, to go and cook her breakfast.

As she tread along the path, she sang the favorite song of her childhood. The song of the mighty. The song of the waters. She was still singing it at full sunrise, as she sat on her hearth, eating the trout she'd caught.

Thunder boomed outside the rock hut. It echoed on the great stone cliffs of Dolor. Jael had banked the fire to produce as little smoke as possible, and set an iron pot in its midst. The remains of the trout simmered along with herbs and a few roots gleaned along her journey. She had a bit of dried beef, but held onto that. She may have need of it later.

As yet, she hadn't discerned her purpose here. The leading had been stronger than ever. Why had God sent her back? Was it her time to pass on into the great beyond? Nay, she didn't think it was.

Not far from here, a battle ensued. She'd heard the sounds of it. Heard the cries of men and horses. Smelt the blood in the air. It stirred her heart to mournfulness. No doubt, the good king's men had come to hunt the magistrate. Again.

She hoped with all her heart they found him this time. And destroyed him. Pure evil, he was. He'd killed her own Da. And it was because of the magistrate, she could never stop running. Never live in the open, unafraid.

Jael shook those thoughts loose and turned her mind to prayer. She prayed for the king and his armies, for in her heart she knew they ran to battle. All day long, she sensed it, even when the rain poured down and the lightning struck all around. Thunder crashed. The Falls of Verani roared, echoing through the haven.

William of Coldthwaite sagged forward in his saddle, barely clinging to consciousness. With one hand, he wrapped the reins around the saddle horn. The other hand pressed against his ribs where his life's blood oozed out. He shuddered against the cold and wet that threatened to wring out the last of his strength.

"I must trust to you, Lodan," he whispered to his horse. "You may yet be on your own."

The horse's ears twitched at the sound of his master's voice, but he didn't stop, didn't even slow down, until he came upon the rushing water of the mighty Verani River.

William groaned at the sight as he clung to the saddle. The water ran high from the late summer rains; its voice raised even more by the narrows so close at hand. He gazed up at the towering, jagged walls of the Touri Mountains that closed in upon the river here and squeezed the waters into a funneling mass before dropping fifty feet into a deep river valley. Occasionally, a weary traveler stumbled into the drink, never to be heard from again. Would that be his fate this day?

Exhausted from battle, Lodan was unwilling to proceed into the dark swirling water. He snorted and pawed at the ground, then stretched his long neck and tossed his head, jingling the harness.

Nausea twisted William's gut as the world spun before his eyes. In the next moment, he drifted into oblivion, his fingers losing their grip on the saddle's horn.

Thick, soupy fog boiled over the falls and billowed up at its base, moving like a cloud over the mountains, borne by the wind. Jael stood in the open door of the stone hut, her head tilted at an odd angle, listening to the almost imperceptible sound of the fog cloud's passing. But it was not the fog cloud that had caught her attention. It was another sound, quite distant. Keen hearing, a trait passed down through countless generations of Jael's family, along with the unusual ability to see great distances had saved her life time and again. Today, she hoped to save another's.

She threw a dark cape over her shoulders and slipped quietly down the steps, out to the bank of the river. It was wide and shallow here, but violent due to recent flooding. She stood waiting and listening, for a good quarter hour then stepped onto a rock. She crouched there upon the rock and at the slightest change in the water's voice, jumped in. Her hands found the object that her ears had heard, a solid mass, giving off little warmth. Her heart beat wildly as she towed the lifeless form toward the shore.

Safe on the bank, she fell to her knees beside the body, and pressed her ear to his chest. With her fingertips, she found the slightest pulse at the base of his neck. She gripped his wet garments and pulled steadily until she reached the steps leading up to the porch of the hut. There, she stopped and sat upon the top step. She reached down, slipped both her arms beneath the man's, and pulled until he was at a place where she could drag him up onto the porch.

Throughout all of this, he had not stirred, had not uttered a sound. She feared all her work may be for naught. To her remembrance, no one had ever survived a fall from Verani Heights.

Once inside the house, she left him to build up the fire. After tossing a few dry sticks on the embers to coax it back to life, she knelt again beside him and began a careful examination. She found several injuries, some quite grievous.

"How have you survived?" Jael spoke the words aloud, though she knew he couldn't hear her. She fed the fire several sturdy logs then reached for the kettle, and poured hot water over a mixture of herbs. While the herbs simmered, she made up a pan of warm water with which to cleanse the wounds. She carefully stripped away his garments and covered him with a warm quilt.

By lamplight, she stitched up one of the lacerations with the same swift skill that had created countless sails for the fishing vessels harbored in the cove below. With a fresh cloth soaked in the herbal tisane, she dabbed at each of the wounds. A thick salve and clean bandages finished the work.

She carried the soiled water to the door and opened it. Just as she drew back to toss out the water, her eyes focused on a swiftly moving form near the river's edge. She set down the pan of water and threw on her cloak once more.

Outside, she stood on the top step and watched as the dark shape drew to a halt, sniffing the ground near the place where she'd rescued the warrior. The tall and very handsome stallion tossed his head and snorted before turning his eyes on her. She watched him for several moments. He tossed his head again, jingling the metal of his bridle. She approached with caution, not wishing to startle him, for she suspected he belonged to her patient. She held out her hand. He set his nose in it and sniffed. She smoothed a palm down his neck and along his back to the saddle. He was hot from a run. She had no doubt he had followed his master.

Gripping the reins, she led him to the barn behind the house, speaking softly in a low, even voice—words in an ancient tongue—soothing words to calm him. *"O tre mis corinor, se din a domior,"* Be settled my friend, all is well. Taking a dried apple rind from her pocket, she offered it to him. He took it hungrily. As he munched the treat, she removed his saddle, the saddlebags, and bedroll. She stowed those items until later then wiped the horse down, threw a fresh blanket over him, and led him to a stall.

After she had fed and watered the horse, she brought out a small handcart to carry the gear back to the house. If someone were to find such an animal in her possession, they would know it must belong to a warrior. The man in her front room was from a distant land, and he would no doubt be hunted. If his enemies sought him, she would need to keep him safe. Therefore, she must hide his belongings.

There were many secrets in Verani Haven. The false wall in the front room of the stone hut was one of them. Jael moved a narrow table from in front of an ancient tapestry that hung on the wall. Then she reached behind the wall-hanging and pulled a latch to release a door. She tucked the tapestry back out of the way, and began moving the man's belongings inside. Until she came to the saddlebags. They intrigued her. Should she go through them, find out what he kept within? She weighed the matter for some time, but finally decided against it. Judging by his garments, this was an important man. What his personal things contained was none of her business. She set the saddlebags with the other things then closed the door, replaced the wall-hanging, and slid the table back against the wall.

After returning the cart to the barn, she checked on her patient, still unconscious, but at ease. She drew the quilt tightly about him and tucked the corners beneath. She knelt beside him. He was familiar to her, though she had never actually seen him. She smoothed the matted hair away from his bearded face. Questions churned in her spirit. What color were his eyes? What language does he speak? How had he come to her here?

And then she knew exactly why she'd had to return to the haven. She'd come for him.

The Disappearing Trail

Jael stirred the stew ever simmering on the back of the fire. She prepared another herbal mixture; an ancient recipe passed from the generations. With this, she made a weak tea and spooned it into the man's mouth. Most of it came back out again, but she believed he had taken enough to do some good.

With her own comb, she worked out the tangles in his hair. She cleansed his face and beard. Though bruised and still a little swollen, she could tell he was a handsome man. Crinkles at the corners of his eyes suggested he liked to smile. She imagined him waking to smile at her. Or would he throw back his head and laugh at such a one as she?

She stood and pressed her open palms against the small of her back and arched it, letting her weary head fall back. Then she pushed the loose tendrils of her flaxen hair back into place. She'd fashioned it into a single braid then wound it around her head. It resembled a golden crown or a halo, as her late father liked to say.

As a night bird's voice echoed across the water, Jael prepared for bed. She lay down and slept, ever mindful of the sounds from the pallet on the floor beside the fire. Every so often, her eyes fluttered open to check the motionless form outlined against the glowing embers. Several times during that long first night, he moaned. She thought perhaps he dreamed or suffered from his injuries.

In the gray light of dawn, she crept to his side, checking once again for breath and heart sounds. She built up the fire and started the day's bread. After adding starter to the dough, she forced a little more liquid down the man's throat. She checked his wounds for sign of infection and changed the soiled bandages.

On the second day since the warrior's arrival, Jael rose early in answer to a troubling dream. She went to the barn and moved the stallion, leading him down a path to what appeared to be a solid row of bramble bushes. She disappeared within, following a hidden path known by none but her.

In a small grove of hickory nut trees, she loosed the stallion. The grove opened up revealing a confined meadow, fed by a babbling brook. Here, the horse would be safe, and have all he needed.

She spoke to him in the ancient tongue, "Remain here until I come for you." Then she patted his head, and fed him another dried apple rind ere she left. As she emerged from the thicket, she stopped and listened. Her sharp ears found nothing alarming, so she continued on her way.

After three days, her patient began to stir. She stayed close by him, keeping watch over him. As she worked, she sang the ancient psalm. The song of the mighty.

> *Ascribe to Jehovah, ye sons of the mighty,*
> *Ascribe to Jehovah honour and strength.*
> *Ascribe to Jehovah the honour of His name,*
> *Bow yourselves to Jehovah,*
> *In the beauty of holiness.*
> *The voice of Jehovah is on the waters,*
> *The God of glory hath thundered,*
> *Jehovah is on many waters.*
> *The voice of Jehovah is powerful,*
> *The voice of Jehovah is majestic.^{i}*

As she gave herself over to the song, her voice rose. She sensed she was being watched and sent a glance to the face of the man beside the fire. His eyes were open, observing her. She moved to his side, and knelt. Would he understand her words?

His brows knit, even as his eyelids fluttered. "Who are you?" His words sounded strained and weak. She moved quickly to bring tea. He must have a very great thirst.

As she prepared it, she told him, "I am Jael. This is Verani Haven. I pulled you from the waters."

"How long?"

She knelt again at his side. "Four days ago it was. You have serious injuries. I have done for you what I can."

His slight movement brought a deep groan. "Am I your prisoner?"

She smiled as she lifted his head in her hand and spooned tea into his mouth. He frowned at the taste. She mopped the corners of his lips. "Nay, my lord, you are not my prisoner. You are bound in the quilts for warmth only. I will loosen them, but you mustn't try to rise. You have stitches in your side you must not hinder. They may break open, do you move of a sudden."

He frowned again at another spoonful of tea. "What is this stuff?"

"It is a strengthening tea. You will need strength. I will prepare food for you when you are ready." She set the tea down and loosened the quilts to allow him to rise slowly. She propped him up with pillows. "I have never known anyone to survive the falls. You must be very sore."

"I am." After a moment's contemplation, his eyes widened. "The falls, what?" He jerked forward, causing more pain. "Verani? I went over the falls of Verani?"

At her nod, he lay back again. "It was not your time." Her gaze held his.

He squeezed his eyes shut and turned his head away. "Do not read my thoughts, dear lady. They are not good ones. I've fought a difficult battle and many men died by my hand. I thought my life was forfeit as well. No hope of salvation."

She touched his cheek to bring his attention back to her. "And yet you are here. There is some purpose for your life, my lord."

He opened his eyes to hers. "Do you know me?"

"Not specifically."

"And yet you call me, 'my lord.'"

She checked the bandage at the base of his neck. "I know of you. You are famed even to the borders of this land, my lord. I recognized the crest I found on your belongings, and ... I have your horse."

He sat forward again and grabbed his side in pain. "My horse? Where? Is he all right?"

She pushed against his chest until he had reclined again. "He is safe. I have hidden him in a place where he will not be discovered."

"He did not also come over the falls?"

She smiled. "No my lord, he followed by land, which is no easy task. Now, if you please sir, I will prepare a bit of broth for you. You must be famished."

"I am that." He relaxed with a sigh and grew quiet.

She wondered if he had fallen asleep again, but at her approach, he stirred. He lifted his hand to receive the cup of broth, but no doubt found his strength was not enough even for this small task. She held the cup to his lips. "It takes time, my lord. Your injuries were grave. I thought you would surely die."

He swallowed the broth. "You must be a good healer. What's in this woeful tea you've been feeding me?"

"It is an ancient recipe, sir, passed down from the generations."

A small smile quirked his lips. "So you are not going to tell me?" He scanned the room, his eyes coming to rest on the tapestry. "Is that also passed down?"

She followed his gaze. "It was a gift from a traveler, long before my time."

"A traveler such as I am?"

"Perhaps, why do you ask?"

"I have seen this work before." He took another sip of the broth then lay his head back against the pillows. "I am weary now. I will sleep."

She helped him settle again. It was plain he was used to giving orders and having them obeyed, so she left him to rest. Beside the fire, she prepared more herbs and let her mind process all that she knew of him. He knew her name, but she did not know his, only that he was of the royal house. He was no doubt King George Horatio's only son, heir to the throne at Coldthwaite, but she'd forgotten what he was called.

While he slept, she prepared her father's bed for him. When he was well enough to stand, she would move him there. Perhaps then, he would tell her his name.

As evening approached, Jael prepared their supper. When her ears picked up a distant sound, she rose and stepped out the door, leaving it ajar. Outside, she stood in the peculiar stance, thought by many as strange. How many times had they laughed behind her back, not realizing she could hear their every word?

She turned her head from side to side and closed her eyes, to discern the sound. Recognition stirred memories. She returned inside and straight to the back room. A moment later, she brought out a large fur rug and threw it over her charge, covering all but his head. He startled awake and stared up at her.

She laid her hand upon his shoulder. "Do not move, my lord. Stay perfectly still, and I think we will be safe." She turned to the hearth where she smeared a bit of white ash over her face. Then she covered herself with her cloak and rushed to the door just as horses approached from the west. She glanced back toward the fire. His disheveled form looked like a heap of bedding, as if she had risen quickly.

"Hello the house!" Came a shout from the yard.

She opened the door slowly and leaned heavily upon it. "Who goes?" She asked in a shaky voice.

Four horsemen sat waiting just beyond the porch. The man who had hailed her leaned forward on his horse. "The sheriff's men, woman! We are looking for a man who would have passed this way several days ago. He's quite dangerous and would be suffering wounds nigh unto death. He rides a fine black horse. Have you seen anyone like that?"

She drew in an exaggerated breath. "I have been quite ill, my lord. I have not stirred from my fire."

The man scoffed and cast a glance from one to the other of his men. "A healer ... ill? That's a new one on me! What illness fells a healer?"

His words revealed two things. He knew who she was, and he was making fun of her. Jael swallowed and lifted her head. "I tended a new babe over Fellsburg way a se'en-day ago. The infant carried a fever which passed to me. I do not approach you for this reason. The infant died. So also may I."

With frightened looks on their faces, the men with the leader slowly backed their horses away from the porch. The leader looked over his shoulder at them then turned his own horse. "I reckon you have seen no one. If I find otherwise," he paused to spit upon the bottom step. "I will return. It will not go well for you then, be you still alive, healer."

With his last threat ringing out across the waters, the men turned and rode away. Back inside the hut, she paused at the window and looked out. She saw them downriver, checking for tracks along the bank.

"You have vanquished them, dear lady?"

She jumped at the sound of the warrior's voice. She turned back to him and lifted the rug, tossing it aside. "For the time, my lord." She blew out a sigh then took up a cloth and wiped the ashes from her face.

The day after the riders' visit, the warrior was able to stand, though he leaned heavily upon her. He said he wished to walk to the window and look at the place. Once there, he gazed out upon the peaceful dark blue water, and sighed. "How I long to be home again."

"You live near water, my lord?"

"I live near the sea. Upon a high cliff overlooking it, actually."

She helped him into her father's bed and tucked the covers around him. "Are you comfortable?"

"Very much so, thanks to you. I hope I will not discomfort you much longer."

"You do not discomfort me. This is my father's bed. He has no use for it now."

"I see. You are alone here, then?"

"Since his passing." She would not tell him she'd been in hiding since that time. "It is unsure how long I will be able to remain in this place."

"And why is that?"

She looked at him for several moments before answering. She didn't know how to answer, actually. The truth might sound like a complaint, or worse yet, a request for aid. Her pride would never allow that. "I am the last of my line, and being a woman, the land must pass to a male relative. There being no male relative, it passes to the magistrate."

"That is unfortunate for you. But you are of marriageable age and fair to look upon. Why is it that you are still alone?"

Heat rushed into Jael's face. She turned aside. No one had ever spoken to her in this way. She drew a breath and slowly released it. "No man would want me, my lord."

"And why is that?" he asked, barely above a whisper.

Her eyes met his for the briefest of moments. Still, the heat rose in her cheeks. Why must she always blush? Perhaps if she didn't answer, he would forget and change the subject.

"You owe me an answer, lady."

"Oh. I ... my father was well known in these parts, my lord. As well my grandfather, and many generations back." She stood just inside the door, hoping to make a quick exit. "They were traders ... of a sort."

His eyes filled with recognition as he pieced the facts together. "Verani Haven ... you are the daughter of Jon Rogan?" She nodded, keeping her eyes averted. He smiled and settled back. "Then I am even more indebted to you than before."

Her eyes snapped to his.

"Jon Rogan smuggled my father out of the country many years ago. I grew up hearing the story of the 'disappearing trail,' dear lady. I have often wished to see it."

She pushed through a sudden shyness to offer him a smile. "Oh you shall, sir, as soon as you are able." With that, she quickly left the room, her heart fluttering wildly. Once again, she'd forgotten to ask his name. Oh, he discomforted her. She was skittish and nervous as an untrained colt. Never in her life had she felt thus.

To calm her roiling insides, she raised her voice and sang the song of the mighty waters as she cleaned the hearth.

By the end of the week, Jael's patient was strong enough to sit up. He came to the table and she served him a hearty meal of fish and bread. "You look much better today," she told him.

He pushed a strand of hair off his forehead. "I feel much better. I hope to leave you soon."

She nodded her agreement. Already, she'd felt a warning in her spirit. His safety was at risk. "I know you are anxious to be away. There is danger for you here."

He gazed at her for what seemed a very long time. "My concern is not for myself alone, but for you also. As long as I am under your roof, you are in danger, Jael."

"I know no other life, my lord."

"I think it is time you called me something other than 'my lord.' Please, call me by my Christian name." He smiled. "You probably already know it."

She was not familiar with the term, Christian name—she supposed it must be the name of the region from whence he came. "You give me too much credit. I do not know your ... Christian name."

He grinned at her, his hand on his chest. "You had me believing you had special powers. I am truly disappointed." He inclined his head. "My name is William."

"Will-yum," she repeated. She was not familiar with such a name as that. Furthermore, it was not proper for her to address him as such. So she called him, "Lord William."

This woman was a puzzle to William. Her bright blue eyes seemed always to be wide open, shining with intelligence and strength. She moved with grace and agility in well practiced motions, almost like a dance.

Well-versed in his language, she also spoke the ancient tongue fluently. She sang psalms in that language from morn till evening, yet she seemed unfamiliar with Christianity. She was shunned by her own people, but she would be lauded as a heroine in his region.

Though he longed for the day he could return home, he dreaded the thought of leaving her. What would become of her? He would offer to take her with him, but it would never do. His return journey would be perilous at best. Traveling alone would be the safest way to assure his return, and return he must. His people needed him. He'd been delayed far too long already.

He spent his last few days in the haven, walking about the house, restless. Under cover of darkness, he walked in the yard. Oftentimes, Jael would join him. Though standoffish, she opened up to him now and then. He learned she'd been hiding most of her life. Ironic, really. The Rogan men had given their lives to set the captives free. Now their very own kin, the last of their great family, spent her life in captivity.

Jael woke, a feeling of urgency nestled in her heart. Though she dreaded it, she trusted the leading.

He must be on his way.

She opened the secret room while he slept, and brought out his things. He found them, assembled by the fire when he came out.

"I see you already know what I am about to say."

She smiled up at him from her place beside the fire. "I am prepared, Lord William. As soon as you have eaten, I will take you to your horse, and then you will see the disappearing trail."

His eyes brightened as a warm smile spread over his countenance. "Ah, good. I have wished to see it. So I will be taking that path?"

She turned back to the fire to stir the tea, but also to cover any sign of the sorrow she felt at his leaving. "In the beginning, it will ensure you safe passage."

He pulled out a chair and sat. "In all these years, they've never been able to discover it?"

"Never, though many have tried." She allowed a smile to have its way with her. "The slave traders could never prove its existence."

"Your family cost the slave traders a lot of money, I'll wager."

She chuckled. "You'd win that bet."

His smile disappeared as he watched her. "But it has cost you as well."

For a moment, she gave all her attention to the fire. She served up the meat and bread and set his plate on the table. "It is a price worth paying."

William agreed. After a quick blessing, he began to eat. "So will I have any trouble following this trail?"

"It only disappears after you have taken it," she answered with a smile. "I will lead you as far as the trail extends."

He nodded his understanding. "I wish I could take you along. You are not safe here."

She sat down opposite him. "As I have said, I am used to danger."

When the time came, Jael led Lord William to the thicket. Quick as a wink, she stepped inside. William stopped and stared at the thick briars. He reached out his hand and received a puncture wound for his effort. "Ouch! What magic is this? What must I do here?"

She giggled. "Just step inside, good sir. The briars will part."

He raised his foot and touched the briars with the toe of his boot. They did not budge. "Easier said than done, I suppose. Is there some secret word I've neglected to say?"

From inside the thicket, her laughter rang out. "You must just take a step, Lord William. Surely a warrior such as yourself has more power behind him than that?"

He chuckled then grimaced as he pushed forward. The briars seemed to disappear before him. He emerged on the other side without a single scratch. "I am all amazement. How does it work?"

She folded her hands to hide their trembling. How she would miss him when he'd gone. "I have no idea. No one does. But no one ever questioned its usefulness." She stepped aside. "This way, my lord."

A frown stole the light from his eyes. "Can you not bring yourself to address me as William, even now?"

Jael dipped her head. "I would consider it disrespectful, my lord."

He gazed down at her, as if resigned to her way of thinking. "I would not go against your sensibilities then. Lead on. Where is my horse?"

Within moments, she had delivered him to his fine steed. And he seemed very pleased with the horse's care. "It's fat and sassy you've become, Lodan. So well fed, you will run long without complaining, I daresay."

Jael held Lodan's reins as William secured his saddle and prepared for his journey. She pulled a dried apple rind from her pocket and held it out to Lodan then rubbed his brow and whispered to him.

All the while she spoke to his horse, William watched her. "What is it you are saying to him?"

She peeked around the horse's head to look at Lord William. "I asked him to watch over you, my lord."

"Say it again in the ancient tongue."

Jael kept her eyes on Lodan as she repeated the phrase, just above a whisper. *"Se lunior le amistar mis corinor."*

He stood still, gazing down at her then bent to press a light kiss against her brow. As he straightened, he placed a circular object in her hand and closed her fingers tightly around it, his eyes never leaving hers. "If ever you have a need my lady, send for me. I will come to you. I owe you my life and more. I would tell you to come to me, but it is far too dangerous for a woman to travel those roads." He reached for the reins. She gave them up.

He stepped into place beside her. "Now lead me on."

Jael had not yet recovered from the pleasure of his kiss on her brow. She drew in a deep breath scented heavily of horseflesh and leather then turned north.

After crossing the brook, they walked in silence for several minutes. William looked back only once. The sight nearly stopped his heart. There was nothing there—no trees, no verdant meadow, no thicket—only the rocky riverbank, still and grey. What magic made this place? Jael walked confidently on, her steps never faltered. He could only admire her.

When they came to the river crossing where the trail ended, she stood aside. He was not certain, but it seemed as though her lips trembled as she spoke.

"Here we must part, my lord. I wish you safe journey."

Her bright eyes sought his and seemed to draw something from his very soul. What? What was it she saw there?

He mounted his horse and turned back to look at her. "So may it be with you, my lady. Go with God."

Lodan nudged her shoulder as he passed. Her hand upon the stallion's silky jaw, she gazed into William's eyes and smiled. Was it only a fancy, or did he detect unshed tears? On the other side of the river, he turned for one last look, but she was gone. She had disappeared.

Changes

𝕵𝖆𝖊𝖑 returned along the same path for a short distance then exited the disappearing trail at one of the ancient markers. These markers were set at intervals which allowed the user to exit at a place that provided cover. If by some chance there were any observers, she did not want to be seen coming out of the thicket. Nor would she ever want to appear to be coming out of a rock. That would definitely raise questions.

Whenever she was inside, she couldn't hear what was on the outside, one of the dangers of the passage. She looked around, standing still only long enough to listen. She heard nothing other than the distant sound of a duck on the water. She turned to look seaward. It was a clear day and on the horizon, she could see the harbor, which was a three-day sail by means of a good tailwind. With her keen vision, she could just make out a few bright, white sails there.

"'Tis a good day for fishing," she whispered. Then she remembered the object William had pressed into her hand. She still kept her fingers closed tightly around it. She unfolded them and found there the ring he had worn on the least finger of his right hand. It was gold with a small dark blue stone pressed into the center. Tiny carved hands held the stone in place.

Jael pressed the ring to her lips and kissed it. "God keep you, William," she whispered, wiping away tears with her sleeve. "No use in crying, Jael," she said aloud. "You've always been alone and always will be." But saying the words didn't make her feel one wit better. It didn't dispel her dreams, either.

She picked her way carefully along the shoreline, stopping every now and then. Anyone who may be watching would see her doing what she did every day. Long ago, most of her neighbors had branded her as crazy and she had no mind to change their opinion. They shunned her, but that only meant they left her alone. It was enough the women called on her when they had need of a healer. Folks weren't so choosey when facing sickness and death.

Back at the hut, she stood inside, casting her eyes around the dark and lonely room. She had felt thus only once, after she and Grandmere had laid her father to rest. She built up a lively fire and set the house to rights. When she'd finished, there was no sign of his Lordship's having been there at all.

There followed that day several sunny days of peace and tranquility for Jael. She sought the leading, but never received any, so she settled in for a time. She even discovered a few wild hens, no doubt descended of Grandmere's flock. She found their nests in the lean-to stable and gleaned a few eggs. These, along with the fresh roots she'd dug from the ancient kitchen garden, would add to her diet and help build up her energy.

The opportunity to spend time in her ancestral home was a gift, in Jael's mind. One for which she was quite thankful. The austere beauty of the cove always thrilled her soul. She used the time to prepare for what lay ahead, for she knew in her heart the end was near. Her life would change no doubt in an instant. She wished only to delay that instant. She loved Verani Haven, and never wanted to leave.

William rode, steadily climbing up into the Touri Mountains on the far side of the river circumventing the falls. Though he could not see them, he definitely heard the voice of the waters and thought about the psalm Jael sang daily.

> *"The voice of Jehovah is on the waters,*
> *The God of glory hath thundered*
> *Jehovah is on many waters. "*

"The voice of Jehovah is powerful, the voice of Jehovah majestic," he spoke aloud. His fine baritone echoed in the narrow chasm between the rocks. "The voice of Jehovah causes the cedars to shiver," he continued, finishing the verse as he'd learned it.

> *" ... And in His temple every one saith, `Glory.'*
> *Jehovah on the deluge hath sat,*
> *And Jehovah sitteth king -- to the age,*
> *Jehovah strength to his people giveth,*
> *Jehovah blesseth His people with peace!"[ii]*

By the time the shadowed mountain pass opened into a wide vale, the sun sat at the halfway point. William drew up beside a bubbling spring where Lodan could drink. There was green grass for the horse to graze and a man could lie down and rest.

His recent injuries still troubled him a bit. But he was blessed beyond measure to have his life and breath. He reckoned his close call was the reason he exulted in the beauty of nature surrounding him this day.

After a short nap and a bite of bread, he filled the waterskin with fresh spring water then mounted his horse. He'd a long journey ahead, but he was loathe to turn his mind to it. His thoughts remained in the mystical vale with a lovely blue-eyed lady. Did she think of him, too?

As Lodan carried him farther and farther away, the truth became apparent. He would not soon forget Jael of Rogan, the fair lady of the haven.

Jael was outside when they came. A band of men, looking no better than marauders, though she recognized them as valley dwellers. Her heart stood still within her breast. She'd had a bad feeling all morning that began as a dull ache in the pit of her stomach. As yet, they had not seen her, so she stepped back into the house.

With no time to waste, she pushed the table just far enough away from the wall to squeeze past. Reaching behind the tapestry, she unlatched the door and stepped inside. She pulled the door shut, then pushed her hand beneath a loose board and pulled the table back into position. She backed up quiet as a feather falling, pressing her body against the back wall. Her fingers found the leather pack that had belonged to her father. In it was everything she would need for her journey, if journey she must. She waited in silence, breath abated, listening.

Soon she heard the hoofbeats of many horses. Men's voices echoed in the haven. They were valley dwellers, all right. Their ignorant tongues tripped over the simplest of words, slurring and slanging the beautiful language of the southern regions.

"The witch must be within, for she is not without. My men has searched the place over."

A familiar voice rang out. "Bein' she's a will o' the wisp, she could be here, and ye'd not know it. Look agin. I'll go within."

This statement was followed by a loud crash as the heavy-footed man burst through the door. He stomped through the room, overturning objects as he went. He tossed aside the table in front of the wall-hanging then tore down the tapestry.

Jael closed her eyes, held her breath, and pressed her body even tighter against the back wall of the secret room. She could hear his heavy breathing. A moment later, the man stormed out the way he had come.

Her eyes snapped open. Dare she believe it? He had not found her hiding place.

"Did ye check beneath?" She heard him call from the porch.

Another shouted from the yard. "Ain't no beneath! It's built upon solid rock as ye can see. I say we set it ablaze and be done w' hit. She'll be downriver by now and chasin' after fireflies no doubt."

The man on the porch blew out an exasperated sigh. "Fools, all o'ye! It'll not be burnt until Master has everythin' outen it he wants. Set sentries to keep a eye on things till he comes. I must away. Don't let down yer guard, Cheek. She's wily."

Cheek—Jael knew that name well—one of the Magistrate's cronies. No doubt the Magistrate himself was the master spoken of by the head man. She was not about to wait around until he arrived in the haven. She sucked in a deep breath and released it slowly, so no one would hear. She'd wait until nightfall then make her move.

Cheek set sentries all around the haven and along the river's bank. He set up his own camp on the porch of the fine old hut. He smiled to himself as he roasted one of Jael's fattest hens over a fire. Long had he waited for this moment—to bring down the Rogan stronghold. Jon and his old forebear, Drudan had pilfered the hard won slaves of the river valley for years.

"All done in the name of their god." Cheek muttered as he bit into the roast chicken. "Takin' food from the mouths of our babes is what he done."

Slave labor had long been a way of life for the magistrate-ruled valley dwellers. It was the only way they could work the vast fields and grow enough food to sell to the mountain dwellers. They enslaved the former owners of the property they controlled, and when they ran out of natives, they spread to the settlements round about. So what if they sometimes infiltrated the mountains themselves?

So the children of the mountain dwellers labored in the fields that grew the food sold back to the mountain dwellers. Twas a way of life and it was good. He would fight to keep it so. He tossed a cleaned bone into the fire and chuckled softly.

After he'd eaten his fill, he lay back against the round rocks of the hut's front wall and exhaled. Sleep beckoned. What a good day this had proven to be. She was close, he could smell her presence. He'd no doubt they'd find her by morning. With the daughter of the Rogan as his prize, he could gallop home with his head head held high. He'd be loose of his debt to the master. Free.

$\mathfrak{A}$ waning moon was on the rise before Jael felt safe enough to leave. In the interval, she'd changed into the clothes from the pack. Men's clothes they were, belonging to her late father. They were a bit large, but she wound his belt around her waist and pulled it snug. She threw on a dark cloak, picked up the bag, and crawled out a trap door in the floor.

Beneath the house, she felt along the wall until she found a lever. She pushed until the rock gave way. It had been many years since this opening had been used, so it took all her strength to loosen it. On the outside, she closed the slab. After she brushed away all signs of its opening, she spread fallen leaves to camouflage her path. Under cover of darkness, she scanned the yard and beyond.

One sentry stood near the river's edge. Another sat near the old shed, but his head drooped in such a way, she knew he slept. She sighted another in similar stance. Apparently the man near the water was the only one left awake. She ran fast as she could to the thorn hedge and jumped through.

Safe on the other side, she saw the sentry turn just in time to see the corner of her garment disappear into the thicket. Times like this, she almost wished she didn't see so well. His brow furrowed, he strode to the place and considered the solid row of briars. He reached out one thick hand, tried to push them aside, but true to their nature, they tore at his flesh.

He jerked his hand back and swore loudly then whispered, "Must've been a waking dream, or else it was a bird in flight." Whistling softly under his breath, he strolled slowly back to his post, turning twice to look over his shoulder at the place where she'd disappeared. He shrugged and took up his stance once more.

"It was a bird in flight," Jael whispered from her side of the thicket. She closed her eyes and drew in a deep breath then set to doing the things that must be done before she could leave this place.

First, she dug a hole in which to bury her belongings. She laid her clothes inside. Raising her arms, she let down the thick braid that wound around her head. She loosed it and ran her fingers through the golden mass. With a heavy heart, she cut it until what remained of it fell just below her shoulders.

She pulled the remaining length back and tied it up tightly with a strip of rawhide. Tears streamed down her cheeks as she gathered the severed strands and laid them carefully over the clothing in the hole. She let her hands rest on the silken pile, mourning their loss a moment longer. Then she buried the lot and set a large round rock over the place to mark it. Taking up an old leather hat of her da's, she pushed it as far down on her head as possible.

Rising slowly, she stepped to the brook, where she found Peg, her old white mule. "Well, you are not exactly a Lodan, but you will do," she whispered. She saddled Peg, and tied on the bedroll and saddlebags.

The sky lit up with shades of umber and lavender as she set off along the disappearing trail, leading Peg. She didn't cross at the river, as she had instructed William. She must not attempt the same route, for it was treacherous and steep. Instead, she knelt beside the river's edge and removed her hat. Sweeping aside some of the pebbles, she dug her fingers down into the rich, dark sand and clay. She smeared the dark stuff over her face and up into and through her hair. With a kerchief, she rubbed at her face until some of the pigment set into her complexion.

In just this way, Grandmere had disguised her, so many summers back, to hide the child Jael from their enemies, bent on revenge. The memory tore through Jael, nearly pushing tears out through the corners of her eyes. She sucked in a deep breath, bracing herself for the road ahead.

Lastly, she tied the kerchief around her neck. Bending forward, she gazed at her reflection in the water then replaced the hat, pulling it down low over her forehead. She climbed up on Peg and turned upriver.

$\mathfrak{Far}$ away, where the land meets the sea, William rode into Coldthwaite, amid quite a stir.

Peasants came running out of their close houses and lined the streets, shouting and waving. "He that was dead is alive again!"

Though weary beyond measure, William sat tall in Lodan's saddle, riding all the way up to the crest. Here sat the grand, but weathered castle, the seat of government for the kingdom of Coldthwaite. The bridge lowered at his approach and several riders met his arrival. Among them, Eldredge, Captain of the Guard, and William the Younger, called Young Will, William's nephew, dearer than a brother.

"Twill be a celebration in the keep tonight, I'll warrant," Eldredge said as his master drew near.

William nodded a greeting to the men.

His face aglow, Young Will reached out to grab his uncle's forearm. The two stared long into each other's eyes. "I thought you had fallen," was all Young Will could manage.

"So had I you," William said, with a shake of his head.

After a long moment, Eldredge cleared his throat behind a balled fist. "Your good mother awaits, sir." The three rode into the castle, followed by two other riders, and the bridge was drawn up.

William's joyful homecoming was shortlived. He'd been home for only a fortnight when he packed to leave again. His father, King George Horatio du Frain, had need of him up the coast a three-day journey. The royal herds had been under attack and much good meat already stolen. This was a constant struggle in so barren a land.

A small band of soldiers accompanied William, which included his young nephew. On the morning of the second day, Young Will rode beside William, bent on chatter.

"I'll not part with you so soon after getting you back," Young Will told William. "This will be a fair journey, and the fight is hardly worth the trouble." He sliced at the air with his arm, as if he held a weapon. "You could waste them with one fell blow of the sword."

William laughed out loud at his nephew's antics. "Don't brag too much on me, old fellow. I may be losing a bit of my skill if someone was near able to bring me down."

"It was all luck on their part, or else your mind was on other things. I've seen you do that a bit of late. You've met someone, me thinks."

William tossed a glance at his nephew. He'd no intention of telling anyone about the fair lady just yet. She was his to keep within his own heart and mind. But he could drop a hint or two, just to torture the poor lad. "More recent than my trip down the falls, I can tell you that. She's a beauty in a wild sort of way."

"You were quite taken with her, I think. Why did you not bring her back with you? We could use a bit of wild beauty in these parts."

William's mouth twisted into a sideways grin. "I would have done, if the journey had not been so treacherous. It wouldn't do to leave such a one in a shallow grave along the way."

"Ah, so she has been assigned to someday for you."

William reached over to flick at his nephew's hat. "Alas, my dear nephew, it is the way of the warrior."

Young Will caught hold of his hat to keep it from flying off his head. "But you will not always pursue that way, I think. You must soon take up another way."

"I hope that is long in coming. I've no wish to hurry my father's death."

The younger man nodded his agreement. "Nor have I, but I was thinking you may want to get in the way of it before that time, settle down and make little princes."

William guffawed. "Now you go too far young Will. One of you is enough."

Will's laughter echoed in the wilderness. "But I am not of your own blood, milord."

An arrow zinged past his head, turning their attention to the task at hand. No more time for frivolity. Their quest had begun.

Tod Gudgeon's Caravan

Jael skirted the valley dwellings, keeping far to the south. She had no desire to meet up with anyone who may know her. As dawn approached on the second day of her flight, rain began to fall.

She drew her cloak more tightly about her. "We must ride through the rain and far into the day, if are we to make Touri Downs by nightfall," she told Peg.

She planned to stay the night near the downs, start up into the mountains from the south side on the third day. A long, arduous journey lay ahead of her, but it was the safest route. No one would look for her there. Who would expect a lone woman to make such a dangerous journey?

Near midday, the rain poured down heavily, forcing Jael to seek cover. She found shelter beneath a rock ledge by the side of the road. There was a pile of dry wood left by some thoughtful traveler, so she made a small fire and sat down. She brewed some tea, and leaned back against the rock to rest. Just before nightfall, the rains slacked off. She doused the flame and climbed back up on Peg.

The mule was usually placid enough. She never refused her mistress. But this time, something was different. The animal placed her feet wide apart and held her ground.

Jael sighed. "What is it, Peg?" She looked around then cocked her head from side to side, listening.

In one swift movement, Jael jumped down, yanking the mule's reins to bring Peg beneath the overhang. Thankfully, the mule obeyed this time, just clearing the open space when a large rock fell, followed by scrap and debris.

A landslide. Her heart thumping hard against her chestwall, Jael rested her forehead against the mule's flank. She would have to be more careful. Her senses must be dulled by anxiety.

Once the danger had passed, she led Peg out and down the hillside away from the rubble. Out of harm's way, she allowed the mule to drink water at a narrow stream, while she gathered her wits about her and settled her nerves. A half hour later, she and the mule set off again.

The small village of Touri Downs snuggled against the rolling foothills. A main road began in this spot that she had always heard led to the rest of the world. She'd never ventured beyond Touri Downs, so she couldn't really say, but it was difficult to believe a road could lead so far, for the world must surely be so much bigger than one could imagine.

As a child, she'd met a man who had sailed across the sea to a shining land of green grass and no trees. He'd shared their fireside and told tales of strange animals and men with dark skin. Things she could hardly imagine. She was about to set off on her own journey to a faraway place, only known to her in legend. The land of kings and warriors. Her heart constricted with an unexpected mixture of anxiety and excitement. For the first time in her life, she had no intuitive feelings about what lay ahead. It was a mystery she would need to solve.

That night she slept beneath the dense branches of a Holyoke tree along the outskirts of Touri Downs, within hearing of the river. There was another encampment near her. She listened to their music far into the night. When finally they slept, she rose and packed up her things. She wanted to get ahead of them if possible, to save herself the trouble of joining up with a group of mercenaries. She was too close to home and did not want to chance recognition and discovery.

The way was grueling, arduous for her and for Peg, but the mule plodded steadily on. They climbed into places she was certain only mountain goats had gone before. From time to time, she feared they would become hopelessly lost, but then she remembered the teachings of her father concerning the sun, the moon, and the stars. Within the first few days, their muscles grew accustomed to the new work. Both she and Peg became more agile.

High upon a craggy peak overlooking the river valley, after five days of steady travel, Jael rested. Peg had been weary after the difficult climb, so Jael picketed her in a narrow canyon where she could graze on fresh green grass. Jael gazed down at what had been her home for so many years. With a heavy heart, she strained her eyes to see it so far below. Now, it was nothing but a black sooty mess. A tendril of smoke still rose from its ashes. She brushed away tears with the sleeve of her rough shirt, and stifled the sobs that pressed so insistently against her.

Lying down upon her belly, she pressed her cheek against the sun-warmed rock. She lay there for a while, listening to the sound of the wind as it whistled among the rocks. She heard the gentle call of a sloebird, nested in the cliff below her.

"There is a time for mourning," she whispered, "and a time for rejoicing. What's past is past. With the help of Jehovah, I will not gaze back any longer. The time of mourning is behind me."

After a while, she sat up and began to sing. She'd not lifted her voice in song since the day she left the haven.

"I exalt Thee, O Jehovah,
For Thou hast drawn me up,
and hast not let mine enemies rejoice over me.
Jehovah my God, I have cried to Thee,
And Thou dost heal me.
Jehovah, Thou hast brought up from Sheol my soul,
Thou hast kept me alive,
From going down into the pit.
Sing praise to Jehovah, ye His saints,
And give thanks at the remembrance of His holiness,
His anger for a moment is,
Life is in His good-will,
Weeping remaineth til even,
At morn singing returneth. "[iii]

On and on the psalm went forth, its mournful tune transforming into a song of victory. The sloebird quieted as Jael's voice rang out over the mountainside. Her tears dried up as she breathed in the fresh air of a brand new day. She took one last look at her former abode then began the climb back down to the canyon where Peg waited.

In her heart, Jael knew this day would be different. Today, she would meet up with someone, but there was peace in her heart, no qualms about meeting them.

"Ho there!" A man sang out. "Who-do-ye-be, and where-do-ye-go?"

Jael sat forward and leaned upon the horn of her saddle as she had often observed her father to do. "My name is Jonathan, and I am making a pilgrimage to the far sea."

The funny little man's features were mostly hidden beneath a floppy hat, but Jael saw quite a lot of tangled brown hair, unruly by nature.

"Ho," the man said, propping one foot on a nearby rock. "That's a right far piece from here, dear boy. What makes you to fly over the mountains and on such a fair steed as this one?"

The man was laughing at her. She straightened her back. "Do you belittle my mule, sir?"

He stood up again, his hands on his hips. "No. I would never insult a man's mule. I'd sooner insult his wife. Take a load off, young sir, and join me for the evening meal if you will. I can offer a plain stew of rabbit and trail herbs if you don't mind."

Jael climbed down and gave over the reins to a small boy who ran up to take them. The boy trotted off with Peg to quarter her with the other animals. This was a motley crew of mules, donkeys, and assorted horses. Jael smiled at the sight. Peg would fit in quite well.

Before taking a step, she considered her place, and who she claimed to be. It was not so difficult to walk as a man when you'd been riding for so many hours and mostly uphill. But she must take care, be consistent, if she was to be convincing in her role.

Her host stepped forward and offered a gnarled hand in greeting. "I be Tod Gudgeon at yer service, young sir. That 'er's me least son, Dago."

A moment later, a tall, thin woman appeared out of the nearest tent. Tod swept off his hat, revealing a shiny, bald top. Jael resisted the urge to giggle. He seemed not to notice. "This here's me wife Obie, and a daughter or two be there with her. I know not how many there be any mores. Most of my sons done gone off to fight in the wars, and some may ne'er return. So is that what ye're a doin' son? Are ye goin' to war?"

"Eventually, I'll join up with my brothers there." She wasn't really lying. Weren't all men brothers? She licked her lips and continued her tall tale. "But first I wanted to look upon the sea. My poor late father made me promise I'd do that before I gave up my life to a lost cause."

Tod Gudgeon spat and wiped his lips on the back of his hand. "A lost cause. I hope not son. But I know what yer poor pa meant. He was loathe to see ye go, I've no doubt. Sit yersel' down now son and eat up this food. It's my bet yer hungry for home cookin'."

Jael sat down and took up the bowl Obie set for her. With caution, she sipped at the contents. It wasn't half bad. A little spicier than she liked, but palatable.

A moment later, a young girl brought flat bread. She tore off a piece and handed it to Jael with a slight bow. Jael lowered her eyes, and took the bread. She would have to be careful with her eyes. She knew they would be her greatest problem. She'd always been told her eyes were quite beautiful. Few men would have such eyes. She knew of no way to hide them, other than the broad brimmed leather hat, and a constant downcast look about her. How long could she keep that up?

"Tis Ruth, me least daughter," Tod called out from his side of the fire. "I believe she likes you, eh?"

Jael lowered her head even more and chewed on the bread. The man rolled backwards and laughed heartily. "Ah, he ain't got no time for sech, I daresay. Eat yer vittles then, young man then we'll smoke us a pipe er two before turnin' in. The day wanes and early is the dawn fer the weary man."

Jael shook her head at him. She had no desire to smoke a pipe. She'd much rather brew up a bit of tea. But she'd have to belay that until she was alone again.

"Ain't got no pipe?" Tod Gudgeon asked her later as he packed his full of dark leaves. "Don't smoke yet, do ye? Well, it won't do no harm. It ain't likely to stunt yore growth more'n it already is. What? That was mean I think." He chuckled at his own joke.

"Me ole man's a bit silly, eh?" Young Dago commented in a low voice. He had crept up behind Jael.

She nodded. "That he is."

"But he can tell a tale so well, ye don't mind it's been told so many a time before. It's what he likes to do whilst he smokes yon pipe."

Jael gazed at the young boy, somewhat the worse for his travels and covered in dust. Unlike his father's, the boy's hair was straight, the color of ripe wheat, and cut like a bowl. She offered him a shy smile. "I reckon you like to hear his tales, though they be oft repeated."

He nodded as he crouched beside the fire.

The fire burned brightly, causing wild shadows to dance on the rocks before them. Jael leaned back against her saddle and watched the scene as Tod Gudgeon lit his pipe.

"Ah now, what kin I tell ye this night, younguns?"

"Tell us of the bear, papa!" Ruth called out from her bed.

"Oh aye, that one." He gave a wide grin, his pipe clamped tightly between gapped teeth. He lowered the pipe and blew out a big cloud of smoke. "Twas many a year ago when I was but a lad. The village where I was born was small and poor. The fishing was bad that year. So bad the bears was starvin. My mam left me alone to watch o'er me little brither on the banks of the river whilst she scrubbed the clothes. Ole Jim, he was always squallin' and today was no diffrunt."

Tod stopped talking for a moment to take a long draw on his pipe then blew another cloud of smoke and let his head fall back. "His squallin' brought that bear on, bein' hungry as he was. He come a'runnin'. It was the biggest bear I ever laid eyes on--and mean. I let out a yelp and mam, she came runnin'. She was badder than any momma bear, let me tell ye. She hopped on that big bear and begun a beatin' it with her bare fisties. She kicked and screamed and scared the lively daylights outin' it. He took off at a gallop."

Tod chuckled and shook his head. "Folks never saw that old bear agin in those parts. My mam, she fell off into the water and come up sputterin' and lookin' all the world like a great whale spewing water from its blowhole. I fell over laughin' and folks that had come up to see what was the commotion, thought I'd died. It was funny, it was."

Though she knew they'd heard it so many times before, there was chuckling on all sides of the fire. Jael chuckled too, as she glanced from one face to the next. "Now, young master," said Tod Gudgeon, lowering his beady eyes at her. "What have ye to tell us? Have you some tale of a bold deed or at the very least, a funny anecdote?"

Jael shrugged her shoulders. What could she tell? She thought for a moment. "When I was but a lad, I lived upon the river's edge. Our home was distant from others and many stopped there to break their journey. A man came once who'd been to many far away places. He smoked a pipe too, but the leaf he smoked was red and smelled of leather. He had a red beard that fell clean to his belly and he told of a distant land where no trees grew. It was all green, covered with grass, and strange animals lived there. There were birds that didn't fly, and snakes that swam in the sea. I disbelieved it at first till he showed me pictures he'd drawn and feathers from the very birds."

It was a stretch she knew, but she hoped they would accept it. It was all she could think of on short notice, and the only thing that wouldn't give away too much about her former life.

"Likely, he drawed them pitchers from the dreams of a drunken mind," Tod Gudgeon observed. "But hit's a story all the same, and a good un, I'd say. What say ye, son?"

"I liked it, Papa," Dago said. "I've often heard of places like that."

"Yes, and I've no doubt o' that son. Ye always were a dreamy one. Well now, was that the will 'o wisp I heared? Ain't we better settle in fer the night?" Without waiting for an answer, he stood and tamped his pipe out upon a rock. "Ye may bed down here next to the fire if ye wish, young sir. Thet's where the boy likes to be, and he it is that keeps the embers glowin' through the night. He'd not mind yer compn'y I'll wager."

Jael wished for a stream in which to wash her face and hands before bedding down. But since she could not, she buried herself in the blanket and slept. It was easier than she thought it would be.

After a quick breakfast of cold bread and meat, the family packed up its belongings and set off through the rocky paths of the high mountains. Jael decided to stay with Tod Gudgeon and his family until their paths separated. This meant she would have to maintain her male image completely. So far, there'd only been one occasion when she'd had to turn her back, as the boy relieved himself at the side of a trail. She tried to avoid these situations. But she supposed it was all good practice for whatever lay ahead.

"Ye don't talk much," Dago said.on their second night sharing the fire. Jael's eyes fluttered open again. Each time she nearly drifted off, the boy thought of something else to say.

"I've never had anyone much to speak to," she whispered. "After my father died, I was alone much of the time."

"I don't like to be alone."

"That I know," Jael muttered.

"I heard ye singin' this day, earlier on our journey. What ye were singin'—it's God's word Papa said. Do ye be a Christian?"

This was only the second time she'd heard the word. First, from Lord William's lips, now, this boy was saying it. "I know not what that means."

"Ye don't know? Most everyone knows that."

"I have lived apart from most everyone."

"Well if I knew, I'd surely tell ye. Me Pa kin tell ye likely if ye should think to ask."

Jael had no doubt Tod Gudgeon would tell her, whether he knew or not. That man loved to talk.

When she finally had the opporturnity to ask, Tod Gudgeon told her Christians were people who followed the teachings of the Christ, who was God's son.

She had never even heard God had a son. She knew God as Jehovah, and had believed in Him all her life, because it was the way she had been taught to believe.

Tod Gudgeon pinched the bridge of his nose, as he often did when he was thinking on serious matters. "I don't hold no torch to them teachin's meself. I just know that's what tis. Obie's people follered it, and they's all dead, so I reckon it ain't the way to go. I done fine so far on me own."

Jael shrugged at his answer, not totally satisfied. There must be something more to it, if someone so well educated as Lord William followed the belief. She tucked it away in her spirit for another day. Someday, when she reached the region of Coldthwaite, she'd find out all there was to know about a great many things.

They were nearing the wilds of Touri now, which was a vast valley filled with black fir and scrub grass. In the winter it was nearly impassable due to high drifting snows and danger of avalanche. It was here her path would take a turn east and the Gudgeons would continue on to the northeast.

There was a certain beauty to the wild valley of black fir trees. She came to appreciate their shelter as well. The weather here was unpredictable at best. During the two days they spent there, it stormed just as many times. Wild storms full of hot lightning and thunder that echoed in your ears for hours. How she missed the roar of the mighty river. Even the memory of the sound comforted her heart and gave her peace.

Once again she allowed her mind to wander, wondering what the future held for her. It was difficult to adjust to this new life away from the haven. Here she could not feel the future. She had retained her excellent hearing and acuity of vision, but the other things had fallen away. She must say she missed them.

She said goodbye to the Gudgeons, after the second storm passed through. They'd holed up in a cave on the north side of the valley. Jael couldn't say she was sorry to leave them. Several times, he'd tried to give her his daughter.

If she could manage to steer clear of other people for a while, she could relax and be herself. She may even find a stream warm enough to bathe in. She'd give most anything for a bath.

Danger in Numbers

Her bath would have to wait, for soon after leaving the Gudgeons, Jael came upon what she thought was a small encampment of soldiers. She stayed well behind them, but she didn't trust them enough to chance a bath even when she found a suitable pool. She stopped near the pool, in case the band of men were merely resting and moved on. But they did not. At last she decided to circle around them.

She left Peg tethered to a banbury bush then crept to the edge of the precipice, hoping to get a view of this bunch. Yes, curiosity had gotten the better of her, but couldn't she make a better decision, whether to stay or to go once she'd seen them? After weighing the matter, she lay down on her stomach and peeked over the rocks.

"Who goes there?"

She sat up so fast, she nearly slipped and fell from the ledge she'd climbed. She steadied herself and turned to look down at the man who'd spied her.

"Er … Jon. I'm called Jonathan." She stammered then climbed down and stood gazing up at the scruffy looking character sitting on a grizzled horse.

He jerked his head toward Peg. "That yer mule yon?"

She gave a slow nod. "That's ... aye ... my mule."

"Don't get many visitors in these parts. State yer business here."

"Passing through ... I'm traveling to the coast."

"Ye come from the coast."

"Not the harbor ... the sea, I'm sent there by my family."

"The sea? What family?"

Jael froze. She mustn't say too much. What if this man was from there? She cleared her throat. "They're fishers. I'm a sail maker. They have a need of my services." She hoped this information would cause him to forget about the names. She was right. He was properly distracted. "Come ye with me," he said, nodding to the front.

She stepped carefully past his horse and walked forward. Her mind spun in circles, making it difficult to plan her next move. She swallowed hard. This could be the end of her journey.

The rider dismounted and strode to the place where the men sat around a roaring fire. A shank of beef roasted on a spit over the flames. The smell set Jael's stomach to growling. But when those men looked up at her, all thoughts of food flew out of her mind. She kept her head down as the man returned, grabbed her by the arm and pulled her forward.

"Jonathan, is it?" The man in the middle asked. He stood, towering over her by at least a foot. "Little bit of a thing aren't ye, Jonathan?" This was met by general laughter in the camp. Jael straightened her shoulders, but did not look directly at him, still worried lest her eyes give her away. "Look at me when I speak to ye, boy!" He reached up and knocked the hat off her head.

She turned her eyes up to his face. "Ain't no need to hide them girly eyes, boy. Dirty as ye are, nobody's gonna mistake ye fer a dame." Laughter echoed again. Jael stood her ground. "Ye on foot or do ye have a mount?"

This was met with more laughter when the sentry revealed the truth. Jael's jaw tightened.

"Lookit him! He's full o' spit and vinegar! He's ready to take ye all!"

"Let 'im try it," someone said, "It'd be the last time fer 'im."

A man still seated by the fire seemed the voice of reason. "Ah, leave the boy be. He ain't even got a beard yet. Jes fine face hair and lots o' dirt."

"And lovely yellow hair besides," the leader said, with a grin that sent chills up and down Jael's spine. He shrugged his shoulders. "Pick up yer hat boy. Then go and rescue yer lonely mule. Ye'll stay with us this night, so's we kin keep an eye on ye."

That was not a pleasant thought. With the sentry watching her every move, Jael had no choice but to comply. She picked up her hat and pushed it back in place, then set off in as manly a gait as she could muster across the encampment to the place where Peg stood, looking quite forlorn.

"Ye kin tie up yer animal here," a skinny youth whispered. "They's grass aplenty hereabouts. Don't pay no mind to them others. They's bored and lookin' fer fun where they kin find it. They just come in offen a run and they's full o' themselves."

"Is that different from the way they normally are?" To her surprise, the young man laughed. "Ye catch on quick, don't ye?" He thrust out his hand. "Name's Ferdinand."

She smiled and held out her hand. "Jonathan."

"So I heard. Sit and I'll spoon ye out a plate o' vittles. It's good meat, fresh from the fields below." He smiled as he passed her a plate.

She took it and ate hungrily. Though she'd had little meat in her day, it tasted good. After she ate, the young man showed her to a safe place to bed down for the night. "Them'll drink too much and ye'll be in trouble if ye don't take cover. Don't ask how I know. It ain't a pretty story."

She didn't ask. She didn't sleep either. It was a long night, but as dawn approached, the whole bunch of them saddled up and rode off. "Ye can come or ye can go—its makes me no never mind," the leader told her. She had not even learned his name, but she didn't care. She wanted to be free of them all. She said goodbye to Ferdinand and turned back the way she had come. She planned to watch and see the path they took then she would take another.

The other path was treacherous and steep. She had to walk most of the way, leading Peg behind her. At one point, she thought she may have to turn back, for the way seemed too narrow for Peg to pass, but the mule was determined. She dove through the narrow space, scraping her sides. The animal seemed pleased by her success and when they arrived at the edge of a stream, waded in and rolled in the mud.

"Just what I always wanted," Jael muttered, "a wet saddle."

It was not as pleasant a place as the one she'd passed the night before, but it would do well enough. Jael removed what she could of her clothes, without revealing too much and quickly laundered them. Then she sat down in the deepest pool she could find and washed herself. She dipped down into the cold water and wet her hair, cleaning out all the sweat and mud and trail dust. Afterwards, she lay upon a large rock in the sun. That sun would soon be gone, so she must take full advantage of its warmth. Rested and dry, she built a fire and hung her still damp clothes nearby.

There'd be no meat-laden feast tonight, but she caught a small fish and baked it over the open flame. She brewed a cup of herb tea and sat down to enjoy it. She spent that night alone and enjoyed every second of it.

A strange bird called. Jael woke to full daylight. She sat up and looked around. It was so unlike her to sleep late, but she had not slept at all the night before. She got up and stirred the fire. It had completely died out. She had no wish to waste time starting another, so she went to the stream and dashed cold water on her face and dried it. Then she took a breath and coated her face once more with dark mud. She pulled her hair back, and tied it.

By the time she was ready to go, it was mid-morning. Peg had seemed perfectly happy to dawdle by the stream, chewing water grass. Jael climbed on a rock and swung herself into the saddle.

She urged Peg forward. For now their path was level, but ahead she could see more craggy peaks. The mountains seemed to go on forever, in rows and rows, carved out of rock and sprinkled with snow. How far and how long must she travel?

The white mule's hoofprints left an easy trail to follow. Its shoes, fashioned by the last farrier of Dolor, held the man's mark, a circle with a triangle cut into it.

Dressed in dark gray apparel that closely matched his surrounds, Shinder crouched over the prints near a stream. He fingered the indentations, sniffed the dirt that coated his fingers. He squinted into the distance. She was close. Very close.

He rose, lifting a fingertip into the air then turned about, jutted his chin and sniffed again. Small, beady eyes peered out from the shelter of his hooded cloak. His lips moved, but he never spoke the words aloud. He couldn't risk it, even in this barren land.

He was the best tracker money could buy. Had a talent for finding the unfindable. He'd been following this one for several days. He nearly had her when she traveled with that fool Gudgeon. But then she tricked him by taking off on her own. He'd not expected that. He'd continued to follow the caravan for a good half day before he'd discovered his mistake.

It was her costume that had thrown him. Oh, she were a wily one. Shinder had his sights set on that boy and it wasn't her. Only when they broke away from the hard rock trail, did he realize his error. They'd lost the one set of prints. The one he followed.

He still maintained she'd be an easy catch. Unaware and foolish, she was. And she a witch with special powers. Well, he'd seen no evidence of it. Sang at the top of her lungs, unafeared. He'd show her what fear was when he had his chance.

The one who'd hired him made him swear not to kill her. But they never said he couldn't torture her. He ground his teeth into a grin and wiped his mouth on his sleeve. He'd an old debt needed clearing. He rubbed the back of his neck, remembering. With a surly glance at the lowering sun, he set off down the trail at as quick a pace as he could maintain and still keep an eye out for sign of her.

The Tracker and the Cobbler

Thankful for the rest she'd had, Jael rode along, humming a tune. That respite may prove to be her saving grace, for grace it surely was. The next few days would be trying indeed. She felt it in her heart of hearts.

She came quite suddenly upon the small village tucked away in the depths of the mountains. It sat upon the edge of the stream, and its main thoroughfare wound up a slope. Singing at the top of her voice, Jael rounded a bend seated on Peg and almost came off her seat at the surprise that lay there before her. She sat in her saddle, blinking her eyes and looking about.

Here and there, a native would stop and stare in wonder at what appeared to be a young lad riding a white mule and looking so surprised. Jael had to admit, she was a sight to behold. But did they not often have strangers pass this way?

A little girl giggled as her brother slapped at the mule's hind legs with a stick. Peg kicked high in the air and Jael came off that quickly, smacking her head hard on a rock. For a moment, the world spun around. Stars sparkled in the air. When she came to herself, she heard the loud sound of a child crying. Apparently, Peg had kicked him in her wild craze of panic.

Jael jumped up and ran to the boy. He grabbed his arm and turned away, but she persisted, speaking softly. "Tis all right, I am a healer. Let me have a look at your arm." Slowly, the boy turned and looked up at her. Sniffling loudly, he let her touch his arm. She felt the bones.

By this time, many more had gathered, including the child's mother, drawn near by her daughter.

The woman cried out, pushing her way through the mob. "Get yer hands off him!" She looked about, wild-eyed, screaming at her neighbors. "He's hurting my boy!"

"No, Mam," the boy told her. "He's a healer. He said so."

His mam took a solid stance over the boy, her fists on her ample hips.

"Sayin' and doin' is different things." She faced Jael. "Yer animal hurt my boy, so what do ye tend to do about that?" She looked at the others, and swung her arms like she meant to box Jael's ears. "We knows how to take care of such things in these parts."

Jael blinked up at her. The woman was at the very least, twice Jael's size.

The crowd murmured, and Jael wondered if they were about to lynch her. Then she noticed a small man with a kind expression on his face, making his way through the throng.

"Twas the boy's own fault," he said. "He was taunting the mule."

"He has a broken bone," Jael told the mother. "It must be set. Do you have a healer?"

She glared at Jael. "I thought ye was one."

"I am, and I can set the bone if you have no one you'd rather do it."

Iffen ye can, ye do it," the mother demanded. "We gots no healer here."

The kind man reached out to help the boy. "Here, bring him inside my shop."

Carefully, Jael and the man led the boy to a small wooden bench inside the cobbler's shop.

The man reached for a clean strip of rawhide. "Here son, bite on this. It's going to hurt."

The boy whimpered a bit and looked up at his mother who had followed them inside.

She shook a finger in his face. "Don't ye be lookin' at me, it's yer due. Ye did wrong, ye have to pay."

Jael knelt in front of him. "Think of a place you love to go, or perhaps something you love to eat, more than anything."

The boy bit down on the rawhide and squeezed his eyes shut. In one swift motion, she had the bone set. A slight cry was all the boy would let out before he fainted dead away. The cobbler brought a strip of clean muslin. Jael wrapped the arm and tied it into place. "You must let it stay thus for several weeks until it heals," she told the boy's mother.

His mother frowned. "How will I know? Will ye be here to look at it?"

Jael bit her lip and gave her head a shake. "Alas, I will not. I've a great distance to cover in so little time. I must move on."

"Dom can check it," the cobbler offered. "He's a smithy and he knows horses."

Jael agreed. "That will likely do. He'll know when the bone is knit. After that, you must be careful that your boy doesn't taunt any more mules. They can be quite unpredictable." She offered the woman a tentative smile.

"Ain't much good for mountain travel either," the boy's mother said, watching Jael closely. "Spect ye've found that out already."

"Peg's not so bad. She balks a bit at steep trails, but I walk then."

The woman laid her hand on Jael's shoulder. "Ye done us a good turn. If ye've a mind to stay the night, ye'd be welcome at our place."

"Yer place is rather full, don't ye think, Tess?" said the cobbler. "My wife and I can put him up."

"Reckon it is better," Tess answered, with a curt nod. "Cookin's better, too. Yer Ader's got naught but time on her hands these days."

The cobbler returned a slight frown ere he turned away.

A moment later, the door opened, and two stout men appeared, obviously the father and some other close relative. They huffed and puffed about then picked up the boy and carried him out. Jael winced at the way they carried him. He could be heard all the way down the lane.

When there was none left but herself and the cobbler, Jael made to go. "I'd best see about my mule."

"I'll go with ye. I have a small place, but there be room fer yer mule there. The name is Donol, by the way, and you are?"

She cleared her throat and tried to speak in a low tone, "Jonathan."

Donol looked at her, his kind eyes revealing humor and warmth. They walked to the place where Peg stood placidly waiting. Jael took the mule's lead rope and followed the cobbler through a narrow alley to a small hut backed up against the granite walls of the canyon.

She glanced at Donol. "What is it like here in winter?"

"Cold. The snow drifts down among the tall spires with little to stop it. No tree will grow here. But 'tis a safe haven in many other ways. We are hidden, ye see. Chance brought ye here or providence. We shall see."

Jael observed the cobbler as he reached for Peg's lead and turned to go into a small lean-to on the side of the hut, inhabited by a cow and a few chickens.

"Food is scarce here also, so the men must comb the high valleys for sustenance. But they keep us surprisingly well." He wound Peg's lead around a rail and helped Jael with the saddle. Afterwards, he turned the mule loose in the stall and provided her with hay and water.

Jael mulled over his words. Living in a place like this one would be a difficult existence, even more difficult than Verani Haven. At least there had been plenty of fish in Verani Haven.

Donol's wife Ader was a petite woman with white hair twisted into a tight little bun on the top of her head. She had dark eyes that had once been merry, judging by the lines in her face. She looked up in surprise when Jael followed Donol into the front room of the hut. Here it was warm and smelled marvelous.

Donol strode over and laid his hand on her shoulder. "Ader, we have a visitor—this is Jonathan—he's a traveler."

"Be ye the healer I heard spoken of in the street?" Ader asked in a soft voice.

Jael nodded.

"Ye are welcome here, dear."

Jael followed Donol's example and washed her hands. Then he showed her to a chair at the tiny handmade table. Everything in this diminutive space seemed made for very small people. But the food was a different thing. Ader served up a stew fit for a king, and the bread was the best Jael had ever tasted. She wondered where in the world the men found such things.

As the meal progressed, Donol explained. "The stew is not beef as ye may have noticed. It is elk, from the high mountains. They are as fat as any valley cattle, I'll wager. They feast on the summer grasses in the high vales."

"He's wonderin' about the bread, I think," Ader whispered. "Everyone wonders about the bread."

"The bread is made from a grain harvested in the high valleys, the same grain that fattens the cattle. Only my Ader can make flour as soft as that. She grinds and she grinds with a flat stone like the earlies did. Ye'd be amazed if ye could see."

"I'm amazed at the outcome, that's certain. It's all very delicious."

Ader looked at her husband, then back at Jael. "Ye be thin and hungry. Ye should stay a while and rest."

Jael met the woman's gaze. "I wish it were possible. I must leave soon. I have a great distance to cover yet."

Ader's sad eyes became sadder still. "It is the way of the young. They must always hurry about doin' this and that."

Donol ate in silence. After dinner, Jael made to help Ader with the cleanup, but Ader swept her away. "A young lad needn't trouble himself about the table. Go and sit yon with my Donol. He'll smoke his pipe and tell ye a story or two, I don't doot."

Jael turned to the fire, where Donol sat on a straight-backed chair, filling his pipe. Would he tell as wild a tale as Tod Gudgeon? No, she doubted it, but the memory brought a smile.

Donol paused to glance at her. "Do ye smoke then, son?"

Jael shook her head as she lowered herself onto a nearby stool.

"No? That's a good thing, it is. It's a bad habit, I think. But it's restful and it gives me sommat to do while the wife works." He chuckled and grinned at Ader. "She don't hear me much anymore," he said. "Her ears are not so good. Tell me ... has anyone else guessed yer secret?"

Jael arched her brows at him. "Secret?"

"Ader knew it right away. And I had already guessed it. Then when I seen that ring ye're wearin' ..." He pointed at her hand.

Jael breathed out a relieved sigh. Did he think she was royalty because of the ring? For a moment, she'd thought they knew she was not a lad.

Donol lit his pipe with a sliver of wood which he then tossed on the fire. He puffed until the tobacco glowed in the pipebowl then blew out a puff of smoke. His wizened gaze settled on Jael. "Ye be a female, don't ye?"

Jael's breath left her lungs in a whoosh.

Overhearing his question, Ader turned and looked at Jael, waiting for her answer.

Jael gazed from one to the other. No use trying to deny it. She nodded her head slowly.

Donol sucked in a deep breath and exhaled. "I thought so. What makes a woman don a man's clothes and go on a long and arduous journey? This is the question I must ask of ye."

"My life was in jeopardy, sir," she told him. "My own neighbors sought to kill me. For years they have wanted the land my family lived on. They'd do anything to get it." She was hoping this explanation would quell the cobbler's curiosity.

"But for this they would kill ye? What come of yer folks? Have ye no man?"

"There is no one save me. My good father passed two summers ago—nearly three now I think of it."

"And ... where is the man ... whose ring ye wear?" Ader asked haltingly, barely above a whisper.

Jael turned to her. "How do you know it is a man's ring?"

Ader's gaze slid to Donol before she busied herself with scrubbing.

"We've seen it afore," Donol told Jael. "A great warrior he was, come from afar."

Jael closed her eyes briefly. He had passed this way at some time. "He gave it me so that I may find him again, had I a need."

"And now ye have a need." Donol took a long draw on his pipe and sat back in his chair.

"Tis a long journey and many dangers lay ahead fer ye," Ader murmured.

"As well I know," Jael agreed.

Ader set her cleaning rag aside. "Ye'd best be turnin' in noo. I'll fix yer bed." She took a candle and went through a low doorway to an adjoining room. The room looked quite cozy. Weary as she was, Jael felt drawn there.

As she rose to follow Ader, Donol stopped her. "So I guess you are not really Jonathan," he whispered.

She smiled down at him. "My name is Jael."

The barest hint of gray shone through the window when Jael awoke. The house was already filled with the smell of breakfast cooking and the soft voices of its inhabitants. Outside, a rooster crowed, followed soon after by another farther away.

When she was out of bed, she found a set of clean clothes neatly laid out for her. They were men's clothes, too, but they fit far better than her father's. There was even a thick pair of socks. Her boots were missing, so she crept out to the kitchen in her sock feet.

"Oh, I knew they would fit ye well," Ader crooned. "Me boy don't need 'em no more, bless his soul."

"I'm sorry ..." Jael started to say.

"No, no ... he growed out of 'em, he did. He's off to war noo, but last I saw him, he was greater than when he left."

"And that was just his middle," Donol added, smiling brightly. "Yer boots was in disrepair, so I be fixin' 'em fer ye."

"Oh please don't trouble yourselves so. You've been far too kind already."

"It is what we do, lass. We show kindness to them what's in need. It's what the scrolls teach us."

Jael shook her head slowly. "God bless you both. Your works will not go unrewarded."

"Oh that we know," Ader agreed. "Noo sit yerself doon and eat whilst the food is hot."

She would not leave empty-handed either, for Ader packed a good-sized sack of food for her.

"The bread will last, though it hardens on the outside," Donol told her. "It gets a bit chewy, but it'll build ye up."

Jael bit down on her lower lip as tears threatened. No one had ever showed her such open kindness. How would she ever repay them? "I don't know how to thank you."

"No need, just be safe lass, keep to the main roads, and keep yer eyes hid. Ye'd best keep that ring out of sight, too."

Jael looked down at the ring. She hardly dared to remove it. She almost felt it had some power to protect her.

"Here—put it on this," Ader said, holding out a thin string of rawhide. "It's tough as can be. It'll not break." She helped Jael tie it about her neck. After Jael tucked it beneath her shirt, she bent forward and kissed Ader's cheek.

The little woman's face took on a rosy hue. Her eyes brimmed with tears as she swiped at imaginary dirt on the table.

Stepping outside, they met the father of the boy she'd helped. He held the reins of a small-boned mountain horse, a dappled gray.

He held the reins out to Jael. "It is our way to pay our debts, sir. And if ye've a mind, ye can leave with us. We be ridin' out within the hour."

"Twould be good cover fer ye," Donol whispered with a slight nod. "And if it be all right, I'll keep Peg here."

This was quite a turn of events. Jael blinked back moisture as the truth became plain. Jehovah had intervened, though she hadn't felt a direct leading. She rode out of the village in the midst of the crowd of men, going out to harvest their food for winter. She could ride with them until they turned to the high reaches.

Her heart swelled as the events of the past two days replayed in her mind. If she'd doubted before, here was proof she was on the right path.

By the time Shinder followed the mule's tracks into the high mountain village of Cairn, he was tired and in a fouler mood than usual. With all the foot traffic hereabouts, he had little hope of finding the shoeprints. His only hope was to find someone willing to give her up. Or give the young lad up, as she'd made herself out to be.

He reckoned a good twelve hours had passed since her arrival there. If she'd put up for the night, he may yet catch her. He watched the streets as vendors put out their wares for a market. He tuned his ears to their lilting tongues, listening for a hint of his prey. Before very long, he realized they were well aware of his presence for their tongues stilled. They cast cold glances toward the place where he stood.

Bah! Fool peasants. The whole lot of them was about as friendly as a devil dog, and the ground here was solid rock, making it impossible to track the stinking mule.

He slinked away, keeping his eyes peeled for a clue of her whereabouts. Just outside the village, he found a wealth of tracks, making for the high mountain valleys. He studied them long and hard, but found no sign of the mule's tracks.

Tired, hungry, and seething frustration, he set off after the mob.

Labyrinthine Ways

William stood atop a high, round rock looking over the tidal basin called Tibble. Just beyond that salty basin, green hills rose banking all the way up to the craggy foothills of Touri. He wrinkled his nose at the smell of the place. Dead fish and rotting seaweed.

"What do you see?" Young Will called from the basin.

"Naught but sea birds and cringies."

Young Will winced. "I hates them cringies."

"You'd best get to the grass then, I see one not a leg length behind you."

Young Will jumped up, skittering over the muddy basin to the grass. Those blue-tinged crablike creatures packed quite a wallop if they got their pincers near flesh.

William and the other men laughed at the sight. They all needed a bit of comic relief after the fortnight they'd spent chasing Brogies, a derogatory term for an indigenous black adder, which was what they called the local cattle rustlers. In other words, they were considered less than snake bellies. He smiled at the thought.

A moment later, he jumped down from the rock and joined his nephew on the upper reaches.

"Tis a bit late in the season for them cringies," Young Will complained.

William chuckled. "They smelled you coming and climbed out of their holes."

Young Will gave him a playful shove.

"That'll be quite enough of that young sir," one of the elder warriors called out. "I'll not have ye showin' such disrespect afore the men."

Young Will came to attention. "Sorry sir, I forgot myself."

"Shore and it happens," his captain said. "Ye give a mind to it henceforth."

Young Will held his attentive stance. "Yes sir, I will."

William eyed the burly captain. Solis was broad shouldered and barrel-chested with thick, red hair and a bristling moustache. And he was a stickler for maintaining respect among his men, especially where Lord William of Coldthwaite was concerned. Young Will's familiarity gave him trouble. William watched his nephew with a sense of pride. The lad took Solis' correction with grace. He'd make a good captain himself someday.

"It's time we were on our way Solis," he told the captain. "No sign of the enemy hereabouts."

"Nor seen I any, sir—I believe they've turned west, back into the wilder."

"No doubt feasting on our good beef as we speak. Perhaps we should just follow our noses." The men chuckled at William's levity. He scanned their faces. They were good men, dependable, and strong. He had confidence in them, which was saying a lot. They followed him without question. William tried never to take that for granted.

The day stretched long as they made their inland journey. The narrow canyons of Touri Deep stood between them and the high plateaus where the Cairn people dwelt. The Cairns hunted wapiti and feasted on a rich upland grain called ewt. They were a plain, sturdy tribe who dwelt in a tiny labyrinthine village on the south side of the mountains, as trustworthy as the rocks they dwelt in. For the most part, they kept to themselves, but had often given shelter and sustenance to William's small band of warriors, knowing they could expect protection from them if ever the need arose.

If the Brogies weren't such a lazy lot, they could well take a lesson from the Cairns. The caribou herds ran plentiful in the high mountain valleys. But it took skill and hard work to harvest them. He couldn't see the nomadic Brogies ever putting forth so much effort.

The warriors camped that night at the base of a high cliff, sheltered from the weather on approach from the southwest. The smoke of their fire rose through the mist, bearing a fragrant aroma of roasted meat.

Smoke rose up from the valley floor to Jael's sensitive nose. She was holed up in a cave near the crest of a high precipice. Her stomach growled as she chewed the last few crumbs of Ader's wonderful bread. She'd stretched it to a week's worth.

If only she dared light a fire, as that one had done down below. She sniffed the air. Smelled like roasted stag. "Och, rue," she whispered. "Not even a pool or a stream so I could catch a fish." These high regions were barren and dry, only affording a bit of scrub grass for the pony.

She'd been on her own for five days keeping close to the rock walls, seeking shelter often. She had the uncanny feeling she was being followed, so she'd made many turns and diversions. She was grateful for the gift of the mountain pony. He had proved his worth many times over.

She gazed out at the clearing sky and saw stars sparkling beneath cloud fingers. The moon yet hid behind the clouds, but she could see its light cast there. Where was the warrior this night? Did he ever think of her? Did he remember her kindness to him, as she nursed him back to health?

She fingered the ring on its leather strap then chided herself for her foolish wool-gathering. Even if he did think of her and remember her with kindness, he could never be anything but a friend. He was a royal and she was a commoner.

Not quite a commoner, her heart spoke the words. She reached far back in her memory. Her home and its contents hinted at a different sort of life than what she and Grandmere had lived. The very structure of the hut with its fine woodwork now reduced to ashes, had certainly been built by a master craftsman. But even as a daughter of a craftsman, she was cut off from ever marrying a royal.

A man could certainly elevate himself. By an act of bravery, or rescuing a royal, or even winning a royal contest, he'd be given a princess to marry. She'd heard of that. But never the other way round. Though she'd saved his life from the brink of death, she'd never be quality enough to be William's wife. So she must resign herself, and be content with her lot.

Just before drifting off to sleep, she heard a distant spate of laughter from the camp so far below. Were they the cattle rustlers from weeks earlier? "I must be careful to avoid them," she whispered, nestling into her blanket. She'd no desire to meet up with them again.

Early the next morning, William stood in the rain, cloaked in leather against the wet. He craned his neck to the top of the granite cliff, sensing something there. Of course it was still dark, he couldn't have seen anything anyway. But darkness didn't deter a peculiar feeling—a knowing in his gut—beyond his understanding. After several moments of watching and waiting to no avail, he went to pack up his belongings.

He and his small band of warriors moved out just as the gray tinge of dawn broke through the cloud cover. There was no levity this morning, just quiet hunkering down beneath their cloaks, occasionally shaking off the excess water. William prayed the weather would clear and make their journey less troublesome.

Even the birds stayed their songs and kept themselves hidden in the crevices. Only a quiet chirping could be heard from time to time, giving proof to their existence.

The rocks of the high peaks were slick and treacherous from the wet. Jael had taken shelter after only an hour's push forward. It would be foolish to risk life and limb for so short a distance gained. She lay wearily speaking to herself the words of the psalms she dared not sing aloud. She had not sung for some days, so real was the presence of the tracker. Though she'd not seen him, she felt him. Even thought she'd heard his movement at one time.

Jael knew exactly who followed her, for she knew the habits of Torin Dugold, the Magistrate. Even the memory of Torin Dugold turned her blood cold, raising gooseflesh on her arms. He was an ancient, obese man with a sickly complexion and tangled, dirty beard. He cared not for his appearance, but spent many hours of the day plotting evil against his imagined enemies. He hated even the memory of Jael's forebears. They'd committed numerous transgressions against him and his family by providing a way of escape for the slaves he kept.

The worst crime had been the intentional aid they'd given to his most prized trophy—the warrior king himself—though at the time, the Magistrate had not known who it was he'd actually captured. Jael had heard the tale told at fireside all her life. Dugold thought they'd taken an aristocrat from the mountain village of Cragmorton. When in truth, he had taken the Lord of Coldthwaite, King over the Southern Provinces. He was dressed as the Captain of the Guard, in rough apparel, to hide his identity. He'd been wounded and unconscious when the Magistrate's men overtook him. They carried him back along with the rest of their booty.

When Jael's father discovered the man's identity, he set out to free him and return him to his place. It was a costly voyage for her da. He would live with a crippling injury for the rest of his life, but as he'd told her many times over, it was a price he was willing to pay.

How she missed her da. He was a handsome man, as dark as Jael was fair. He carried a heavy weight of sorrow, for he never recovered from the loss of her mother. But he always had a smile for his only child. She never doubted his love for her. The memory of it still warmed her heart, even on such a bleak day as this one.

It was late afternoon before the wet tapered off and the sun and wind dried the rocks of the high peaks. Jael set off walking and leading her horse. Bone-weary from the long journey, she desired more than anything to see the end of these mountains. But as yet there was none in sight. She continued along through serpentine canyons and had nearly given herself up for lost again when she came upon an enclosed green space where a thin cascade of water fell from high above. It was beautiful and the sound came like music to her ears.

She decided at once to camp there beside the pool. Her horse was soon tethered in a grassy retreat to eat and rest. She waded into the shallow pool and found it rife with trout. Jael caught several, intending to smoke them over a low fire. But a distant sound brought her cautiously to her feet. She stood in the listening pose for several long moments. Even her horse raised his head and paused in his ruminations to listen and sniff the breeze.

She crept inside an opening in the valley wall to spy out the sound. Just below the enclosed vale, a string of ponies laden with merchandise moved slowly along a well worn trail. Thankfully, no one seemed to notice her. She counted five men of varying ages and sizes, undoubtedly merchants from some distant land returning with goods gained from the bounty of the mountains.

She heard them call to one another and could not understand their tongue, so stayed hidden in the cleft of rock, cowering in the darkness until they had passed. Not long after their passing, just as she went to turn away, she heard another step and turned back. Her blood chilled in her veins as she recognized the countenance of the one moving stealthily along the path behind the merchants.

It was Shinder, the tracker. His gray complexion and clothing blended perfectly with the granite walls behind him. She narrowed her eyes and watched his progress. He crouched beside the trail and studied the prints. He lifted a pinch of dirt to his long nose and sniffed it. Then he stood and studied his surroundings for some time. When his eyes lingered in the area of the crevice, Jael froze. She dared not even breathe until he finally relaxed and mounted his pony.

She waited until there was not even an echo of hoof beats before she ventured back to the vale. Darkness fell quickly there, but with the tracker's presence known to her, she felt safe no longer. She must think of a way to outwit the man whose name was used to describe an animal known to most as a ferret. He'd been given that name for obvious reasons, especially if you came face to face with him as Jael had, on occasion. He had sharp teeth and a long nose, dark beady eyes, and the innate ability to find anyone and anything he went after.

She whispered a prayer as she left the safety of the green vale, asking that God give her wisdom to know how to proceed. She lifted her fingers to the ring on its string about her neck and thought of the man who had given it to her. How she longed to see him, but she dare not even pray for guidance to him. Until she could lose the tail of the tracker, her very presence would be a danger to anyone with whom she came in contact.

Snagging a Ferret

As Young Will stood first watch on Sabbath's eve, his keen eyes picked up a slight movement. He'd been watching for some time when William moved near.

"What is it?"

"We are being followed." William looked, but could see nothing there. "Did you actually see someone, or did you catch his scent?" He whispered with a wry smile.

Young Will glanced at his uncle. "I've been watching his progress this last hour, milord."

"I see—any clue as to who it may be?"

"Nay, not a clue, sir."

"Let us send an interceptor then." He turned and whistled softly. Lodan approached.

Young Will stepped forward. "Not you, sir ..."

"And who best? With your keen eyes upon me, I shall have no fear." He mounted his horse and whispered, "Put the others on alert if you will." Then he set off down the trail.

William rode as quietly as possible, glancing up at Will from time to time. When he saw the young man hold up his hand, he stopped and dismounted. Then he moved forward on foot. He saw the tracker, crouched over the trail, his dark hand moving along, tracing the hoof prints there. When he glanced up, William ducked behind a rock. After a moment, William ventured to look again and found the tracker nearer than he liked. He slipped into the cleft of a rock and waited for the right moment.

$\mathfrak{Shinder}$ knelt over the tracks, examining each set in turn. At a slight noise, he lifted his head and sniffed the air. A badger waddled near at hand, fouling the air with its scent. He must be very careful, lest another come upon him before the air had fully cleared.

Shinder was well aware of a party of warriors ahead. He thought at one point, he'd come up on his prey, so drew back. He didn't like to be surprised. He would much rather observe the men first. It should be easy enough to see whether there was a woman with them. He'd identified what he thought were the prints of a mule, but it seemed to be a pack mule, so deep were the tracks.

This woman he followed was light of weight. Unless she was also carrying extra baggage, he knew it could not be her. He was beginning to believe she had obtained a pony or even a mountain horse, since he had lost her so many days prior.

If she had fallen in with a merchant train, she may have traded her mule for a better mount. That mule may now be carrying merchandise. It was also probable, due to the rough terrain, the mule was no longer shod with its original shoes. Which would explain why he hadn't found any tracks to match. It seemed to be the only possible conclusion. He could not have lost her completely. She was sly, but not as sly as he.

$\mathfrak{As}$ William watched the tracker, the man rose from his crouched position and stood looking up to the place where Young Will hid in the shadow of a large rock. No doubt the tracker sensed a presence there. While he was thus preoccupied, William got the drop on him. The tracker struggled, but to no avail. When William had him in an arm lock he asked, "Who are you and why do you follow a band of warriors in Touri Deep?"

Angry at being caught, the tracker spit out his ire, barely missing William's boot. William took a step backward and turned the man around. He fastened his hands with a rope and tied it to his saddle horn. He brought the tracker's pony alongside then mounted his own horse.

The tracker glared at him and tried to break free. William urged his horse up the incline, leading the pony and the tracker.

Back in the camp, Young Will ran up, took the tracker into custody, and pushed him to the fireside. Here he was greeted by severe looks all around and prevailed upon, none too politely, to sit down. William joined his comrades in questioning the man. Solis had a tight hold on the tracker's fur collar and bent his head back until they could see his eyes glowing in the light of the fire.

"What's yer business, sir?" Solis demanded. "Ye'd best say or ye'll not be leavin' here still breathin.'"

Shinder narrowed his eyes. He'd already scanned the camp. He'd not seen the woman he was following, but that was no certainty she was not hiding somewhere near. She knew him, after all. "I be a tracker, hired to find a prey. If ye have her among ye, ye'd best give her up. She's a evil one, not to be trusted."

Several of the men chuckled at his words. "Only a dimwit would think a band of rough warriors would have a woman along o' them," one of them said.

An alarm had sounded in William's mind at the mention of a woman. "Did you say, 'she'? We are warriors of the Crown, sir. What makes you think we would have a woman in our company?"

"Don't make no nivver mind to me who ye are. As I said, she's a evil one and iffen she wanted, she could be most anywheres."

William drew back. "So you've lost her trail then?"

The tracker struggled against Solis' hold. "I've not lost it. I'm just checking all the possibilities, sir. If not w' ye, she may be w' the band of merchants whose trail ye crossed back a ways. Ye did see them?"

Solis knocked the man in the side of the head. "We seen ye, did we not?"

William crouched before Shinder and stared into his eyes. "Have a look about our number, if you will, and see that we have none but what stands here before you. Any one of us is willing and able to take you out at any time. Not a one of us has a high voice, an unbearded face, or a rounded bosom."

This brought raucous laughter from his men.

William stood, still looking down at the tracker. "Now tell me of this *lady* you follow. You say she is evil. Let us decide if it is so."

In a low voice, the tracker growled out his answer. "Oh, it is so, my lord. She is a witch as it be—hails from the low valley beyond Verani Common—slipped away in the dark of night. None but the devil hisself could be coverin' her to gimme the slip."

William had come to alert at the name Verani. "Has she a name, man?"

Shinder narrowed his eyes and sneered. "Nay, I'll not be givin' ye that. She be mine own prey."

William kicked at the tracker. "I don't argue a right to her bounty, sir. I just want to know who she is and why someone seeks her so diligently. If she is so very dangerous, as you say." He looked toward Solis. "Loose the man, Solis, that he may better make an answer." William hoped to persuade the tracker through kindness to deliver the name of his prey. It didn't work. Shinder did not respond to kindness, only to more deliberate persuasion. William was also capable of that. He quickly pinned the rodent-like man to the back wall of the canyon.

"I know her only by the name of her sire. She is the daughter of one Jon Rogan and no fouler breath was ever breathed in the Verani Vale, sir. She has the same gifts as her old man and his afore 'im. Wicked they are, and devious—iffen ye get a whiff of her—ye'd best steer clear. Eye contact w' her will only get ye unpleasantness. A evil spell she'll set on ye quicker'n ye can pass water. You let me go. I'll come upon her soon enough no doubt."

William stood erect, but kept his hand tight on the smaller man's neck. His eyes sought an answer from the stars above, but none came. She was here—possibly nearby—and he had no way of protecting her. What could have driven her from the safety of the haven? What could have possessed her to come into the wilds of Touri? He released the foul little man and bid his men to secure him near the fire for the night. "Give him some supper and don't let him out of your sight." He turned back to Shinder. "We'll give you passage in the morning, but not before."

Shinder spit again, making sure to turn his head far enough to miss William's feet. William figured he had no desire to anger a warrior, if he had any brains at all, and he did have a certain degree of backwoods canniness. If he had his freedom while darkness still enshrouded, he would probably find a way to exact his revenge.

William hoped to delay him enough to give Jael a chance, though small. He strode quickly to his horse.

"Where do you go now, sir?" Young Will had followed him and stood watching as he mounted his Lodan.

"I ride ahead to spy out that merchant train. If I see no sign of a woman among them, I'll return quickly. Keep a close watch on that one, Will. He's dangerous if I'm any judge at all."

"Do you know the lady he seeks—if lady she is?"

William spoke quietly, not wanting anyone else to overhear. "Oh, she is a lady, nephew. I will explain in detail upon my return, when we are free of this vermin. Now I must be away." Young Will stepped aside, and William set out down the trail, illuminated only by moonlight and rife with shadow. It may be a fool's errand, but he must at least try.

He came upon the merchants' camp within the hour. It wasn't difficult. The noise alone led him to them. There was no sentry, which William thought quite foolish.

A pack of burly turbaned men sat around a large fire spitted with a roasting animal, drinking and singing uproariously as if they were celebrating something.

He circled the camp in the darkness and spied out all the inhabitants. He checked their mounts then still without drawing anyone's attention, checked each tent. Only one held an occupant who was snoring loudly. William stifled a chuckle. "Probably their sentry.

After having satisfied himself there were no females in the ranks, he strode into their circle of light.

"Hale there, comrade," one of the merchants called out. He was a round man with a large red nose. "Come share our fire and our bounty. We've roasted a goat on this most holy even. Though you are obviously not of our ken, and would have no knowledge of our holy days, we are inclined to share with whatever stranger shows himself at our fireside. It is our custom."

William gave a curt nod of his head. "It is a good custom. I'm glad to give you the opportunity, sir." He sat down among the very happy lot and took the meat offered to him. It was very good and so was the wine being liberally passed. He took only a sip, enough to wash down the roasted goat. He had no intention of joining their inebriated state as well.

After the feasting, the men took to dancing to a tune played on a paddle-shaped stringed instrument. William rather enjoyed the revelry. He took ample time to observe each one and satisfy himself that none was of the female persuasion. When he had completed his survey, he thanked the headman and took his leave.

"Feel free to share our fire for the night," the headman answered, laughing loudly. "I suppose though, you wish to sleep." He lifted a limp arm and made a circular motion, William supposed was meant to encompass all of his party. "They will eventually fall into some sort of stupor and quiet may reign. We'll not be on our way until the even tomorrow, when the holy day ends."

William thanked him again and moved away. He was anxious to be gone. No doubt, Young Will was most anxious for his return. He was met by that young warrior halfway along the trail.

"I was concerned for your safety, my lord."

"You need not have been," William told him with a grin. "I have feasted on goat and wine this even, and sung songs with a very strange lot. They are in the midst of celebrating a high holy day I believe. I saw no female among them for certain. I will rest a bit easier for that."

"Now fulfill your word to me and tell me of the lady, sir."

William sat back on his horse and thought a moment. "She is no witch, though strange she may be. She heard me fall into the drink above the falls then came out in fog so thick you couldn't see your hand so close to your face. She found me driven like a dead tree on high water. I've no inkling whatsoever how that could occur, for I was all but dead at the time. She pulled me to her fireside, though quite small she is, up so many steps to a high porch. I couldn't fathom it. I made her tell me it over and over, just to be certain."

He smiled at Young Will. "She is the daughter of an old friend as well, you see. You've heard of her father, though you didn't know him by name. He was the guardian of the disappearing path."

Young Will's head came up. He jerked so hard, he nearly stopped his horse. "You don't mean—he—the one who saved the king?"

"The very same—his daughter is the fair maiden spoken of earlier."

"Ah, the wild rose you spoke of upon your return."

William nodded. "So you see the need for my nocturnal excursion. I sought her out in hopes to find her before this ferret we have in custody. I did not find her, but perhaps we have given her a few extra hours to make an escape."

"But would she be traveling alone up here in the wilds? Tis dangerous for a man, let alone a woman."

"Of course it is. Only the direst of circumstances could have driven her here."

"Can we not rid ourselves and this fair lady of this vermin?"

"Nay, t'would alert a stronger menace and he would only send out more. She has avoided the tracker thus far." William took up his reins and urged Lodan forward. "May her powers serve her well."

Young Will turned his horse and followed his uncle. "She does have powers, then. But you say she is no witch?"

"What power she possesses is given of God, of that I am convinced."

When they arrived back at the camp, they found Shinder snoring by the fire along with the rest of their band, except the night sentry.

William and his nephew lay down upon their beds to see what sleep they may glean before first light interrupted them.

Wooly Winter

As the days grew shorter the cold mornings warned Jael she must make haste to find a safe place to winter. All her witless wandering had delayed her arrival in Coldthwaite. She couldn't put all the blame on Shinder. She'd been lost more than once and still wasn't completely sure she followed the correct route.

Wherever she ended up, she'd have to continue her masquerade. She was not pleased by the thought. But would it be possible to suddenly appear as a woman alone, and not bring suspicion with it? A woman with no family or friend save a prince and his father, the king of some far and distant place. A friendship her own dear father had forged. She was grateful for that hope. It warmed her during the dark days of this grueling journey. But it provided her no escape at the moment. She must keep her secret.

Now she had not even her old friend Peg to talk to. This witless pony she rode was ample for his job, but he had no desire for companionship. He did not even seem to listen to her as Peg had done. She longed for an animal like Lodan, whose loyalty had driven him to seek his master even to his own endangerment.

She smiled at the memory of the spirited stallion. Where was he now? Did he proudly carry his master still? She had no doubt of it. If only she could discern them—if only her senses were working properly—if only she could understand the deep pressure of her heart. The presence of the tracker, breathing down her neck kept her mind and heart so fully occupied. Her head ached from the pressure, and the constant searching of the gray sentinel-like columns of stone that marked this part of the mountain range as Touri Deep.

Seven long days later, Jael stood at the southern base of the Touris, where sat a rather odd village. It seemed to be carved out of stone. Its small houses were all built of that material, buried half beneath the hill they sat upon. According to the folks who lived in them, they were nearly impervious to the cruel storms that came at various times during the year.

Jael had heard tales told of this place. It was called Duflec, *stronghold*. Her da had told her of it. Beneath the hill, ran a deep spring. Caves provided storage to the harvest of their crops. They were a stout, muscular people, known for their steadfastness. It was here Jael decided to winter, could she find a safe haven.

Near the edge of town, she gained entrance to a cozy, warm hut inhabited by a very old woman. Enora Longarden had recently been widowed. She had great need of help to finish the harvest. Jael could provide that.

"It is providence," Enora told her. "I prayed ... for a sign ... and so ye have come ... before the words ... let go of me lips."

Jael spared the woman a small smile, wondering at the whispery sound of her voice. And it seemed to come in spurts as if she struggled to breathe.

Enora gave Jael a bunk in the barn, a stone structure half buried in the hill. A long narrow window was cut into the front to allow the flow of air in summer. With winter coming on, Jael searched the place for something to cover the opening. She found an old broken wagon bed and after gaining permission from the owner, made sort of a flap that could be fastened when necessary. There was a stone bowl structure in the middle of the barn where she could build a fire.

"It was for smithing ... ye know," Enora told Jael. "But ye may ... use it for warmth. Jest do take care ... innit, lad."

Jael hated to deceive so decent a woman, but she knew there was no other way. She spoke no more than necessary, worked hard, and ate little, not wanting to take advantage.

"I have a full ... harvest ... ye needn't fear," Enora said, noticing Jael's hesitation at supper.

Jael shrugged her shoulders. "I've never had much appetite."

"Ye look as if ... ye'd blow away ... on the wind. Ah ... we have such ... wind here."

"I'll not blow away, I assure you. I only need shelter until spring if it pleases you."

"Then and on ... if only ye would ... I cannot see ... what will come after."

Jael dreaded the onset of winter. Enora told her it came to this place with little warning. It blew in like a tempest and once the snow arrived, it wouldn't leave until spring thaw. The snows just piled up, one upon another.

She was constantly amazed by the stamina of the natives. How did people learn to survive in such cruel circumstances? Yet they thrived, existing on goat meat and milk and what crops they gleaned from the valley.

Jael dearly missed the mild climate she left behind so many miles ago. Was it thus where William dwelt? She only knew he lived near the sea. It must be cold there, she decided, for it could not be much farther away.

She spent her days helping Enora prepare wool for spinning. The neighbors brought a good deal of it to the elderly woman, knowing she had time to work on it over winter. When spun into fine wool thread, she knit it into sweaters and thick socks for the villagers.

"So they have done ... for years past," she told Jael. "I keep ... whatever I need."

It seemed a fair exchange. Enora loved the work and the lanolin from the wool kept her hands soft. Jael marveled at the woman's dexterity with the needles. She knitted scarves and sweaters faster than Jael had ever seen done.

Jael took up some of the rough work and stitched hems. This was something she knew how to do. Enora fingered her work on one of the sweaters.

"Ye have a way ... with the needle ... I see. What ... have ye done ... to make that? Do ye be a tailor?"

"I was a sail maker."

"A sail maker? Oh ... and marvelous ... it is ... the ships on the sea." She took a shallow breath and halted.

As Jael watched Enora work she began to understand the woman's breathlessness. She suspected Enora was breathing in bits of the wool and it was clogging her windpipes. But there was no help for it. She would never give it up.

She did like to talk though. As her knitting needles flew from stitch to stitch, she did just that.

"I seen the ships ... once ... out on the fair sea."

Jael's attention snapped to Enora. "Is it near here?"

"Ah ... it is some ... days ... or is it perhaps weeks? I have no ... proper recollection ... I was but a child."

Jael nodded, masking her disappointment with a smile.

Enora seemed not to notice. Her eyes had that faraway look Jael had come to recognize.

"There be a king ... he lives by the sea. Once he came here ... I did not see him ... but my 'Enry did. He ... told me all about it. A fair ... man he was, I believe ... a warrior."

"The warrior king?" Jael had oft heard this description of William's father, King George Horatio.

Enora nodded, her mind traveling back to a time so distant. "The Gatherer ..." She paused so long, Jael assumed she'd forgotten her train of thought.

"The Gatherer?"

"He will bring us together ... they say. He will unite the kingdoms ..." Enora looked at Jael, her eyes sparkling. "His wife is ... fair as the dawn ... I hear tell. Tis such a story ... how he come by her ... she was lovely ... he was ... so handsome. To my ken ... they did not know ... one another ... beforehand. There was a ... a treaty ... ending the war ... and the daughter ... was the prize." Enora grinned, showing several large gaps in her teeth. "Would ye like that, lad ... such a prize?"

Jael shook her head and made no comment. As a woman, she could find no fault in it, but how would a man feel? Would he not rather have a mate of his own choosing? A woman had not always that luxury.

Enora chuckled, punctuating the laughter with a cough as she often did. "If there is enough ... reward in it ... I expect ye would."

Jael shook her head. "If the woman was contentious or unsightly, the reward would have to be very great indeed."

This set Enora to laughing so hard she couldn't breathe. Jael was immediately sorry and jumped to her aid, but the old lady just waved her away.

"Och ... a good laugh ... clears ... me up fer a bit." She cackled often over the next few minutes, bringing a smile to Jael's lips.

Several weeks passed in similar fashion, with Enora spinning and Jael helping wind the yarn. By midwinter when the hard cold was at its worst, Enora insisted Jael stay in the house near the fire.

"Ye have not ... mortored me by now ... so I think I kin trust ye. Do not say nay ... to me. Ye'll freeze ... to death out yon."

Jael was only too happy to accept Enora's invitation. She'd been dealing, but not well. It was difficult to sleep when one was so cold and the room so drafty. The tight little house, on the other hand, was much cozier. Jael slept on a pallet near the fire, making it easy to keep it stoked during the night. And there was certainly no shortage of firewood. A seemingly endless supply was stored below the house in a cold room.

According to Enora, the storage room below the house led directly into a cave. "It opens on the river ... miles from here. Some of it ... is so narrow ... ye must crawl ... to get out. In the old days ... when trouble came ... the children hid down there."

"But did not the enemy know?" Jael asked. "They must have found the caves?"

Enora shook her head. "For many years ... twas a secret ... known only to us that lives here ... and we be a ... tight-lipped lot. Ye'll see ... if ye get a chance ... to know many of us."

Jael felt a bit more secure. If the tracker showed up, which she could foresee happening, she could escape through the caves—if she could find her way—without getting lost and roaming in the deep for the rest of her days. She shuddered at the thought of wandering in the dark for even a few hours.

Enora chuckled. "Rabbit runned ... over yer grave."

Jael glanced up at her. Had she been visibly shaken? She looked at her hands. They still trembled.

To calm her frazzled nerves, she began to sing in a low voice. She was a little afraid of giving herself away.

"Ah, such a ... lovely voice ... for a laddie. It minds me ... of my dear son ... he could sing. Go on ... please."

Jael kept her voice low and made sure to sing in the Anglican tongue, not the ancient tongue that seemed to get her into so much trouble. She sang a psalm of praise. Then sang the song of the waters, though it made her heart ache.

"Oh that one ... made ye think ... when ye go to the sea ... ye'll hear the mighty ... roar again."

Jael smiled through watery eyes. "I do miss it. It calmed me so to hear the water. It put me to sleep at night and woke me every morning."

"Oh ... aye ... and so it is here ... but with the wind ... instead."

Two days later, the two were working quietly on the wool when there was a sudden knock at the door. Jael froze. What if it was the tracker?

Enora rose and drew her shawl close about her, anticipating the cold draft. Jael pushed her chair further back into the corner wishing to disappear as much as possible.

"Ah ... I thought ... it may be ye." She heard Enora say and relaxed a bit. It must be a neighbor needing the warmth of a sweater or some other knitted goods.

"I come to check on ye, Enora. I heared tell ye had a helper this season, but I did not know were it true."

"Tis true, aye." She turned and pointed in Jael's direction. "That be young Jonathan ... over there ... working the wool. He's ... a good lad and a ... hard worker. I'll be that sorry ... to see him go ... comes the thaw."

As Enora spoke, a well-bundled form moved through the door. He looked like a giant furball. Upon entering, he peeled off a couple of layers of wool and revealed a shiny bald head and sleepy eyes. He nodded in Jael's direction. "Pleased to make yer acquaintance there lad, name's Thaddeus." He turned back to Enora then. "I come to see ye fer me eldest too, he's done growed plumb outta the shawl ye made fer him last year. He's a full foot taller'n before. Ye got somethin' made up already, or do I need to come back?"

Enora held up her hand. "I think I have ... somewhat. I'll be right back."

Thaddeus cleared his throat and moved nearer the fire. He held out big, dark hands and warmed them. He gazed at Jael for several seconds. "I come partways because they's been a stranger among us—another—not ye."

Jael looked up at him, her heart in her throat. Shinder.

Thaddeus hesitated. "He be lookin' about fer someone. A woman. Nobody knew of anyone new to the village proper. Not a woman, leastways. I only knew a ye, and ye be a lad." His brow lowered then rose as his gaze moved over her and back to the flames. "I reckon."

Jael sat very still.

"Iffen they's trouble and I know aforehand, I'll send word," he whispered. "Ye jes go below."

Did he guess her secret? Or was he just fishing? She bit her lip and nodded as Enora came back into the room.

"I found a good un ... it'll do quite nice ... I think." She handed a folded woolen cloak to Thaddeus. "Drink a hot cup wi' us ... be ye a mind."

"I must away," he told her. "I told me good wife I'd only be gone a bit. My boy is hankering to get out and needs proper cover. I be thankful as usual, Enora. Take care and ye also, young Jonathan." He nodded in Jael's direction and strode quickly to the door.

Jael wondered if his son really had such a dire need after all, or did Thaddeus only come to warn her?

Coldthwaite

William came home to Coldthwaite for the winter. Here, so close to the place where the Southern Sea flowed into the Northern Sea, the weather was mild year round. Farther north, great cliffs tumbled to the water and even the surf carried ice, but in the southern kingdom, a warm wind blew from the sea and beyond, in the land of great, wide deserts. It could be cold, but not frigid.

His Majesty, King George Horatio, William's father, preferred the milder climate. Of course he placed the blame on William's mother, the Lady Bethalyn, who bore it well. They were preoccupied this winter, having married off their youngest daughter.

With William's return, they had received wonderful news. The fair Lady Elizabeth was expecting her first child. Her husband, one of William's most trusted swordsmen, was quite proud of his accomplishment. He and his young wife were waiting out the winter at Corwinder-by-the-Sea, near the base of the Touri Mountains.

"My dear," Lady Bethalyn said to her son over dinner the first evening. "Tell me again how you found Elizabeth. She is well, you said?"

"Yes, Mother, she is quite well, and asked after you most earnestly. She was wondering whether you would travel there in the spring." He graced her with a bright smile. "She frets lest her confinement will be quite a bore without you."

Her hand fluttered to her breast. "Oh dear, I had not considered." She turned her eyes on her husband. "What do you think, my dear George?"

Her husband leaned upon an elbow and cupped his chin in his hand, thoughtfully stroking his short dark beard. "I think I can well do without you. Spring is a busy time. But after the holiday, I suppose you could be away for some time. Yes, I would hardly notice your absence."

William grinned to see the arc of his mother's eyebrows reach so far northward. He knew that look well.

Young Will was barely able to stifle a guffaw from his end of the table.

The slight noise drew Lady Bethalyn's attention away from her venerable husband. "What is so funny, grandson, heart of my heart?"

William nearly choked on a bite of bread. He quickly washed it down with a draught of wine and leveled his gaze at his nephew.

Young Will straightened, returning Grandmother's look with alacrity. "Not funny, Grandmother, endearing. How I have missed these times with you."

She held his gaze, brows still in their arched position. "Have you then? Well, it is due course, you know. You must grow up, though I would wish it otherwise." She waved her hand in the air. "No sooner is a child born than he begins at once to grow up then he wants to go away. When he is away, he wishes to be home again. Is it not so, William?" She looked at William.

He paused in cutting his meat long enough to smile at her. "Yes, Mother, it is so. I am constantly longing for the comforts of home."

His father laughed out loud. "I suppose this is why you have never thought to settle down, my son? Then you would have even more reason to regret your lifestyle. Following in my footsteps is a difficult path, I suppose."

"More than you know, Father." With a wry smile, he set to work cutting his meat then forked a bite into his mouth.

Father's brow furrowed as he changed the subject. "Heard you anything of the Lady of the Haven?"

William smiled to himself at the title his father had given Jael. When he raised his eyes, they held a more serious expression. "I wish I could say I had. I have no idea what may have become of her. I can only hope her fortune holds."

"If she is anything like Jon, I would expect to see her here by spring. He had nine lives, I believe. And he lived them fully until the last."

William nodded then sipped his drink. "From all you have told me of him, he must have been quite a man."

His father chuckled softly. "More than a man I always thought. I confess I was quite surprised to hear of his death. I believed him to be among the immortals."

"Myth only my love," his wife interjected. "I always told you that. Unless he was an angel come down to earth … and then I think they can actually perish. I do not know. Our dearest apostle never explained that to my complete satisfaction."

Her husband touched her hand. "There is so much we have yet to learn.

As much as you search the Holy Scriptures, I've no doubt you'll come across it one of these days, dear."

"Speaking of the apostle," William began, "brings a question to mind."

Both his parents turned their attention to him.

"I know it is said the apostle lived among us for many years, but do you know if he may have crossed through Verani Haven on his journeys?"

"I do not know," his father said, straightening in his chair. "It is said he landed here in a sailing vessel, so he must have traveled by sea from the Holy Land. I don't know where he ventured after he left here. He would've been quite an old man by then."

Lady Bethalyn's gaze bore into William. "Why do you ask?"

Young Will cleared his throat and reached for his flagon.

William gave him a slight kick beneath the table before turning an innocent expression to his mother. "I heard Jael … er … the lady, speak in the forbidden tongue, and she sang the psalms. But she seemed to know nothing of the Savior, so it was a puzzle to me."

"That she speaks the forbidden tongue is not a mystery, considering her lineage," his father said. He drummed his fingers on the table, thinking. "And I did hear Jon often sing the psalms. I believe his family may have descended from one of the ancients. Most likely, they were descendants of Abraham, prior to the birth of the Savior. Do you not think this is likely, my son?"

"Perhaps, and yet ... I sensed a deep faith in her. I suppose she could be of the Hebrew persuasion."

His mother ventured a thought. "I believe God honors the knowledge we have until we are given the opportunity to believe in the Son. If she has never heard of our Savior, then she could not believe in Him."

"Had I only known more at the time," William's father said, "I was young and ignorant. If I had shared my knowledge with Jon, perhaps by now ... but then we never know ..."

"He was a good man," Mother answered. "He lived his life for others, and he believed in the God he knew. He certainly did us a good turn, so also his daughter." She reached across the table to take her son's hand. "I am so grateful to God for leading you to her. Someday I hope to thank her in person."

William sighed. "I really hope you have that opportunity Mother—more than you know."

He felt her eyes upon him, long after their conversation ended. She watched him throughout the remainder of the meal. He knew what she was thinking, without being told. Because he knew her well. He sensed trouble ahead. The Lady of the Haven may have ancient roots, but she was not of royal blood. And his mother would never approve anyone who was not of royal blood.

After Winter Solstice, William and a few of his men packed up for the trip back to Corwinder-by-the-Sea.

"Father has a ship at the ready," he told the men. "A supply ship headed to Corwinder."

"Sounds good to me," Young Will said. "I'll take a day's sail over a two-day hard ride any time."

William smiled down at him. "You aren't getting lazy on me, are you?"

"Nay, sir, not so. Just thinking of my horse is all."

The younger man's pursed lips and averted gaze told William all he needed to know. "Aye, I thought so."

Together, they strode to the wharf where a mid-sized galley stood at anchor. Once aboard, Master Sharpe and his second mate, Oeghan saluted William and accompanied him to the quarterdeck. Young Will stayed below to oversee the loading of the horses.

After the ship set sail, William stood at the rail, arms folded over his chest, gazing into the distant peaks. His mind traced Jael's possible journey. Was she alive still? Or had Shinder managed to capture her?

William suppressed a shudder at the thought. He smoothed a palm over his jaw to ease his taut nerves. She was smart and seemed to have a sense of danger, so he wanted to hold to the belief that she could outwit the tracker. He hoped she'd found shelter. The safest place for her would be Duflec. She could hole up there till spring then catch a fisher vessel to the sea. Was she smart enough to figure that out?

He gripped the rail and leaned into the wind, hoping to clear his mind. When he heard the gush of the water against the bow, memories rushed in. How had such a little thing managed to drag his waterlogged frame out of the swift-running currents of the Verani?

He couldn't fathom it. But he was thankful to God she had.

At midday, William joined Master Sharpe in his cabin for a light repast of salted meat and aged cheese. William especially enjoyed the master's intelligent conversation.

"I've had a good report of this latest crop of trainees at Corwinder. What're your plans for them, if I may be so bold as to ask?"

After a sip of the master's good ale, William looked him in the eye. "At snow's melt, I plan to launch a campaign against the Brogies."

Master Sharpe nodded his approval. He rested his forearms on the thick oaken table. "Those foothills around Corwinder seem a perfect place for the Brogies to hide."

William agreed. "They're wintering somewhere in those vales. I'm thinking they'll set out early, hoping to cull the herds before the royal herdsmen arrive."

The master lifted a pitcher and offered William more ale.

William shook his head. "No, thanks. It's delicious, as always, but I've a long evening ahead of me."

Master Sharpe filled his own cup then set the pitcher down. After taking a sip, he sat back in his chair and propped his feet on a stool. "So once you've routed those Brogies?"

William stared out the porthole, watching the seemingly endless expanse of snow-covered shoreline slip by. "I have determined the need to train as many men as I can find, in order to defend the royal herds. After we've accomplished that, they'll be ready to take on bigger prey." He leveled his gaze at the master. "And I have just the prey in mind."

It was nearly five bells as they sailed into the tidal basin near Corwinder. They had only a couple of hours to unload their gear and supplies before the tide receded.

After bidding farewell to Master Sharpe and his men, William's party headed to the keep.

Solis greeted them just inside the gate. "Your Majesty, good day to ye. I daresay your voyage fared well?"

"Aye, Solis. They left your supplies on the dock. About three carts' worth, I'll warrant."

Solis gave orders for a contingent of men and carts to bring up the supplies then led William and his men inside the keep for a briefing.

"Our watchmen in the foothills have detected nothing thus far, sir. But they have sent back sore tidings. The harsh winter has claimed more head of cattle than is usual."

William scowled. "That is bad news. Add those to the Brogies' haul last summer's end and we've deep losses indeed."

"Aye, sir," Solis said. He sat back, folding his arms over his chest. "And here's another interesting tidbit. That weasel we captured back in the Deep's been nosing around. There's been three sightings of 'im. Doesn't seem interested in the cattle, or the Brogies. Just tracking."

William came to immediate attention at the reference to the tracker. "When was this?"

"It were, as I said, three separate times. Once, afore Winter Solstice. Then after the year changed over, they seen 'im again. And more recent, he was scouting out the woods just east of the harbor."

William wanted to jump out of his chair, but suppressed his inner excitement. If Shinder was still searching ... that meant he hadn't found her. He'd managed to quiet an outburst, but he couldn't stay his smile.

Young Will leaned forward and whispered, "That's good news, isn't it, Uncle?"

William nodded. "Aye, it is." He made eye contact with Solis. "Send word to your spies. I want to know the man's every move."

Into the Caves

Shinder developed a case of cabin fever ere winter ended. Though the snows still lay heavy on the mountain, he fashioned a pair of snowshoes and took off for a walk. He'd wintered in a cave near a tiny village on the edge of nowhere. The place held a secret, of that he was certain. The small rock huts were built over caves and for centuries, it'd been rumored that an underground network connected this place to the river, perhaps even to the sea. Many a slave had disappeared there.

He'd found the natives tight-lipped and dull as the stone they dwelt in. One even told him right out there was no network. "Them caves is dangerous and filled w'water so cold it'll freeze a man in a pig's wink."

Shinder hadn't believed it. Lying, blitherin' idiots, all.

Before heading outside, he ventured a short length into the dark interior of the cave he dwelt in, but it was a dead end, closed off to the other caves. Afterwards, he stood long at the mouth of the cave, searching the bright white landscape, letting his eyes adjust to the light. He sniffed at the air and wrinkled his nose. His prey was nearby, he sensed it. She would not escape him this time.

Enora lay abed late one morning, "… feeling her age," she'd told Jael. "Sometimes … I hates the bitter cold. It seeps … into these old bones … and my body aches … so."

Jael wished she had access to her supply of herbs. She could brew an "old age" tea. It brightened the eyes and warmed the belly. It'd be just the thing for Enora.

Enora was just easing her way out from under the furs of her bed when they heard a sharp knock. "Now ... who could that be ... at this early hour?"

"I'll see who 'tis," Jael told her. Since she was already dressed and closest to the door, it only made sense. She did go carefully, however, peering out through a narrow crack in the door before unbolting it.

Thaddeus stood there. Jael started to open it wide, but he caught hold of the handle to keep her from opening all the way. He came not in, but stood just outside the door, speaking in a low tone. Alarmed, Jael closed the door again and turned to face Enora. "I'm afraid I must go."

Enora moved forward as quickly as her stiff old legs could carry her. "Who was at the door?"

"Thaddeus—he told me to go below. There's a tracker lurking about, who's looking for someone somewhat like me. It isn't safe for me to remain. Thaddeus said you'd tell me how to find my way."

Enora bustled around, packing up a few things. "Wrest up them coverlets ... I gi'ye and ... all o' yon socks. Ye'll need 'em below." Enora tugged at a wool carpet and brought up a section of the floor with it. She threw it back and glanced at Jael. "Take up yon candle and ... make yer way down this ... ladder. Ye'll find yerself ... in a small room. They's a ... lantern ... on a table. Light it ... with the candle then hand me up ... the candle."

Jael did as she was told. Enora took a deep breath and coughed behind her fist. "Now ... I'm going to shet ye up ... in there. After I've done it ... turn yer back ... to the ladder ... and step forward to the wall. Feel ... along that wall ... straight in front of ye ... until ye feel a ... bowl in the rock. That ... is a step. Directly up from there ... is another. Ye put ... yer hand in that one ... and yer foot in the other and ... pull yerself up.

If I ... throw a switch up here, ye'll go up ... into another room. If I don't ... throw the switch, ye'll come up ... into this room ... just aside the fireplace." She paused for a moment to breathe. It was a lot for her to say all at once. "I'll throw the switch ... and when ye've gotten in there, push it down. Ye'll see it ... when ye're there. Oh yes, push the lantern through first ... and tie them coverlets to ye ... the best ye kin so as ... ye kin make it ... all in one trip." She shook her head from side to side. "They's no second chance."

"Where do I go from there?"

Enora looked down at her. "Iffen ye need to go farther ... someone will come. If not ... I'll open the slider again. If ... I don't see ye again ... take care, Jonnie. Ye be a good lad ... and a hard worker." She swiped at the tears parading down her rosy cheeks then closed the trapdoor. Jael could hear the sound of furniture being moved about. Or, perhaps it was the slider.

Jael glanced around, taking in her surroundings. She'd been down here before, but only to get more wood. Firewood was neatly stacked all around the square room. The ceiling was less than an arm's length higher than Jael's head. She bundled up the blankets and threw them toward the wall. Picking up the lantern, she stepped forward as she'd been told.

She found the foothold, and the handhold, set the lantern down and pushed the coverlets up through the opening. Then she picked up the lantern and held it while she pulled herself up. She set the lantern on the floor above her and climbed through the opening. As soon as she was up, the slider closed. She'd barely made it inside. Could Enora see her? How else would she know to close the latch?

In two breaths, she heard someone banging on the door. She sat perfectly still. Her sharp ears picked up the tracker's nasal voice.

"I hear ye have a boarder."

Enora answered, "I did indeed, but no more. He set out ... a while back."

"Then ye'll no mind me having a look."

Enora sucked in a breath. "I do mind, but ye kin ... look iffen ye wish. I've nothin' to 'ide."

A moment later, Jael heard the sounds of furniture and heavy objects being pushed about. She could hear Enora's objections amid heavy coughing. "Ain't no call ... in tearing up the place. Me hut's ... tiny, no one ... could hide in here."

"What about below? Where's the door?"

"Below?"

"Don't mess with me, old woman! I could crack all yer bones with my teeth."

Jael's ire rose. She searched for an exit, but found nothing. A moment later, the front door of the hut crashed open. She heard the voice of Thaddeus. "Unhand that woman, sir!"

"I ain't got no cause to hurt ye, sir—or this woman—I just want what I came fer. Ye tell me where she be, and I'll leave. No?"

Jael closed her eyes tight, straining to hear every sound. She heard enough to piece together what was happening. Her heart thundered in her chest. She felt along the walls to find a way out. She had to help them. Finally, she found a tiny crack that must outline the trapdoor. She pressed her face against it and lined up her eye so she could at least see what was happening.

Thaddeus threw his weight against the wiry tracker, but Shinder was faster. He tossed Enora aside, striking her head on the stone wall. Jael almost cried out, but she bit her lip to guard against it. She watched in horror as Enora fell against the floor near the fire and lay still. Was she dead?

Shinder sidestepped the bigger man and ended up behind him, a short sword at his neck. "I'll thank ye to tell me what I need to know sir."

"Ye can go below if ye wish, ye'll not find no one. The young lad ye spoke of moved on a fortnight ago." Thaddeus told a valiant lie, but Jael could tell Shinder wasn't having it. He tossed Thaddeus aside and crossed to the carpet. He threw that aside too, found the trapdoor, and pulled it open.

Before Thaddeus could come to himself and get to his feet, Shinder grasped the iron tongs from their hanger under the mantel, lifted a large burning ember, and dropped it into the cellar. The ember caught some of the dry wood and flames jumped.

Shinder slammed the trapdoor, pulled a heavy chest over it, and turned to sneer at Thaddeus. "If there ain't no one down there, it'll no matter." Then he fled to the door and let himself out.

As Thaddeus jumped up and ran to the chest, putting all of his strength into moving it, Jael tried not to panic.

What now? Already, the smell of smoke drifted through. Was she going to roast like a duck in an oven? "Thaddeus, what do I do?" She screamed the words, then peered through the crack again. He seemed not to hear her. He had thrown the trapdoor open. Already the flames had caught the dry wood. Smoke poured into the main room of the hut. He jumped up and grabbed Enora, tossing her over his shoulder like a sack of potatoes then ran out the door.

Jael's heart sank as heavy smoke oozed through the crack and burned her eyes. She stepped away from the slider, feeling her way along the opposite wall. Surely there must be a way of escape. In the farthest corner of the small room, she took a deep breath and tried to force herself to think clearly. Enora told her someone would come for her.

Already, her nose burned from the smell of smoke. She tore a length of material from one of the coverlets and stuffed it into the cracks around the slider. That helped a little. Then she crept back to the far corner, and sat on the coverlets with the lantern out in front of her and waited.

She didn't know how long she waited. In the darkness, it was impossible to tell. It seemed like an eternity. Finally, she heard a sound like the scratching of a mouse. A moment later, she heard a muffled voice.

"Jonathan, be ye in there still?"

She followed the sound. "I am here!"

A blackened face appeared in the lantern light. Where had he come from?

"It's Thomas, son of Thaddeus. He sent me to lead ye to safety. Follow me and bring yon lantern."

Jael threw the coverlets over her shoulder and tied a knot to hold them there. She snatched the lantern and hurried out. "What happened to Enora?" She had to struggle to keep up with him.

"She be all right, just a bump to the head is all. Her house has no insides though. Plumb burned out it is. Da feels the loss of the wool most keenly." His voice echoed off the rock walls of the cavern they traversed.

"I am sorry for that. It must be a great deal of work gathering such a lot of wool."

"Ye are not a shepherd then?"

"No, I am a sailmaker."

"Ah, well it is not so very different as losing a sail ye worked mighty hard to make, I reckon."

A level-headed lad. She followed him through the maze of caves along an intricate route that she could not fathom in the deep darkness. Finally, he stopped and waited for her to join him. She lifted her lantern to see him better and try to get an idea where she was. He pushed the hood of his cloak back, revealing tousled dark hair and small round eyes like his father's.

He held out a rucksack he'd toted over his shoulder. "Da sent ye this. Ye must proceed alone from here."

Jael took the sack and asked, "How do I know where to go?"

He held his lantern high. "Ye see them sparkly things along the top of the cave?"

A dim spot reflected the lantern light. "I see it."

He turned back and grinned at her. "It's made from snail slime and ground up shells. Shines in the dark, it does. It be an old trick."

She matched his grin with one of her own. "It works. So I follow those spots?"

"It'll be slow goin' fer ye, I reckon—but aye—ye follow them spots. Comes out above the river. If ye follow the river's flow, ye'll come to the sea. It's several days' journey on foot in good weather. It'll take longer while the snow lasts. And there won't be no boats this time o' year. Da says to say he's that sorry ye couldna have yer horse. There was no way, ye see. That ferret fellow is watchin' too close."

Several days' journey to the sea. Och, rue. She watched the glow of Thomas' lantern fade into darkness before she set off on her own.

She was alone again—hungry, cold, and sore—but alive. She hated the tracker, all at once. She hated him for forcing her to weave all over the rugged Touris, stretching her journey from weeks to months. She'd been forced to hole up over winter, now thrown into a twisted labyrinth of dark caves.

She felt like sitting down and crying bitter tears, but what would that accomplish? She sighed and straightened her shoulders. She had never been one to give in to emotion. She'd always pushed herself onward, even in the worst circumstances.

Besides, it wasn't the tracker, not really. The blame fell solely on the Magistrate. He had hated her family for years. Had done everything in his power to hurt and humiliate them. His hate was a festering sore. She would not let bitterness do that to her.

The teachings of her father rose up within her. At least now she could sing again, albeit softly. She raised her voice and sang a psalm of praise and wonder.

As she lifted the lamp to seek out the guiding lights, she was reminded of several things. Enora had not died. Thaddeus was safe. She, Jael of Rogan, was alive and free and within days of the sea.

Soon, with the help of the Almighty, she would find William, and she would be safe. She stood still a moment and closed her eyes. Could she really be so close to realizing her dream?

Strange Bedfellows

Jael had no idea it would take so long to find the end of the cave. How many miles had she walked? And she was so tired. Why, it must be late night, nigh on to morning. She trudged wearily on following the dim lights, praying the oil in the lantern would hold out.

The pack she carried grew so heavy, she moved it to the other side. Whatever it contained, it was certainly weighty. As soon as she found daylight, she'd see what Thaddeus had provided.

Every muscle in her body was screaming a protest when finally, she detected a spot of dim gray light in the distance. As she neared the end, struggling as she was to put one foot in front of the other, she tripped over a rock, and fell headlong.

She woke to darkness and confusion. What had happened? She went to move, but pain shot through her body. Her side hurt the most, so she carefully felt along her rib cage.

"Cracked a rib," she whispered, fingering the bones, one by one. "Does not seem to be broken." She tried to move again, but cried out, as nearly unbearable pain stabbed her to the quick.

Turning, she blinked into blinding light. She'd been facing the back of the cave. After her eyes adjusted, she looked for the lantern but remembered the crashing sound just before she fell. At least she'd made it all the way to the end before losing the thing. She felt along the dark floor for the sack until she found it. Then she pushed herself up and took a slow step forward. Soon the pain settled into something she could endure. She continued on toward the light.

As she neared the entrance, she realized most of the light was reflection off a heavy blanket of snow covering everything. She stood there and looked out, shivering. It was cold, so very cold.

Near the mouth of the cave, she sat shivering on a rock and picked up the rucksack. Inside, she found a bundle of bread and meat, a small hatchet, and a knife. She turned the sack upside down and shook it to be sure she had everything. Two small, flat stones fell out. Flint. She grabbed them up quickly. She could build a fire.

A dead tree lay near the entrance, so she soon had enough dry wood to build a small fire. By this time, her side was really inflamed, so she lowered herself to the ground and leaned against a rock for support. The ground was so cold. But there was nothing for it. She'd have to tough it out until the heat of her body warmed it. Thank goodness she'd thought to tie the coverlets around her shoulders like a cloak before she left Enora's. At least she had that.

The fire brought almost immediate warmth. She laid more wood on top then leaned back and rested. She thought about the food, but was too weary and sick to eat. She fell into a deep sleep, making up for the hours she had trudged through the dark cave. Strange dreams troubled her, finishing with one that seemed very real.

A gray wolf stood looking down at her. At first Jael was frightened, but the fear abated as the animal continued to stare at her. Soon it moved away, but stayed near the fire. It lay down on the other side, still watching her. After a bit, it dropped its head and slept. She also slept, unafraid.

When she woke, she remembered the vivid dream with unnatural clarity. She pushed away from the ground and sat up, squeezing her eyes closed against the pain. Her first thought was for the fire. When she went to move, however, she realized another need. A full bladder. While attending to that, a slight movement across from her caught Jael's attention. What she saw sent bolts of raw fear through her.

It had not been a dream. She watched the gray wolf, afraid to avert her eyes. How could she have missed the smell of the wild animal warmed by the fire? Its feral eyes shown as it watched her. A low sound emanated from its throat as it warned her. She sent up a desperate plea to God for help. What shall I do?

A memory from the dream returned to her. She had not been afraid. She took a deep breath, and moved ever so slightly, to place another stick on the fire. Tiny embers rose on the hot air, quickly burning away to ashes. The beast didn't move, but watched her. After a moment, it raised its head. She pushed away from the fire, keeping her head and body low.

Back to the coverlet, she retreated then reached for the sack. She extracted the bundle of food, and slowly unrolled it. There was a portion of salted meat, and two small loaves of bread. Enough for several days. Her eyes found the wolf's. It lifted its head when it smelled the food. Should she try to share her meat? She took a bite and chewed it slowly. Then broke off a larger portion and using a small stick, slowly edged it toward the fire. When she heard the warning growl, she tossed it the rest of the way then withdrew. The wolf did not move. It watched her, not the bit of meat lying on the ground in front of it.

She wrapped the remaining meat and tore off a bite of bread and ate. When she had finished, she wrapped it up and replaced both bundles back inside the sack, closed it, and placed it behind her. She leaned back slowly, wishing she had something to wash down the dry bread. She knew she could get a handful of snow and satisfy her thirst, but decided she must wait and give the animal time to settle. After several minutes, it moved forward just enough to grab the meat, nearly swallowing it whole. On its belly, it inched forward and cleaned the hard-packed dirt floor where the meat had lain.

Jael reclined against the rock, watching the wolf through half-closed eyes. After cleaning the floor, it licked its paws then lay back down, stretching out full-length on the other side of the fire. It watched her for several minutes until its eyes closed in sleep.

What would draw a wild animal in to a human's fire? Was it some sort of sign? She watched the wolf until her own eyes drooped in weariness. Quietly, and with great caution, she reached to place another stick on the fire. There were only four such sticks remaining. She'd need to cut more, but not now.

Shinder spent a frigid night trying to stay warm beside a weak fire beneath a hastily built lean-to. He was not in a good mood. He hated cold weather. Hated the fact that he was here, still chasing after that silly woman. How had she managed to elude him for so long?

He struck off across the top of a snow covered ridge, determined to make progress. There were so many caves in these parts, and each one led to another. He ground his teeth in frustration. Shading his eyes with a fur-covered hand, he looked out across the river valley. He could see another, just a short distance ahead. He set off in that general direction.

As he neared the cave's entrance, he stopped. He almost thought he smelled a fire, but no, there was no sign of smoke. Perhaps it was the smell on his own clothes. The weak fire he'd managed with damp wood had been nothing but smoke in the beginning, so his clothes were well permeated.

After a moment, he ventured forward again. It was still early, just beginning to lighten. When he was only a few short yards away from the entrance, a movement above it caught his eye. A gray form limped down and around to the front of the cave. Shinder was downwind, so it didn't catch his scent. He stayed still, hoping it wouldn't see him. The wolf limped into the cave and did not return. Shinder stood there for several long moments, processing the scene before him. If a wolf—or possibly even wolves, as they usually ran in packs—was living in that cave, there'd be no human presence there. He sniffed the air again then lifted his arm and sniffed the fur of his overshirt. He frowned and turned away. He'd no time for foolish pursuits and certainly no time to battle a passel of wolves.

He set off down the incline and onto his former path. He'd head back out to the foothills. It made more sense. Who could survive in this barren place? Certainly not a wispy twig of a woman like that one.

When Jael woke next, it was daylight again. She'd slept through the night. The fire had died back, but some embers still glowed with warmth. She sat up slowly, startling the wolf. It jumped up quickly, but made no sound, looked at her, then turned and limped away.

It was wounded. "We are alike then," Jael whispered. She moved forward and hacked at the fallen tree. Each blow brought renewed pain. She would have to bind the injury in order to go on. She could not stay here much longer.

As the fire burned, she took account of the things she had. She wore underclothes, leather britches, a wool shirt and an over-shirt, besides the thick knitted sweater Enora had made. She had one coverlet and the cloth used to wrap the food. She did not know if this cloth would be large enough to wrap around her. Then she thought of the muslin she had used to tightly bind her breasts, in an effort to disguise her femininity. She would have to use that, because it was necessary she bind the injured rib. If she did not, she could injure it further, break it, and do worse damage. She knew the consequences all too well.

Building up the fire until it glowed, she set to work. Under the coverlet, she removed the shirts and the undershirt, revealing the tightly wound muslin girdle and the ring, hanging around her neck. She removed the ring first, and held it near the fire, watching its stone sparkle. Ignoring the longing in her heart, she laid it aside then worked at the knot in the muslin. It took several minutes to untie it, during which time, the wolf returned. It ran up rather suddenly, startling Jael. She sat still, watching it limp slowly forward where it dropped into place on the far side of the fire. It groaned slightly as it settled in.

Jael gave a soft chuckle. "I feel the same way." It perked up its ears and lay watching her as she worked at the knot in the muslin.

Finally, the knot came loose and she unwound the cloth. Her skin itched beneath it. She rubbed at the creases. It had been some days since that skin had seen daylight. Sitting up straight, she rewound the muslin, taking in more area this time. When she was finished, it was tight lower down and just covering her upper chest.

She would have to be very careful in the interim, not to be found out. At least it was cold and she would be well covered by layers of garments. She replaced the ring, along with her other clothes then sat back to rest.

One more day. No matter what, she must leave at first light in the morning. She could delay no longer.

But during the night, a wind arose and by morning, fresh snow blew with such force, she couldn't see anything.

"Look at that weather," Elizabeth said to her husband, Toldar. "I shall be a prisoner here forever."

Toldar threw her a charming smile as he pulled on his boots. "Oh, stop complaining, my love. You're a princess of the realm, and you are safe and warm. You have a handsome husband who adores you. What else could you possibly desire?"

She sighed as she gazed into the looking glass. "But you are preparing to leave, and you'll be gone all day."

He stepped forward, encircled her with his arms and kissed the back of her neck. "Yes, I'll spend the greater part of the day training young whelps to wield a sword. Oh, how exciting."

She smiled at his image in the mirror. "And in answer to your former question, sunshine and a beautiful white horse to ride along the tide."

He chuckled. "Sorry my love, I can promise you neither at the moment, but in a few months perhaps." He turned her around and kissed her forehead then her lips. "I must go."

"Oh, and I was just beginning to thaw a bit."

"Hold that thought," he whispered. "Your brother will be at the door if I do not go at once. I am already late." He let go of her and moved to the door where he removed a heavy cloak from its hook and tossed it over his shoulder. "I shall return."

"You'd better." Elizabeth turned back to the window after her husband left. She pushed the shutter open a crack and watched the heavy snow as it fell. She was so very homesick for the coast. The large castle there was drafty, but still warmer than this awful place. She turned when a maid entered with fresh water. "Can you coax more warmth from that fire?" Elizabeth asked her. "I am freezing in here."

The maid smiled and nodded. "Yes, milady."

After building up the fire, the maid stood. "Would you like for me to fix your hair now, mum?"

"Yes please do. It's quite lost its moorings, I'm afraid. And when you've finished, please let Abigail know I will take my meals here today."

"Are you unwell, milady?"

"It is only my condition, I think. I am so tired and cold."

"Yes, milady. I've often seen it thus. After the first few months have passed, you'll feel better."

"I keep hearing that. I hope it is so. Otherwise it will be a very long season."

William watched the men as they practiced at swords. A large fireplace on either end of the room was filled with what looked like burning tree trunks. All about the room, the young men stood in sets, and practiced in rounds. Their movements were studied and balanced. Some were quite agile, but most still needed a lot of work.

When Solis approached, William turned and shook his head. "It begins again, does it not?"

"Ain't they a sad lot? But I have seen worse. We'll whip 'em into shape. It may take longer than we have though."

"We've nothing else to do. That wind howls with renewed force. Ah!" He grimaced as one of the young men he was watching struck too hardy a blow. "It is just practice, Drumwalt, have a care!"

"Sorry," Drumwalt said, bowing to William.

Solis chuckled then turned toward William, a serious expression on his face. "Did ye hear the latest of the ferret, sir?"

"He's back?"

"Aye sir. I heared tell he was roamin' about the streets of Corwinder."

"Here? When did you hear this?" William's mind moved swiftly. Had he trailed the lady here? Could Jael be so near?

"Just last evenin' in the pub, my lord. Twas Alton what said he seen 'im."

"Alton—he is usually very observant. No doubt it is Shinder, and can his prey be far?"

"Are ye familiar with his prey then, sire? A witch, he said it was."

William glowered at the captain, but did not reply. Instead he strode from the room. Bad weather or no, he must get outside. All at once, it seemed the walls were closing in on him.

CHAPTER 13 – THE BROGIES

The Brogies

The snowstorm continued three days and nights. When finally the clouds parted and blue sky showed through, Jael gave praise to God. Her friend the wolf departed at once. Jael gathered her few belongings and made ready to depart. During the worst of the storm she'd built up walls of snow to fend off the worst of the drifts, leaving only a small opening. She worked one entire morning, chopping extra firewood, since she had no way of knowing how long the storm would last.

Only a small twinge reminded her of the injury, which meant her wrapping had done its job. Before setting out, she covered her feet with the cloth from the food and took off across the snow. It was slow going, but she pressed on. Hunger drove her. If she could make the river, perhaps she could cut through the ice and find a fish to give her strength. A cup of hot tea would be better, but for now, that was only a dream.

Keeping to the edges of the foothills became impossible. Great drifts of fresh snow made it too treacherous in many places. She found a windblown vale where the snow was not so deep, and traveled along more easily. At the approach of darkness, her anxiety grew. She'd found no food, and where would she shelter for the night?

So far she'd experienced great favor. Surely God was watching over her. She'd managed to travel in comparative safety and was now closing in on her target.

She must be very careful not to lose her concentration.

There was a scent of smoke in the air. She stopped to get her bearings. Somewhere close by, there may be a dwelling or a camp. As dusk lengthened the shadows, the temperature dropped. She struggled on, so weary, she nearly fell asleep on her feet. The snow was thick and dense enough in places she could just lean forward and be supported, but to fall asleep would be certain death.

The sound of music assailed her now. Someone played a jaunty tune on a lute. As she drew closer, she whispered a prayer. "Let them be friendly and safe."

She never heard anyone approach, but was startled by a sudden crunch of snow directly behind her. Then pain more acute than any she'd ever felt, and darkness.

Jael awoke to warmth at least, but her limbs were tightly secured. She lay on her side almost too near the fire. All around her, she heard raucous snoring and sputtering. Whoever they were, they slept. Panic churned in her breast. She struggled to break free of her bonds, but to no avail.

"Don't bother," she heard a familiar voice whisper. "Ye'll not loose them strops. Newly tanned leather they be, and the warmth of the fire dried 'em tight."

"Where am I?" Stars of sharp pain nearly blinded her with the effort to speak.

"Ye are warm and dry. It is better than ye were before, though ye are not free. Ye've seen these men before and I seen ye, in the wilds of Touri."

She knew who he was. The camp in the mountains, where the men were drinking and singing far into the night. Marauders, she'd assumed at the time. Later she'd realized they must be stealing the beef they were eating.

In the dim firelight, she could see red hides hanging on the walls. "Newly tanned leather ..." the young man had told her. They were Brogies and she was their prisoner. What would they do to her? Her heart constricted in her chest. She could barely get a breath. What if they found out she was not a man? What would be her fate then?

Tears burned her eyes. She blinked them away. She could not show weakness—that would only be worse for her. She tried to take deep, slow breaths to still the panic in her heart. The calm voice behind her helped a bit.

"They'll likely require ye to work as they do me. They don't really need it now, but when the snows clear, they'll be goin' arter the cattle they left in them hollow places."

She grimaced at the thought. When the snows cleared? That could be weeks away. No, she could not stay here. She must break free as soon as possible. And they must not find out her secret.

"We've seen this one afore, have we not?" A heavy man with a long black beard ran his dirty fingers beneath her chin. "I believe we have. Up in the wilds of Touri it was. Still wanderin' about, lad? Ye shoulda stayed w'us then. We'd a toughened ye up by now." He stood and warmed his hands before the fire. "He's ain't much. Don't know if we'll get a lot of work outin' 'im."

He spoke to another man who looked enough like him to be his brother and probably was, for Brogies tended to run in packs like wolves. The other man was somewhat younger, and even less clean than the first.

"M'hap we can make a trade with the mule runners?"

Jael knew this was what they called the merchant trains that passed through at regular intervals during spring and summer.

The big man nodded thoughtfully. "They ain't so picky. 'Til then, set him to work helping Rudeness there. He kin scrape hide and iffen he gives ye any trouble, scrape hissen."

Jael closed her eyes. At least they'd have to free her hands and feet to scrape hide. Then maybe she could manage to escape.

"Don't even think of it," the boy they called Rudeness whispered when they set her to work next to him.

Jael looked at him, her eyes narrowed.

He jabbed her in the arm with his fist. "I kin see what ye're thinkin' and it won't work. They got the drop on ye when ye came here. They'll no be lettin' ye get away free. Believe me, I've tried. Here, scrape it this way, it's easier." He showed her how to scrape the hide then they stretched it over a frame and he hung it on the wall beside the others. "We only have one more. But don't worry yer head about it, they'll find something else just as bad fer us to do. What's yer name?"

"Jonathan."

He looked at her for several long moments and she prayed he did not guess her secret. "I members it now." He grinned at her. "Do ye member mine?"

Jael studied his face, trying to remember. All she could think of was the rudeness thing. Then she looked up at him and it popped into her head. "Ferdinand."

"That's it. Ye'd win a prize was there any."

"How long have you been here?"

"Most of my life. Folks is dead, nowhere else to go no ways."

"But you'd be free."

"Free? A orphan? No my friend. I got more brains up here 'n that." He pointed to his head. "Maybe you ain't been a orphan long enough, if indeed ye is one."

Jael turned away a moment. She was an orphan, but she was not as young as he supposed, neither was she a lad. So life would be different for her. She supposed it would be quite difficult for a young boy who had nowhere else to go. "You could go with me," she offered. Bringing a smile to Ferdinand's dry, cracked lips.

"And where would that be?"

"To the sea—I've friends there—I just need to get there."

He raised his eyebrows. "To the sea?" He leaned in close. "Well it just so happens, we're a goin' to the sea, soon's the snow melts. So bide yer time, lad. We'll see do ye have friends. When I see that, I'll maybe go wi'ye. Otherwise, don't be botherin' me with dreams and wishes." His voice grew hard and his eyes narrowed. "I've had me fill."

Jael held her tongue after that, no use in alienating her only hope. She worked at whatever was given and did her best to stay out of everyone's way. She greatly regretted that she'd moved the binding around her chest. She really felt the need of it now. But at least she didn't need it as much as others she'd seen.

Days passed with no hope of release. The snows clung to the ground and the awful cold set in. On billowy days the men stayed inside and it was worse then. It was close quarters and smelly and they drank too much. They almost always ended up fighting and the language nearly burned her ears. She found herself blushing too many times, but if they ever noticed they made no comment. They probably just attributed it to the warmth of the fire.

She'd been with them for nearly a fortnight when the leader's brother who was called Gort, asked her to go out into the snow and dig him up some potatoes. He was drunk, and she thought he was funning with her.

"He means fer ye to do it, so ye'd best get out there," Ferdinand whispered in her ear.

"You mean he's serious?"

Ferdinand's brows knit together in a straight line. "Dead serious, if you catch my meanin.'" He started to move away, but Jael caught hold of his sleeve.

"Where are the potatoes?"

"There are none, fool, and it's winter."

Och, rue! Was this her day to die? "But, what must I do?"

"Use yer noggin I reckon, I dunno."

Amid jeers and laughter, Jael bundled up and went outside. Perhaps if she took a while out there and stayed out of sight, he'd either forget or fall asleep. She hadn't been outside long, however when she was accosted by

Black Dog, the sentry. He'd been given the name because he looked a bit like a shaggy dog, and he was mean to boot.

"What business have ye out here?" He demanded in his usual grumpy tone.

Jael kept her head down as she answered. "Master Gort wants potatoes for his dinner. He sent me out to gather them."

Black Dog erupted into hilarious laughter, taking Jael completely by surprise. "'E does, does 'e? Well ye'd best be about it then. Bah-hah-ha!" He continued to laugh for several minutes. Jael was quite tired of hearing it, but when it ended, he stood watching as she tromped about in the snow. "Ye ken what 'e's askin' fer don't ye lad? Ain't no taters this time o' year." He sniggered. "Ain't no taters no time o' year round these parts."

"Be there taters or no, good master," she answered, "I mustn't go back inside empty-handed."

He slapped his leg. "That's a fact, me laddie. It is. Ye learns right fast. But I dunno can ye avoid a stroppin' this time. He's asked ye fer taters and do ye show up without taters, he'll no doubt whip ye." He held his sides and laughed harder, thoroughly enjoying the joke.

In that moment, Jael hated them all and wanted desperately to be free. She looked out upon the barren wintry landscape and fought hard to hold back the tears stinging her eyes.

She sucked up every drop of courage she could muster then turned slowly and headed back toward the cottage. If it was a whipping she was to receive, let it be over and done. Then they could all get on with their day.

Black Dog watched her go, a smile still tugging at his lips.

It was a bit of diversion Gort was craving, not the potatoes he'd asked for. He was wide awake and full of vinegar when Jael entered. As soon as she had set down the bucket she carried and peeled off the cloak she wore, he was upon her.

"Where's the potatoes, lad? Did I not ask ye fer potatoes?"

She saw Ferdinand turn away. He knew what was coming and had no power to interfere. Jael stood waiting for the punishment. At least he did not tear away her garments in order to inflict more hurt. He flung her down near the fire and took down a rawhide whip from a nearby hook.

Amid much shouting and laughter from the other men, he cracked the whip, first above her head, then on either side, near enough to her ears she felt it snap. She didn't dare move, but held her position, knowing he would only inflict further hurt if she flinched or tried to escape.

The first hit cut through the thin shirt she wore. The next brought blood. Eight more times he hit her. Then he seemed satisfied. He slowly recoiled the whip and hung it upon the wall. "Next time I asks ye fer taters, I'd best get taters and not a bucketful of air."

She stayed put until he had gone back to his chair. When things had quieted down a bit, she crept back to the corner where Ferdinand worked, cutting hide into strips.

"Ye took it like a man there, Jonnie. I has to give ye that. Jes try to stay out of sight fer a while. Let them welts heal."

She hurt long into the night and wished mightily for just a bit of the salve she had at home. Without it, the welts would likely leave a nasty scar, but there was no help for it. She closed her eyes tightly, and prayed for strength to endure this test of her will. Surely that's all this was. Why else would she be here among such as this?

Where is your protection now, God? Have I left off following your ways? I've not, to the best of my knowledge, save a bad thought or two. If you could forgive your servant David, you can forgive me for such as that.

After her prayers, she repeated every psalm she could pull from her memory until she finally drifted off to sleep.

Captured by Freedom

Little by little, the days grew longer. The sun broke through the overcast skies. The snow began to melt with an incessant dripping from the eaves of the old cottage.

"We pull out tomorrow," Jael heard the big man say when she had nearly given up hope. "The thaw is coming all over now. I want to be in the folds afore it gets clean underway. We must beat the clearin.'"

She supposed they were trying to round up the cattle before the owners came and did it. They meant to be in and gone, leaving no trace once the snow melted. It was a good plan, though devious. She didn't care, just so she could get to the sea. Once she got there, she had no doubt she could find William. She had no idea of how far the coast stretched or how many long days it may take to travel south. If she could gain her freedom and it was warmer than this, she'd be happy.

Ferdinand was watching her. He had not spoken a great deal of late. He did warn her once when he heard her speaking to herself in the ancient tongue. "Don't do that, ye dingwilter. Do they hear ye, they'll cut out yer tongue. It be forbidden."

What was that woesome fear she heard in his voice? Why was the ancient tongue forbidden, and who had forbidden it?

"**They're** movin,'" Solis informed William with a glint in his eye. "Our bird of prey come back."

William nodded. The bird of prey was a young man who could blend well into his surroundings, get information then get out unobserved.

"Get the men ready to pull out. We'll leave at first light. Which way are they moving?"

"Seaward and one guess as to where."

William grinned then let his head fall back in a full guffaw. His plan was working. The Brogies were walking into a trap.

The next morning he and his men set off for the dells, fully loaded for a long stay. They hoped to arrive ahead of the Brogies. Soon after they started, a horseman moved up beside William.

"Your sister sends her regards," Toldar said, reining in his horse to match Lodan's stride.

"I hope she is well."

Toldar flashed him a grin. "You know her as well as I."

"That I do, and as I've said in the past," he thumped his fist against his chest. "I feel your pain."

Toldar chuckled. "Where is Young Will? I haven't seen him."

"I sent him to the harbor. He'll go by boat."

"Ah, well we've got quite a surprise for the Brogies this time, eh? They'll not get away again."

"That's my greatest hope. Keep it to yourself, if you will. I've no wish for word to get out. The men don't know where they're going."

Toldar frowned. "Do you think there's an informant among us?"

"There have been too many coincidences where the Brogies are concerned. I'm taking no chances this time."

Toldar leaned forward, crossing his arms on the saddle horn. "Good. I'd like to have this over. I'm for settling down—how about you, brother?"

William averted his eyes, pretending to check the horizon. "If I could find what you've got, perhaps." He urged his horse into a cantor. Toldar pulled back to rejoin his men.

Jael was riding a mule again, but this time sharing it with Ferdinand. She was thankful for the need for layered clothing, since they must ride so close. So far no one had challenged her and by God's grace she had managed to maintain her disguise.

The journey was hazardous at best because of the high drifts in places, but the snow had begun to melt. This also meant the river was high and so was every little brook and rivulet along the way. Twice she nearly lost her seat on the back of old Kit. "Hook yer claws into my belt this time so's ye don't slip no more, 'tis makin' old Kit skittish. We don't want him skittish, believe me."

Jael did as she was told.

Though Ferdinand was younger, he was more experienced in the ways of this troupe than she, so she was willing to take orders from him. He seemed to appreciate having someone to order about instead of always being the tail end of everything. When something went wrong, it was Jael who received the blow. Poor Ferdinand was happy to give over.

As they rode along, she wondered what all he had suffered over the years. She had noticed that he was little more than skin and bones though the Brogies certainly fed themselves well enough. And they were all dirty. Dirtier than she'd ever thought possible.

She looked down at her fingers, covered in crud. The nails were so embedded with it, she feared they would never come clean. Her hair had long ago lost its golden glow. It hung in ugly limp strands whenever it was not pulled back.

She closed her eyes and dreamed of a frothy warm bath. How wonderful it would be. Her eyes came wide open as the mule slipped again and she had to struggle to stay on. Her very bones ached. In her mind, she began to sing her favorite psalm, *"The God of glory thunders 'pon great water, Tis a powerful voice, tis full of majesty ..."* as they moved along beside the mighty river.

She tried very hard to concentrate and not let the words slip out.

When they stopped to make camp that night, she could barely stand, but she must not show her weariness lest she fall prey to such abuse, she feared she may die. She had learned that lesson quickly. To her very great relief, the others were as tired as she. After a major ruckus over who would stand sentry, they all lay down upon the cold ground and slept.

It did not look like morning when they rose to leave. It didn't feel like it either, but they were soon on their way. The poor mule seemed to be as weary as his riders. He poked along, stopping often, causing the men to yell at them more than once.

"Ye kin walk quicker'n that and will iffen ye can't git yer animal to move any faster." Barto called out.

He was the big man, head of the Brogies. His patience waxed thinner than normal. Twice he had his hand on the whip at his side. Jael winced at the thought. She'd felt its bite more than once already, and had no desire to feel it again.

"I'm all fer walkin'," Ferdinand said. "How about ye?"

"What must be must be." She slid off the back of the mule and stepped carefully through the thick slush. They learned fast to hold onto the mule's bridle in order to keep their own feet on the ground. It was very slick going, but by the end of the day, they'd made up some ground.

According to Barto, they were halfway along. Jael's heart sank a bit. She was most anxious to get there. She hated to entertain any hope, but it was difficult not to. At times she felt she couldn't breathe.

It was well into the third day of their journey when the feelings started. She had had no inkling of anything for so long she had given up ever knowing again. She was alone in a small thicket, making a necessary stop. The men often teased her because she could not relieve herself in front of anyone. She would stand with them sometimes, her eyes carefully averted. They didn't seem to notice nothing came from her. As soon as possible she would find a private spot.

They joked about it often. "The lad has the runs agin." She tried hard not to let it affect her work. That was all they really cared about anyway.

The feeling crept into her heart and it was almost as if it warmed her. She raised her fingers to the ring, caressing it for a moment, wondering if what she was feeling concerned William.

As she made her way out of the thicket, she glanced up to the ridge behind them. It was the last of the tall ridges. Before them were low rolling hills called the Dells. As her eyes followed the spine of the ridge, she thought she saw a movement there. Her keen vision detected the gray form and she smiled. Could it be the same wolf? Did it follow her then? She ran forward to rejoin Ferdinand.

He glanced at her, furrowing his brow. "What? Does yer friend come to save ye? I've seen no sign. Have ye seen a sign?"

She knew he was teasing her, so she ignored him. "I thought I detected a bit of salt on the air."

"Ah, does that make ye smile? I detest the smell of dead fish which is all it means to me."

"If you smell only dead fish, it could be the places you frequent, Ferdy. Perhaps ye'll find that not all seawards smell the same."

At that moment they were interrupted by Gort. He came to order them to set up camp. "Bring in all the dry wood ye kin find if ye must cut down a dead tree. We must have plenty of fire this night."

"What's that all about?" Jael asked Ferdinand.

"I don't know, but I'll find out." With that, he was off. After a few minutes, he returned to find her already gathering wood. There was a strange look on his face. "Barto says the wolves are gathering. It's a sign, he thinks."

Jael's mind immediately went to her wolfish friend. "A sign of what?"

"The cattle are near. It's been a bad winter. The beasts are hungry, and we must keep them at bay until we have first catch."

Well, that would certainly make things more interesting.

Once they had plenty of wood assembled, Ferdinand made the fire and started the food while Jael continued to cut up wood.

Throughout the night more Brogies arrived, coming in from all over. They talked and laid plans until late. There was little chance for sleep that night anyway, for Jael's eyes wouldn't close. She kept hearing strange noises—the howling of wolves, and some strange bird that called all through the night—she was unfamiliar with the breed.

She rose up early to tend the fire, allowing Ferdinand to catch a few more winks. The bird sounded nearer than before. She kept looking about her, hoping to see it.

She sat with her back to the fire when she heard the whooshing sound, followed by the hoofbeats of many horses. A cry sounded as the sentry caught sight of them. She jumped to her feet and stood there, frozen. They were being overtaken by some mighty army of men. She bent to shake Ferdinand. "Wake up! We're under attack!"

"What? What is it?" Ferdinand jumped up, rubbing his eyes. "Who comes? Make for the trees!"

He took off running but was soon accosted by a horseman. "Stand yer ground, lad. Ye'll no be hurt if ye doan try to run." The man leveled his gaze at Jael. "That goes for you, too."

"We must," Ferdinand whispered once the rider had left them. "I think we must. What—do we stay here and be slaughtered—do ye see what's happenin' there?" He pointed to the place where the men had been sleeping a few minutes before. Most had run already, but many had been cut down. The snow was stained dark red.

Jael's heart thumped hard against her chest. "He said not to run. I think he meant it."

"Look—I see an opening. I'll take my chances there. Are ye wi' me?"

"They could've cut us down already if they wanted. I don't think they intend—" Ferdinand was already running. She took off after him.

Two riders circled around. One of them drew back his arm and hit Jael in the side of the head, sending her flying. She fell against a rock and was knocked silly. Ferdinand tried to run harder, but was taken up by the forward rider, a man twice his size. Jael tried to reach out to him, but couldn't seem to move her arm.

"Where do you think ye're going little man?" The rider asked Ferdinand. He turned his horse back and faced his comrade. "It's as Solis said—a slave—see the markin's?" Ferdinand had an S-shaped brand on the back of his neck. The man pointed it out. Jael watched as if in dream, still unable to move.

"What of that one?" The other man asked, pointing his lance at her.

"He be a slave, too." Ferdinand said. "Ain't got a brand yet. They just caught him a short time ago."

"More'n likely true," said the big man. "Too small to be anything else. Take 'im up and bring 'im in like Master said." The other rider dismounted and tossed Jael over his shoulder. "No bigger'n a fly. What were they thinkin' a doin' with him?"

"Oh he'll grow. They train 'em up from babbies to do their work."

Once Jael was lying over this man's saddle, she lost all hold on consciousness.

Jael woke sometime later, after having some very strange dreams. The whole world had gone off-kilter. It was heaving and hoving like a ship at sea.

"Bout time you waked," Ferdinand whispered.

Jael gazed skyward, seeing nothing but fuzzy white clouds. Her stomach heaved. She swallowed the bile and sucked in a breath. "Where are we?"

"We're on a sailing vessel. We're bein' taken far away to serve new masters, no doubt. So much fer yer friends."

Jael sat up slowly, coddling her sore head. So there was a reason for the motion in her dream. "But … we're not in chains, nor even tied up."

"I thought o' that, too. The others is all fettered. At least the ones 'at lived. It's a puzzling thing to me." He grunted. "And yet I do enjoy seeing it."

Jael was enjoying the fresh air. They were on deck, lying against some ropes. She sat back on them and looked out to sea. On one side, land slipped by at a goodly pace. On the other, there was only water for as far as she could see. She took in a great gulp of air. It was marvelous and salt-tinged. "How long did I sleep?"

"Hours—ye missed all the excitement—them bringin' the wounded on board. Then the ones what could stand, but they was in chains. They gimme a bowl o' somewhat. I dunna know what it was, but it was hot and it tasted of the sea. Some kind of fishy stew. M'hap you'll get one soon."

Jael wrinkled her nose and frowned. She did not feel at all like eating. In fact, she was quite nauseous. What she wouldn't give for a cup of tea.

As if reading her thoughts, a slender young man approached. She kept her head down and her eyes averted as he spoke to her. "You're awake, I see." He crouched before her, and touched the knot on her head. "Sorry about that, but you cannot go running when you've been told not to. You must learn that now." He cocked his head at Ferdy. "Master Ferdinand here said you were also in bondage to these men?"

Jael processed that thought and nodded her head, still staring at her hands. His voice held a familiar timbre. Her heart ached at the sound, even as her memories caressed her.

"Well then, you're free now, laddie, and if you're hungry at all, you can go below and get a bite to eat."

She gave a shudder.

He laughed. "I've seen that look many times. Tell you what. I'll see what I can do for you. Stay above where you can get the air and if it overcomes you, please move to the side and let it go into the sea." A grin still illuminating his face, he rose and made for the hold. She watched him go. Something about him was very familiar to her.

When Jael looked up to see him returning, she knew. He had to be related to William. He was so like him, only younger. She longed to ask, but held her tongue, not knowing how it would be received. He handed her a hot cup of strong tea. She thanked him then sipped it slowly, savoring every drop. It had been so long.

The young man left them and Jael looked at Ferdinand. "From what country do these men come?"

"How would I know? Do ye think I would have the stomach to ask such a thing? Ye don't know me so well, do ye?"

Jael frowned. She let her head fall back on the coils of strong smelling rope and took in more air. The tea was working. She'd just needed something in her stomach. Her legs felt weak when she tried to stand, so she sat back down on top of the coil of rope. From there, she could see more.

All along the coast now, she could see dwellings and fishing vessels. Her eyes nearly clouded over with the strain of it. And all over—all around her—she could feel a presence. She had no idea at the time what it was, but it was comforting, like being held in a huge pair of arms.

The sun was setting by the time they dropped anchor. They had not sailed very far, but apparently, they were to disembark here. Jael stood slowly, looking up and down trying to find something that looked like a castle. Perhaps they had not gone to the right place. Was her journey still not ended?

Corwinder

"𝔜oung Will!"

Jael looked up when she heard someone calling that name.

Could it be? Her heart raced, drumming in her breast. But no, the kind young man who favored William, the same who had talked to her earlier and had shown her kindness, responded to the call.

She knew by his age he could not be William's son, so he must be some other relation—a brother—a cousin, perhaps? She watched as the older man seemed to give orders to Young Will, who turned to look at her and Ferdinand.

He strode to them, set his hands on his hips and said, "Time to go, lads. We have all the prisoners ashore. You'll go with me and the rest of the men." He stood aside for them and waved a hand in the direction they should go. "Don't delay, they're waiting."

Ferdinand got up first, but his legs seemed unsteady beneath him. Jael followed behind him and Young Will, her mind teeming with questions. "What is this place?" she asked Young Will.

He glanced over his shoulder at her. "Tis Corwinder-by-the-Sea."

"Corwinder," she repeated. It had a pleasant sound, especially when Young Will said it. He even sounded like her memories of William's voice. "If I may ask, sir." She started another question, but Ferdinand gave her a wilting look. However, Young Will's expression showed patience, so she finished her question. "What will become of us here?"

"Ah, you may well ask, and I would wonder if you did not. You are free now, young lads. You may choose your own future. You may train here with the others and become warriors," he glanced back at Jael and winked. "When you've grown a bit more, perhaps. Hard work will put on muscle. Or, you may seek a trade as fishers or farriers. There are many merchants in this town, and they're willing to train if you're willing to work."

By now they were ready to disembark. They had to give their full attention to climbing down the rope ladder over the side, into the waiting small boat. Then on their landward journey, Young Will continued to regale them with facts about Corwinder. "If you choose to join the warrior band, you'll serve the finest captain ever in Solis. He's well liked, though a bit stern. And of course the finest Prince that ever lived is in charge of our lot—my esteemed uncle, William of Coldthwaite."

Jael bit down hard on her lower lip. It wouldn't do to let loose the smile that threatened. But the name tickled her ears and thrilled her heart. He was in charge, if indeed it was him, and it must be. Her heart swelled to bursting.

Young Will pronounced Coldthwaite with an r, as she'd heard the locals tended to do, making it sound like Cold-thrate. Jael spoke it under her breath, over and over, to memorize the saying of it. She fingered the ring beneath her garments. She half expected to see him on the docks where they climbed ashore. She cast about for him, examining every tall and slender man who appeared there. But he wasn't on the docks. Neither was he present when they entered the long, low room where the men spread out to recover from their latest bout, or quest, as she heard them call it.

Young Will sat Ferdinand and Jael down near the fire and promised to return for them soon. "You'll be hungry, I don't doubt, but you are both ... in need of a bit of ... ah ..."

"They could use a bath," the man called Solis said with an overabundance of mirth, in Jael's opinion. He was joined by others who sat nearby. The whole room erupted in laughter.

She felt a quick panic rise in her throat. Would they be sent to bathe together or near other men? If so, she'd be forced to confess. She'd have to reveal her identity and she had hoped to lay eyes on William first, just to be sure she was safe.

She scanned the room, time and again, but to no avail. She didn't see him at all. Her head and eyes ached with anxiety and leftover pain from the blow she'd suffered. Soon, the heat of the fire produced a lethargy. Not long afterwards, she dropped her head on her arms and joined Ferdinand in a nap.

Jael didn't know how long she slept, but when she awoke, she heard the excitement in the room and sat up. She blinked her eyes several times to clear away the sleep. Several men entered the main door and a huge roar filled the room.

"William! William!" The men cried. "He has vanquished the enemy!"

She stood up slowly in order to discern whether it was really him, but she was too short to see over the men's shoulders. She stretched onto her toes. Then her eyes found his face. He did not see her and would never have recognized her if he had. She was content for now to hang back and remain unnoticed.

Sucking in a deep breath, she was startled by a voice behind her.

"Wake yer comrade." She turned about to see a short but very sturdy man standing quite still and straight. "Me name's Stoker. I'm to take ye to the stables."

To the stables? She wanted to ask why, but thought better of it. Perhaps she'd find the reason when they got there. Perhaps that was where they would have to bathe, and the time had come when she must confess everything.

She shook Ferdinand who stood clumsily, still heavy with sleep. He followed her lead as she followed the man called Stoker. The two of them had been assigned to him for the time being. He told them he was the stable master and began giving orders straightaway.

"First order of business is to muck out them stalls. Won't make no nevermind that ye're so dirty. When ye've finished it, ye can get cleaned up. They'll no doubt be wanting to burn them clothes. Just keep clear of the horses, yer smell may spook 'em." He chuckled as he strode along.

"Ye'll have to earn yer keep here, but it ain't like ye ere a prisoner or a slave. Ye are free—young Master Will wanted me to say—no more a slave." Jael smiled at Ferdinand, who perked up a bit at the words.

"What do you think of my friends now, Ferdy?" she asked, when Stoker had moved away.

"Yer friends, what? Who among this lot knows the likes of ye? I ain't seen no reco-nizins."

"I haven't seen my friend yet, at least not close enough for him to recognize me. When I do, you'll be surprised."

Ferdinand chuckled as he worked, then held up a forkful of manure. "Ye're full of this stuff, fine young laddie. But I must admit, it is nice to think of bein' free if truly we are free. Yes, a taste of freedom is heady stuff indeed."

Halfway down the long line of stalls, Jael came across an old friend. A tall young man brought him in just as she turned to exit the neighboring stall. The stallion's fine head went up and his ears perked at the sound of her voice.

"Careful, lad," the young man said. But he remained quiet as she moved near the stallion without incident.

Lodan stretched his long beautiful neck to her and sniffed at her pockets. Her face fell. "I am sorry, old friend. I don't have any apples today. I haven't had any for some time as you'll know by the complete lack of the scent." She leaned her forehead against his neck and whispered in the ancient tongue, *"Se dun mis corinor, se dun. Lune de amistar a stordor."*

At her whispered communication, the young man reacted by pushing her aside. "I haven't seen him act so with a stranger, lad, but he can be quite fractious. Ye must take care and step aside now. I and I alone gives the care to His Majesty's horse."

Jael bowed her head and stepped out of the way. "I am sorry sir, but he is such a beautiful animal. I was drawn to him."

The young man glanced at her from time to time as he groomed Lodan. As soon as he finished his duty, he looked at her one more time before turning to go. Jael wasn't sure she liked the expression on his face. She had a sneaking suspicion he was mistrusting of her. Had he overheard her words to Lodan? Did he hear her speak the ancient tongue? Or was he merely jealous of Lodan's obvious acceptance of her?

"What makes him think the lad's a spy?" William asked Solis. "You did say it was a young lad?"

"No bigger than a yellow-bellied marmot, sir. He was evidently a new capture of the Brogies, a slave in training, so to speak. The other young lad who was already a branded slave, put us onto 'im. Then your own groomsman heard the little 'un speak in the forbidden tongue. An' 'e was speakin' it to yer horse, sir."

William drew back. "My horse?"

Solis nodded. "Yes, and that devil-dog was calm as could be, searchin' out the boys' pockets fer treats like a kiddie. What do ye think of that, sir?"

William stared into the fire, a small smile quirking his lips. Could it be? He turned back to the captain. "Where is this lad, Solis? I want to see him."

Solis scowled his displeasure. "He's a bit dirty, sir. Just come in from the trail and all. They put him straight to work muckin' out the stables."

"Just bring him to me, Solis. No need to prepare me for the worst. I can stand a bit of dirt."

"Aye, I reckon ye can, Your Lordship, sir. I'll send for 'im at once." With that, Solis strode to the door, called to one of the men and said,

"Bring that young Jonathan lad to the Prince. He wishes to interview him. Make haste."

William frowned at the name, then released a full-on smile. Jonathan, eh? He chuckled under his breath.

Solis had no sooner closed the door than a knock came upon it. He swung it open again. A servant stood there. "Beggin' yer pardon, sir—but the Lady is come down and wishes to see His Lordship." Solis scowled at the servant then turned to William. "My lord, the Lady Elizabeth wishes to see you."

William exhaled loudly and shook his head. "Make sure our little 'spy' is here when I return. I'll not be long."

"Yes, my lord." Solis stood aside and held the door open for William, who took it in three long strides. He strode through the outer door and stood looking up to an exterior staircase where he knew she would be standing. He smiled and walked to her, climbing the steps to meet her halfway. Taking her hands in his, he bent to kiss her forehead. "You are looking well sister, much better now, I believe."

"I am, dear William, now my lord husband has returned to me. It is too much to have you both scurrying off on these dangerous rounds. I fear one or both of you will fall. I have already lost you once and do not wish to go through that again."

Jael followed the messenger out of the stables, just in time to witness William's exit from the long room. The expression of his face was one of joy. She looked to see what brought such pleasure. When her eyes found his destination, her heart nearly stopped. She watched in chagrin as he rushed across the open space to the steps and met the most beautiful lady she had ever seen.

Jael bit down on her lower lip. This thought had never once occurred to her. At the door of the long room, she paused for one last look. A breeze flattened the lady's garment against the swelling of her middle. Jael's keen eyes took in the roses in the lady's cheeks, the adoration in her eyes as William dropped a kiss upon her forehead. That last was a fell blow to Jael. Her breath caught in her throat. He is married!

Herself Again

"**Come,** lad, the prince awaits. Don't daudle," the messenger told Jael.

With an aching heart, Jael kept her eyes on the stone floor as they passed through the great hall and into the side room where Solis waited for her. His face held such a stern look, she faltered.

"Stand away from the fire, so's ye doan smell up the room," he said, further humiliating her.

Jael forced down the lump in her throat and moved to a place near the corner. She kept her head down, but ran her gaze over her surrounds to occupy her mind and calm her nerves. She stood in a large square of a room with solid rock walls like all the others here. Strong dark beams formed the ceiling and a massive fireplace provided heat. A window opened out onto the parade ground, still white with snow.

Solis strode near, and dropped his head back a bit to look down his nose at her, narrowing his eyes.

She met his gaze, though briefly, wondering what he was thinking and why she had been called here. The door opened and William strode into the room. She caught her breath. For so long, she had yearned for this moment. Now that it had come, she felt no joy, only the deepest sorrow.

She could not bring herself to meet his gaze, but watched his movements furtively from beneath her lashes. He crossed to the fire and stood at a distance, watching her.

After what seemed an eternity to Jael, he spoke. "Solis, leave us. I will speak to the lad alone."

"Sir?" Solis prompted, as though unsure of what he'd heard.

William tipped his head to the side and repeated, "Leave us."

"Yes, my lord," Solis answered, throwing one last scowling glance at Jael.

After Solis' departure, William stepped nearer, his eyes never leaving Jael's face. "My men believe you are a spy. What say you?"

Jael's eyes darted to his in surprise, but quickly found the floor again. She was not sure if she should reveal her identity to him. She'd depended on being welcome, but now she didn't know. She almost felt anger at him for leading her on, but then it had been many months since he had seen her last. More than likely, he never expected to see her again. His little parting kiss had meant nothing. She'd read more into it than what was really there. What a fool she'd been.

All of these thoughts swirled in her mind as William stood waiting for an answer.

"You do speak, do you not? My men have heard you." He stepped nearer. "By matter of fact, they have heard you speak a language long forbidden in our land. It has long been the language of spies bent on mischief. Are ye a spy then, lad?"

She opened her eyes wide. Lodan's groom. No doubt he'd run straight here to tell what he'd heard. So this was why they'd brought her here to Lord William. She raised her lids to gaze at him and as she did, her face began to burn. She dropped her gaze to study the floor. Her fingers trembled as she pushed at a strand of hair.

"I ... did not know ..." But then she had. Had Ferdinand not warned her how it would be? She shook her head. "I am no spy, my lord, just a humble servant."

William took another step, more convinced now than ever. He had heard her voice. Jael's voice. He kept his own low, mindful of the prying ears just outside the door. "What have you done to yourself, Jael? How have you come to this?"

She pressed her lips together as her eyes filled with moisture. Then she lifted her chin and forced her eyes to meet his. "I had no choice, my lord." She closed her eyes, forcing out tears that coursed down her dirty cheeks.

William was not angry at her, but at himself. If only he'd brought her with him in the beginning, she wouldn't have suffered so much. That she had suffered greatly, was evident in the gaunt, sunken eyes that had once held so much light. Her beautiful flaxen hair hung limp, chopped short. He folded his arms behind his back to hide a tremor that shook his limbs.

"What am I to do with you now, lady? I leave on the morrow to go into battle once again in defense of our lands." He watched her expression. "And what of you?"

Her eyes widened, reflecting hope. "I could go with you."

He shook his head. "It is not possible."

She covered her cracked lips with the back of her hand. "My lord, I have traveled these many months as a man…"

He barely hid a smile and shook his head. "And no one guessed your secret?"

She opened her mouth, then closed it again. After a moment's hesitation, she answered. "Only one … or two …" she frowned. "Not more than three …"

He laughed outright. "It is as I thought. Nay, my lady, I cannot take you with me. There is nothing for it, you must stay here."

She lifted her dirt-stained palms, ready to plead with him. "But why? I can work—I can take care of horses—I can …" her voice tapered off. "No one will know."

William scowled at her. Not used to being contradicted, he watched her, weighing his response. "I will know." He took a step back and jerked a cord that hung from the ceiling. A moment later, a woman entered and curtseyed before him. He greeted her. "Abigail." He looked up to see Solis standing in the doorway. "Close the door, please, Solis."

Solis' brow arched.

William stood his ground. "With you on the outside."

With a curt nod, Solis backed out the door and closed it.

With a glance at Jael, William turned back to Abigail. "I have something for you to do. It is very important, and you must keep it as quiet as possible."

Abigail nodded, peering up at him. "Yes, my lord?"

"You see this … person?" He gestured to Jael. "This is my friend, from a distant land beyond the Touris. Not a lad, as you would presume, but a young woman."

Abigail gave a soft gasp.

"Yes, Abigail. It is quite shocking, but it was a necessary ruse, for her safety. I would like for you to prepare a room for her in the main house. Then see if you can find the woman underneath all of that … filth." He gazed at Jael.

Abigail bowed again. "Yes, my lord. I'll go at once, and make the preparations. If it is all right with ye, I will return for hi … ah ... her … then." With another glance at Jael, Abigail bowed out, closing the door behind her.

William faced Jael. "Abigail will give you whatever you need. You can trust her completely."

Jael kept her eyes on the floor. "Thank you, my lord."

He sniffed. She still couldn't speak his name. He sucked in a deep breath then released it. "I have another reason for wanting you to remain here." He watched as with some reluctance, she raised her eyes to his. He frowned. She seemed not to trust him. Why was that? What had she suffered? He took a step nearer, observing her more closely. What had been done to her?

He fought the desire to touch her, examine her for bruises, or other physical signs of abuse. Assure her of his continued care for her.

Then he shook himself, forced his mind to concentrate on the matter at hand. "My sister is nearing her confinement. Her husband travels with me as one of my most trusted warriors. We will be much more at ease, knowing you are here with her."

She blinked her eyes several times as his words seemed to penetrate the darkness of her mood.

When she did not immediately speak, he continued, wondering at the strange expression on her face. "You met the man called Young Will, I believe?"

She nodded.

"He is my nephew, the son of my eldest sister who—tragically—died in childbirth. So you can see why I'm concerned, and her husband, also."

She licked her lips. "Is there no midwife?"

"Aye there is, but ... she is quite old. Believe me when I say your presence would be a great comfort."

He smiled, ever so slightly, hoping to relieve her mind. She bit her lip again. William took a breath. "Have you ever ... assisted in a birth?" Aye, a touchy subject, but she, being a healer, shouldn't be as sensitive to such things.

She gave a slow nod, watching him with a look of caution. The door opened, startling her. She took a backward step.

Abigail entered and stood before him, hands folded in front of her. "The room is ready, my lord."

William turned his attention back to Jael, almost loathe to see her go, though of course, she needed immediate attention. "Go with Abigail."

Turning to the servant he said, "Take good care of her, Abigail. Give her whatever she needs." He spoke the words softly, having seen Solis standing just outside the door. He was not prepared for questions yet. He stood aside, and Jael looked up at him. Oh, the depths of pain in those eyes. It fair stabbed his heart. And he would bet she'd also seen Solis. For she kept her head down as she softly whispered, "Thank you, Your Majesty."

Jael followed Abigail out of the room. All eyes in the longroom seemed glued to her as they passed through. A young warrior held the outer door open for them. Oh, the questions that would fly around the room after they'd gone. Well, let them question. They'd not come up with the answer. Especially since Jonathan would never return.

Abigail crossed the muddy compound to a set of stairs on the other side. The same stairs where only a short while earlier, Jael had seen William with the woman she now knew to be his sister. What a relief that had been. Her knees had gone weak. If only she'd been clean, and dressed in an appropriate outfit. Och, rue! What must he think of her? She mustn't think of it. She gave the housekeeper her full attention.

Abigail was slight of stature and pleasantly full about the middle. Her round face sported rosy cheeks and full lips. She had white hair piled neatly on top of her head, with little wisps slipping out here and there. Small, round brown eyes completed an overall friendly face, but today Jael sensed she was anxious. Occasionally, she cast a glance over her shoulder. A very sobering experience for Jael. She could well imagine the woman's thoughts. *Who is this strange person given into my care? What kind of woman would dress in men's apparel and travel unknown miles across the rugged Touris unescorted?*

Jael would no doubt think the same given the circumstances. Here was a trusted servant of the man who had come to mean so much to Jael, and more than anything, she found herself wanting to please that trusted servant.

On the landing, Abigail opened a door and entered the rough stone building that stood opposite the main headquarters. They traversed a long corridor, their footsteps echoing on smooth wooden floors. The structure seemed to be a private residence, though quite a lot larger and grander than anything Jael had ever seen. They passed room after room before turning a sharp corner and coming to a pleasant, though sparse corner room. Dark drapes covered the closely shuttered windows. Inside, two other women worked diligently making preparations, while others brought hot water, and built up the fire. It was quite warm within the room.

Once inside, Abigail closed the door then led Jael into an inner room, perhaps some kind of dressing area. An entire wall was made up of cabinets and doors and in the middle of the space, there sat a padded stool, and a dressing table with a looking glass. The latter object was something Jael did not want to see at all. She turned her back to it.

"Sit there," Abigail said, pointing to the stool.

When she took up a pair of shears, Jael's eyes widened.

Abigail set her lips and tilted her head to the side. "I'll just be cutting away these rags ye're wearing. They be filthy and will need to be burned out of doors."

Jael made no comment as heat rushed into her face, burning at her cheeks. In truth, she was flooded with relief at the thought of being free of the rags. How clean they'd been when Ader gave them to her. How shocked that little woman would be now, could she see their condition.

Snip! Abigail began to cut. The garments fell down around Jael's waist. As she turned, Jael caught a glimpse of something quite shocking in the dressing table mirror. She turned her head away at once, but that quick glimpse brought on a flood of tears, she could not seem to halt. Of all the things that could happen, this was by far the worst.

Abigail stopped her cutting and stood back. "I'm sorry, miss. Were ye attached to them garments? Would ye not wish them destroyed?"

Jael shook her head in misery. "It's not that. I ... I've not seen myself like this." All at once, this struck her funny, and to Abigail's obvious confusion, Jael began to laugh. The two other women in the room stood still and looked at her, no doubt wondering if this creature was cracked in the head.

Then Abigail smiled. "I see yer concern," was her pragmatic reply. "If I looked as ye do, I would cry also." She gripped Jael's shoulder. "They be cleansin' tears, ye'll see. A little soap and hot water's all ye need. We'll have ye back to yer old self in no time."

Her kind words settled Jael's strained emotions. But as Abigail began cutting at the muslin wrapping, Jael heard a swift intake of breath. To her credit, the woman did not speak. Jael closed her eyes, knowing her back must look quite shocking, since she'd been whipped several times while with the Brogies.

Jael lifted the ring from about her neck and laid it on the dressing table. Abigail looked from the ring to Jael, inquisitive. But she didn't ask the questions Jael knew she must feel. She simply resumed her task, and when the clothing fell away, she gave a sigh of relief. "There. You are free of them things for good." She kicked them aside and gave a nod of her head to one of the other ladies, who picked them up and left the room.

Abigail and the remaining maid lifted up a sheet to give Jael privacy as she stepped into the waiting bath. It was all somewhat humiliating, for she had never stood unclothed before anyone, save her grandmother and possibly her mother. But oh, the warm bath felt wonderful. She closed her eyes in ecstacy, relaxed, and let her head fall back against the rim of the tub.

How many months had she longed for this?

"Help me scrub her, Hazel," Abigail whispered, refusing to let Jael move a muscle. It felt good at first, but then Jael thought perhaps they had removed the top layer of her skin. After they had scrubbed the rest, Hazel poured warm water over Jael's head then Abigail scrubbed her hair with strong soap, taking care around the egg-sized knot on her head. She worked up a powerful lather that smelled of pine tar.

When the bath was done, Hazel rubbed her down with sweet oil while Abigail tried to tame the snarls in her hair. "I know you're fagged, miss, but if it should dry this way, we would never get the tangles out."

Jael sat in a large and very comfortable chair and nearly fell asleep while Abigail finished her hair with a loose braid. Then the woman propped Jael's feet on a tufted hassock, covered her with a soft blanket, and left her there to rest.

Jael was barely aware of Hazel and the other maid cleaning up the mess from the bath. Abigail banked the fire, pushed open a shutter just a crack then let herself out.

Jael let the lanquidity take full hold and drifted off to sleep.

When Abigail knocked at William's door, he sent Solis out again.

Solis glared at the housekeeper as he crossed the room and closed the door.

William hid a smile behind his wrist, pretending to scratch his nose. He could picture Solis standing just on the other side of the door, straining to hear what passed within.

Abigail curtseyed. "My lord."

William nodded. "How is she?"

"She's resting peacefully now."

He stood with one hand on the fireplace mantel, a thumb hooked in his belt. "But how is she, Abigail? Is she well?"

Abigail frowned then gave a nod. "I believe so, but she is gaunt and thin. Ye could see her bones poking through and ... I believe she may have been beaten, sir. There're scars on her poor back, and bruises, some old, some new. As well there's a largish knot on the back of her head. I do not know what she may have suffered, for she didn't complain, but it must have been bad." She shook her head and clucked her tongue. "It must have been very bad indeed, sir."

William winced at the thought of Jael being beaten. He knew most of her suffering would have been at the hands of the Brogies, since they were known for mistreating their slaves. He only hoped that was all they'd done. If they'd discovered she was female—he did not even want to consider what could've happened to her.

He turned away from the fire and looked at Abigail. "You say she's sleeping now?"

"Aye, sir. She liked to fell asleep in the bath, sir, she was so very tired. I've put her in the corner room, where she'll have plenty of privacy. It's not the finest of rooms, but ..."

He held up his hand. "No, that is good. I have only one more thing to ask of you, Abigail. We leave early on the morrow, but I do wish to speak to the lady before I go. Would you go in early and see that she's awake and decent? I do not wish to disturb her, but I will be gone for some time, and it is needful that I speak with her ere I go."

Abigail bowed her head. "Aye, my lord, I will do as ye ask." With that she turned to go, but drew up short when the door opened, and Solis stood before her.

William resisted the urge to roll his eyes.

Keeping a close watch on William, Solis stepped aside to allow Abigail to pass.

When she'd gone, William addressed the captain. "Close the door, Solis. I have something to tell you."

William knew full well Solis always liked to be in the good graces of his leader. He held a great deal of respect for the man. It was earned respect, which made it all the more valuable.

Solis stood at attention as William related the events of the day then gave him a solemn charge. "You are now in possession of an important secret, Solis. Her presence here must not be noised about. The lady has come to me for protection, and I mean to give it."

Solis nodded. "Ye are thinking of the tracker, sir?"

"Aye. He is still out there. I don't want him causing trouble while we're away. So I shall need four trustworthy men to leave behind. I'll trust you to do the choosing."

"Whoever they be, they'll be none too pleased at being left behind whilst everyone else is on campaign."

William rested his palms on the worktable and leaned forward. "I understand that. You must make them grasp how important a mission is theirs. Not only will they protect the lady, but also my sister, and most likely, the queen herself. I expect my mother will join the Lady Elizabeth for her confinement."

He stood and strode to the door. "You tell them that, Solis, and I've a notion they'll volunteer their services."

Elizabeth

Jael was awake when Abigail entered, set down a tray, and stepped to the chair where Jael had spent the night. "Are ye awake, my lady?"

"I am, and have been watching the first rays of the sun. It is so wonderful to lie abed." She offered Abigail a smile.

"I am quite certain it must be," said Abigail.

Jael suspected the woman never had that opportunity.

Abigail spoke again. "I am sorry to disturb ye so early, but Lord William wishes to speak with ye. He says it is a matter of great importance."

"Of course, I will get up right away."

She held out her hands to stay Jael. "Oh no, he says ye are not to rise by no means. He will come in when ye are decent. I've brought ye a cup o' tea and when ye've had it, he'll no doubt be ready. He leaves this morn, ye ken, and he'll be gone for many a day."

Sorrow blanketed Jael's spirit as she confessed her knowledge of Lord William's imminent departure. She took the cup of tea and sipped it slowly. Abigail took a brush to her hair and afterwards, braided it again. Then she slipped quietly out to inform the master, the Lady Jael was awake.

William took a quick account of Jael's appearance as she looked back at him. She was still pale, but the dark circles beneath her eyes had lessened somewhat. And then her eyes—there was just a glimmer there of the old Jael—the girl he'd known so many months prior. "I hope I didn't wake you."

"No my lord, you did not."

"I am sorry to disturb your privacy, but I must have a word with you ere I go." He stood near her, gripping the back of a chair Abigail had provided for him. "I have informed my staff that you shall have whatever you need. I want you to be comfortable here. Please feel free to ask for anything that will help make you feel at home."

She gazed up at him, but didn't speak. When she did not respond, he continued, "You are free to go about at will—but not alone." The look on her face caused him to waver, but only for a moment. He held up his hand. "You are not safe, my lady. Not even here. Not while the tracker is still out there."

She drew in a quick breath. "The tracker? What do you know of the tracker? Has he been here?"

William stepped around the chair and lowered himself onto it. "I met up with him on the trail some time back. My only regret is that I let that ferret go."

Jael fingered the lace coverlet Abigail had thrown over her. "You've met Shinder, then. If you believe he will find me here, then I must go."

"Absolutely not," he said, probably with more force than was necessary. But the mere thought of that foul creature made his blood boil.

She sat forward, insistent. "By my presence, I endanger your family."

He gave her a small smile. "Then our situation is much the same as it was last summer, my lady, when my presence endangered you. Here, at least I can see to your protection—out there—I cannot. You must stay here, Jael. There is no question of that."

She relaxed again, but the look in her eyes still troubled him. Would she stay, or would she run as soon as he had gone? He must make a stronger case.

"As I have explained to you, my sister's husband travels with me. He … and I will be much more at ease, knowing you are here with Elizabeth." He held her gaze until she dropped her eyes to study her hands. Leaning forward, he covered one of her hands with his own. "Don't force me to exact a promise from you. Because I will do just that, Jael."

Her eyes snapped to his. "I will do as you ask."

He smiled an apology. "Thank you." He sat back, resting a palm on each knee. "I am sorry I will not have time to introduce you to my sister Elizabeth. I must leave that to Abigail. I have explained the situation to my sister." He rose to go then, but Jael reached her hand toward him.

"Lord William."

A tremor shook him as he gazed at the small hand, rough and red, so changed from the first time he had seen it. She removed his ring from her finger, and held it in the palm of her hand. "I wanted to return this to you. I suppose ... I will no longer have need of it."

He shook his head. "Nay, my lady. I gave it you. It is yours to keep." He turned to go, but looked back at her. "I would that you wear it. It will give you clout here, among my people." After a moment's hesitation, he added, "In the event I do not return ... I have left instructions for your care, Jael. You will have a home, and the protection of the crown."

Leaving her no time for a response, William rushed from the room. The look in her eyes pierced his soul. He longed to touch her—hold her—stay with her, but he knew he could not. This campaign was of great importance.

He longed to tell her of it, but he dare not. She would think he did it for her. Was it fate, or providence that she should find her way to his doorstep on the eve of this journey? After standing outside her door for several long moments, he strode away. With great effort, he turned his attention to the task at hand.

After William left, Jael sat for several minutes, fingers on her lips, trembling with emotion. Why had he left her so suddenly? Why did he treat her so? Was he angry with her?

Hearing the noise from outside, she crossed to the window and pushed open the shutter. She swiped at stray tears with the back of her hand and stood looking out at the men who were gathering. There were so many of them, dressed for battle, mounted on horses. They were in for a long ride. But, where were they going?

As she watched, William walked out of the building to join his men. Dressed in a long tunic of indigo, a black leather belt at his waist, he strode across the compound, hand upon the hilt of his sword. He swung easily into the saddle, and sat for a moment, looking up at the place where she stood. She raised her hand to him. Then he turned to his men and addressed them.

"We go forward in battle this day, to meet the enemy who threatens our very existence. For many years, he has pricked us and torn away at the boundaries of our lands. He has taken our children captive, and killed our women. He has feasted on our crops and our livestock, and laughed at us from the safety of his high tower. But no more! We will bear no more of his mockery! While the river runs high, we will sail its length. We will camp at his door, and stand in his face as he awakes from his stupor! On the very eve of the Holy Day, he will reap what he has sown!"

The men went wild, yelling and clanging their shields and spears. Jael stood in awe of it all. As the meaning of his words penetrated her mind, her knees gave out from beneath her, sending her back to the chair for a moment.

The magistrate! He means to attack the magistrate of Verani Deep!

And then his words returned to her, piercing her heart. The words he spoke ere he left her room. *In the event I do not return...* The breath left her lungs in a whoosh. He feared he may not return!

When she heard another man speaking, she returned to the window. He was dressed in a brown cloak and he stood on the ground, facing the men, his arms upraised. All the men on horseback sat with their heads bowed. Her heart filled with wonder as his words reached her ears.

"Blessed are the meek; for they shall inherit the earth. Blessed are they which do hunger and thirst after righteousness; for they shall be filled. Blessed are the merciful; for they shall obtain mercy. Blessed are the pure in heart; for they shall see God. Blessed are the peacemakers; for they shall be called the children of God.

O Lord, watch over my brethren as they ride forth in the name of righteousness. May they be ever in your sight and under your secure graces, Amen."

With that, the speaker stepped aside and the battery of men moved into place behind Lord William, Young Will, Solis, and another man she must assume was William's brother-in-law.

"'Tis a sight to behold, is it not?" said a female voice from behind Jael, startling her so that she almost fell out of the window. She turned about to see the beautiful woman who had met William on the steps the day before.

"I beg your pardon, I never meant to startle you. The door was open."

Jael gave her a shy smile. "No, it is all right, I've quite recovered." So, this was Elizabeth. Her long, dark hair fell in graceful waves around her shoulders and down her back.

Dark eyes and full lips smiled back at Jael. "My name is Elizabeth. My brother has told me so much about you."

Jael nodded, feeling dowdy and self-conscious standing in front of the window in nothing but a nightdress. She gathered it about her and went back to the chair. To her surprise, Elizabeth took up a soft coverlet from the bed and threw it over her. "You must be chilled to the bone, standing in the open window like that. I can understand your distraction, though. The warriors are quite impressive." She stepped back to the window and peered out at them.

Jael's courage rose a bit. "Who was that man at the last, who spoke with so much eloquence?"

Elizabeth cast a glance at her. "That was Stephen. He is the pastor of our local congregation. We depend upon him to pray for our men before they go off on such a great campaign."

Jael was still a bit confused. "Pardon my ignorance, Lady Elizabeth, but what is a … pastor?"

"You are unfamiliar with the term? He is like a shepherd, only his flock is mankind. He cares for their spiritual needs, in much the same way a shepherd watches over his sheep."

Jael nodded her understanding. "I see."

She glanced out the window again, raising her hand in farewell, then brought both hands to her face. She glanced at Jael, bright tears brimming her eyes. "I am sorry. I've said my farewells, but it breaks my heart to see them go."

Jael wondered whether she should rise and go to the woman. But with a final glance at the retreating warriors, she closed the shutters and came to sit in the chair William had so recently vacated. She wiped her eyes and gave Jael her full attention. "I had heard you are a follower of the one God. Is this not true? My brother said you often sang psalms, with which he was quite familiar."

Evidently, her brother had said quite a lot about Jael. She was not certain how to answer. "I do follow a belief in the one God, Lady Elizabeth. From times past, my family has sung the psalms. I know not when they had their beginning."

"It is much the same with us, only we also believe in the Son of God."

"I have heard this before. You are Christian. Elizabeth is your Christian name."

Elizabeth smiled. "You have a singular way of saying Christian, enunciating each little syllable. I like it. And I know you must be aware, both our names come from the Holy Scriptures."

Jael's caught her breath. "Do you have the Holy Scriptures here?"

"Pastor Stephen has many of the manuscripts. He often reads from them in our services. You must come next time and hear it."

"May I? Though I am not a … Christian?"

Elizabeth leaned forward to lay her hand on one of Jael's. "Of course, you may. Now, you must tell me all about your journey. I am so fascinated. And it will help keep my mind off the fact my husband has gone into battle." She pressed her fingertips against her lips. "It'll be so nice to have a friend to talk to."

When Abigail entered a short time later with a tray for Jael, she seemed surprised to find Elizabeth there and the two of them conversing as if they were old friends. Jael decided Elizabeth had a gift for making people feel at ease.

Abigail dropped in a curtsey before Lady Elizabeth. "Shall I bring you something, my lady?"

"Oh no, Abigail, not now. I will wait for the midday meal. I'm a bit ... queasy this morning, perhaps because Toldar has gone. It always upsets me so."

"Have you Morningstar blossoms here?" Jael asked Abigail.

Abigail pursed her lips and knit her brow. "I believe so my lady. Does it blossom in May?"

"Yes, but I thought perhaps you may have the dried blossoms. A tea of simmered Morningstar blossoms will relieve nausea."

"I will see if they may be found." Abigail dipped her head and left the room.

Elizabeth turned back to Jael, an amused expression on her face. "So you will begin at once? My brother wanted you to rest for several days at least."

"I am resting," Jael answered with a smile. She took a bite of the porridge Abigail left and closed her eyes. "Mm…"

Elizabeth giggled. "You intrigue me, lady. Perhaps this separation from my dearest will not be so bad after all." She laid her hand on Jael's arm. "I think I shall leave you now. I am tired, and you are wishing to be alone with your food."

Jael returned her giggle. "I'm sorry. It has been so long since I've eaten anything as wonderful as this."

Elizabeth rose and padded to the door. "Come to me later and we will speak again. I must learn all there is to know about you if you are to be of help to me."

After eating everything Abigail brought her, Jael promptly fell asleep again. When she awoke, she laughed out loud. She'd been in this fine house with the wonderful big bed for twenty-four hours, but had never actually slept in it.

Abigail and Hazel were in the room, hanging up several dresses they'd managed to find for Jael. Momentarily halting their work to look askance at her, they soon took it up again. She supposed they would grow used to her strange ways in short order.

When they were alone, Abigail told Jael the servants were all very curious about their new houseguest. "They're nosing around and trying their best to get the information out of me. But the master cautioned me, he did, saying we must keep you safe at all costs. I'll not let the master down." After this long speech, Abigail presented Jael with one of her new dresses and several articles of underclothing. "I took it upon meself to find ye these dresses and the maids stitched up some under things for ye. They worked well into the night and early this morning to produce them. Now, ye must make haste. Lady Elizabeth has requested ye for luncheon in her quarters. Hazel will help ye dress, if ye've a mind."

Jael had a necessary detour to make first. When she returned, Abigail had gone, and Hazel stood waiting to help her into the new things.

The undergarments were well made, even if they were done quickly. They were much finer than anything Jael had ever worn. The dark blue dress she chose was heavy and warm, much to her liking and it looked well on her.

While Hazel fixed her hair, Jael took in the woman's appearance. Her wiry red hair fought to free itself of the braids she wound into a bun at the base of her skull. Freckles dotted her hands and face. The dots pinked when Hazel was pleased, which she often was, in Jael's presence.

Jael widened her eyes as she gazed at her own reflection in the looking glass. "I can hardly tell it's been cut. Thank you so much, Hazel."

Hazel curtseyed, green eyes brightened by the praise. She showed Jael the way to Elizabeth's quarters then left the two alone.

"Do sit down, please Jael. You look quite well, by the way. Hazel did a wonderful job with your hair. Did you have a maid where you were from?"

Jael laughed. "Nay, my lady, I was quite alone."

She made a grimacing face. "I find that appalling. I've never been alone in my entire life."

Abigail served up a feast. At least it seemed so to Jael. She'd never seen such a fine outlay all in one place. Instead of the rude pottery Jael had grown up using, there was fine hand painted porcelain. She tried really hard not to show her awe over everything. When they'd finished the meal, Abigail cleared it away.

Elizabeth suggested a walk. This was the first time Jael noticed the guards. As soon as the door opened, two men appeared at their side, and stayed with them everywhere they went.

"I fear I shall not get used to this," Elizabeth whispered to Jael. "I know 'tis for our safety, but it is so ... confining."

"I'm sorry, this is my fault."

Elizabeth gave her pretty head a shake. "Nay, do not be sorry, my friend. Besides, have you noticed the one on the left? He is quite fine, do you not think?"

Jael feigned shock and whispered back, "Are you not a married lady?"

Elizabeth giggled. "Married, yes—dead, no—besides, I believe I was thinking of you."

Verani Deep: Growing Darkness

Lundar Cheek rubbed the back of his neck to relieve a bit of his distress. The Magistrate had called a meeting of his officers and as usual, the man was late.

Darkness had descended on Verani Deep by the time Torin Dugold took his place at the head of the memory table. A new chair had just been crafted for him, carved from a single tree trunk and fortified with iron bands. He'd outgrown the last one. He sank into its well-padded depths with a heavy sigh. "Ah, ye have done yerselves proud, boys. Ye may live to regret it, though, I'm quite cozy." He chuckled deep in his massive chest as he lit his pipe. "What have ye heard from the plains today?"

His first officer frowned and spoke in a rumbling voice. "We've heard no good news, milord. The rains have made it impossible to ready the fields for planting. The dampness has brought on much sickness."

Lundar near jumped out of his chair when Torin slammed his fat fist upon the table, upsetting the nearest flagon of ale. "Blast it all! Does my comfort mean nothing to ye? Give me news I can sink my teeth into." He gazed around the table. "Link? What of thee?"

The slaves working at the fire paused in their labors, dashing frightened glances at the master's table.

Link swallowed, nearly choking on a draught of ale. "I've had a missive from Shinder," he managed to spit out amid spewing ale.

"Ah, Shinder—now there's a man after me own heart—evil through and through. Let me have it." Torin's bulging eyes found a spot upon the far wall to concentrate on as he blew out a lungful of smoke. He pursed his lips and replaced the pipe.

Keeping his eyes trained on the table before him, Link swallowed again, his adam's apple traveling up and down his scrawny neck. "He's come upon the wench in a fishing village full of caverns. She thinks she's safe and sound, is what he says, and he 'tends to let it be for a time until she grows careless. Then he 'tends to burn her out. She's a sly one, Rogan's daughter. He says she's dressed in man clothes and done covered hersel' w' filth."

Lundar scoffed and several of the men at the table made noises of surprise. Torin dropped his over-sized head back and laughed heartily. "Och, ain't it astonishin' what one will do when one is scared half out of one's wits? That's news indeed, Link, and so very ..." he smacked his lips loudly, "satisfying. Yes. We did well to send Shinder. He'll not give up until he has her. I longs to watch her roast like yon pig. If only we could have her here by the Holy Day. Would it not be diverting?"

His men agreed, banging the table with their fists.

Lundar Cheek feigned his approval of Dugold's plan. With one long, bony finger, he pushed at a bit of leaf he'd pulled from his cloak. These meetings were a terrible bore. They took him away from more pleasant pastimes. If only he'd been able to capture that wily woman. That will o' the wisp. It would have been so different. He'd be on his own now, instead of lookin' at that uppity fat hog. How he despised the man and every minute spent in his presence. But Cheek was bound to the magistrate, until he could manage to free himself.

One favor so long ago—one itsy, bitsy favor—had indebted him for a lifetime. And had it been worth it? Nay. Most decidedly not. The wench had up and died on him. He spit his ire upon the floor, bringing a swift glare from his master.

An eerie screeching sound filled the room as a bone-thin servant turned the spigot over the flame, sending chills up and down Lundar's spine. The roasting pig filled the room with its heavy scent, but his stomach churned.

It should have been he who'd taken Rogan's daughter, he ruminated. If he'd not waited for word from the fat man, he'd have had her. For he was convinced she'd been there, in the house, when they'd first arrived. Her witchcraft had been her salvation that day. She'd faded through the very walls. He could still smell her presence within. He ground his teeth and sat forward. Now there would need to be another way to gain his freedom, but he wouldn't find it here, shut up in this hell-hole of a broken-down castle.

"Is that ye, Cheek? Volunteering to go into Dolor Heights? I am surprised. I thought ye did not like it there."

Lundar Cheek's eyes widened. He looked up. What had he missed?

There was snickering all around the room.

Shaking off the confusion, he swallowed his pride and asked, "What will ye have me do there, milord?"

Torin screwed up his face, stretching his large mouth into an oval. "Spy out the land, me hardy!" He sent Cheek a grotesque wink. "Find me a reason to roast a few peasants. It's been too long since we've had some fun. What think ye?"

"With yer permission, I'll leave at once." He punctuated it with a light fist pounding on the table, as was their custom.

He was more than happy to go, so made a quick exit. Several of Dugold's cronies looked as if they'd volunteer to go with him. No one loved the magistrate's meetings. But he didn't need or want their company. He must use the time well and come up with a solution to his problem.

Ever since that fiasco at the Haven, the master had been more aggressive than ever. Lundar and his men had done the master's bidding, but the silly dawds feared the haven. They'd cried about it constantly. *Who knows what curse we've brought on ourselves?* Wah, wah, wah! Babbies, the lot o'them.

It was well known to any and all the place was mysterious, guarded by some great power. Else, why could they never find the path nor ever the source? The magistrate himself was most likely cursed, that much was plain to see. He'd never been the same since he struck the Rogan. He was constantly sick, grew sallow, and ever fatter.

Outside, Lundar stood for a moment, looking out over the fog enshrouded valley. His tongue sought a sore spot on his gum whilst he scratched his chest.

A stupid night bird sang its song, oblivious to the fact so much evil lay close upon its doorstep. Lundar shrugged his bony shoulders. He'd go to Dolor. And if there be anyone left alive there, he'd bring them back to please the magistrate, perhaps to satiate his evil hunger for a time.

But Lundar knew the day would come, and was even fast approaching, when he would have his revenge. He did not know how it would come. He only knew 'twould come.

$\mathfrak{Shinder}$ set out on the road to the coastal village of Corwinder-by-the-Sea. He was a patient man. He'd learned the art of patience long ago. Chewing his lower lip, he spat in the weeds beside the road, licked his forefinger, and held it up, testing the direction of the breeze.

He'd learned, if you waited long enough, your prey lost its fear and grew over-confident. Then you could walk right in and take the prize. So what if it hadn't worked the last two times he'd tried it with this 'un. He prided himself in knowing when to call it quits. But he'd never call it quits on this foul offspring of the Rogan. It was a matter of wills, and his was stronger.

He'd spent several weeks wandering about Corwinder. It seemed a pleasant town and the people were well used to strangers, so they paid him little heed. He'd come there within days of the arrival of the ship. The Prince of the Realm had beaten back the Brogies. Interesting. But that wasn't all he'd learned.

He heard tell of two young slaves who'd been taken in at the fort. He bided his time and was well rewarded when he heard a tale passed on by one of the young maids working there. She told a man friend at the pub, who told another, who was persuaded to tell Shinder. A woman had arrived, dressed as a man. Yes, he knew who it was before they whispered the name. *The Lady of the Haven.* They whispered it with apparent awe.

Bah. Such nonsense.

He ground his teeth then ran his tongue over his lips as if he was about to consume something delicious. For he also knew the main body of warriors had gone away and they would not be back for a long time, which meant he had plenty, and he planned to take it.

He removed to a small cove, where an old fisher's hut stood, and there he stayed, watching and waiting.

True Friends

After several days of pleasant occupation, Jael began to think about her position in this household. She was higher than a servant, that much was certain. Having been raised in solitude, she was usually unaware of such things, but several times in their conversations, Lady Elizabeth had alluded to the differences.

"It has been so long since I've had anyone to commune with," she'd told Jael. "Of course I may talk to the servants, but not on the same level. One mustn't fraternize overmuch or they will take advantage."

Jael thought about her words for a long time. Lord William had ordered her to stay so she'd supervise the birth of his sister's child. Did that not constitute some sort of servanthood? Would it be insensitive to introduce the subject at this time? Perhaps Lady Elizabeth hadn't thought of it in this light. On the other hand, it may discourage her friendship. Jael was loathe to do that. She'd never had a true friend, other than Peg, and Peg hardly qualified, since she was a mule.

After spending much time in thinking on this, Jael made a discovery. A little too slow in coming, by her way of thinking. Surely she was losing her touch.

Abigail, who was definitely on the level of servant, but in the management category as housekeeper, gave a curtsey to Jael whenever she entered, and addressed her as "Lady Jael" or "my lady."

Why had she never noticed this before? Should she try to set this to rights? Would they not resent her when Lord William returned and her true role came to light?

Jael lifted her hand and looked long at the ring she wore. She'd placed it on the first finger of her right hand, since it was quite large. Even then it sometimes threatened to slip off. She'd pressed a glob of wax behind the stone to hold the ring in place. Lord William had made her keep it, saying it would give her clout among his people. Is this what he meant? Did he mean to give her some authority here? Did he mean to elevate her from her low estate, to one that would serve him better? And why was that, exactly? It was a puzzlement. One of many presented to her in this place.

After several days of rest, Jael took the time to familiarize herself with the house. She discovered a passage that led to the roof. It was a wonderful place with a full view of the surrounding area, including the shoreline. It had evidently been built for this purpose, for a low wooden railing ran about the entire area of the flat roof. She supposed it was a lookout of some sort.

She found a very comfortable hideaway here as well, which was bathed in sunlight in the mornings from the time the sun arose until midday. Someone had placed a stone bench there, where one could sit with one's back against the wall of the turret and look out to sea. What a wonderful place to commune with God.

She sang her psalms softly and no one heard. No one knew, because the only time she was guarded was when she actually left the confines of the house. Here too, she could hear Elizabeth's voice when she called to her, for Elizabeth's rooms were inside the turret.

"You look unusually bright today," Elizabeth told her after one such retreat to the roof.

Jael smiled into Elizabeth's eyes. "The sun is out."

"Ah, is that all?" Elizabeth laughed. "It is often present here. You shall probably grow very tired of it."

"Nay, I don't believe I ever shall. I have had enough of gloomy days."

Elizabeth was sitting in a large chair, with a beautifully woven cloth spread over her lap. She was making colorful designs on it with a needle and this fascinated Jael, who'd never seen such fancy work.

"Have you really never seen embroidery?" Elizabeth asked her. "Do you sew?"

"Well, yes, we were sailmakers." She wondered what the lady would think of this.

Elizabeth seemed unconcerned. "Yes, but that is crude cloth, is it not? Look at this fabric." She picked up a corner of the cloth with her fingertips and showed it to Jael.

Jael touched it lightly. "It is a wonderful thing, so soft, and the designs you are making are so beautiful and colorful."

"It is for the baby, you know, for the cradle. Would you like to learn it? If you can sew, you will be able to learn these stitches easily."

Jael doubted her clumsy fingers could turn out such intricate work, but she was willing to try. It did seem a good way to pass the time when she wasn't otherwise occupied.

Elizabeth's health fared well. Dora, the elderly midwife seemed pleased with her progress. But the old woman didn't like Jael.

With a sour glance at Jael, she expressed her concern to Elizabeth, though Jael stood not ten paces away. "She's too young, and hasn't the experience. There's some 'at says she has witchin' ways."

Elizabeth's beautiful brows knit in a frown. "My brother says she's an excellent healer."

Dora scowled and raised a single eyebrow. She looked Jael up and down.

Elizabeth was adamant. "*He* wants her present for the birth."

Jael noted Dora's evident lack of enthusiasm, even after being told the master wanted Jael. But what could be done about it? What else could be said? Elizabeth could hardly say her brother didn't trust old Dora and wanted Jael there in case of problems. That would not sit well with the woman, nor would it please the servants, who had utmost respect for Old Dora.

Dora bowed her head and muttered, "What Lord William wants will certainly be done." She said no more out loud, but as she left the room, Jael clearly heard her mutter, "The young prince will do well to worry over his own men and not fret over women's concerns."

Jael hid a smile behind her hand. Sometimes acute hearing was a blessing, sometimes not.

Three days had come and gone before Jael ventured forth into the fresh morning air to look for herbs. She needed to build up a supply in order to function in the office of healer. Abigail seemed not to know anyone in all Corwinder who dealt in herbs. "Is there no apothecary?" Jael asked.

"Ah, the 'pothcree—aye, my lady, we have that. I will send to him at once so he may come and speak w'ye. That would be best in light of Lord William's orders."

Jael arched a brow. "Lord William's orders?"

"Aye, my lady. He said fer me to be sure ye doan try to go into the common area. There be danger there. I will send for the 'pothcree and mayhap he could come this very day, but he is a right busy man."

Jael would've like to go into the common area and had just been considering it prior to Abigail's pronouncement. Of course, the woman was only following orders, so Jael tried not to get her hackles up over it. She resigned herself to wait upon the man's visit, and hoped he didn't take too long.

He did come that day and Jael found him to be somewhat helpful, though he was unfamiliar with many of the herbs she liked to have on hand. He made do with a much smaller inventory, which worried her a little. Perhaps they were unavailable in these parts. She thought with regret of the many wonderful plants she had passed on her journey. If she had only known how things would be.

No use wasting time on regret. They would all have been lost, either at Duflec, or certainly among the Brogies.

There was nothing for it then, but to venture forth on her own. Surely the guards would allow her to walk about the grounds, and perhaps even down by the sea?

The young man who had caught Elizabeth's discerning eye that first day introduced himself to Jael. "I am Courin, my lady. What may I do for you?" He stood nearly a foot taller than the others, and evidently outranked them.

"I would like to go in search of herbs, in order to build my inventory," she told him. She didn't see the need in telling him about the Apothecary's visit.

His handsome face showed signs of doubt. "Nay, my lady, I dunna like it, Lord William says ye are not to go about where there may be danger."

She stood looking up at him. "Lord William told me I was free to go about, as long as I was accompanied by a guard." There was a soft snicker behind him and Jael stepped aside to see from whence it came. Someone crouched before the fire, feeding its flames with fresh wood. Noting the silence, the man turned, and she immediately recognized his face. She almost spoke his name, but bit back the word just in time. Ferdinand.

His face darkened when he realized they'd overheard. He stood and bowed low before her. "Beggin' yer pardon, my lady."

She stepped back then glanced at Courin, hoping to distract him from Ferdinand's blunder. "If you will, sir, I could do with a bit of help. I must prepare for Lady Elizabeth's confinement. I must have the necessary herbs on hand. It will take some time to prepare them properly." In order to punctuate her request, she raised her right hand to her throat, displaying the ring.

Courin's hard expression softened. He inclined his head. "Aye, my lady, I will see ye have your escort, but ye must give me time. Can ye return in half an hour?"

Just outside the door, Jael heard the young officer chide the poor young man. "Ye will make yerself ready to accompany the lady. Go to the gardener and ask for the necessary tools. And Ferdinand, do not humiliate yerself further. Keep a civil tongue in yer head." Ferdinand hurried away, passing close to the spot where Jael stood. He didn't look back, or he would surely have seen her standing there.

When she returned half an hour later, she found Ferdinand waiting with two of the guards. He'd assembled a wheelbarrow filled with tools for their excursion. She smiled at the sight. She could do a great deal of gathering with all that. As she set out, she felt his eyes upon her. Did he guess or know her identity? She'd seen no recognition in his face, yet he watched her. When she spoke, a strange expression crossed his countenance—puzzlement, perhaps.

It took great patience on the part of the guards to accompany Jael, as she stopped often, to examine the flora. Some she did not recognize at all, but most were quite common. Nearer the shore, she found Lamb's Wort and Endergazen, a delicate blossoming plant that grew from bulbous roots. The dried roots could produce a deep and restful sleep, but too much would result in death. She harvested only a few of those.

Lamb's Wort thickened the blood and fought infection. This thought sent her eyes to the trees where she soon located a yew. She would need that also. By the time she'd finished for the day, the sun was past noon. She apologized to the men for keeping them so long. They shrugged it off, but she suspected they were not happy about being late to midday meal.

As she collected her things from the wheelbarrow, she smiled at Ferdinand. The puzzled look returned to his expressive face. She almost perceived recognition there.

"And where have you been this morning, dear friend?" Elizabeth asked as she entered Jael's room.

Jael dusted her hands together. "I have been out harvesting herbs. Come and see."

Elizabeth regarded the plants strewn about on the table. "Are these not weeds and grasses?"

"Weeds and grasses containing powerful chemicals that can help your body heal itself."

Elizabeth looked askance at Jael. "Is this not sorcery, dear friend?"

Jael gave her a mischievous grin. "Some would call it so. At least until they have a need for its power. I would say instead, God's provision for our life on earth."

Elizabeth clapped her hands. "Well said. These are the things you were asking Abigail about? Are there Morningstar flowers here?"

"Nay, I purchased those from the apothecary. The Morningstar flower blossoms only in the woodlands, and our fine guards will not allow me to go there."

Elizabeth sat in Jael's favorite chair. "Well, you have been out all morning, so you missed the delivery of the letter." From the look on Elizabeth's face, Jael knew it must be good news.

"From my husband, of course. They are well, though he cannot tell me where." She lifted her eyes to Jael's. "They will leave their horses and proceed by boat. He didn't tell me this in the letter, I knew it already. Before he left, he told me he would send me a note when they reached that place. The rest is ... personal, but they are well, and apparently, right on schedule." She refolded the letter and sat looking at Jael. "Tomorrow is our Sabbath. Will you accompany me to the service?"

"Yes, I'd like to. What time shall I be ready?"

The services were held in a chapel built for the men, so the main floor was theirs. Any family, ladies in particular, sat above the pastor behind a silk curtain. This not only provided privacy for ladies, but kept the ladies from becoming a distraction to the men. Jael could only feel excitement the first time she sat there, waiting for Stephen to arrive. When his family entered the alcove and sat down, Elizabeth introduced his wife Elenor, and their children, three daughters, and two sons.

Many of the female servants of the household also sat in the alcove. It seemed a bit strange to Jael, because the main floor held only a few men, since the main body of warriors was away.

A hush came over them when Stephen entered. His hair shone bright white through the silk curtain. This morning, he spoke on the history of the church, beginning with the prophecies foretelling the birth of a savior. He ended with:

"Let us begin to prepare our hearts to celebrate the Holy Day, when this very Savior, the only Son of God gave up his life and then as he foretold, received it again. He is risen to live in our hearts."

She felt quite stimulated by this message, though numerous questions filled her mind. Especially when he read, "Let not your heart be troubled, believe in God, also in me believe..."[iv]

She squeezed her eyes shut and let the words permeate her being. These were new thoughts. She must have time to think about them.

But not now, for directly following the service, she accompanied Elizabeth to the house where they would receive guests for dinner. Fortunately, Stephen and his family were among those guests. Jael waited for the opportunity to speak with him. There was none until he was leaving.

"It was so nice to meet you, my lady," he said. "I have heard so much about you."

Heat rushed into Jael's cheeks. She could only imagine what he had heard. "I enjoyed your ... I believe you called it a sermon? I have many questions, sir."

Stephen smiled into her eyes. "I love questions. An inquisitive mind is a definite sign of intelligence. You must come to our house two days hence. We have small informal meetings there, and we discuss many things that may interest you."

Jael watched them as they walked away, the man and his wife, with the children running ahead. There was definitely something different about them. They fairly glowed with a presence of something she could not put her finger on.

New Roads

Ferdinand felt Courin's eyes upon him as he worked with the horses. It was unnerving. What was the young master thinking? Had Ferdinand somehow offended him again? When he had done all he'd been ordered to do, he began to clean the stalls without being bidden, hoping the man would move along so he could relax. But no.

Courin called out to him. Ferdinand stepped forward. "Sir?"

"How many years served ye among them Brogies?"

Rubbing the back of neck, he looked up at Courin. What had prompted such a question? "As long as memory serves me, sir."

"What are yer plans now, lad?"

Ferdinand chanced a grin. "It is just good to know I can have plans, sir. I've no laid anythin' out yet."

Courin quirked a sideways smile. "I reckon that's true. I been watchin' ye work and ye done well. Ye follow orders and more. If ye'd like, I could put ye on as apprentice when the master returns. It'd mean a life of follerin' the warriors, but ye'd have all a man needs and a bit more besides. It ain't a bad life, lad."

"Not a bad life fer a lad what ain't got stature enough to be a warrior, is thet what ye're a sayin,' sir?"

Courin laughed. "Ye've got a quick mind besides. 'Tis true yer a bit of a lightweight, but them makes the best apprentices."

"I wouldn't say no to such an honor, sir." While the young man was being friendly, Ferdinand decided to press his luck a bit. "Do ye member the lad came in w'me—Jonathan his name was. I was just wonderin' sir, if it ain't presumin' fer me to ask."

Courin frowned slightly. "I do remember another, smaller lad. They must have taken him for the kitchen. It's the usual practice fer one so small. I ain't seen hide nor hair o' him by the by."

Ferdinand gave a solemn nod. "I thank ye, sir."

"Don't worry now, lad, they'll be takin' good care o' him. Like as not, ye'll see him sometimes hereabouts."

Ferdinand turned back to his work. That's just it, he thought. I believe I have seen him hereabouts, only he ain't a he no more. As Courin moved away, Ferdinand shook his head and murmured to a nearby horse, "It's a confusin' thing, that. Me head's all messed up about it."

The horse tossed his head and whickered. Ferdinand gave him a hard look. It sounded just like a laugh.

Jael watched the progress of a dodger bird's building its nest on the eaves of the turret. The funny little bird brought various bits and pieces of cloth and wood, which it pasted in place with a liberal amount of mud.

She'd always liked dodger birds. They were plain little homebodies who seemed always able to survive, no matter what was thrown at them. And their unobstrusive song pleased her also. "Chip-chip-a-dee," and sometimes, "chipper-chipper-chipper."

On this particular day, she felt very much like that little bird. She strode to the edge of the roof and stood looking out over the tidal basin, mostly dry at this hour. Seabirds circled and dove, catching food in the tidal pools.

She closed her eyes and tried to imagine where Lord William might be now. Was he drawing near Verani Haven? At a sudden chill wind off the sea, she crossed her arms over her breast and hugged herself to keep warm.

She tried not to think of him, but he would come to her like a whisper on the wind, and she imagined he called her name. She had no hope of ever knowing him as more than a friend, but her heart tended to entertain thoughts of him.

"You are a foolish girl, Jael of Rogan," she said to herself. "You are a little dodger bird, and he is an eagle." Sometimes she felt as if her heart would break. But she must comfort herself that she now had friends and those who cared about her. Perhaps one day, she'd meet someone more suited. But right now, she couldn't imagine loving another.

When the evening came for the meeting, Jael heard things she had never thought to hear. She was dumbfounded. There it was, in writing on this fine old paper. Though she'd never learnt to read, she watched as Stephen read the ancient script, translated by Patrick so long before.

"In the beginning was the Word, and the Word was with God, and the Word was God; ... In him was life, and the life was the light of men, and the light in the darkness did shine, and the darkness did not perceive it.[v]*"*

Though the words made perfect sense, and it was plain to her that someone had carefully written them, she continued in her confusion. She'd worshipped God her way all her life. She trusted in Him to show her if that should need to change.

On her own again, she handed her confusion off to Him in prayer. "Holy Father, you have never left me. In the wilderness, you sent a wolf to be my companion. Who knows what dangers he kept away? You kept me constantly and never let me be found of my enemy. You kept me alive through captivity and made me strong. Even there among the foul Brogies, you hid me from a worse enemy. You brought me to this place where I am free and have so much. But I am confused. I do not know about this Jesus. If He is real and I should believe in Him, let me know. Help me to see it and help me to understand."

The sun was setting and the sky filled with brilliant colors. She breathed deeply of the fresh air blowing in off the sea and sighed. Whatever the outcome, she knew she could find peace here.

𝔄 heavy rain pelted William and his men as they rowed up the overflowing Verani River. It was slow progress against the currents. Camp that night was uncomfortable at best, but the food was good.

Toldar smacked his lips over the roasted crowfish. They had hit upon a school of them which had to be eaten quickly. They couldn't smoke crowfish. It grew tough as old leather.

William chuckled at his brother-in-law. "One would think you were the one carrying a bairn, man. You eat for two."

Toldar frowned at his comrade and continued to clean the bones of the large fish. When finished, he tossed it into the fire and wiped his hands on his pantlegs. "Admit it. You envy me, brother."

"Of course I do. But not for the reason you think." William finished off the last drop of fresh wine then smiled.

Toldar picked at his teeth with a sliver of wood. "What then?"

William grinned. "I envy your healthy appetite and vast capacity for food. But I wonder if perhaps you've a tapeworm on board."

"Bah!" Toldar tossed an empty wineskin toward William. "Just because I haven't the delicate du Frain appetite, I must have a parasite? Is that what you're saying, brother?" He turned about, glancing at the others. "Are ye hearing this, men?"

Once the laughter died down, Fegan took up his lyre and began to play upon it. Soon the men began to sing. Even Solis joined in. It'd been a long and weary day and they had need of merriment to prepare their aching bodies for sleep.

William took it all in, letting his eyes rest on each one in turn. Each day brought them nearer their destination, when no man would rest until they had victory. It was the greatest desire of each man's heart to rid the kingdom once and for all, of the carnivorous magistrate. He was evil beyond measure in their eyes.

The younger ones had grown up hearing tales of his wickedness, but none as sick and mind-bending as the one Young Will told as they reclined near the fire after their meal. He related it as he'd heard it from his grandfather. William's own eyes closed in pain at the remembering of it.

Quite a good storyteller, Young Will's voice captivated his audience. "How one Jonathan Rogan, a peace-loving man died. A sailmaker by trade, a healer by nature, a deliverer by heredity, he never set out to harm any man. But he did great hurt to one Torin, the magistrate and that was never forgotten nor forgiven. The trail of freedom ran through Verani Haven and Jon Rogan was its willing servant, following in the hallowed footsteps of his father and his father before him.

Early on, he paid most dearly for his good works. The magistrate stole his beautiful young wife and gave her to one of his men who beat her and abused her until she died a short time later. You have all heard how our own King was taken wounded and sick after a great battle and enslaved, though the magistrate knew him not. Jon Rogan heard of it, and came to his rescue. He spirited him away to Verani Haven where he kept him in a secret room until he recovered enough to make the long journey home.

When the enemy came too close, Jon Rogan escaped with the ailing Warrior King and carried him on his own horse to the edge of the Touri Mountains. Wounded he was, but he managed to send a signal to the army there. They met him in the heights, and carried their young king home. For years afterwards the magistrate hunted Jon Rogan, but always came up empty-handed. He sent his men time and again to bring harm to Jon's family, but the women could never be found, only heard as they walked upon the shore of the great Verani Basin, singing in the wee night hours.

'Twas a dark day when Jon Rogan was taken by the magistrate's men as he stepped off the disappearing trail. They took him to the magistrate's foul castle and tortured him for three days and nights while the men feasted and drank their fill. Then the magistrate himself with his own hands cut out some of Jon Rogan's inward parts and fed them to the dogs while Jon watched. He had one of his men sew up the hole and sent Jon Rogan home to his mother and his daughter to die. They left him lying beside the cascade, where they knew the women would find him.

The magistrate knew it would torture the women, them being healers, too. They would do all within their powers to cure him, but Jon Rogan would die anyway, because his inward parts were gone. A fouler tale I've never heard. But don't you doubt its truth men—the King himself gave witness to it."

Past to Present

𝕮𝖑𝖎𝖟𝖆𝖇𝖊𝖙𝖍 had grown large with child, so entered her confinement. Jael sat with her many days, learning the intricacies of embroidery. To her surprise, she was quite good at it, and enjoyed it immensely.

She enjoyed talking to Elizabeth about her faith. Elizabeth's belief in the Son of God was every bit as deep as Jael's belief in Jehovah. It was making the two one that gave Jael a bit of trouble. Then she found out there were actually three. But the Holy Scriptures plainly said the three were one. This so befuddled Jael, she didn't know what to think of it.

"It is much the same with us," Elizabeth told her. "Toldar and I were two people until we were wed, and then we became one."

"And now there are three," Jael answered with a smile.

Elizabeth batted at her with the embroidery hoop and giggled. "Aye, I think you have it."

This might be simple for Elizabeth, who had grown up under those teachings, but Jael only grew more confused.

"We are all three in one," Pastor Stephen told her. "We are spirit, soul, and body. But do you see them all?"

As her understanding grew, she noticed other things as well. Some of her old feelings were returning. She sensed things keenly, heard distant sounds, and could see beyond words into a man's mind. It was an amazing thing.

She stood upon the high reaches, gazed out into the distance, and sensed things happening far away. When she prayed for William and his men, she felt their presence with her, sensed their mood, and sometimes even heard what they heard. Or so she believed.

She sang the psalms with renewed vigor and spoke words in the ancient tongue that had been long forgotten.

She also began spending more and more time in Ferdinand's company. The guards took to letting the two of them wander farther out, while they stood watch at a distance. There had been no further sightings of Shinder, so the threat had faded somewhat. The men remained vigilant, but with time, grew confident all was well.

Even as their trust and friendship grew, Jael had never confessed to Ferdinand. She sensed he knew something, but he never asked until one day in late spring.

They'd wandered to the base of a cliff where she found a good supply of Drumwort growing. Its dark green leaves and stems carried a powerful antiseptic. Ferdinand was helping her harvest it and had complained more than once about its odor.

She brought out a small box and handed it to him. "Drumwort will linger on your hands for days if you do not rid yourself of it properly. This mixture of herbs will cleanse the odor. Use it when you wash."

He sent her a look she recognized. Mischief. He was up to no good. "Speaking of bad odors, how long did it take ye to get rid of the stink of our journey?"

Her mind was preoccupied with plans for what other herbs they may find, so Jael was not as attentive as she should've been. Too quickly, she answered, "I thought Abigail would scrub off the top layer of my skin." She stopped herself, pursed her lips, and turned back to Ferdinand.

A knowing look met her gaze. She drew in a deep breath then blew it out slowly. "How long have you known?"

"Many days, milady. Since I first followed ye out with yon barrow. There be certain things ye cannot hide. At first, I thought ye may be a sister, or even a cousin o' Jonathan's. But then, I seen ye walk."

Heat crawled up Jael's neck into her cheeks. She turned her face away. How should she respond? He knew the truth.

Ferdinand passed by her to dump a bunch of Drumwort leaves into the barrow. "Aye, there be some things ye cannot hide." He glanced over his shoulder, a worried look in his eyes.

Did he think she was angry at him? Finally, when she'd recovered enough, she sought to reassure him, so added one of her brightest smiles. "So, what do you think of this place now, Ferdy?"

He faced her, his hands on his hips. "It's still nice to think o' bein' free my lady, though I must work to earn my keep. Could ye not ha' found somewheres we coulda rested a while? And where's this grand friend o' yours?" He jerked a nod toward the men. "Be it Courin there? Or is it … the Lady of the Haven?"

She looked askance at him. "You've been listening to fairy tales. The Lady of the Haven faded into the mist a while back. I'd not be expecting to see her again." Jael stood aside and brushed her hands together. "We have enough for now, let's be on our way before those two come and get us."

It wasn't long before they'd renewed their friendship. She even had him at the service once, but he told her it was too hard for him. "It's confusin' that. I've enough to think on just learnin' the work they gimme daily. Did I say they're goin' to make me a 'prentice when the warriors return?"

"Aye, you did tell me, and I'm that proud of you. You've earned it."

He narrowed his eyes at her. "It was not o' your doin'?"

She shook her head. "I don't have that much influence here, Ferdy. I would've done if it had been in my power. I owe you a large debt of gratitude."

He looked away out to sea. "Nay, my lady. I done nothing much." He shrugged as he plopped down on a nearby rock. "I'm only glad they never realized your secret." He gave a shudder. "If Black Dog had known ... I don't want to think what he'd a done." He glanced at her then quickly away again. "I don't think ye'd have made it out alive, did they know ye was woman."

Jael could only agree. She'd thought about it often and each time, found herself thankful to God for His divine protection. Had he blinded them to what Lord William thought was obvious? Perhaps He had, and if God had done that for her, how could she ever doubt His purpose for her now?

Abigail set Jael up in a spare room where she could spread her herbs out to dry. She had some of the menservants bring in more tables. Then she called for a carpenter to build a shelf with cubbyholes to hold the different roots. When it was finished, Jael spent many hours within the room, preparing the herbs. She wanted to be ready for anything, within reason.

Pastor Stephen found her there one day and seeing Ferdinand and a female servant with her, felt free to enter. "May I have a look at your inventory, my lady? I have always had an interest in the good things God has furnished for us. Tell me what are these used for?" He held up dried bulbs that looked like spring onions.

Jael smiled as she took them in her hands. "That is Endergazen, my dear pastor, and it is a very powerful sedative."

"Ah, it helps one to sleep?"

"Aye, and too much brings on eternal sleep."

Stephen arched his brow as he laid the thing carefully down. "How did you come into all of this knowledge, fair lady?"

"I grew up with it. My father was a healer, as was his father and mother before him and so on ... and so on."

He folded his hands behind his back and moved on, gazing at the herbs that hung from the rafters. "So it was passed down from father to daughter."

She rolled a dried Drumwort leaf and tied it with a bit of twine. "Well, there were no sons this last. I was the only child of my father. He and my grandparents taught me many things."

He stopped, turned about, and looked at her. "And the rest of the family?"

"I am sorry to say we were the last. Verani Haven lies empty these days."

He gave her a wry smile. "Thanks to the magistrate."

Jael nodded then placed the rolled leaf in a cubicle. "Perhaps he was the instrument, Pastor. What if it was time for me to go from there? I was alone, and would've been alone, forever, I suppose." She shrugged her shoulders, looking down at the Drumwort leaves. "I was content to stay. I never minded being on my own. But then ..."

"But then you were meant to come here," he finished for her.

She brought her gaze to his. "I believe that is true. Since I've come here, some of my ..." She stopped herself before she confessed something she'd never told anyone, realizing she mustn't tell it. Not now, leastways, especially since Ferdinand still worked nearby. She cleared her throat as she rolled another leaf. How she wished she could tell Pastor Stephen everything. She had a feeling he would understand.

How that lately, since she'd been seeking God, her powers had returned. She'd know before the knock sounded, Elizabeth was coming to her room. And on the night previous, she'd been on the roof when she felt a presence behind her. When she turned, there was no one there, but she felt there would be, even saw his face. A face not totally unfamiliar to her, though she couldn't say his name nor when she'd ever seen him.

Pastor Stephen watched her as if he knew her thoughts. Perhaps, being a man of God, he understood her as no one else did.

Behind them, Ferdinand cleared his throat. "Lady, I am finished here. If I may ..."

Pastor Stephen turned to him. "Ah, good. I've wanted to talk to you, lad. Let us walk out together."

Ferdinand glanced back at Jael, a grimace on his face.

With a smile on hers, Jael returned to her work. Elizabeth's time was nigh. Jael wanted to have everything prepared.

At the approach of even, she made ready to join Lady Elizabeth for tea.

When Jael entered, Elizabeth stood at the window, gazing out at the compound. "Is it a boy, or a girl?"

Jael went to stand beside her. "How should I know?"

Elizabeth spared her a smile. "Oh you know. I know you know." By now, her smile had grown to a full grin. "What's more, you know I know you know."

Jael laughed at Elizabeth's joke. She did have a definite feeling, but she had no intention of making it known. "I can only tell you this, Lady Elizabeth. 'Tis a babe."

Elizabeth shook her head then proceeded to lower herself onto a chair. "And so you refuse to tell me?"

"You will know soon enough. How are you feeling of late?"

Elizabeth let go of a breath. "Heavy, so very heavy. Will the child ever come forth?"

"Oh, I think it will be soon now."

"Just tell me it will come before the Holy Day."

Jael sat across from her, took her hand, and gazed into her eyes. "I do not know about that, but I can promise you, when the child is ready, it will come."

CHAPTER 22 – THE SIGN OF THE LOON

The Sign of the Loon

Lundar Cheek rode swiftly to Dolor Heights. It was a forlorn place of misery and he did not like it. How anyone could think of living here was beyond him. But long ago someone had come and had managed to hold on. He wrinkled his nose at the stench of the place as he rode into the village. He felt rather than saw them staring at him, for they hid away inside their dank cottages as he drew near. No doubt they knew his face and feared him. He'd been responsible for the deaths of many of their men, and he was proud of it.

For the most part, Lundar saw nothing to rile the magistrate. They were not withholding anything as far as he could see, for they had nothing, save mud and rot. At the far edge of the village, he halted his horse and sat looking out over the adjoining fields. It had been too wet to work. There would be no crop this year and the people would starve, most likely. If he had any compassion at all, he would turn and ride back to the magistrate. But he had none. He had never received it, and so had never given it.

He slid down from his horse and strode into the nearest cottage, where he heard a babe screaming. Disturbing the peace, it was. He took all within and herded them out, where the sickly mother fell down upon her face into the mud. She'd be more trouble than she was worth. He gave her a good, swift kick.

By this time, several other women had come out grabbing at the child and the sick woman, trying to rescue them.

One more vocal than the others cried out, "Let them be, ye dirty bastard!"

Lundar turned on her at once and knocked her down with the back of his arm. He stooped and wrapped her hands tightly with cord and pulled her to her feet. Amid screams and curses from the others, he tied her to his horse then climbed into the saddle. By the time he'd made the end of the village, he had three of them bound together and stumbling behind his horse. It would be a long journey, but he had accomplished his goal.

"It'll not be enough," he muttered beneath his breath. He must have some great accomplishment in order to free himself of the magistrate. He was weary of the drudgery and hated even the sound of the magistrate's voice. All the way back to the old fortress he thought about it. When he came within sight of the place, he smelled the smoke of many pigs roasting. Preparation for the Holy Day had begun.

He stopped his horse and dismounted, kicking at the women to make them sit. "Take yer rest whilst ye can," he growled. "Soon the air will be filled with the stink of yer bodies roasting on the spit!"

"Why do ye do this?" The vocal woman cried. "We've done nothing."

"Aye, and that's why I do it. Ye've done nothing. Ye should have done something. Now shut yer trap."

He strode to the nearest tree to relieve himself and in the silence that ensued, he sensed something. He could not say exactly what it was, but he edged nearer the overlook and peered out. His squinty eyes cast about from horizon to far horizon, but there was nothing there. An overcast sky lay heavily over the lifeless, gray landscape. He wanted to raise his fist to that silent sky. He hated the rain, hated this place, and hated what he had become. Still fuming, he returned to his horse and the women.

William gazed at Young Will, who had just returned from spying out the old fortress.

"It was Lundar Cheek. I'd recognize him anywhere. We were very nearly seen by him, but in the end, he moved on. He led three unfortunate creatures behind him. No telling what he plans to do with them."

"They likely need more slaves fer the galley," Solis said, rubbing his beard with the back of his hand. "It bein' the Holy Day and all."

"Let's hope that's all it is," said William. He slapped his young nephew on the back. "Good work lad, set your men at the ready. We'll move into place after dark. There'll be no moon tonight."

Lord William strode to the fireside and addressed his men. "From here, we will travel overland to Verani Deep, where the magistrate dwells."

They'd set up camp in the forest along the banks of the Verani, within hearing of the great cascade. William had to raise his voice in order to be heard above the noise of the water. "Those of you who were with me the last time, will remember it well. He has commandeered an old fortress which stands in ruin. The hardest part will be finding him in the maze of broken down walls."

He gazed about, making eye contact with individual men. "We must not underestimate this man. He is devious. We hope to find him and his army well gone with drink and all set to celebrate the Holy Day. We will cut them down. They will celebrate among their forebears."

A low echo of approval rippled through the men, for William had ordered a general silence. He did not want anyone to become aware of their presence. He kept his battalions close for the night and posted sentries on all sides.

Jael awoke in the deep of night. She thought she heard a loon. She frowned and rubbed her eyes. It could not be. Loons didn't live near the sea, but in the river valley she had left so long ago. Her heart ached at the thought. Sometimes she was so homesick.

She heard the sound again, and sat straight up in her bed. Throwing her legs over the side, she crept to the window, hardly daring to breathe, lest she miss the sound again. She was puzzled by what she heard, so much like a loon, but perhaps something different.

She threw a shawl about her shoulders and went out to the passageway, climbed the spiraling stairs to the roof, and stood watching and waiting in utter darkness. There was no moon, only stars twinkling in the distance.

Somewhere out across this vast expanse, William and his men prepared to go into battle. She knew it, though no man had told it to her. She stepped to the railing and looked out over the sea, where white-capped waves rolled inward in quick succession. She closed her eyes and relished the mesmerizing sound.

When the cry of the loon came again, she turned about and there upon the roof of the turret sat the great bird.

"But, a loon doesn't fly," she whispered.

What magic was this? She moved nearer—stealthily—not wanting to spook the thing. It was a loon, or had been a loon, for when she drew nigh, it disappeared. A cold chill coursed through her. She gathered the shawl about her shoulders and leaned back against the wall of the turret, praying from the depths of her heart for William and his men.

It had to be a sign.

A sound from within startled her—a human sound of

suffering—Elizabeth! Jael ran all the way to Elizabeth's room and did not stop to knock.

Elizabeth stood near the foot of the bed, holding on to the bedpost. Jael lit the lamp then returned to her friend. When the pain had subsided, Jael helped her sit.

"I am sorry, Jael. I had hoped to be so much braver than this. Here I am crying at the first twinge."

"Twas more than a twinge, from the looks of you," Jael assured her. She was still shaken by the sign of the loon, and could not seem to cast it off. "I'll send at once for Dora, but you must calm yourself. It may be a long time yet."

She went to wake Abigail, who would send someone for Dora. Jael returned to Elizabeth for a moment, to check on her. She was resting, so Jael went to her room to get dressed.

She stopped in the herbal room and gathered what she needed. She would have Abigail bring water and set a tea kettle to boil over the fire in Elizabeth's quarters.

All the while, she thought about the sign she'd seen. What did it mean? Her heart constricted at the thought that it may be a bad omen, either for Elizabeth or for the men, fighting their battle on the morning of the Holy Day.

Was it wise to do so? She had never been superstitious, but she didn't fully understand the laws of Christianity, if there were any laws. Grandpere had told her many times, "If you truly love the Lord with all your heart, you need not fear the law." It was one of his favorite sayings, and she had always understood what he meant. If you truly loved God, you wouldn't break His laws.

Why was she thinking about such things? She pushed them out of her mind, along with the sighting of the loon. She must give her full concentration to the task at hand.

When she returned to Elizabeth, she found her writhing in pain in her bed. Jael bent over her. "You must calm yourself, dear Elizabeth. Let your body do its work, don't fight it."

Elizabeth sucked in a breath. "But it hurts so."

"I've no doubt the pain is very cruel. But it will be less so if you can relax." She began at once to rub Elizabeth's back, settling her a bit.

When the pain had lessened, Elizabeth turned to look at her. "Is there nothing you can give me? No herb to ease the pain?"

Jael blew out a breath. More than anything, she wished it was possible. "Not at this time, my lady. Anything I give you may harm your child.

Something that would relax you and help you sleep would slow your labor, and make it even longer. 'Twould be cruel, my lady."

Elizabeth heaved an exaggerated sigh. Jael helped her to a sitting position. "When you feel up to it, you should get out of bed and walk about. It'll help you."

Elizabeth did get up after a while, and Jael helped her to walk around the room. She sat in the chair to rest just as Abigail entered, carrying a large pot of water. Hazel followed soon after, with the requested teakettle. The two of them built up the fire and set the water on to boil. Not long thereafter, Dora entered, and sent Hazel to get the rest of her things.

The peaceful atmosphere of the room changed at once as Dora moved briskly about, making things ready, snapping out orders like a chieftan.

Hazel returned with the birthing stool and Dora had her set it in the corner near the bed. Then she ordered more water and some food and drink for herself. Jael watched her with interest, but stayed near Elizabeth, determined to keep her easy.

After several hours of little progress, Elizabeth began to weep. Dora wiped her brow. "There, there child, it ain't so very bad. Often the first is hard, and takes its own time."

Jael wasn't so sure. She didn't have the experience Dora had, but she couldn't seem to rid herself of the feeling something wasn't right.

Elizabeth raised large, pain-filled eyes to Jael. "What do you think, Jael?"

Dora glared at Jael, turned and huffed away to the fire. Once there, she pivoted so she could watch. Jael reached for Elizabeth's hand and stood still, whispering a prayer. Then she opened her eyes and said, "Stand up for a moment."

"I ... I don't know if I can."

"Yes, you can. Here, I'll help you." Jael moved around the bed and took both of Elizabeth's hands in hers. When Elizabeth was upright, though not quite steady, Jael placed one hand on either side of her belly. She closed her eyes and let herself concentrate. She could almost hear the heart beating and the blood flowing. She also heard Dora's muttering in the background.

After a moment, Jael dropped her hands, stood and looked into Elizabeth's troubled eyes. "The baby is turned wrong," she whispered.

"What does that mean?" Elizabeth asked. Jael heard the panic in her voice, and slipped an arm around her.

"It means you must rest, my lady. Lie down upon your right side, and I will prop you up with pillows. If you can calm yourself—truly let go—I believe the child will turn on his own."

"Humph!" Dora muttered again. "Ain't likely. It'll be a breach birth. Ye shouldn't make her think it can be any diffrunt."

Jael ignored the old woman and helped her friend to lie down. "Don't let it trouble you, Elizabeth. Lie down and let everything go." Jael moved to her basket and brought back a small box containing a thick ointment. When she had Elizabeth settled, she rubbed her back and belly with the soothing ointment that smelled of lavender and balm. She washed her face with warm, lavender-scented water.

All the while, she sang her favorite psalms ever so softly. When Abigail entered with more water, she stood still for a moment and watched.

Dora muttered something about the young thinkin' they know it all.

Abigail gave Jael a knowing smile. "Can I get you anything, my lady?"

Jael shook her head. "I'm fine, Abigail. Why don't you and Hazel rest a bit, whilst you can?"

Elizabeth slept for nearly two hours then awoke suddenly, her eyes large with pain. Jael jumped up and stood by her, holding her hands. "'Tis all right, my lady, 'tis a good pain. The child moves."

After the pain subsided, Elizabeth tried to rise. "Check it again, dear, if you please."

Jael stood and laid her hands on either side of Elizabeth's belly. With a smile, she spoke, "He is ready to come, my lady."

"*He* is?" Elizabeth said, grabbing Jael's wrist. "You said he."

Jael nodded, still smiling. Still facing Elizabeth, she said, "Dora, come and help her to the birthing stool. She is ready now."

Dora was still muttering, but she did come. She seemed a bit taken aback when Jael stepped aside. Jael waited until Dora had Elizabeth settled, and had fully taken over. Then she moved behind Elizabeth and took her hand. Once again, she began to sing the psalm of the mighty river. She sang for Elizabeth and for the child, but also for the men who moved into place for a mighty battle to be fought this day, the anniversary of the Savior's return.

𝔄 great distance away, a loon called out of the heavy mist lying over the river valley. William looked heavenward and whispered a prayer. He laid his hand over his heart and prayed for the safety of his men. That's when her face came before him, so near, he could almost discern her breathing.

"If you can hear me," he whispered, "and you can know, say a prayer for me this day, my lady, and for the men who follow me."

It was difficult going into battle on such a day, a gray dawn filled with the rank smell of pork roasting. Long into the night, the air had been rife with revelry and pierced with an occasional feminine scream. William was sorry for it, but he must delay until morning when he knew the magistrate's men would be sleeping off their drunken stupor.

All around him, the men readied themselves. There was no talk, just motion, as they set themselves in order and polished their weapons. When every piece of light armor was in place and every weapon set, they assembled in battalions, awaiting their master's orders.

He knew they waited for a word from him and many good words rushed through his mind unattended. Finally, he drew in a deep breath and spoke. "This is the moment for which we have long prepared. Now it is time to go forth. We will have victory this day, men. Great is the army whose God is the Lord!" The men reached their swords skyward and repeated his words, pledging their lives to God, to William, and King George.

William held his stance until the men quieted then raised his hand. "No matter what this day brings, we shall still sing His praise, but stand assured, my brethren, this day will bring victory! God will vanquish the enemy!"

Toldar and Solis rounded up the men and William gave last minute instructions to the battalions. "There's a cave on the far side of yon hill. A back way out allowing escape if the occupants of this fortress become trapped. Many years ago, the tunnel collapsed, but Young Will saw signs of recent digging there. No doubt they've made a new passage. We can't let any of them escape."

He looked at Young Will. "Station a small band of men at the entrance of the cave and don't let anyone pass. Toldar, take your battery of men to the north. Solis and I will move in from the south. We will surround them then we will squeeze them. Leave no stone unturned."

With that, they moved into position and began the descent into the valley where they were blessed by a mist, providing them cover.

Somewhere in the distance, a loon called again, its eerie voice echoing across the valley.

153

An Alpha and an Omega

Elizabeth was delivered of a boy as the sun came up on Holy Day. Almost an hour had passed since Jael had turned her over to Dora. It probably wouldn't set well with Dora, as it would make her look bad and Jael had no doubt the news would spread quickly. But everyone else in the room was happy.

Abigail helped clean up as Jael assisted Elizabeth. When mother and son were comfortably situated, Jael sat on the edge of the bed and smiled at them. "He's a good size."

"Aye and I still feel that. It is good to have it over and done. I do not think I want to go through that again."

"Famous last words," Jael leaned forward to kiss Elizabeth's forehead. "You did well. He is healthy and strong and he looks like his father."

Elizabeth gazed at her son. "He does, doesn't he? That's all right. He has a very handsome father. Would you send a message to my mother and father?"

"Of course, is there anything in particular you wish to say?"

"Just that I am fine and the boy is fine. He has no name as yet, for Toldar and I could not agree upon one. He wanted to name the child Dartok, after his father." Elizabeth grimaced. "They are a fine family, but ... Dartok."

Dora scoffed. "Dartok is a good strong name. It is right and proper for a father to choose a name for his son."

Elizabeth smiled at Jael.

Jael rose to go. "I'll just go and send that message. We'll talk later."

A courier pigeon carried a message to Coldthwaite. This process fascinated Jael. She stayed to see the bird fly away, then while Elizabeth and her son slept, it seemed a good time to go and gather more Drumwort.

Jael could not fathom her urgency in this matter. She had a strange feeling and wished to stay busy. Ferdinand accompanied her, glad of the opportunity to escape the stuffy interior of the stables.

"Is this how I am to celebrate the Holy Day, then?" he asked as he pushed the wheelbarrow behind her.

"I did not know you observed the Holy Day, Ferdy. I didn't think you were religious at all."

"Don't mean I can't celebrate. We takes every opportunity to have a good time. Besides, even the Brogies celebrated Holy Day. It was a big drinking day."

Jael frowned. "I doubt that is how God would have us honor it."

He shook his head and muttered as he followed along behind her.

Jael smiled. He'd never noticed her ability to hear so well, and she'd never confessed it. Best kept secret, anyway. She never knew when it may come in handy. She didn't like always listening in on folks, though.

"She's becoming strange," Ferdy muttered. "It be that man, Stephen, talking all the time about the Son of God. These Christians are just odd."

Jael squinted into the distance, noting that the guards had stopped to sit upon a large rock at the edge of the sandy shore. She and Ferdinand proceeded to the base of the cliff, where gulls flew about and guano fertilized the ground. Here Drumwort grew in abundance.

Ferdinand grunted as he pushed the barrow into place. "No wonder it smells so bad, if it likes gull poop." He took up the short-handled shovel and began to dig at the plants. "I hear there was a man-child born this morn."

Jael knocked excess sand off the roots of a plant and tossed it into the barrow. "Yes, a fine, big boy."

"No one seems to know his name."

"He has none yet. She awaits the return of his father."

"Blast!" Ferdinand yelped and bit his lip, swinging his hand in the air.

She could tell he wanted to say more, but restrained himself. He'd taken a splinter in the palm of his hand. She drew near to look at it then pointed to a nearby rock. "Have a seat there on the rock. I will get it out for you."

When he was sitting down, he lifted his palm to her and looked away over his shoulder.

She chuckled. He had never liked pain and most likely didn't want to see what she was doing with that knife.

He winced and shut his eyes tightly as she pulled at the splinter. When she had most of it out, she cut into his flesh just enough to remove the remnants. "There, I believe I have it all, now go down to the water and wash. When you return, rub it with the leaves of this plant. It will help the pain."

"And it will stink like ..." He turned quickly, without finishing. He started down the beach to the water, leaving a smile on Jael's face.

She turned back to the base of the cliff and as she did, a strange feeling came over her. She swung back around to check on Ferdinand, but he was still walking, murmuring as he went. She drew back from the cliff and looked up, her sharp eyes taking in every angle. The gulls that flew incessantly overhead had stopped their cries. They stood like silent sentinels upon the ledges. A cool breeze pricked at the back of her neck and she crossed her arms over her chest. She began to sing softly in the ancient tongue.

Ferdinand crouched beside the water and dipped in his hand, which had bled only a little. The briny water stung a bit, but he supposed that to be a good thing. He cleaned his hands and shook off the excess liquid then stood looking out to sea, patting his hands against his chest to dry them.

He turned back toward the cliff and for a moment, could not see Jael. Shading his eyes with his hands, he soon caught sight of her. She stood with her back to him, looking up. His gaze followed hers, just in time to see movement among the rocks, too far back for her to see.

He glanced toward the place where the guards sat, idling away their time. They were too far away to reach Jael if there was a need. He moved swiftly to the nearest rock and crouched there, watching the stealthy figure as it moved nearer to the ground, picking its way carefully down among the rocks.

Ferdinand dared not call out, for fear Jael would look away and not see what was coming at her. As he drew near, he halted in his tracks and blinked his eyes. For he had seen Jael turn, facing outward. And then ... she disappeared.

"What in blazes?" He blinked his eyes again. The black-clad figure was almost upon her, or at least the place where she had been. Ferdinand sprinted nearer, undercover of some rocks. Then he saw the ferret-like creature standing in front of the spot where she'd been, as if he too was wondering what had become of her.

The noise of the waves diluted the sound of the man's voice. He stayed where he was, his back to the sea, and to Ferdinand.

Ferdinand's heart beat wildly in his chest. He must do something to protect the lady. Drawing a long knife from its sheath at his waist, he dashed forward.

Jael did not at first realize what was happening. She only knew she felt quite peaceful as she turned and stepped back into the shadows. She could hardly believe it when Shinder stood in front of her, looked right at her, yet seemed not to see her. She could hear him breathing, could almost hear the beat of his heart. She heard him speak foul words, cursing her very existence. It was as if time slowed and the world outside did not exist. It was like ... being inside the disappearing trail.

But then she saw Ferdinand.

As Shinder turned to meet his attacker, Ferdinand's gaze met Jael's. It was sudden and mystifying, and she feared for a moment, he may lose his concentration. But just as Shinder turned to him, Ferdinand cried out and hit Shinder, plunging his knife deep into the man's side. He seemed a bit off his mark because in the moment of impact, Shinder sunk his sword into Ferdinand's belly.

Jael screamed as she swung the shovel with all of her might. It came crashing down on top of Shinder's head.

Out of the corner of her eyes, Jael saw the guards, alerted by her scream, race forward, weapons drawn. Shinder flailed his arms as he groped about for his weapon, never taking his eyes off Jael.

She kicked sand in his face, then fell down at Ferdinand's side and gripped his hand. He fought for air, his face a mask of pain and panic. Her own breath caught in her throat. She lifted his torn body onto her knees. Still too shocked to cry, she leaned over him. The deep gash in his side oozed dark blood and bubbled with air from his lung. She tore off her shawl and pressed it tightly against the gash.

His lips moved then he pushed out words. "I seen ye there, and then ye were not, my lady. I could not trust my eyes. I could not let him find ye." He closed his eyes as he struggled for breath. Jael tried to quiet him, knowing his condition to be very grave.

After a moment, he opened his eyes again and looked at her. "I wish I had believed ye now and listened when ye tried to tell me ... for I am convinced ... 'tis true, my lady."

He closed his eyes again and she despaired of his life, leaned forward over him and cried. She began to pray aloud in the forbidden tongue, not caring who may hear.

He opened his eyes again. "I understand now, is that not diverting? I know what ye are saying. 'Tis true. 'Tis all true, for He stands here, by me. Do ye not see Him, my lady? He says ... he says there is still time. He will lead me there himself."

He exhaled and she thought he was gone. He sucked in a breath. "I think I will go with him. There is a path beyond ... 'tis the greatest of all disappearing trails, I think." His eyes found hers. A smile curled his lips. "'Tis lovely there."

Jael bowed her head over him. If she could have done it, she would have given him her own breath, her own life, so he could live in her stead. He quieted again, and she looked to his face. His eyes were open, staring up at the sky. She laid her fingers tenderly over them and closed the lids. For a moment, she left her hand there, and whispered to him. "Oh, Ferdinand, you were the truest of friends. I will miss you so."

Behind her, she sensed movement and glanced back as Shinder caught hold of the downed sword. With all the strength he could muster, he lifted it and drew back to swing at her. She froze in place, not willing to leave Ferdinand, even to save her own life.

Another sound caught her attention. The unmistakable zing of an arrow. An arrow which found its mark. Peirced above the elbow, Shinder's arm fell, losing its grip on the sword. A moment later, the second guard swung his sword and severed Shinder's arm.

Disbelief sparked in Shinder's eyes as he continued to glare at Jael. He looked up into the faces of the two guards and growled, "Have it over."

Jael turned her face away, but she couldn't shut out the sound of the blade piercing flesh and twisting, tearing asunder. She leaned forward and let go the contents of her stomach then covered it over with sand.

Courin helped Jael to her feet then swung her up into his arms. She let her head rest against his shoulder as he carried her to the house, where he left her in Abigail's care.

"What a day," Abigail clucked sadly, as she washed Jael's face. "One life begun, and one life ended."

Jael looked at her. Two lives ended, if you could count Shinder. Most would not, but Jael could not help feeling sorry. She drew in a shaky breath. "How is Lady Elizabeth?"

"She is fine and dandy, taking care of that new infant." She leaned in close and whispered. "I did not tell her what had befallen ye. I told her only that ye was abed, so ye rest now. She'll be glad to see ye whenever ye feel up to it. It's good ye have somewhat to keep ye occupied."

Jael nodded and closed her eyes.

The Battle

The men were in place before the mist began to rise. William had to admit, the old fortress made a good place to stage a battle. There was certainly plenty of cover. It was nothing but jagged walls reaching hither and yon. Only the main section remained intact. Piles of rubble and filth lay about the yard.

At their approach, very little noise could be heard from the interior, as only the servants went about, beginning preparations for the day. One of them, an emaciated creature dressed in rags, came outside carrying buckets to fill with water. One of the warriors pulled him aside.

"Have mercy, young captain," he begged when he saw William.

William shushed him, but he continued to whisper, trembling and cupping his hands in front of his face.

"I pray thee, young captain, let me go inside and warn the other slaves. They be innocent, my lord. And there be three women there. Peasants from Dolor Heights. They's tied to trusses and meant to be heated slowly over the flames when the master wakes."

Solis looked at William, but William shook his head. "We cannot. Have him gagged and tied. We'll do our best to distinguish slave from ... whatever you call those ... creatures. Send it among the men, but take no chances."

"Aye, sir." Solis said, urging the slave forward.

"There's no need for to gag me sir, I'll no make any noise except fer the sound of me footsteps runnin' away."

"After we've finished here, you'll be free to go. Until then, you'll do as yon captain says." Solis scrambled away with the servant in tow.

William led the first company of men into the interior rooms of the old fortress. Their footsteps echoed on the cold, damp floor. They followed their noses to the main room, where one entire wall was taken up by a blackened fireplace with ovens on either side. William's eyes took in the tall ceilings built of massive timbers. This had been quite a place at one time.

The floor was a mass of snoring bodies everywhere in all shapes and sizes, but so far, no magistrate. William would never forget that man's face. He circled back and motioned for his men to spread out. "He's not within. Let Solis and his men go and clear out that mess."

Lundar Cheek could not sleep. He lay upon his blankets in an inner room of the old fortress trying to keep out the cold. It was difficult, because the cold seemed to be coming from within his very heart. Things had not gone well with him since his return. He did not trust Torin Dugold, not one jot.

He could not forget the look in those swollen red eyes when he returned with the three women.

"Is that all ye come by?"

When Lundar told him how Dolor Heights stood nearly abandoned, its fields a muddy mess, he'd shouted obscenities at him.

"Have ye not brought me a boy at the very least?"

"It is as I have told ye, there were no others."

Torin spewed angrily. "Get thee from me!" He turned his eyes to the women, raking over them in so disgusting a way, the most vocal of the three spat out curses at him. He dropped his huge head back and laughed loudly. "Well, at least ye've brought me one with spirit! I will enjoy watching her melt over the fire. Cover them in candle wax, just to add to the excitement," he ordered. "First thing tomorrow, we'll set them ablaze and roast them like yon piglets!"

The whole thing disgusted Lundar. They had their fun with the women, rolled them in mud and excrement, dripped hot wax all over them then tied them to tree limbs to await their fate. He could still hear them screaming for mercy.

His stomach twisted and churned. He got up from his pallet and stepped across the puddles to a window, looking out upon the lower heights. He saw movement below, but dismissed it as servants going about their business. The Holy Day required much preparation.

The soft sound of a footfall behind him brought him quickly around to stand face to face with a young warrior, fully armed. In an instant the warrior had Lundar pinned against the wall.

"Wait!" he choked out. "Spare me life and I can show ye the

whereabouts of the magistrate. Ye'll never find him without my help." Blood ran down from the beginnings of the wound where the sword pressed hard against his throat. He dare not breathe.

Hearing a ruckus, William ran to the place. A young warrior turned, keeping Lundar in a tight hold. "This man says he knows the whereabouts of the magistrate, sir."

William glared at Lundar. "No doubt he does—hello, Cheek. Why should I trust you?"

"Because, like as not, ye've already come up empty-handed. Ye think that fat slug would sleep in the open? Nay, he's hiding away in the depths with a good many men, none of whom was allowed to drink so much as a drop last night!"

William turned his face away to hide his panic. He'd sent Young Will with a small band to guard the very place. "Bring him and follow me." He ordered as he swept out of the room and into the main corridor. He yelled to the men, not caring who heard.

Solis' unit was well occupied in the interior. They'd taken the slumbering men completely by surprise. Solis ran up when he heard William's voice. "These cannot be all, master, there's not so much as a thimble-full and the magistrate ..."

"Is not among them, I know. According to Cheek, here, he's in the cave." He took no time to explain, but continued on his way, followed by as many men as were free. "Finish up here then go to Young Will's aid." Solis nodded and turned back to his men.

Lundar ran behind the young warrior, his wrists fastened with leather thongs. "If ye would but listen, I can help ye!"

William glanced over his shoulder at the man. "Why should I listen to you? Are you not a long-time follower of the magistrate? Are you not the very one who committed countless atrocities against the good citizens of this region?"

"Aye, I admit ... it was me. I done it, but I doan want to go out this way. Allow me to make some atonement. There be a quicker way. If ye care fer yer men there, ye will take heed."

William stopped. He looked Lundar Cheek in the eye. "What do you think to gain by this? If there is a quicker way, tell me now, and I'll settle up with you later."

"Nay, my lord, but let me go with ye, that I may have the satisfaction of seeing his demise with my very own orbs."

William's patience was at an end. "Tell us the way, then."

"Take the south road by the river. Cross over at fallen rock. Ye'll come upon the lee side of the cave. They'll no see ye comin' on 'em from that direction."

Once again the men were on the run. William figured he was taking a chance, but lives were at stake. Cheek was a snake and would turn on anyone in a moment. But the magistrate did not inspire loyalty. Most of his subjects hated him, but they also feared him. It was no wonder Cheek hoped to see the end of Torin Dugold.

When they came to the fallen rock Cheek had spoken of, they broke into a single file of men, led by Toldar, who refused to let the Prince endanger his life.

"Nay my brother, you are the heir," he whispered. "You must return." The men never addressed William as "Lord" or even "my lord" in the field, lest his identity become known, making him a target.

"You must return also, or my sister will put an end to my existence," William replied. But he held back as Toldar wished. As they neared the area of the cave, they heard the sounds of battle and quickened their steps.

When his uncle ordered him to take a small band to the nether regions, Young Will was disappointed. Once again, he was relegated to clean up. He tried to take it well, but it rubbed him wrong.

His men felt the same, for they slogged along, barely speaking. Young Will's legs seemed made of iron. He had to push himself to go on when he wanted desperately to turn about and be in the thick of it.

As they neared their destination, he stopped the men, hoping to rally them a bit. "Listen, I know how you feel. Be assured, what we do here is important. It may become very important, indeed. We know not who may find their way through this dark hall. Let us keep our eyes open and our ears attuned. Be at the ready, men!"

And so they descended upon the cave's dark mouth just in time to surprise the swarming mob of enemy ranks who preceded the magistrate. The battle began at once. Young Will swallowed hard at the lump in his throat. He had never anticipated such a brutal attack. Within seconds, several of his men had fallen around him.

Arrows flew from above, striking all around. Twice he'd been hit, but his armor shielded him. He swung his sword valiantly, cutting down several men. Within moments, he was coated in blood, but there was no time even for thought. Because each one he felled was replaced by another. He and his men were grossly outnumbered.

Never looking back, he pushed into the interior. The new opponent he faced was taller than he and much more powerful. His men tried to press in around him, but the big man had singled him out. With a low growl, the man pushed his sword past Young Will's and drove it deep into Young Will's thigh.

Will doubled over in pain and was immediately caught up by strong arms. "Have a care, Will." Toldar's voice rasped in his ear.

Relief flooded Young Will. Help had come at last. Toldar laid him down behind a large rock then ran back into the battle. Will lay in excruciating pain, tugging at the belt around his midriff. He cut it loose with his knife then pulled it tight around his leg, hoping to stop the bleeding. As soon as that was done, he fell back, the knife still in his grip. He was ready to defend himself if necessary.

Theirs but to Do and Die

William fought like a wild man, pressing into the mouth of the cave, giving no ground. He was soon joined by his brother-in-law, who fought alongside, determined to watch over him. The enemy's men were large, but lacked true skill in battle. William flew at them with both speed and skill. His sword cut through flesh, broke bones, and ended many lives.

A giant of a man ran at him from the shadows and caught him by surprise. William spun about, barely avoiding a blow from a powerful weapon with scalloped edges. The man pressed in hard upon him, nearly catching him again. William dodged at the last moment, but caught one foot in a depression and slipped forward. In that moment, the man's weapon would surely have cut him down, if not for a sudden flash of light and a powerful presence.

Astonished, William pushed away from the floor of the cave and staggered to an upright position. He could not say what had caused the bright glow, but in its ethereal rays, he swore he saw the outline of a man. The thick-legged giant stood in momentary shock, but then let out a guttural roar and waved his cruel sword in the air. He dove at William with great force. The bright visitor had given William time to recover himself and he was ready. His sword pierced the big man's neck. William pushed him aside. With an unexpected strength and swiftness, he made an end to the man's life, severing a necessary artery.

Afterward, he bent near double to catch his breath then whispered a quick thanks to God. He rushed back into the fray with renewed energy and determination.

When Toldar took a hit from an opponent, William moved in quickly to cut the man down. He struck so swiftly and with such strength the man's head rolled free of his trunk, while the body still stood for several moments before it fell forward. Toldar stood in near shock, blinking at William.

"Are you all right?" William asked.

Toldar grabbed his upper arm and grinned. "He barely nicked me." The two raced forward, pressing deeper into the interior.

The battle lasted less than an hour in true time, but seemed an eternity to the valiant warriors. When they had finished their work, the field was littered with bodies leaking out their life's blood upon the ground, their empty eyes staring up at the early sun.

Even after all of this, they had not found the magistrate, so William pressed forward.

As soon as the fighting had begun in earnest, Lundar managed to break free. No one noticed as he pressed forward clenching the bloodied sword of a fallen warrior. He had only one thought in mind and cared not whether he survived it.

He found his prey, cowering alone in an inner chamber carved out of the solid rock, where he had intended to remain until all had ended. Until his enemies had given up, and returned home. Torin Dugold had plenty of provisions packed inside this room and only the closest of his men knew of the room's whereabouts. Lundar Cheek was one of those men. The plan was, to wait until such a time, Torin could replenish his army and move to another location.

When Lundar unexpectedly stepped inside the room, Torin squealed, "Close the door quickly man!"

Lundar Cheek closed the door, but stood brandishing his sword and listening to the big man wheeze. He grinned an evil grin.

"What think ye, Cheek? Have ye come to stay them off?"

"Surely master, do ye think I would come fer any other reason? Ah, and we was to have such fun today. Is that not always the way?"

Torin's expression changed as he realized what Lundar was up to. He fumbled about for his sword, but Lundar quickly knocked it out of the way with his own.

"Not fair, man," said Torin, "'twould not be a fair fight. I've never known ye to cower in fear. Ye are not afraid now, I daresay, so let me have my chance."

"Ye've had yer chance. Ye've had more'n that. Ye've taken all and given nothing. Now I'm takin' back. I'm going to enjoy watchin' ye suffer, I am."

Torin's bulbous eyes darted this way and that. Lundar grinned. He knew the man's thoughts. He was trying to come up with a way out of his predicament. Lundar had always known this day would come. He just didn't know it was going to be his victory. He thought it'd be someone else's. Any one of Torin Dugold's captains would love to be standing right where Lundar was now.

Of course, Torin had hoped to stave it off until he could establish his kingdom and reward his constituents well enough to keep them by him. But he'd run out of time. Lundar swung his sword, filling the small room with a swooshing sound. Torin cringed, but it did not strike. Lundar played with him, enjoying the game.

"Do not toy w'me man. Whatever ye mean to do—do it quickly."

"As ye have done time and again? Ye who will have mercy ... show mercy? Nay, my lord," he sneered. "'Twould not be a fittin' end fer one such as ye." Lundar passed the sword from one hand to the other and grimaced. "Perhaps I should turn ye over to yer enemies."

The sword slashed again and took a bit of flesh with it this time. He had a great deal to spare and this could go on incessantly. Tears filled Torin's eyes, but he set his massive jaw. Lundar caught the motion and grinned. Now he had Torin right where he wanted him. He was angry. Lundar fed the anger and it became much more.

Torin stood as quickly as a man his size in a very small room can. Lundar rushed him before he had time to make another move.

William crashed through the door just as Lundar Cheek lunged at Torin Dugold. Toldar and a battery of men followed close behind him. The crashing of the door and the extra movement throughout the fragile tunnel was too much for the old structure. William heard rumbling overhead as dust filled the room.

Cheek had not turned to face William. He had the fat man pinned against the back wall with the sword pointed at his throat. In the shifting of the rock walls, dust clouded the room. Torin got a lungful. He began to cough and pushed hard against Cheek, but the smaller man would not budge. As Torin's face darkened, Cheek called out. "Make yer escape Lord William, whilst ye can. I will rid the world of this vermin if it takes me life as well! Get ye hence! This cave will not hold!"

William glanced over his shoulder at Toldar. "Order the men out!"

The men turned with some reluctance, probably disappointed they would not seen the end of the magistrate. Then William ordered Toldar to follow his men.

Toldar gripped William's shoulder. "Do not you hesitate, brother, lest you be buried alive with that monster."

William gave a curt nod then turned back to the two men locked in a death struggle.

Torin was choking. "End it, Cheek!"

William weighed his sword with one hand. "Cheek, you can still get away."

Lundar Cheek kept his gaze on Torin. "Aye, but to what end? Will I go free? I think not. If ye wish to see this man's end then," he stepped suddenly back and slashed Torin's throat, "ye have seen it. Now leave me. Seal this room if ye must. I will die here rather than ride out w'ye and be put to death before the masses. Give me that much at least for my effort."

The ground rumbled again, leaving little doubt as to the fate of anyone left inside. William gave a quick nod and started to turn, but in that moment, his eyes caught movement at Cheek's feet. Torin had gotten his fat paw around his fallen sword. Even as William reacted, he drove the sword upward into Cheek's side.

William would never forget the look on Cheek's face as the man realized what had happened.

In one swift movement, William put a final end to Torin's hateful existence, severing his head, therefore rendering the rest useless.

Dust filled the room again and Cheek managed to whisper. "Get out, ye fool!"

With one more glance at Cheek, William dashed out as quickly as he could with dirt and rocks licking at his heels. He saw the light of the entrance just as the main part of the roof gave way. Toldar grabbed hold of William's shoulders. Holding his shield aloft, Toldar dragged him out of the falling debris. Together, they stumbled forward until they cleared the great cloud of dust and rock.

Many of the dead and dying were buried in its collapse. William and Toldar fell upon the grassy banks of the river, lying on their backs, filling their lungs with fresh air.

Solis strode up and stood looking down at them both. "May we assume the enemy perished, or do we need to dig into that mess?"

William pushed up slowly and shook his head. "I made sure Torin was dead before I got out."

"What of Cheek?" Toldar asked, wiping his face with his forearm.

"Torin drove his sword into Cheek before I could get to him. I believe they have both perished. It was Cheek's desire to die in the attempt." He took a deep breath and leaned forward. "What is the tally, Solis? Were you able to free most of our men?" His eyes were on the mound of rock and soil that now covered the mouth of the cave.

Solis cleared his throat. "Aye my lord, but ... yer nephew ... he is gravely injured."

William jumped up. "What? Where does he lie?"

Toldar stood and followed.

Solis strode along beside William. "We have moved him to the front, awaiting yer orders, sir."

William rushed forward, afraid to think what he might find. "How bad is it?"

"He took a sword in his thigh, so there be a lot of blood, sir. He staunched it somewhat, usin' his own belt."

As they approached the place where Young Will lay, William gave orders to Solis. "Gather the worst of the wounded and take the quickest route to the sea. There, send them by boat to Corwinder."

They'd laid Young Will in the deep shade, upon a bed of moss. William knelt beside him, leaned forward, and whispered his name.

Young Will's eyes fluttered at the sound of his uncle's voice. "I've lost a bit of blood, Uncle."

Laying his hand on Young Will's shoulder, William told him, "You must be strong, lad. You must hold on until we can get you to the lady. If anyone can help you, I know she can."

Young Will opened his eyes, but did not speak.

"Think only of getting home," William said. "Your journey is not done. I will need you in the days to come."

"Then I will surely stay," Young Will murmured as his eyes fluttered shut.

William squeezed his own eyes closed, battling his emotions. If the boy died, it was on him. He'd placed him in harm's way. Surely, if he'd been more attentive to God's voice, he'd have known the danger. How could he return home without Young Will?

Someone touched his shoulder. He looked up to see to Tom standing there. Tom was the closest thing they had to a doctor. William swiped at moisture on his cheek. "Do what you can to keep him alive, Tom."

"Aye sir, I will do what I'm able."

"I know you will." Standing up, William turned to Toldar and Solis. "Commandeer whatever you can to make their journey more bearable."

When they had gone, he turned to visit the other wounded, giving hope where he could. He said a prayer over the dying. Amongst the lesser wounded, he found Fegan, who had suffered a head blow that needed stitches. William sat beside him. "If you're able, Fegan, take up your instrument and sing to them. Accompany them upon their journey, to give them hope and comfort. Perhaps it will help to take their minds off their pain."

Fegan gazed out at his companions. "This I can do. I thank ye kindly, sir." He found his things and pulled out the lyre, sat down upon a rock and began to sing the psalms of praise.

The pleasing sound filled the camp and the words followed William as he moved about, checking on his wounded warriors.

"I love Thee, O Jehovah, my strength.
Jehovah my rock, my bulwark,
And my deliverer,
My God my rock, I trust in Him:
My shield, and a horn of my salvation,
My high tower.
The `Praised One' I call Jehovah,
And from my enemies I am saved.
Compassed me have cords of death,
And streams of the worthless make me afraid.
Cords of Sheol have surrounded me,
Before me have been snares of death.
In mine adversity I call Jehovah,
And unto my God I cry.
He heareth from His temple my voice,
And My cry before Him cometh into His ears."[vi]

$\mathfrak{A}$ new sound brought Jael's heavy lids open. She lay still for a moment, noting the lateness of the hour. Again the cry went forth. It was the child.

She forced herself to rise. Her head ached, but not nearly so much as her heart as the memories came flooding back. She leaned forward for a moment, nearly doubled over by the pain of it. She crossed to the window and pushed the shutter open. The afternoon was peaceful and would have been quite pleasant if not for the heaviness of her heart.

She stepped to the table and splashed her face with cool water, dried it, and straightened her hair. Then she made her way to Lady Elizabeth's quarters. She must see to her patient.

As Jael entered, the child cried again. Elizabeth handed him to the nurse. Catching sight of Jael, she shook her head. "Where have you been, dear lady? I have been in despair." She gave a loud sigh. "The boy is hungry and gets no nourishment from his mother. I am intent upon sending him away so I can get some rest."

She patted a spot on the bed. "Come sit by me. You have rested, from the looks of you."

Jael forced her lips into a smile. "I think perhaps that is a wise idea, Lady Elizabeth, sending the child away for a bit. I see you have found a suitable substitute."

Elizabeth nodded. "This is Obi. Abigail found her."

Jael glanced around the room. "Where is Dora?"

"Also gone. I have been abandoned."

Jael leaned forward to lay her hand on Elizabeth's. "I am sorry for it, my lady. I'm here now. What can I do for you?"

"Sing to me, Jael. You know how it calms my nerves. Perhaps then I can sleep. What a way to spend Holy Day."

Abigail and the nurse, Obi, quietly left the room. Jael took up her embroidery and sat down opposite the bed. Once she was settled, she began to sing. The only interruption came when Abigail returned with tea. It was not long before Lady Elizabeth slept.

Not until her friend had spoken those last words, did Jael remember today was the Holy Day. This very evening, a special service was being held in honor of the day. Jael leaned her head back and closed her eyes against the pain. So much had happened. In all her life to come, she knew she would never forget.

Abigail crept in, bringing the evening meal. "It is early for it, my lady, but everyone wishes to go to the service."

Jael nodded as she folded the cloth she'd been working on. "All right, Abigail. Will you go also?"

Abigail shook her head. "I'll stay here. But ye should not miss it, my lady. 'Twould comfort ye much."

"Aye, I suppose it would." Jael closed her eyes.

Abigail set the tray on the table. "But first ye need to eat."

Elizabeth sighed, but did not otherwise stir, so Jael ate a little bit of the food.

Abigail returned later and motioned her out. "Hazel awaits ye in yer room."

After Hazel made her a bit more presentable, Jael left to go to the chapel. She wondered as she walked along where they had laid Ferdinand. Certainly, she would hear of it. When she reached the chapel, she was surprised to find so many in attendance. She climbed to the family section and found a seat, just as Pastor Stephen entered. From the moment he opened his mouth and began to speak, she began to cry silent tears.

> *"Let not your heart be troubled, believe in God, also in me believe; in the house of my Father are many mansions; and if not, I would have told you; I go on to prepare a place for you; and if I go on and prepare for you a place, again do I come, and will receive you unto myself, that where I am ye also may be; and whither I go away ye have known, and the way ye have known...I am the way, and the truth, and the life, no one doth come unto the Father, if not through me."[vii]*

She understood it all now, what he had been trying to tell her. It was all too real. She had doubted it until Ferdinand spoke his final words. "He is here with me ..." echoed the story Stephen read: "I go to prepare a place for you ..."

In his mercy, He had come and introduced himself to a humble servant like Ferdinand, who stood on the brink of death, unafraid. She drew out her handkerchief and brushed away the tears. Elenor laid her hand on Jael's arm. Jael turned to look at her. On the other side of the curtain, Stephen was closing the sermon, so Jael whispered to Elenor. "I believe now. Tell me what I must do."

It was dark when Elenor, Jael and Stephen emerged from the chapel. Everyone else had gone. Jael felt much lighter. She felt peaceful, almost happy. In the morning they would lay Ferdinand to rest in the sepulcher beneath the chapel. This was a place of great honor, reserved for warriors who had given their lives in combat for God and King. Pastor Stephen and Courin had agreed that this is where Ferdinand belonged.

As Jael climbed the steps to the house, she stopped and looked out upon the shining water in the distance. She stood there basking in the soft light of a crescent moon, the gentle ocean breeze and the sound of Stephen's words echoing in her heart. *I am the way, and the truth, and the life, no one doth come unto the Father, if not through me.*

William stood on the crest of the hill, enjoying a moment of solitude. He looked out at the verdant river valley. From a nearby bush, a night bird called. It all seemed so peaceful. One would never know what violence had just ended here. He hated war, but because they'd fought, peace would reign. For a while, at least. Until another tyrant came forth. There'd been an ugly succession of them over the last few decades, since the reign of his great-grandfather.

Torin was by far the worst and the most devious. He had always managed to evade his attackers at the last moment. Until this one, and only now, because one of his own had stood against him. William shuddered to think what would have been if they had not happened to run into Cheek.

His brother-in-law stepped into his line of vision.

Catching sight of William, Toldar strode up the hill.

William watched his approach. Where did the man find so much energy? Must be the quantity of food he ingested.

Toldar reached for a blade of grass, set it between his teeth then looked at William. "We've a stew of fresh fish and herbs, brother, if you're hungry."

William met his gaze with a solemn one of his own. "What of the captives?"

Toldar stood at ease, his arms crossed over his chest. "One woman was dead when we reached her, but the other two remained alive. Several of the freed slaves promised to see them safely home. They are camped just over the hill."

"Have they food and necessities?"

"I made sure of it sir," Solis said, as he strode in from the encampment.

William ran his fingers through his hair. What he wouldn't give for a bath. He sucked in a breath then released it. "Stay with the men, if you please, sirs. I will go and speak with the exiles."

Solis looked at Toldar, who nodded and sat down.

William strode into the small camp, startling the inhabitants. Several of the men jumped up and bowed. William held out his hand. "Nay, stand. I would speak with you. Where are the women?"

A man pointed to the place. William noticed it was downwind. He found the two in deplorable condition, hardly recognizable. One of them sat up, eating. The other lay alongside her, moaning softly.

"Her is badly injured, my lord," the first lady whispered.

William crouched before them both, wishing for a cloth with which to cover his nose. "You come from Dolor Heights?"

The woman nodded. "Aye, my lord." Her lips trembled. "I be Lenore. At one time, my husband was chief of Dolor Heights."

"How is it there?"

Her shoulders slumped. "It is very bad, my lord. The men has been gone these many months, and the rains have washed away our crops. The few women and children left behind are sickly, nigh unto death."

William turned his head just enough to catch a breath of fresh air. "Where were the men taken?"

The woman sniffed and wiped her nose on her sleeve. "We dunna know."

Overhearing the question, one of the former slaves stepped near. "If I may be so bold sir ..."

William stood to look at the man. He was small and very thin, his gaunt face marked by scars. "Yes?"

"The magistrate sent 'em to the mines, sir. They be workin' there—men and boys from Dolor and beyond."

The woman sucked in a breath. "Our men and our sons, all of 'em, gone."

William frowned. "The mines—at Touri Deep?"

The gaunt-faced man nodded. "Aye, sir, he goes after the gold, sir."

William set his hands on his hips. "The gold?"

"Aye, the fabled gold, sir. We knew 'twas a foolish quest."

The woman covered her mouth with the back of her hand and began to cry aloud.

William shook his head and faced the speaker. "Foolish quest or no, I will send men to free them." He turned again to the women. "Do you have all you need for now?"

"Aye, my lord," the woman answered, still sniffling. "We been given food and drink. Tomorrow we go back to our home, such as it is."

"Be assured, I will give you whatever assistance you need there." He lifted his voice to the others who had gathered around. "And to all of you. With God's help, let us make every effort to recover as quickly as possible from the effects of this tyrant's reign. Return to your homes, and do what you can to ensure survival through the coming winter. I realize the crops will be late, and perhaps nonexistent in some places. But be certain of this, your neighbors stand ready to help in time of need."

A few weary cheers went up. Before returning to his camp, William took the time to visit with each of the men, giving more personal assurances. He intended to do all he could to help them.

His father had long been determined to return this region's hereditary titles to power, but William was uncertain. He'd seen too many weak among them. And they were spread too thin. Most had been forced to flee their hereditary lands.

Not one who had taken up arms against the magistrate had survived. In William's opinion, only the weak had managed to subsist, and that because they ran. He could not respect that. It would have been better if they had joined their countrymen in battle, instead of cowering in fear. In the end however, his father's word would decide the matter.

Jael sat on the lower corner of Elizabeth's bed, watching her feed the child. It was a joy to behold. Even the smallest things produced such pleasure. She laughed at the sight of the tiny fisties batting the air. "He'll be a warrior like his father."

"Oh, fie. I hope not," Elizabeth said, but her face shone with delight.

At the approach of a vehicle and sound of many horses' hooves, Jael jumped up and ran to the window.

"It is probably only my mother," Elizabeth told her. "It sounds like a coach and six."

Jael nodded. "Six white horses pulling a shiny black coach with covered windows?"

"That's her. Be prepared, Jael. She will come in and take possession of everything and everyone."

Elizabeth's tone was light, and punctuated with laughter, so Jael didn't worry, but she wondered about it. She had not long to wait, for soon the hall filled with the sound of the queen's arrival.

The door opened and Abigail stood aside. "Lady Bethalyn, Her Majesty, the Queen."

Jael stood and dropped into a deep curtsey. Lady Bethalyn paid her little mind for the moment, moving quickly to the side of the bed where she leaned down and kissed her daughter's cheek. "Oh dear, you are ... feeding him, yourself?"

Elizabeth snuck a peak at Jael, who stood waiting at the foot of the bed. Jael met her gaze with a small smile. Elizabeth gave a soft chuckle. "Yes, Mother, I am feeding my own child. Myself."

"Well of course you are, dear. I just thought ... but then you always did like to do things your own way. I will try not to interfere. But do you think it wise?"

"It is wise, Mother. Why should I let a nurse have all the fun? I shall mother my children as I see fit. So far I am quite happy. If I find myself feeling otherwise, I may enlist help." She waved a hand toward Jael. "I'm sorry Mother, I didn't introduce Lady Jael to you."

Lady Bethalyn turned to look at Jael. She looked at her very well. After the passage of several long moments, she said, "Lady Jael? Where have I heard that name?"

"From my father no doubt, or perhaps your son," Elizabeth said. "This is Lady Jael of Verani Haven."

"Verani ... ah ... I see." Lady Bethalyn frowned then nodded then turned back to her daughter.

Jael bit down on her lower lip to stay the smile that threatened. She gave a quick bow and backed away. "If you need me, Lady Elizabeth, I will be in my room."

Elizabeth nodded in return, obviously suppressing laughter. "Thank you, dear lady."

The door was not completely closed before Jael heard the words spoken by the queen in lofty tones, "Why do you call her lady?"

This was going to be interesting. She spent the rest of the day going over the inventory of herbs in her room. Though she tried hard not to think of it, she still fought melancholy when she handled them. Ferdinand had been so constantly with her.

When dinner was served, she was informed, "Lady Bethalyn will eat with her daughter," so Jael was on her own. She did not really mind.

Immediately after her meal, she climbed to the roof and sat looking out to sea. As the sun dipped beneath the horizon, she went inside. The quiet evening bored Jael, sending her to bed early.

She'd been there for only two hours, when the chapel bell began to ring. Its tolling broke into her dreams and sent her flying to the window. At a loud knock on the door belowstairs, she grabbed her shawl and threw it over her shoulders as she ran out into the hallway. A masculine voice rang out with, "Lady Jael! Lady Jael! Come quickly!"

Jael ran to the top of the stairs and looked down to see one of the guards. "The ship has come in bearing wounded, my lady. You must come at once!"

Jael ran back to her room, followed closely by Abigail who helped her into her clothes. Then she grabbed a basket and filled it with the herbs she had prepared. She ran down the stairs just as Lady Bethalyn was calling for Abigail. "Abigail! What is all this commotion? Abigail! What is happening?"

The men were arriving in the long room across the lawn. They set up a makeshift hospital and built up the fire. Jael was immediately ushered to the table nearest the fire where she saw a familiar face and her heart nearly stopped. He was so like his uncle in appearance.

The man called Tom stood by, saying, "The wound was quite deep, my lady, and cruel. He lost a lot of blood. He stopped the flow himself, by tightening his own belt around it. But I'm afraid the damage was too severe. Aboard ship, I cauterized the wound, but it stinks of rot. I'm afeared we'll have to take it off."

Jael looked at the older man who served as a doctor. "Has he been conscious at all?"

"Nay, my lady, none at all since we set sail. But he promised his uncle to hold on and he has. The lad's got strength."

Jael went to work quickly. She carefully unwrapped the bandages and revealed the ugly wound. "I need boiling water." She made a tisane and carefully washed the wound.

As Tom held the lamp, she examined the leg carefully. A moment later, Tom was called away to attend to others. He left the lamp and Jael went to work. When he returned some time later, he spied the fresh bandage and looked at her inquisitively. "What is your opinion, my lady?"

"I have cut away the rotted portion of flesh. I made repair where I could then coated it with a liberal paste of Lamb's Wort and Drumwort. We will look at it in the morning."

Tom opened his mouth to object, then shut it again. As he turned away, she heard him mutter, "If the boy dies of gangrene, it willn't be my doing."

Jael sponged Will's brow with herbs then forced the same tea down his throat that she'd fed to his uncle so many months before.

Throughout the long night, she worked with Tom by her side. He was determined to watch what she did. Several times he stood amazed as she uncovered wounds he had not even noticed. She laid her hands on many and prayed over them silently. He scratched his chin and asked questions as often as he dared. While he stood by her, she always told him what she administered, so maybe he would remember and know how to help in future.

Near dawn, they ministered to their last patient. Jael met Tom's eyes. "Will there be more?"

Tom blew out a weary breath. "Tis all for now, my lady. Lord William sent us on ahead out of concern for his nephew. He wanted you to have a chance w'him." He rubbed his brow with his thumb and forefinger. "Two never made the journey. They was buried at sea. We lost nine at once and then the other two made eleven. Not bad for so brutal a fight as it was and 'twould have been much worse except ..." he glanced up at her. "I'm sure ye'll hear account of it all, my lady."

He'd say no more about it, but assured her he'd left Lord William and Lord Toldar quite well, though not entirely unscathed. "No one can fight such a battle as that was and go completely unhurt."

They returned to Young Will and found him much the same as before. She sent Tom away to try to get a bit of sleep while she stayed by Young Will. He'd not been gone long before Lady Bethalyn came to visit her grandson.

"He must be moved from this place. He must be in his own room. Please have him removed there at once."

"Yes of course, Your Majesty." Jael answered, dipping her head. "As soon as we are certain we will not have to ..." she allowed her voice to trail off. It was a difficult thing to say.

Lady Bethalyn's eyes widened. "You do not think ... he will lose his leg?"

Jael placed her hand over Will's brow then upon each side of his face, checking on the progress of the fever. It still had not broken. She hesitated to discuss this in front of him, even though he was not awake.

She needn't have worried, for while she'd been checking for fever,

Lady Bethalyn caught sight of the ring on Jael's finger. She reached for Jael's hand and lifted it for a closer look, in order to be sure. Then she dropped her hand, lifted her royal chin, and looked down her nose at Jael. "Where did you get that ring?"

Drawing in a deep, fortifying breath, Jael glanced at the queen. "Lord William gave it me." She made no explanation, simply stated the answer to the question. Upon hearing her answer, Her Majesty the Queen left the room.

Jael held her place for several minutes, watching Young Will breathe. She blinked her eyes. What had just happened? No doubt, she would hear about it soon enough.

Missions of Mercy

Elizabeth pressed her lips into a straight line. She lowered her eyes as her mother let loose a most diverting tirade, albeit in low tones, so as not to disturb the child.

"You know very well, I am usually quite good-natured. I am in possession of an even temper and merciful disposition. I believe, though you can tell me if I'm wrong, I am well loved by my family, well respected and loved by my staff." She paced to the window, turned and paced back.

"But, and I think you will agree, I have a very strong sense of place. I am after all, wife of a monarch, daughter of a monarch, and the mother of the man who will someday take his father's place as monarch." She turned again and paced back to the window. Turning her head, she spoke over her shoulder. "For years, I have guarded my children from the modern contagion of mixing what I like to call ranks." She turned to face her daughter.

Elizabeth glanced up. "Yes, Mother. Ranks."

Mother nodded. "To this end, I have kept a constant flow of high-ranking guests moving through your lives. I was honored when our eldest daughter, Young Will's own mother, married a prime minister. Then you married slightly lower in Toldar, whose father was Mayor of Corwinder. But it was a good match, for Toldar is heir to much good property in the northern region of Cragmorton. Though I hope you'll never go there, of course."

She paced across the room, her hands at her waist, fingers intertwined. "I have a confession to make." She gazed at her daughter. "You mustn't speak of it."

Elizabeth nodded, her brow furrowed.

Mother set to pacing again. "For many years, I've had my eye on a young lady from Coldthwaite. She has grown into an excellent young woman. Clear of eye and well spoken. Her background is unquestionable, since she is your second cousin."

She stopped, her back to Elizabeth, so she couldn't see how Elizabeth glared at her as the identity of this "excellent young woman" became known to her.

Mother drew in a shaky breath and exhaled. Her hands at her sides, she formed them into fists. "Now enters this usurper from a foreign land. A woman of doubtful origins and no rank, except what was given her out of respect for something her forebears accomplished years ago. Certainly, she's partly responsible for William's return, but ... this cannot be. She cannot possibly expect to be accepted as one of the royals."

She faced Elizabeth. "I cannot abide it."

"Mother," Elizabeth said, "you cannot be serious. Euthagenia is not an excellent match for William. He would never agree to such a match. Besides, I think you are jumping ahead of yourself. I do not believe Jael has any designs on my brother. Nor he on her."

Her mother plopped down on the chair. "She wears his ring."

"He gave it her for her protection, Mother."

Mother smoothed her skirt. "Protection—from what?"

Elizabeth weighed her answer. Shaky ground lay ahead. If she told her from what, Mother would be upset and angry that William would allow such a one to bring a possible threat upon his family. And if she told her about the journey Jael made across the great mountains, her mother would probably succumb at once to shock. She must proceed carefully, therefore. "How is Young Will doing, Mother? You have not said."

Mother glared at her. "You are changing the subject."

"Only because I am not fully aware of the circumstances. I feel ... you should speak with your son about it." Yes, it was a lame excuse. But at this point, her own son began to wake, detouring Mother's attention far better than Elizabeth could do.

After a brief incursion into baby talk, Mother caught Elizabeth's eye. She continued in soft tones, emphasizing each word as if she was still speaking to the infant. "You will see how it is when this child is grown up. You will want only the best for him, my dear." She rubbed the baby's tummy. "I am not finished with you on this subject, Elizabeth. We will speak again later."

Elizabeth could not hold back her smile. "I do not doubt that Mother, not one bit."

"He has passed the point," Jael told Tom. "The fever lessens, as you can see."

Young Will's eyes fluttered at the sound of her voice and soft touch of her hand.

Tom nodded in tentative agreement. "I would like to see what lay beneath them bandages, though." He pointed at Young Will's wrappings, now stained with fresh blood.

"It is a good bleed," Jael told him as she began to pull away the bandages. "The Lamb's Wort has a drawing effect. I believe the herbs are working."

When the wrappings were completely gone, Tom looked at the wound, his mouth agape. "Praise Jesus, it's a wonder, for true."

Jael cleansed it again and applied a fresh coating of Lamb's Wort. After rebandaging it, she checked the rest of his leg, down to his foot and his toes. Everything seemed fine. "If it is acceptable to you, I will have him moved to his room."

Tom cast her a sidelong look. "I heared of the ruckus, milady. Ye was brave to go agin Her Majesty."

Jael smiled back at him. "Brave, Tom, or foolish?"

Tom grinned, his face pinking up. "A bit o' both, I ken." He stepped around the bed toward the door. "I will oversee the move myself. If ye want to make him your priority, I will see to the others and only call upon ye if there is a need."

"Thank you, Tom." A few minutes later, a very weary Jael climbed the outer steps on the way to her room and hopefully, some rest.

She was met at the door by Abigail. "You mustn't think ye can rest like that, my lady. I have ordered ye a bath."

Jael let her head fall back in frustration. Oh well, a bath would feel awfully nice. While the women prepared the water, she sat down at the dressing table and began to brush out her hair. It had grown a bit in the past weeks and most of her color had returned.

When they were ready for her, she went gladly. Being waited upon was one of the nicest things about being here. If she ever had to leave, she would miss it terribly.

William sat astride Lodan, gazing at one of the most depressing scenes he'd ever laid eyes upon. "Dolor Heights."

Toldar reined in beside him. "Pain. How very apt. I've often wondered, who would name their village thusly?"

"I believe its original meaning was 'birth pangs.'" William unhooked his waterskin and drank.

"It matters not, I suppose. It is pain in one form or another. I would call it Misery."

William gazed at Toldar's face, rugged with new scars and overgrown beard. "Perhaps we can lessen their misery a bit ere we proceed with our journey."

The rain had at least held off for several days and the mud was a bit less thick. The few remaining inhabitants of Dolor received their women with joy. Their situation troubled William greatly.

"This is not truly our jurisdiction," he confessed to Toldar, "but I am finding it difficult not to interfere."

Toldar winced as he gazed at the ground. "But the mines at Touri Deep—it would mean another long journey, sir—the men are spent and tired."

"Yes, they are and beyond. What say you, Solis?"

"Some of the men was wonderin' could they go huntin' sir? They mean to feed these people, I ken."

William gave a nod. "That's a good idea, set them to it at once. We'll camp here a day or two, hunt and fish and leave this place better. That'll give me time to make a decision based on the welfare of our men."

After Solis left, Toldar turned to William. "There are some who will need to go on to Corwinder, should we decide to make the journey into Touri, sir."

"Aye, I realize that. We can send word by them of our delay, and the reason for it. I desire word from there, as well. I must confess my anxiety for my nephew is great. And then we must consider you also, Toldar. Most likely, you are a father by now. Perhaps you would wish to return with the wounded. We will need someone to go along."

"Nay, my brother, could I return without you? Allow you to go on and gain all the glory for yourself?" He finished with a broad smile. "I think not."

William slapped him on the back and they moved forward, listening as Solis directed his men.

Early next morning those remaining wounded prepared to make the journey home. These men were not severely injured enough to go with the first evacuees, but not well enough for further sorties. Joseph of Coldthwaite, Solis' second in command, would make the journey with them then return with news of Corwinder.

What men were not hunting and fishing were working in the village, repairing huts and digging drainage ditches. Fresh food and assistance energized the inhabitants of the village. They busied themselves smoking meat, tanning hides, and cleaning their houses.

When William felt satisfied with their labor, he prepared his men to set out for Touri Deep. Lenore approached him and gave a curtsey, albeit a bit clumsy. William received it with a grin. He supposed she might be out of practice.

"My lord, we wishes to thank ye fer all ye done and offer ye our prayers fer what ye are about to undertake on our behalf."

William nodded. At least she smelled a bit better these days, and was already beginning to recover from her injuries. "You are welcome, lady."

"We ain't had so much since our men went away. They was a great loss and then when the lady left ..."

William's ears pricked up. He turned his head to the side. "The lady?"

Lenore nodded. She covered her mouth to hide her teeth when she smiled. Several of her front teeth were missing. Those left behind were not pretty. "The Lady of the Haven sir, she come regular like to check on us, her bein' a healer an' all. And she never did come empty-handed."

William hardly knew how to respond. Everywhere he went he was reminded of her. He nodded politely to Lenore. "Perhaps she'll return one day."

"I do hope and pray for it, sir."

Most of the village turned out to watch as the warriors rode away.

William's standard-bearer lifted a new flag along with their own. A flag made by the women of Dolor. All their hopes rode with the warriors.

A soft knock at Jael's door woke her from a long, restful sleep. She got up at once knowing it may be Tom. "Young Will has wakened, my lady."

"I will come at once." She washed her face and dressed. Then she went to the room on the lower floor where the men had carried Will. He was awake, but very groggy from the tea she had administered. Jael bent to look at him.

"I believe his fever has broken," Tom whispered.

"Aye Tom, you are right." She smiled into Will's eyes. "You are home now, Will, recovering from your injuries."

He opened his mouth slowly as if he had to force his lips to form words. "My leg?"

She patted his hand. "You still have it." He breathed out a sigh then closed his eyes. When the door opened behind her, Jael knew without turning, it was Lady Bethalyn.

"I heard he was awake."

Jael turned to look at her. "He is resting peacefully now, Your Majesty. The fever has broken."

Lady Bethalyn pressed her palms together. "Oh, that is good news. I could not rest knowing what he must be going through." She moved to his side and took his hand in hers.

Tom cleared his throat and began to back away. "If that is all, Lady Jael?"

"Thank you, Tom. I will stay with him now."

When Tom had gone, Lady Bethalyn watched Jael as she worked near the fire, mixing dried herbs for tea. "Surely you do not mean to stay? Can you not have one of the men sit with him?"

Jael frowned as she poured hot water over the herbs. What was she asking? Did she object to Jael's presence because she was a woman, or because she was not a servant? She looked up at Lady Bethalyn's face, trying to discern her meaning. "There are several tasks only I can do and when those are done, I will leave him in the care of a page, Your Majesty. He will most likely sleep for some hours yet."

"What is it that only you can do?"

Jael stood and carried the bowl of tea to the bedside. She set it down to steep for a few minutes while she changed the bandages. She spoke in a quiet voice, "I will change his bandages and administer this tea, which contains a powerful sedative. It will help him sleep."

Her eyes on her grandson, Lady Bethalyn asked, "And what do you give him for pain? I suppose you give him something, since he lies so still and unhampered."

Jael smiled. "Those herbs I use to coat the wound also relieve the pain. The sedative I mentioned relaxes the muscles. When he is able to bear the pain a bit, I will reduce the amount I give him."

"This is how you treated my son?"

Jael hesitated. "Yes, Your Majesty, it was very similar, though Lord William's injuries were nigh unto death."

"But you were able to bring him back."

Jael began to cut away the bandages. Mindful of Lady Bethalyn's sensitivities, she kept the wound covered. "God's Providence brought him back, Your Majesty. I was only the instrument He used."

"And a very capable one you do seem to be," Lady Bethalyn's eyes never left Jael's face as she probed a bit deeper. "Will you return to Verani Haven when all of this is over?"

"You may wish to turn away for a moment. It is quite a gruesome wound."

Lady Bethalyn set her chin in the air. "I am sure I have seen worse."

Jael watched her for a moment, before returning to her work, carefully lifting away the soiled bandage. She checked the wound thoroughly, cleansed the outside of it then applied a fresh poultice and covered it with a new bandage.

Throughout all of this, she watched Lady Bethalyn. That lady barely breathed during the entire process, but she seemed determined not to cringe. When it was finished, she sat down in the chair beside the bed, visibly shaken.

Jael disposed of the soiled bandages and washed her hands. Then she returned to Will and spooned a bit of the tea into his mouth. His eyes fluttered a bit then opened. Lady Bethalyn stood immediately, no doubt wanting him to see her there.

Will's eyes soon found his grandmother's. He gave her a wan smile. "Grandmother," he whispered.

She touched his lips with her fingertips. "Shh. There, there do not speak. There will be plenty of time for that. Just see if you can swallow a bit more of this tea." She held out her palm for the cup. Jael handed it to her.

Jael stood aside as the queen administered the tea. When Will had had enough, he fell asleep.

Lady Bethalyn faced Jael. "Thank you ... Jael. A grandmother must feel she is of some use in times like these."

Jael nodded and took the cup. "Of course, Your Majesty." She moved to the bell and pulled it then returned to the fire to put her things away.

Lady Bethalyn stepped close behind her. "You did not answer my question earlier. Will you return to Verani Haven?"

Jael stood to face her, though several inches of height required that she lift her eyes. "I ... there is nothing there ... anymore. My home was destroyed."

"Well, can it not be rebuilt? Surely you have family there."

Jael wiped her hands on her apron. "I am the last of the Haven family. I have ... not thought ... where I will go after this."

"You will stay as long as you are needed, of course?"

Before she could make an answer, the door opened. Jael glanced into

Abigail's inquisitive face. "Abigail, would you send Young Will's page up to sit with him now?"

Abigail bowed and exited. Jael turned back to the queen. "Of course, I will stay as long as I am needed."

A moment later, Young Will's page entered. Jael gave him his orders then turned to go. The queen bent to kiss her grandson ere she followed Jael out of the room.

"Do not think I am ungrateful. You are surely a gift to our family. I ask God to bless you, daily in my prayers. But there are certain ... lines that are drawn ..."

Jael gave a curtsey and lowered her head. "I am very well aware of the differences in our stations, Your Majesty. I am most grateful for your praise and your prayers. If you will excuse me, I must go and tend to the others."

Lady Bethalyn dismissed her with a wave of her hand. "Yes, of course, go. I hope all of your patients are doing as well as my grandson."

Dark Vision

Jael took the stairs slowly, her heart a jumbled mess of emotion. The message was clear. The queen wished her away as soon as may be. She thought her unworthy and feared her son may mean more by his gift of the ring than Jael had ever dared to think.

She stopped halfway down the steps and stood looking out over the courtyard. Visions passed quickly before her, so quickly she barely took it all in. She saw William, sitting tall in the saddle, saw Toldar and Solis beside him. They rode into darkness until the craggy peaks of Touri loomed over them. With a mighty flash of light the mountains came crashing down upon them. She saw strange men with wiry frames bent and bruised from long abuse, running before them, their faces twisted in fear. And then she saw an eagle take flight, its powerful wings touching William's head as he rode forward, skimming the mountain peaks.

A familiar voice spoke out of the mist surrounding her. "My lady ... be ye all right?" She came to herself, and gazed into the eyes of Courin, standing on the steps above her. At some point, she'd sat down, her basket forgotten. She frowned. When had that happened?

"My lady?" Courin repeated.

She looked back at him. "Oh, aye. Yes, Courin, I am quite well." At least she thought so. She looked down at her hands, blinking her eyes to clear her mind of the powerful vision.

Courin stepped nearer. "Let me help ye then. Do ye go to the Long Room to minister to the men?"

"Aye. Aye, I do. That is where I am going."

Courin took her arm and helped her up, stooped to pick up the basket, and led her down the remaining steps. He led her across the open area to the door of the Long Room. There, he let her go, opened the door and stood aside for her. Still a bit dazed, Jael stepped into the dimly lit room and looked about her.

The room was nearly empty. The patients were slowly thinning out. One by one, they were gaining strength and leaving. Some were going back to their duties, others were being sent home for a while, to recuperate.

"Are ye certain, then? Ye are well, my lady?" Courin asked again.

She turned back to him, feeling rather foolish. What must he think of her? "I am ... well, yes. I suppose I must have ..."

He offered her a kind smile. "Ye're tired is all. Ye've worked day and night, my lady, and not one among these is sorry for it. We've a great deal to be thankful for, and that's certain. I'll be right here, my lady—should ye have need of me."

Jael thanked him again then forced her body forward to the task at hand. All the while, the scenes of the "waking dream" played over and over in her mind. What did it mean?

As soon as she finished her work, she set out for the chapel. Pastor Stephen would know what to do. He wasn't in the chapel, so she walked next door to the residence. A servant answered her knock and led her to Elenor's parlor.

Elenor rose from her chair as Jael entered the cozy room.

"He is studying for tomorrow's sermon," Elenor told Jael. "But I will tell him you are here."

Jael looked down at her hands. "No, please don't disturb him. I'll come another time."

Elenor touched Jael's arm. "But you are troubled, my lady. Please, at least sit and have tea with me. I was just about to pour myself a cup."

It took only a moment for Jael to decide. She nodded and sat in the chair Elenor offered. She glanced around the room. "The children are very quiet this evening."

Elenor smiled as she poured out the tea. "We have a rule that they must keep to their rooms of a Sabbath eve. They respect their da's need to study the Holy Scriptures."

"It is a good rule." She also appreciated the peace. This was a happy household, usually filled with the laughter of children.

When Elenor was seated opposite Jael, she gave her an anxious glance. "I hope you are well? It is only a few days since ... you lost a good friend."

Jael breathed out a sigh. "So much has happened since then. It has all gone so quickly."

Elenor smiled and shook her head. "Sometimes that is good, but ... sometimes, not. The grieving finds ways of coming out and making its presence known to you."

Jael nodded. Perhaps that's all this was.

Elenor stirred her tea. "I suppose you do know that, full well."

Jael raised her eyes to Elenor's and smiled. "Yes, I do. Actually, I ... perhaps you could help me with something. I ... I had a waking dream."

"A waking dream? You mean ... had you a vision?"

Jael nodded. "I believe so ... I suppose you would call it a vision. I saw something."

Elenor frowned in concentration. "What did you see?"

Jael explained the vision, as best she could. "What do you think it means?"

Elenor had not taken her eyes off Jael's face. She set her tea down and took Jael's hands in hers. "Oh my lady, you must tell this to my husband." She let go Jael's hands and left the room.

Jael sat in silence, a jumble of nerves, wondering what Elenor must think of her. Would she bid her husband come see this wild woman who sees visions? Perhaps they would feel the need to pray for her, or cast out an evil spirit.

She had not long to wait. Pastor Stephen sat down across from Jael, with a look of expectation. Jael repeated her story while Elenor served her husband some tea.

After hearing the tale she told, Pastor Stephen sat back and looked thoughtful. He sipped his tea slowly, seeming to savor its taste. He was quiet so long, Jael grew fidgety. Finally, he set down his cup and leaned forward. "This is a true vision, I think. It may be a ... warning ... if you will. I am glad you came to me. We must pray for the safety of our men, Lady Jael. Something is going to happen, or perhaps already has." He glanced at his wife then back at Jael. "We cannot know."

After a moment's hesitation, he continued, "But the eagle ... is a good sign."

Jael regarded him. "How so?"

He nodded. "In the Holy Scriptures, the eagle is a sign of strength. In your vision, he brushed Lord William with the tip of his wing. I believe he imparted strength to Lord William, perhaps even helping their advance. We will pray that they will surely make it to safety."

After a time of prayer, Jael excused herself. Exhaustion set in as she made her way slowly back toward the house. Here, she was halted by the sound of Lady Elizabeth's voice. She looked up and spied the lady sitting on her balcony, taking the air.

Elizabeth stood and leaned against the stone balustrade. "Dear friend, please come and sit with me. I am bored almost to tears."

Jael smiled up at her. "How can you be bored, with a new baby nearby?"

"All he does is sleep. Except at night of course, when he cries. And eats. And messes his nappie."

Jael gave a soft laugh. "I'll be right up." In truth, she wished to be alone, but a diversion might do her more good.

When she reached the balcony, Elizabeth waved her to a chair. "I am not fit for pleasantries, my friend. I am skittish and desperate for word from the front. Why have they not returned? I blame my brother, for he cannot stop once he has started..."

Jael listened with little more than a polite smile as her friend droned on. She knew the real issue here. Elizabeth was nervous and upset over her husband's lengthy absence. As Jael watched her prattle on and on, she noticed the telltale signs, especially the anxiety in her eyes. Finally, she leaned forward and touched Elizabeth's hand. "He is all right. He has God's divine protection. I believe we will hear news of him very soon."

For a moment, Elizabeth only stared at Jael. She made a strange sound, as if the wind had been knocked from her. Then her lower lip trembled, and she began to weep. Jael moved to her side offering a handkerchief. She sat with her until the tears were spent.

"I'll go and make you a comforting tea." When she returned, her friend looked up, offering a wan smile. "How do you always know these things?"

Jael thought a moment. "Perhaps because I'm a healer." She handed Elizabeth a cup of the fragrant tea.

Elizabeth took the cup and held it between her palms. "Or is it because you've known so much sorrow of your own?" She sipped the tea. "This is most excellent. What is it?"

"A mixture of chamomile and lavender blossoms, sweetened with honey." She poured herself a cup then sat back in her chair and inhaled the fragrance. "It's quite calming. I'll leave extra. If you drink a cup before retiring for the night, you'll sleep better." She gazed over her cup at Elizabeth. "It may also calm the child."

"Oh, my dear, where have you been with this?"

Jael giggled.

Elizabeth sat forward in her chair. "How is my dear nephew? Mother was so cryptic."

"He's recovering well. In a very short time, I predict he'll be able to visit you and take away some of the unbearable monotony of your life."

"That is such a different tale than the one my esteemed Mother told. But she was most impressed with your work."

"I'm surprised to hear that, for she seemed ..." Jael stopped herself before she confessed too much. After all, Lady Bethalyn was Elizabeth's mother, and also the queen of the realm. She'd no wish to speak ill of her.

Elizabeth quirked a smile. "Believe me, I know how she is." She glanced about then leaned forward in a conspiratorial manner. "There is a reason for it. You see, she noticed my brother's ring on your finger and assumed it meant ... well ... that he had designs on you. Not that he couldn't have—or doesn't have—I would be very glad of it. But she has always planned our lives for us, you see. And you are most definitely a distraction from that plan."

Jael hardly dared speak. She knew no proper answer, unused as she was, to so sisterly a conversation. She found herself both flattered, and alarmed.

Elizabeth touched Jael's hand, no doubt to gain her full attention. "This is quite diverting, because she has in mind a young lady who is so much the opposite of anyone my brother would choose." She hid a smile behind her hand.

Jael arched her brows. Again, she had no words. As their eyes met, both of them burst into giggles.

News from the Front

Two days later, Courin stood at the door of Jael's room. Hazel was just finishing her hair, so she bid him enter.

Courin seemed a bit embarrassed by that, so he stood at some distance and called out the particulars of his errand. "My lady, another ship has docked with wounded aboard. These are not so serious as the first, but Sir Thomas requests yer assistance."

"Thank you, Courin. Tell Sir Thomas I will be there directly."

After Courin left the room, Jael noticed Hazel's expression of alarm. Her hands trembled as she finished Jael's hair.

Jael took hold of her fingers. "What is it?"

"Oh my lady, I do hope it ain't my Roy among these."

Jael stood and turned to look at her. "Well, Courin did say they weren't so serious. Would you like to accompany me? We will know right quickly whether he is among them."

"Oh yes, milady, I'd love it above all things. And if he ain't there, someone may have news of him."

Jael nodded and threw on her cloak. "I just need to stop and pick up some supplies." Upon their arrival at the door of the Long Room, they were met by Joseph, who bowed low and spoke to her.

"Good day, my lady. I bring a letter to Her Majesty, and to Lady Elizabeth. "I return at once to the front, if ye have any messages ye wish to send."

"Thank you, Joseph." She started to move on, but for a whisper behind her. "Ask him, if you please." She had nearly forgotten Hazel. "Oh, Joseph, Hazel wishes to know if her Roy is among the wounded."

Joseph smiled and bowed again. "No, my lady, Roy has not returned. He is still at the front."

Hazel breathed an audible sigh of relief. "Thank ye, dear Joseph, and when ye see him, tell him I asked after him." Joseph nodded then stood aside for Jael to pass.

Hazel turned back, saying she had a great deal of work yet to do.

Jael began at once, tending the injured. While there were no mortal wounds this time, some were still badly injured, mostly broken bones, and wounds mended on the battlefield. Among them was a young man of medium height, whose leg had been broken in a fall. The men had set it and anchored it in place with smooth branches. When Jael examined him, she noticed the fine workmanship of a leather belt cinched round his waist.

"Me Da made it," he told her. "He's a cobbler of Cairne, milady."

Jael paused her examination. "Cobbler?"

"Aye, and a fine one too. He works with his heart upon the leather, formin' as it were a regular masterpiece of each bit."

"Would his name be Donol?" she asked, already knowing the answer, for his eyes were like Ader's eyes, as well she could remember, and his voice was quite like Donol's.

His Ader-like eyes lit with pleasure. "For sure and certain it is—but do ye know them?"

"Aye, I had the very great pleasure of making their acquaintance a short time ago as I passed through the Touris."

"Imagine that. A lady such as you, meeting my poor Ma and Da. They must've been that honored."

Jael smiled and nodded. "Oh no, the honor was all mine, sir. And when you return, you will tell them we have met. Tell them Jonathan has done very well for himself." He seemed a little puzzled by that last, but happily agreed to carry the message. "Once I have healed enough to make the long journey there, I will carry yer message, milady. I would be honored for it." She finished the new bandages and gave orders for him to spend some time resting.

The stories she heard them tell of Dolor wrenched her heart. She'd known them well, attended them in childbirth and sickness. Many times, her father had rescued their children from slavery, only to have them taken again.

When she finished with the wounded, she assembled a good supply of the antiseptic herbs to send along with Joseph. Since she could neither read nor write, she dictated directions for their use. This was all she could do, except to send word Young Will was recovering well.

"I don't know whether to be relieved or angry." Elizabeth confessed to Jael at dinner. They sat together on the terrace outside Elizabeth's room. "He is not among the wounded, though he was injured, or so his letter tells me, but they are proceeding into the Touris to free some slaves from those hateful mines. Oh Jael, what shall I do? How much longer must I bear this?"

Jael plucked a fat grape from its stem and held it between her fingers. "At least you know he is well, my lady and he thinks of you."

"If he thought more of me, perhaps he would return. The men could do very well without him. He's never even seen his son."

"Your husband knows his place." Both Jael and Elizabeth startled to hear Lady Bethalyn's stern reprimand. Neither had heard her enter.

She stepped out onto the terrace, nestling her grandson in her arms. "He will not leave his liege's side."

Her back to her mother, Elizabeth frowned. Jael returned the look with a playful smile. "Do not despair, my lady. They will accomplish this last thing then they will return. You'll see."

Still, Elizabeth sulked. "But that poor little boy goes nameless still. He'll be walking before his father cares enough to return."

This comment brought Lady Bethalyn to her side. She glared at her daughter. "If you continue in this manner, I will be ashamed to call you my daughter. It has ever been our lot to wait upon our husbands, and we do it gracefully, and without complaint. You should not speak thus before your ... subordinates."

Jael saw the flash of fire in Elizabeth's eyes and wondered if she could affect a quick retreat, but it was too late.

"Mother, I would thank you not to interfere in my relationships, either between myself and my husband, or myself and my friends. Lady Jael is my friend. She is not my subordinate. She means a great deal to me, and if I wish to vent my frustrations to her, I know that I may. For I know she can be trusted to say nothing of it. She has proven herself to me. My brother believes her to be of the finest character and recommended her. If you cannot take his word, then take mine."

Shaking with rage, Elizabeth sat back in her chair, her eyes on the setting sun.

Jael watched as Lady Bethalyn progressed from outrage to a degree of calm. At that point, she leveled her regal gaze at Jael. "Jael, please take my grandson back to his cradle for me. He sleeps so peacefully. Then, I ask that you give me a few moments alone with my daughter."

Elizabeth started to object, but Jael held up her hand. "It is all right."

After tucking the child carefully into his cradle, Jael crept quietly from the room, closed the door and made her way to the spiral staircase. She climbed to the roof, seeking solitude.

From this observation point, she watched as the final preparations were made, the ship weighed anchor, and hoisted its sails. She wondered how long it would be until it made its destination. After traveling up the coast it would anchor in Verani Harbour and the supplies would be taken overland to the rendezvous point.

How she wished she could be with that shipment. Far from the tension she felt in the queen's company. She did not despise Lady Bethalyn. On the contrary, she understood her alarm. Jael was well aware of who she was and from whence she had come.

In the Deep

Twill Duggin was a son of Dolor, raised in the shadows of the Touri Mountains on the banks of the river Verani. In all the years of his life, he never remembered a time as idyllic as the dreams that had come to him of late.

In the few hours of slumber allowed the slattel, as the miners were called, dreams were rare. He dreamt of Dolor, lush and green. Crops flourished, cattle grazed, the children grew tall and strong. It was indeed a far-fetched fantasy. More and more he let his mind wander there as he slagged away in the mine.

Most likely, it was starvation setting in. He was slowly dying and it was his mind's way of handling it. He swallowed hard against the pain in his throat and wiped his brow with his forearm. The cracking of a whip nearby quickened his pace and darkened his eyes. He beat at the rock, his strength oozing out with each blow.

He had stopped praying long ago. The words ceased to come. In the deep darkness, his hope had dried up. Next to him a boy of ten summers lay on his stomach and crawled into a narrow passageway, a rope tied to his ankles. When he called out, another man pulled on the ropes and hauled him out. He brought out a pail of rock shards he had chipped out of the interior of the tunnel.

In just this way, the men had dug out hundreds of miles of passageways throughout Touri Deep. If they were lucky, very lucky, they came out with a bit of ore that would yield the gold or silver. If they were very, very lucky, they came out. Sometimes the tunnels collapsed on them. No one bothered to dig them out unless they'd been hitting a rich vein.

Their captors were evil grey men who had sold their souls to the devil. No one knew why they continued in the magistrate's service. They were merciless. What of theirs did the magistrate hold? Did he hold their women and children captive? Twill leaned forward and touched his dry tongue to a tiny rivulet of black water dripping down the cold rock wall. If only it were more. He closed his eyes and pictured the dream again, making it real inside his head.

A loud horn blew somewhere off in the distance. The slattel set down their shovels and picks and hammers. They pulled the boys out of the tunnels and helped them to their feet. Slowly, they made their way to the main corridor of the mine, where a great fire burned and over it, a soup pot bubbled.

Here in the darkness, they would eat. They would lie down and sleep. The lot of them worked eight hours, ate, slept four hours, worked eight hours and slept four hours. They knew not whether it was day or even. They worked thus until they died. Their lifeless bodies were dropped down a bottomless pit into oblivion. Such was life for those taken into servitude by the magistrate. There was no mercy. No one gained freedom. If someone was hurt, they continued to work until they could no longer move. Then they were disposed of in the same way as the dead. By that time they no longer cared.

Twill chewed a bit of meat that had found its way into his soup. It was a good sign, he thought wearily. He would sleep and perhaps he would dream the dream again. He looked forward to it. When he lay down, a boy came, and lay close to him. Twill put his arm over the boy.

"Goodnight, Da," the boy whispered.

"Goodnight son," Twill whispered back. And then they slept.

In the dream, Twill looked and beheld his dear wife looking back. She stood across the vast expanse of green rolling fields. He ran to her then he stopped, because he had forgotten his son. He stood and waited for the boy to catch up. Desperation raced in his chest. He couldn't return to the mother of his child without the child. He looked back and saw the boy's face, bright with wonder and joy. His heart broke and Twill cried.

"Da!" the boy shouted, his hands cupping his lips. "Da! Hurry! Something is happening!" A look of panic came over the young face.

Twill turned to look into the light. The light grew ever brighter and sound filled the dream. Then he awoke and realized the dream was real. His son shook him and cried. "Da! Awake, please! Something is happening!"

Twill sat up, his heart pounding wildly. He blinked his eyes hard. The room was filled with the light of many torches.

"Get up!" A voice cried. "Get up ye men and follow us. Do not speak. Make no more noise."

Slowly, the slattel rose as one and stood blinking and rubbing their eyes. Accustomed to following orders, they moved into their usual single file and stood in place, ready to go back to work.

"Nay, men, turn and follow." Puzzled, the men turned and walked after the dark figures framed in light. Who were these men? Twill scanned his fellows. No one seemed to care, they only followed.

William let his head fall forward. The sight before his eyes sickened him as these once proud men plodded along in blind obedience.

"They are a pitiful lot," Solis whispered to his master.

William grimaced. "Do you wonder at it?"

"Nay, the monster. Pleased he was to sell his silver and gold bought with blood. I fear they'll never make the journey though."

"They'll make the journey right enough. They are strong, else they'd not be living still. Take your time with them. Toldar and I will go ahead and make the way safe."

"Have a care, my lord, they are still about. Probably went for reinforcements."

"Oh aye, of that I am certain." William moved ahead of Solis and spoke quietly to his men along the way. Some held back to help those who didn't have the strength to move more quickly. When William joined Toldar, he found him standing at the mouth of another tunnel.

"There is a noise I cannot fathom, my lord. Listen and see what you think." He motioned to the men to halt.

William stood in silence, listening. His heart nearly stopped. He looked at Toldar. "Get these men out of here as quickly as you can!"

Even as he spoke, the ground began to rumble. William ran ahead urging the men forward. "They've set off an earth-shaker! Carry those who cannot run!" The warriors grabbed boys and men alike, tossing them over their powerful shoulders then running through the tunnels, following Toldar and William as they led the way. They had carefully marked the trail with smudge from the torches and it was a good thing, since they had to make such a hasty retreat.

When the long arm of the tunnel they were following began to lighten, they ran faster. The end was near, but so was the flashing of the earth-shaker. Rocks were coming loose and tumbling down all around them. A large fissure overhead widened with each explosion. As the men began to spill out of the narrow mouth of the mine, they fell down upon the ground with their burdens. Then others took them up and moved farther away from the mouth, knowing that at any moment, it could all break loose.

"Do not stop now," William shouted, waving his arms. "We are not safe here! We must run! We will make for the crown!" The crown was a small oasis in a narrow canyon whose craggy ramparts very much resembled the points of a crown. Here they could rest and regroup, but it was several miles away yet. William felt certain they'd be forced to turn and fight at some point.

When they'd first arrived at the mine, he sought to make peace with the guards, called gallots. Gallots were a mixed lot of rogues. They were eunuchs, encouraged in their anger from childhood, which made them a fierce enemy. They gave not a moment's consideration to his proposal of peace. They did not believe their master was dead. Torin Dugold had convinced them he was like a god and could not die. They would never turn against him, for to do so would bring eternal damnation. They would fight to the death.

After a brief encounter which left several of them dead, William's warriors were able to gain entry. When they located the miners, they infiltrated the few gallots who stood guard and took them out quietly. But even as they strove, they knew some had escaped and run for reinforcements.

They were nearly half way down the sloping slag heap outside the mine entrance when the main blast occurred. They took cover where they could or just fell to the earth covering as well as possible. Rocks spewed heavenward and soon fell earthward again, coming down with great force. A thick, dark cloud ascended, heavy with dust and dirt.

There was a secondary explosion as fumes released from the earth ignited and blew mightily. The men remained in place then slowly rose to take count of any wounded or lost. They found only two. One of their own and one elderly miner who died with a smile upon his face, for he had tasted freedom.

Here Toldar and William meant to take a stand against whatever gallots remained, so they sent Solis and a few others ahead with the miners and the wounded of their own men. "Make for the crown and wait for us there." William spaced his men out so no great number would be found in one place. They took cover, watched and waited.

It was quiet for nearly an hour, but at last it seemed the gallots were giving chase. They came from several directions, looking to surround the small party of men. William kept quiet and made no move until the gallots came near.

"That's it," he whispered. "Come into the circle, boys." As soon as they cleared Toldar's group, that man gave a whoop and set upon the gallots from his side. William's men held their ground as another group took up the other side. A fierce battle ensued, for the gallots were strong and well-trained in battle.

A large gray-skinned gallot took aim at William and bore down on him. William fought with all his might. They were equal in physical strength. As men and gallots began to fall around them, they battled on.

When Toldar's force had beaten down the enemy on his side he ran forward, to join his brother-in-law. He climbed upon a rock behind the big gallot and crashed down upon him just as another blow struck hard against William's sword. For a moment, all three struggled then the big gallot succumbed to a deadly wound from William's sword, driven upward toward the heart. The man's eyes never fluttered, but remained open and staring up at the clear blue sky.

The moon was high in the sky by the time William, Toldar, and their men made it to the crown. They had buried the dead then walked there straight away.

They were greeted by a large welcoming fire and what was left of two roasted hinds. "It seems as though the men of Dolor are celebrating," Toldar told William.

"Can you blame them?" William answered with a smile. "Come, brother. Let me have Lukas check that injury."

Toldar's brow furrowed as he glanced back at William. "How do you always know everything?"

"Because I am in charge, brother—and also very observant—I saw you favoring the arm when you fought that great beast of a gallot. Now sit down and let me call Lukas." After everyone had eaten their fill and most had joined the miners in blissful slumber, William, Solis and Toldar laid plans for the return journey.

"Them Dolor fellas are not able to make the journey just yet, my lord," Solis told William. "I believe they could do with a day or two of rest. The Sabbath approaches, so ye may consider waiting till it passes."

William looked to Toldar. "What think ye?"

Toldar laid his head back against a rock and closed his eyes. A long gash down his arm had been cleaned and bandaged, but the pain of it wearied him. "I think it could not hurt to rest. Most all the men are weary and many are injured."

"Including you, so shall we remain here? It seems as if the hunting is good and there are trout in the stream there."

"A good place to bathe, too. That will be a necessary function as soon as possible. Those miners are pretty rank," said Toldar.

"That they are," Solis agreed with a chuckle. "Covered in years of dirt, so it seems. Do ye know they've not seen the light of the sun in all that time? Who knows how long they've been in captivity. How did they survive?"

William gazed at the star-filled sky. "Men can survive much when they have no choice."

Toldar's only comment was a soft snore. William looked at Solis and smiled. The two nodded at each other then laid down to rest.

"You look a bit dazed, Twill," William said, upon noticing the man had wakened.

"Everything is different, save one." He pointed to his son lying beside him in blissful slumber. Twill laid his hand on the boy's mud-caked hair. "I returned a prayer of thanks to the Father God for sending his emissaries to rescue us. I know God sent ye, for you're such good men, come all the way from the coastal regions, by your speech."

William laid his hand on the man's bony shoulder. "I've no doubt God sent us to you, Twill. He's given us victory at every turn. Now our main concern is to get the lot of you home, where you can begin again."

Twill looked as if he would cry, but William doubted there was enough water in the poor, emaciated man to form a tear.

After feeding the pitiful looking lot, Solis' next move was to order them all into the pool. They would have to scrub the clothes they wore and dry them in the sun, because there were no more to be had. Thus it was, the group sat about the fire all afternoon in their skivvies, covered with borrowed blankets. But they were clean, and well fed. There was not a single complaint among them.

William's men were another story. They were anxious to be away. He kept them busy following orders, hunting and fishing and putting up whatever food was left over.

It did his heart good to watch the young ones move languidly about in the beginning, but as the day proceeded, they began to take up childish ways again. One of the youngest of the warriors spurred them into a game of hide and seek, which kept them occupied for some time.

William sat down with the elder freedmen and explained to them the situation at hand. He did not want them to carry false hopes in their hearts only to be sadly disappointed at the sight of their hometown.

Some of the men grew angry. Others sobbed outright, but this was truly more humane in his mind. They would have the journey home to prepare their hearts and minds and by the time they reached there, they'd be ready to take up their tools and remedy the situation.

William took Toldar and his heartiest warriors and left ahead of the miners, to make certain the way was clear. They didn't want to come under attack from any of the former magistrate's sympathizers. He need not have worried. Along the way, the warriors were cheered by countrymen and stranger alike. The news of the magistrate's demise had quickly spread.

The battalion set up camp on the edge of the Verani, and waited for Solis and the rest of the company. Nearby, their horses grazed, and grew strong for the return journey. William's heart had turned toward home and he did not doubt, his brother-in-law also thought of little else.

That night, William sat upon the bank of the river and listened to its music. He was transported in time to the quiet days he'd spent in Jael's company, alone at Verani Haven. How peaceful and calm she was at all times, even when the enemy was near. She moved with such grace, her movements could almost be called fluid, like the river as it flowed.

A loon called in the semi darkness. Its eerie call struck a chord in his heart. He whispered a prayer on her behalf. He waited for her. He hoped she waited for him.

Family Traits

Elizabeth had managed to calm her mother, though it had taken many words and an honest apology. "Mother you know I am troubled over Toldar's long absence. You don't help by lecturing me. I'm spoiled from years of pampering and used to having my way. I need time to grow up. You must let me do it on my own."

"But you don't always make wise decisions, my love."

"Wise in whose eyes, Mother? They are my decisions to make. This is my home, after all."

"I know that, and I realize I was out of line. I embarrassed you before your friend, but I am not at all convinced she is the best friend for you. Who is this woman? What sort of upbringing has she had? A mother must concern herself with all of these things."

"I know you mean well, but I trust my brother when he says I may have complete confidence in her. And then she has recommended herself in her actions. What would I have done had she not been present during the birth?"

"I give ground to her in that and in her doctoring in general. She has done miracles for your nephew. He sits up now and will no doubt be walking before too many days pass."

"And I have not been to see him, not once. Oh, Mother, my mind is so troubled I can think of no one more than myself."

"There now, you have come upon the answer. You are not getting out of your quarters enough. If you like, call upon your friend to take you out for a walk. Stop and visit Young Will along the way. I will sit with the baby." After a moment's thought, her mother continued. "Are you quite certain you cannot name the infant? I tire of calling him 'the baby.' The poor thing must have a name."

When Abigail came for Jael, she went forthwith and found Elizabeth preparing for an outing. Jael was more than happy to accompany her.

"I hope all is well between you?" Jael asked when the door was closed on Lady Bethalyn's quiet presence.

Elizabeth linked her arm with Jael's. "Yes, I smoothed it over very well. She urged me to call you and go out. That is a good thing, I think."

"Aye, it is. I do not want to be the cause of trouble between you."

"Oh you needn't worry over that. We are often at odds, my mother and I. Come; I wish to visit Young Will. Mother tells me he is improving daily."

"He is indeed. He is quite strong of mind and body."

Elizabeth lifted her chin. "It is a family trait. You see how quickly recovered I am?"

A broad smile on her face, Jael gazed at her friend.

Young Will beamed when Elizabeth entered. "I am only disappointed you did not bring my young cousin with you, Aunt. I would like very much to see him."

"You can come to my quarters at any time. Lady Jael tells me you will be up and about very soon."

Young Will inclined his head toward Jael. "Thanks to her, I shall. I begin to understand why my uncle is so enchanted with her."

Jael sucked in a breath at his words.

Elizabeth's face lit with a pleasant mixture of mischief and humor. "Enchanted, is he? I did hear the patient often falls in love with his nurse." In a lower tone, she spoke to Will alone, "I would not repeat that in the presence of your grandmother."

Will eyed her inquisitively. "Do I detect difficulty?"

"You know her as well as I do."

"Indeed. Don't say she still favors Euthagenia?"

Elizabeth inclined her eyebrows slightly.

"No, Aunt. Has my uncle not convinced her these last several years? He would go to the ends of the earth to avoid that lady."

Elizabeth spoke no more on the subject, but turned instead to the welfare of her husband when Will last saw him. "Everyone suffered some injury in that battle—we fought in such close quarters—but many were negligible. I heard a few more had been transported ahead of the main company."

"I hope it will not be much longer before they are all returned to us. I can hardly bear the expectation."

"Yes well, you did marry a warrior, Aunt. It is the life you, and you alone chose, if I remember correctly."

Elizabeth turned away, adjusted her skirts and strolled to the window. "Yes I know, and now everyone reminds me of it incessantly."

Jael had remained silent throughout their visit. Young Will turned his eyes to her. "I was very sorry to hear of the loss of your young friend, Lady Jael."

Elizabeth turned back to them, eyes widened. "What friend? Dear Jael, why have I heard nothing of this?"

"It was … the day of your son's birth, my lady. I could not trouble you."

Elizabeth crossed to her and took her hand. "I am all astonishment. You could not trouble me? Who was it? Who has died?"

"Oh dear," said Young Will. "Have I misspoken?"

Elizabeth looked to him then back to Jael. "No. I want to know. Dear Jael, I like to think that we are friends. Have you gone through some great sorrow without my help because I was so caught up in my own troubles?"

Jael patted her friend's hand. "You are upsetting yourself, Lady Elizabeth. Please allow me to speak." She then related the events surrounding Ferdinand's death.

"Dear Ferdy. He was such a good young man and he saved your life." Elizabeth looked as if she may cry. Young Will found something of interest outside the window.

Jael continued to speak softly. "He would have been proud to know you thought of him so well, my lady. He died an honorable death, and was buried as befits a warrior. He lies even now in the sepulcher beneath the chapel. But soon afterwards, the ship arrived bearing Young Will and many other wounded. There was little time for mourning, and it was just as well."

"Yes, I suppose it was. But to think of you nearly losing your life, bearing the loss of a friend, and yet saying nothing. I think my mother underestimates your character greatly."

"Please do not seek to elevate me in her sight, my friend. She must come to that on her own, if I am to be comfortable in her presence."

Elizabeth leveled her gaze at Jael. "Then you may never be so, for she is quite stubborn."

Jael turned again to Will. "I believe it is a family trait."

Young Will released a loud guffaw that proved to be quite contagious.

The men sang joyfull as they descended Touri Heights.

"I exalt Thee, O Jehovah,
For Thou hast drawn me up,
and hast not let mine enemies rejoice over me.
Jehovah my God, I have cried to Thee,
And Thou dost heal me.
Jehovah, Thou hast brought up from Sheol my soul,
Thou hast kept me alive,
From going down into the pit.
Sing praise to Jehovah, ye His saints,
And give thanks at the remembrance of His holiness,
His anger for a moment is,
Life is in His good-will,
Weeping remaineth til even,
At morn singing returneth."[viii]

When they'd finished the psalm, Twill added on to it, singing loudly, though a bit off key. "No more will we live in darkness. No more will we wonder whether tis morning or night."

Another man took up the melody with more words of his own. "No more will we drink the blood of the earth, and eat the leavin's of the gallots."

This went on and on in rounds, to the great delight of all the men.

William smiled from his heart to see the joy on their faces. This was his reward. Yes, they had fought a difficult fight, but it was definitely worth the pain to hear the rejoicing of the freedmen. By the time they reached the river camp, they were weary, but light of heart, if you judged by their chatter.

William knew his men were anxious to be away, as was he, but they must wait one more day till the others had rested from their journey. It seemed only fitting that they celebrate. He ordered the men to build a bonfire. They roasted fresh fish and game. Someone took up the lyre and flute and began to play. The men sang and danced far into the night. William had not the heart to stop them, for he understood their jubilance. They were almost home.

He sat alone near the fire's edge, observing the celebration, but his mind was elsewhere. He looked at his hands. He could still see the blood on them, though he'd washed them time and again since the last battle. Tears stung his eyes. Would he never be free of the horror of battle? Was he to be a David, and not a Solomon? He had always secretly desired to be a man of peace. Not that he feared the fighting, just the aftermath. Living with knowledge he'd ended so many lives. He rested his head on his folded arms and fought the threatening darkness.

A small sound brought his head up. Alert. A soft step. Then a young boy crept nearer. William relaxed.

"If you please, sir," the boy whispered. "May I sit wi' ye?"

"Of course," William said, patting the ground beside him. "What is your name?"

"Asa, sir."

By the light of the fire, other boys gathered. William wondered at their expressions.

Near at hand, Toldar spoke. "You are their hero, brother. They'll tell the stories all their lives, of how you rescued them."

William frowned. If they knew the darkness of his soul, they'd run from him. He glanced into the faces, lit by firelight. Saw hope reflected there, expectation lighting their eyes. A little encouragement was all they needed. He opened his arms to them. He regaled them with stories of his travels and was rewarded with laughter that warmed his heart as nothing else. Then he realized what an opportunity this was, to impress upon them the importance of what had just happened to them.

"Hold not bitterness in your hearts against the memory of those who enslaved you. Think only of rebuilding your lives and becoming good, strong men. You will be free to live upon the land again. You will plant crops and harvest wheat then eat of its bounty—not this year—but next. Learn to protect yourselves, train as warriors for your defense and hunters to make up the slack while there are no crops."

"I loves to fish!" one boy called out. The others gave a hearty laugh. William joined in. "Aye, that's a good way to feed your families. The Verani runs full from the heavy rains, and fish are abundant. Catch what you can and smoke it over slow fires that your families will have somewhat to eat this winter. Be good helpers to your parents. Most of all, love the Lord with all your hearts, my sons, for He is the one to whom you can be most grateful for your freedom."

Some of the boys had already fallen asleep. William spoke to a couple of the men nearby. "I think it's time these young ones find their beds."

After they'd gone, Toldar sat beside William. "You will make good little followers of them all."

"I desire to help them upon their journey, my friend. Their lives have been nothing short of a slow death until now. They will run free like young colts for a time and they must learn to live again."

"The same could be said for the men. Some of them are like empty shells. They do not even speak."

When morning came, the men seemed pensive. Their steps were slow and heavy. Did they dread the sight of their homeland? As they drew near, a cry went up, for the women had caught sight of their approach. They came running, looking about blindly for their husbands, fathers, brothers, and sons. Some did not at first recognize one another, but to the last, they found someone to welcome them.

Many came home to find great loss, and some of the women found no husband, no son returned to them, but they welcomed those who did arrive. The sight squeezed William's heart until he had to look away.

As soon as the villagers had gone their way into their dwellings, William ordered his men to mount up. They turned toward home. "Into the wind, my brothers," he said, as he urged Lodan into a gallop.

𝕵ael stood in Elizabeth's quarters, holding a fussy baby. Elizabeth was concerned. Jael weighed him in her arms. "He is a good weight. He seems healthy besides. There is no fever." She offered Elizabeth a playful smile. "I believe he may be spoilt."

"Spoilt. No. How so? I have not spoilt him," Elizabeth said. "But he is so beautiful and I do love to hold him."

"And that is enough to spoil a child," Lady Bethalyn said.

Jael hid her surprise by lowering her face to the baby's, making him smile. Was the queen actually agreeing with her?

Lady Bethalyn continued her speech. "You do hold him more than most mothers, but I would rather it be so, I suppose, than the other way around."

Elizabeth released a soft sigh. "It is just that ... I miss his father so. He is to me the next best thing. He is warm, and he looks at me with eyes full of love."

Jael giggled. "Ah, so now the truth is told." She looked down at the child. "Your mother needs your attention, little one, though she uses the excuse that you need her." The child smiled and stretched and yawned. "I do believe he has a dimple, there in his right cheek."

"I have seen that," Elizabeth said. "Just like his father."

At that moment, the door swung open and there stood the man himself. "What is just like his father?" In the next moment, his wife was in his arms, crying and covering him with kisses.

Lady Bethalyn stood so suddenly, she dropped her needlework. Her lady-in-waiting stooped to pick it up and set it on a table. Lady Bethalyn seemed unaware of anything but the spectacle before her. "There, there, what a show. Leave the man a bit of decorum, will you, daughter? At least let him see his newborn son."

Jael's heart leapt within her at the sight of their happiness together. As Toldar cleared the door and went to greet his mother-in-law, the door filled again with another, just as strong and tall. He said not a word, but stood looking back at her. Surprise flashed in his eyes.

Jael's gaze flitted to Lady Bethalyn's. When she saw him, and discerned where his gaze rested, she moved with swiftness, blocking Jael's view of the door. "Bring the child to his father, Jael. Do not make him wait another moment."

Jael stepped lightly to Lord Toldar who immediately received the child and stood gazing down at the boy.

Lady Bethalyn turned to the doorway and exclaimed, "Good heavens, dear William, you have come at last."

Jael watched as the queen pretended she'd not just belittled Jael and managed to shut her out of Lord William's sight.

Lady Bethalyn took her son's arm and moved past Jael. "Come in and greet your nephew."

In her confusion, Jael sought only a means of retreat. As soon as Lord William cleared the door and turned away to receive greetings from his mother and sister, Jael fled the room. It was cowardly, but she must have time to recover from so great a shock.

She fled to the spiral stairs on to the roof where she stood for a moment, her back to the wall. In another moment, she collapsed to the floor, her face in her hands. She wept bitter tears and cried out to God. "Oh, dear God, what must I do? I cannot go on in this way. I love him too dearly to be near him. And yet I am not welcome. I am so unworthy."

"How oft have I uttered just such a cry to God?" said a nearby voice, startling Jael so severely, she stopped mid-sob and looked up. Her shoulders still shook and eyes still flowed. She swiped at her eyes to clear them, for in the evening light, she couldn't make out the face of the one who stood above her. He reached down his hand to her and said, "Get up and come near, my dear young woman, and tell me what troubles you so."

His voice was gentle and caring, yet held a familiar timbre. Jael found she needed a friend at this moment. She set her hand in his and he pulled her to her feet. When she stood face to face with him, she knew him. The speaker was none other than King George Horatio du Frain.

"Your Majesty," she whispered, dropped into a curtsey, and bowed her head.

He took a step back as she rose. "You know me? What a good memory you have."

She said nothing because it did not seem good to tell him she had seen him more recently, in a waking dream or a vision, standing upon this very spot.

He set her hand upon his forearm, covered it with his own, and moved toward the railing. "Come see my favorite lookout."

"Your Majesty, I do apologize for intruding upon your privacy."

"Nay, do not apologize. I am a guest in this place and I was not expected. I should apologize to you. I overheard a very private dialogue between yourself and your God. But since I did overhear, you must explain yourself, and tell me what troubles you so."

Warmth flooded Jael's cheeks. To think he had overheard. Oh dear, what she'd said. She cast about for some explanation to throw him off the track, but he would not be treated so lightly.

"Nay, my dear, I know who you are. You are Jael, daughter of Jon Rogan. You are the Lady of the Haven. You are not unworthy of anyone here. How is it that you think so? Who has beset you with such feelings?" He paused to gaze into her eyes. "And who has won your love so well? Would that I was twenty years younger and unattached."

He chuckled softly then continued, "Ah, but such is not the case and besides, I have a wife I would not trade. But then," he paused, as though in thought, "could she be the very one? Ah, I think it is so by the look upon your face. You are too transparent, my dear. If I were to put it all together, I would say that my fair lady thinks you unworthy of her son."

Now Jael could not return his glance. She dared not, for he had just called her too transparent, and every feeling stood exposed in her eyes. She wiped at tears with her fingertips and looked out to sea where another ship sat at anchor. An extremely fine vessel, adorned with the King's own crest.

He squeezed her hand. "Say no more. I know your feelings. But, you may rest at ease. I will say nothing of what I have seen or heard. But promise me this. You will join my family for dinner this evening."

Jael looked up at him, ready to object, knowing her presence would be a most unwelcome one for Her Highness.

He raised his chin to look down his nose at her. "Do not make me order you to come, my lady, but stand assured, I will do so if necessary." After a moment, he asked, "I will expect to see you, then?"

She nodded slowly and he left her. She stood for some time afterward, still feeling the warmth of his touch, the brilliance of his smile. Like a father, he had reined her in, accepted and encouraged her. She turned her gaze to the sea and wondered what the evening would tell. The sea was calm at the moment, but there were surely rough waters ahead.

The Royal Family

After that short interview with his sister and mother, William left his sister's room and started down the hall, desperate for another sight of the lady who had filled his thoughts for many weeks. The door to her room stood open and upon closer examination, he found the apartment empty. He stood in the corridor for a moment then strode to the stairwell. Perhaps this was a good time to make his rounds of the wounded. Who knows but he may find her there, working among her patients.

As their leader, he liked to speak with each one, thanking them for their part in the campaign. On his way, he came upon Young Will at the base of the stairs, walking about with the aid of a cane.

Young Will gave him an ear-to-ear grin. "Dear Uncle, I had not heard of your return. How wonderful to see you."

"And you, Will, how is it you are up and about so early? Your wound was gruesome when I last beheld it. I feared you may lose your leg entirely."

"Ah, but you sent me to your miracle worker, and she did a mighty work. Of course she gives all glory to God, but I think she had a bit to do with it. As for the wound, it is still quite gruesome. The scar will be an ugly one, but the leg is still attached."

"You have not lost your sense of humor at least."

"Nay, nor shall I. For it is humor that brought me through the worst. Along with the hope of seeing that dear lady's face every day. She was a wonder, Uncle. I am not surprised you…"

William waved a hand, glancing about. "Enough, Young Will. I will not have you announce such things to all within hearing."

Young Will leaned forward. "Surely you don't mean to keep it a secret now, Uncle?"

William look away. "I am sure I do not know what you are talking about."

Young Will scoffed. "Ah, I see how it is. All right then, I can be patient. Do you go to the Long Room? There are still several wounded in residence, but many have gone home."

"Have they really? I was hoping to see most of the men there."

"Well, you should not have hired a healer, my lord. She did too good a job of it, I suppose. Oh yes, I was not to talk about her anymore. Sorry about that. I will try to remember."

"You needn't be facetious. And I didn't hire her. She's not an employee, neither is she a servant. She's an invited guest. Are you able to come to dinner? My father is here and he was hoping to have all of the family together."

Young Will coughed behind his fist. Eying William circumspectly, he made an answer to his question. "I should be able to come, if Grandmother will allow it. She has been very protective of me, but I have managed to get about when she is occupied with the little one."

"I will look to see you at dinner then." William got as far as the parade ground before he was accosted by his mother's servant, Eloise. "My lord, Her Ladyship wishes to have an audience with you in her quarters before dinner. May I tell her that you will see her?"

William turned his face away for a moment, to hide his chagrin. Then he turned back and smiled pleasantly at Eloise. "You may tell my mother I will come to her room at seven bells. Thank you, Eloise."

Why was she insisting on a private audience with him in her rooms? He massaged his brow with this thumb and forefinger. He hoped it was nothing to do with his cousin. She'd been trying to pair the two of them for several years and the harder she tried, the further he ran. Had she no understanding? He strode quickly to the Long Room and stepped inside the door. Here it was decidedly calmer. Among the men he felt no distress.

𝔚hen Jael left the roof to go to her room, she found Hazel rushing about. "Oh my lady, I was given orders to help ye prepare for the dinner tonight. Abigail has sent up a very prettyish dress and she wishes ye to try it on for size. Will ye bathe now?"

"That's such a lot of work for you, Hazel. I can just…"

"Oh no, milady. Ye mustn't think of it that way. I will start at once.

There will be plenty of time."

Jael put the dress on and found that it fit almost perfectly. There was a little extra room in the waist. She turned to look at it just as Abigail entered. "Oh it needs a tuck there. Here, let me pin it. I'll set the girl to work on it at once. It is most exciting to have His Majesty with us again. I ha' been wonderin' when he'd make the trip. It's wonderful he wants to include ye, but not too surprisin' since ye've done so much good here."

Jael had never expected such praise from Abigail. She opened her mouth to answer, but closed it again as Hazel and two other young women came through, carrying steaming buckets of water.

Her bath done, Hazel spent more time than usual on Jael's hair, jabbering away constantly about "her Roy." When she had finished, the dress was ready.

Fully dressed, Jael stood before the looking glass and gazed at her reflection. She had never been vain, but she could not help but admire what she saw this night. Her cheeks were flushed, her eyes bright. Hazel had threaded primroses in her braided hair. The soft rose color of the garment complemented them perfectly. Abigail brought a pair of soft slippers and put them on her feet. The outfit was complete. However, there was still nearly an hour to go before dinner, so she sat down in the big chair and waited.

She was still sitting there when seven bells began to sound. Half an hour yet. Perhaps she should take a walk. That would help calm her frayed nerves.

When she opened the door, her breath caught in her throat, for Lord William stood there, his eyes reflecting the bright candlelight directly behind her. She caught a whiff of soap and leather and a less defined odor of a spicy nature.

"My Lady," he said, bowing his head before he moved away.

Her hand at her throat, she stepped back inside her room to catch her breath and wait for the shock of seeing him to subside. She chided herself for her weakness. Of course, there would be many times when they might meet in this way.

She had no idea what he wore. Funny, her eyes had been so drawn to his, she'd noticed nothing else. She couldn't help the memory of his look. Was that a flash of admiration she'd seen in his eyes? After a moment, she stepped back out into the corridor, looked this way and that. Satisfied, she set out for a walk.

William paced back and forth in his mother's room, waiting. After several very long minutes, the door to the dressing room opened and she made a regal entry. He had to smile. It was ever so. She was very dramatic. He bowed and kissed her hand.

"William, it is so wonderful to have you here with us. Do sit down."

He would not sit. "There is not much time, Mother."

"There is plenty of time. If we are late, then we are late. They will wait for us."

To his relief, she did not sit. They would stand, apparently. He gestured toward the door. "Can we not talk on the way?"

She leveled a gaze at him. "No, we cannot. What I have to say is of a most ... delicate nature."

Fie. She means to impress Euthagenia on me again. "Then perhaps I should rather speak with Father?"

Lady Bethalyn laughed. "Oh no, my son, not that delicate. No, I wanted to ask you something my dear, to clear up a matter that has me most puzzled."

"I am glad to oblige, Mother."

"I was certain you would be. You are looking very well, by the way. You were not injured this time out, I hope?"

He took a step toward the door. "Mother, do not dilly-dally. I am anxious to be away."

"Yes, I can see that." She sighed softly, and turned her face away. "I was wondering whether ... well, you see ... I observed that Jael woman wearing your ring." She turned again to face her son, watching his countenance. "I was curious about it, my dear. Do you think it wise?"

"Wise?"

"Yes, do you not think it would give her—and everyone else—the wrong idea?"

William arched one brow, but held his tongue.

She smoothed her dress then straightened her sleeve. "Well, you know how people are. They will assume you meant to favor her."

He watched the exaggerated movement of her lips as she pronounced that last part. "She saved my life. I gave her the ring as a gift, and because her life was then in danger. I told her to use it if she had need. To bring me to her. I would have gone to rescue her."

"I see, and when she came to you here, was that not very presumptive of her?"

William released an impatient breath. "No, not at all presumptive, when I had invited her and promised to give her aid. She had no other place to go. I owe her my life, Mother. I should think that instead of treating her so rudely, you would rather be grateful to her for that at least."

"Rudely, I do not treat her rudely."

"Perhaps rude is a bit strong. But what is the real issue, here? Why not treat her rather with kindness for the good she has done, and for that matter, the good her family has done."

She swung away from him. "Do not throw that at me. I have had enough of it, these many years. All I wanted was to caution you, my son. You must not form a foolish attachment. You will be king one day, after all."

She had finally hit the crux of the matter. William drew a deep breath and released it. He must be calm. A soft answer turns away wrath. But he could not let anyone speak ill of Jael, not even in private. "I am well aware of what my future holds. But I would not consider an alliance with the Lady of the Haven to be foolish."

His mother pivoted slowly, her eyes widened. "Of course it is. Who is she? Who was her family? Are they of royal blood?"

William had done with this line of conversation. He felt the need to be on his way. "Royal blood is in short supply these days, Mother. Inbreeding is not the answer. As for the lady's family, in my opinion, they are among the highest and wisest to have lived upon this earth. She has made a name for herself everywhere she has gone. Everyone she has touched speaks her name with reverence. I have seen it in my travels, and I have seen it here."

Her face a stony mask, she spoke, "Do not make me order you, William."

"Do not make me say something we will both regret." He turned to go, but she called him back. "William. Just promise me you will go slowly and think about what you do. Take counsel from your father. I know he will direct you wisely."

William bowed low. "I know the truth of that, and you may rest assured, I will follow his advice."

𝔍𝔞𝔢𝔩 passed by the door of the dining hall, on the way to the receiving room. The table was elegantly set, with gleaming candlesticks and polished silver, pretty porcelain dinnerware and lovely floral arrangements. Elizabeth had gone all out.

Even more intrigued by the many odors emanating from the area of the kitchen, she could hardly wait to see what delicacies came from there this evening.

The room was full when she entered at half past seven, but most of the royal family had still to arrive. Young Will sat in the corner with his leg elevated on a footstool. Jael went directly to him.

He smiled up at her. "I hope you will not be offended if I remain seated, my lady. I have overdone a bit today and my leg is making me pay."

Jael gave him a stern look. "Did I not tell you this would happen?"

"You did indeed. But as a man, I must prove it, as most young men do. Ah, here is my uncle. Is he not a grand sight?"

Jael turned to look. Lord William was indeed splendid in a tunic of royal purple with gold trim. She'd never seen him dressed so well. He was immediately followed by Lady Elizabeth and Lord Toldar.

Lady Elizabeth rushed to her side at once. "It is wonderful, is it not? I am so happy you will be here to see it all."

Jael was not certain what the lady referred to, but she made no reply. A moment later, they were joined by the men and Pastor Stephen, who bent near her to whisper, "I was just going to tell Lord William and Lord Toldar about that vision when it occurred to me, I may be breaking a confidence. Shall I not tell them? I was hoping I may, for it would encourage them to know God so cares for them."

Lord William leaned forward to add, "He has already begun the story and I begged him to finish it."

Once again a prisoner of his gaze, Jael had no choice but to agree.

Pastor Stephen related the vision. As he told the part about the eagle's wing, Lord Toldar and Lord William exchanged amused glances.

Jael noticed the exchange. She made a mental note to ask about it. As soon as the pastor finished, she addressed the two young lords. "What meaning does the eagle hold?"

Lord William answered. "I have had a nickname for my brother-in-law since we were at studies together, as children. His nature is that of a protector, dear lady, especially vigilant. Therefore, I called him the eagle."

Lord Toldar took up the story from there. "He'll not tell you the rest. Lord William was pressed hard in battle, Lady Jael. He was near to being overcome by a man of twice his weight and nearly half again his stature. He fought valiantly, but needed a little extra help. As soon as I was free, I jumped down upon the big man and upset him just enough to receive a deadly blow from my brother."

"As for the Touris falling upon us," Lord William finished, "they very nearly did, for the gallots blew the top off the deep."

"And the thin, emaciated men running before you, did they exist as well?" Pastor Stephen inquired.

Lord William nodded. "The miners—men of Dolor who had not seen the light for many months—perhaps even years, and they were half-starved, mere skeletons."

"They did look a bit peak-ed," Toldar added.

"Your Majesties, Ladies, Lords, and Masters, dinner is served," said the royal butler, with a sweeping bow. They moved to the dining hall, where all of the guests took their places at the table. Seating had been prearranged, and Jael found herself between Elenor, and a man she'd never met. She looked across the table at Elizabeth and Lord Toldar. Young Will sat on the other side of Elizabeth and Lord William was seated on the end. King George sat at the head of the long table, with Lady Bethalyn on one side and Pastor Stephen on the other.

Within the first few moments of the meal, directly after Pastor Stephen had blessed the food, Elizabeth introduced Jael to the stranger on her left. "Master Abraham Worther of Coldthwaite has come down with my father on a mission of some importance. He won't say what it is," she finished with a smile.

Jael returned her smile. Abraham Worther was a smallish man of medium build with thin white hair and a broad face. He had round, dark brown eyes full of merriment, shaded by wispy white brows. His full lips were overshadowed by a nose that held its place solidly in the middle of his face.

"Are you familiar with the name Worther?" he asked Jael after the introduction.

Jael nodded. "I know its origins, sir. You come from a family of weavers?"

Abraham smiled. "Aye, lady you are quite right and not only that, but my interests run much farther."

King George, who was listening to their conversation, insisted upon interrupting at this point. "Abraham is an historian, dear lady."

Jael nodded and smiled at the king. He sent her a kindly wink. Thankfully, Lady Bethalyn's attention was taken by Lord Toldar, who was explaining the root meaning of the name 'Dartok.'

After exchanging an amused glance with Elizabeth, Jael turned back to Abraham. "What is your area of expertise, sir?"

"Families—Lady Jael—families. It is a most interesting occupation." At this point, they were again interrupted by the passage of several main dishes. Jael began to feel very uneasy, dared a glance in Lord William's direction and found him watching her. This was followed closely by a quick glance at Lady Bethalyn who was definitely watching her. Jael turned her concentration to the task at hand then to Elenor, who was quite taken up in tasting the food.

Then she found, that if she listened intently, there was much to glean regarding the royal family. To be sure, they had their share of quirkiness, but it was mostly pleasant. Jael wondered how many among their number had to strain to keep it that way.

Pastor Stephen and Elenor were oblivious, but the newcomer was obviously quite preoccupied. He watched Jael as a fox watches its prey, while pretending not to be watching at all. This was not lost on Jael, making it hard for her to enjoy the meal. Hard, but not impossible. The food really was quite delicious.

An Ancient Tale Told Well

When the main part of the meal had ended and drinks came around, His Majesty stood and held his cup aloft. "I thank you all for joining us tonight in a quiet celebration of our family. I am very thankful to have my sons and my grandson safely home again. The victory they have won has not yet been fully realized." When everyone had taken a drink, he continued. "Now to the entertainment for this evening, I have received permission from my daughter to adjourn to the formal parlor."

They moved to the parlor where they spread out in the chairs farthest from the fire, since it was a warm evening. A footman threw open the main doors, which provided some relief in the form of an ocean breeze.

King George conferred quietly with his son and afterwards called Abraham to come. Then he took his place at the head of the room. "I have something I want all of you to see."

Abraham brought a large rolled tapestry and stood with it near the center of the room. Two pages waiting nearby moved to either side and assisted him as he carefully and lovingly unrolled the thing. As the full picture was revealed, Jael's eyes widened. She covered her mouth with her hand.

King George set his hands on his knees and leaned forward, to better observe the work. "What have you discerned, Abraham?"

Abraham gave a nod. "It is quite authentic, Your Majesty."

"So it is the original?"

"Without doubt, the original," Abraham agreed.

Jael could not keep her seat. Hardly knowing what she did, she rose and moved slowly forward, her eyes never leaving the tapestry.

"It is beautiful," Elizabeth whispered.

As Jael drew near, she felt, rather than saw King George smiling down at her. She reached out her hand and gingerly touched the spot where a nail had torn the wall-hanging years before. Her grandmother had carefully stitched it back in place. It was the very one that had hung on the wall in her home all of her life. She looked up at the king. "Where did you find it?"

He smiled and gestured toward Lord William. "I believe you must ask my son."

Jael nearly turned her head, but found she could not. Tears burned her eyes and more than anything, she wanted to flee the room.

A moment later, Elizabeth stood beside her, an arm about her waist. "It is the story of Ruth, is it not?"

Jael turned to her friend, grateful for her assistance. "Yes, Ruth—when Boaz first sighted her, gleaning in his field."

"Tis marvelous. Tis one of my favorite biblical stories."

Jael nodded. "Mine, also."

"But I would think your favorite would come from the Book of the Judges, My Lady," Abraham suggested with a smile.

Jael's eyes darted to his. "I beg your pardon, sir?"

"I speak of the story of Deborah and Barak, My Lady, in the Book of the Judges." His gaze held hers for a long moment.

Jael's breath caught in her throat.

Elizabeth took her hands. "Come and sit down, Lady Jael. I believe Master Worther has a story to tell."

Jael followed her friend, her confusion increasing.

Lady Bethalyn looked uncomfortable also. "What is going on?"

King George signaled to Abraham, who handed over the tapestry to the pages. They carefully rolled it and withdrew. Then Abraham began to speak and by the look on several faces, Jael knew they had enjoyed his stories before.

A spirit of calm descended over the room. She gave herself up to the pleasure of hearing a master storyteller at work.

"It began centuries ago in a place called Bethsaida in the Holy Land. It is not clear whether it was before or after the birth of Our Savior. 'Twas a time of great famine in the land and so cruel, the children were starving. Many left their homes and went seeking green pastures. One of these was a man named Jebuel. He took his family and set out for the north, where he had heard he could find water and a means to make a living.

The famine had spread farther than he expected, so they made their way to the coast and followed it north for many weeks. There they joined a merchant train and traveled clear around the Mediterranean Basin. After months of seeking a dwelling place, they came upon a river emptying into the sea and followed it for several more days. This great river was full of fat trout and Jebuel was able to feed his growing family well. They came to a small fishing village where he learned a trade and taught it to his sons.

When barbarians attacked the village, he escaped with his family, farther into the wilderness. Here they found a tranquil haven pressed up against a great rock wall, called Dolor where they could dwell in safety. Because of brutal winter weather, he was forced to dig deep near the base of the great cliff and as time went on, he strove among the rocks and built a sturdy foundation. Slowly a small cottage grew seemingly out of the rock itself. No one thereabouts had ever seen such a dwelling. It was built high to withstand floods and deep to withstand snow and ice. It was like a tiny fortress.

He did not realize it at the time, but he had come upon a place of enchantment. No locals lived there, because they feared it. And they left him quite alone. He raised his sons to be strong and mighty. Their hearts stayed true to their God, who had forbidden them to take wives of any but their own race. In time all returned to the Holy Land, save one. That was the youngest son of Jebuel, who stayed to keep his elderly parents well. God saw his true heart and sent a man of like faith to them, having heard their story told among the inhabitants of Dolor Heights. This man had a young daughter, Risha, whom he willingly left in Jebuel's care, to grow into a woman and become a wife to Jebuel's son, Ithiel. Ithiel and Risha continued happily for many years, raising a family of their own.

I will skip now, several generations, for the sake of time. The family prospered in that place, but the time came when they could no longer remain as faithful to the earlier promises unless they, like the early brothers, returned to the Holy Land. They continued to practice the faith and to tell the stories of old, and took great care indeed to bring only those who promised to follow that faith into their household."

Jael could not take her eyes from Abraham's face. She had never heard such a talented storyteller. He spoke as if he loved it, told it faithfully and well. She had no doubt, from the very beginning, he spoke of Verani Haven. So enthralled was she that she no longer cared about the queen's icy stares, brought on by her son's inquisitive glances. King George seemed unconcerned, so neither should she be. Abraham met her gaze and spoke as if only to her.

"Though the Haven family was protected from many things, sickness still struck, and bad years came. The family dwindled. Those who remained were strong and loved the Haven more than life. The children grew up learning about the enchanted land they lived in. Like as not, they loved nature, spoke to animals, and common among them all, was a strange tongue known by no other but themselves. Twas an ancient language of the region, learned from early inhabitants, long dead.

In the days of the one kingdom, much evil was allowed to spread. The great King of Coldthwaite Common had too short an arm to keep all under control. Villages were constantly being attacked, their children taken into captivity. So when the twin sons of the great king inherited the kingdom, John settled among the Mortons in the Touris, where he built a great castle in a high valley and called it Cragmorton. Joseph stayed in Coldthwaite. During the beginning of their reign, the lands were safer and more pleasant, but for only a short time, for evil does constantly return.

When John's heir was taken into captivity, he called for help, and the men of the Verani Basin came forward to fight. Their army was powerful, but no match for the barbarous armies that moved in upon them from the east. John's only son seemed lost to them. At this time, there were two sons of Jebuel living in the Haven. The younger was called Justus and the elder was Rogan. The two were gifted beyond any former inhabitant of the Haven. They had learned the secrets of the grove, where laid the disappearing trail.

When they heard of the young heir's plight, Rogan set off on a lone quest to find and rescue him. His tracking skills were unmatched. He soon picked up the trail and followed a merchant train for many days. When he returned, he went by way of the disappearing trail and his track was lost. No man could discover him at all. When the king heard of his son's rescue, he went at once to the Haven and was there reunited with his son. He dubbed the place 'Verani Haven,' blessed the ground and promised never to forget Rogan and his family. From that day henceforth, the family was no more referred to as the sons of Jebuel, but as the Rogans."

The end of the tale was applauded by most of the family, but Jael felt disappointment. There was more, though she knew not what it was. She watched Abraham, wishing for an opportunity to further probe his great knowledge.

"These mighty warriors are weary and must go to their beds," Lady Bethalyn announced. "We have kept them too long, I fear."

"Nay, my lady," her husband replied. "They love Abraham's stories above all things. I have only prepared them for a good night's rest."

"You speak of us as if we were still children," Elizabeth chided them. "We are all grown up now, Mother and can make our own decisions. But I must confess myself to be weary and anxious for a look at my son." She inclined her head and with a goodnight to one and all, departed, followed closely by her husband.

Young Will was the next to go, making his way carefully upon his cane. Lord William accompanied him, to see him safely to his room. Pastor Stephen and Elenor seemed a bit loathe to go, but soon took their leave also.

Lady Bethalyn turned her eyes upon Jael, who still watched Abraham, hoping for more. "You know more of my family, Master Abraham?"

He graced her with a pleasant smile and nodded, but before he could make an answer, the queen interrupted. "Master Abraham, I know you to have made a strenuous journey this day. A servant waits here to show you to your room."

Abraham bowed to the queen and to Jael and left at once. Jael was cruelly disappointed, but she did not forget to show her gratitude to King George. "I am more grateful than you can ever know, Your Majesty," she said, in a quiet voice. He glanced down at her with just a wisp of a smile and the very slightest wink.

Lady Bethalyn was not content to watch her go, but would accompany her to her room. Jael supposed she wanted to be sure she went straight to her quarters and made no detour along the way. Jael was content, however, in knowing her heart. She could forgive her, though she longed for just one moment alone with Lord William, to discern his thoughts about Master Abraham's story.

"I do hope you realize," Lady Bethalyn said, as they climbed the steps to their rooms, "that Master Worther is quite a gifted storyteller. The full truth of his stories often stands in question."

"Thank you, Your Majesty. I will keep that in mind."

Finally at the door to her room, Jael bid the queen goodnight. She stood with her back against the closed door. As Lady Bethalyn's footsteps dwindled, she breathed a sigh of relief. What a trying time of it she'd had this night.

A lamp burned in Jael's room when she entered. Abigail always left it for her. She knew the bed would be turned down and her night things laid out. She was quite weary in body this night, but her mind worked as she digested all she had heard. She turned and sat on the chair to remove her slippers and as she did, noticed a difference in the room. There, on the inside wall, hung the tapestry.

She drew in a breath. She stood, and taking up the lamp went to get a closer look. She smiled and blinked her eyes to dispel the tears. Who had done this? Where had it been found?

Her heart ached with a longing she didn't fully understand. She knew who brought it back. The King had told her she must ask Lord William. Of course, it was he. He would have known the tapestry, for he had commented on it during his stay in Verani Haven.

She fell asleep gazing at it, under the light of a full moon. For the first time since she had come to this place, it seemed like home.

"You forget yourself, lady," King George said to his wife as they prepared for bed. "She is a guest in your daughter's house."

"She is no guest, husband. She is employed here. She is a healer."

She'd spoken the words 'employed' and 'healer' with such disdain, he grew impatient with her. "Nay, my dear, she is the woman who saved your son's life. If not for her ..."

"Oh, do not weary me further with a list of her accomplishments. I have heard too much already."

"I do not understand this jealousy, my love.

She caught her breath and glared at him. "What? Jealousy? I am not jealous."

"Ah, but I believe you are. You had another path in mind for our son and he has chosen his own way. Beyond your feelings that the lady is of a lower *rank* than your son, have you any other objections?"

"I do not see how you cannot object to her. You ... men cannot see beyond a pretty face."

He grinned at her. "Aye, I'll warrant you that. If not for a pretty face, I would not be here, right now, with you."

Lady Bethalyn arched one brow and frowned at him. "You are playing your usual games. But you will not win this time. Now, I am weary, my love. Please let us give this subject a rest. You see I am ready for sleep."

"One more thing I will say upon this subject, then I shall 'give it a rest,' as you say. Trust me, my darling—I know things that you do not—things that will come to light in the very near future."

"Oh fal-de-lal! Now I shall never sleep."

George smiled a wicked smile as he climbed into bed beside his wife.

By the Sea

The sea blew its breath over Jael, caressing and thrilling her. It lifted loose tendrils of her hair and sent them dancing about her face. She closed her eyes and breathed deeply. With eyes still closed, the sound of the water pressed in about Jael, and for a time, she was completely caught up. She could not be seen.

Since that day at the cliff, she had tried it only once. It was utter abandon, sheer ecstasy. She was in the presence of God. He called to her at times and she came here, walking alone upon the beach of an early morning. Overhead, the sea birds called out unheard. Only the sound of the water penetrated her reverie. She lay back upon the cool damp rock and opened her eyes.

Then it was, she saw him, walking along the strand. His shirt hung open, his leggings rolled up, hair pulled back and tied with a leather string. He stopped and stood with his back to her. He watched the sunrise.

She watched it too, as it framed his silhouette. Did he sense her presence? Because he glanced over his shoulder to look straight at her. He seemed taken aback. She giggled to herself. He hadn't seen her there before. He hesitated for a moment, as if indecisive. She felt the same. Should she stay, or should she go?

His mind made up, he turned and walked toward her. She bit her lip at his approach, his face so handsome—his eyes—full of the morning light.

She looked down, saw her bare feet sticking out from under her skirt, and quickly drew them up. Her hair—too late to think of it—she smiled. "Good morning, my lord."

"Good day to you, my lady." He glanced around. "Are you certain it is wise to be here ... all alone ... at so early an hour?"

"But I am not alone, my lord. And the danger is past, is it not?"

He smiled, ever so slightly. "You may not be totally out of danger yet.

We know not what stragglers may be seeking still."

"Stragglers? Yes, I believe I may have seen one, or perhaps just an under dressed prince."

He glanced down at his attire, but made no attempt at a remedy. "I beg pardon, my lady. I did not expect formal company upon the beach ... at so early an hour."

"At so early an hour? How oft you do repeat that phrase. Is it unusual for you? For it is not at all an unusually early hour for me."

He smiled then and cast a look toward the shore. "I would offer to accompany you back to the house, but I fear 'twould be taken in a very bad light, should anyone else be about."

She smiled into his eyes. "I am certain you are right, my lord. I would not have your honor sullied by *my* actions."

He laughed outright. The sound was more beautiful than any song she'd ever heard.

He shifted his stance. "I cannot in good conscience, leave you here. At least go ahead of me that I may guard your way."

She lifted her chin. "How is it that I have existed on my own so long without your aid?"

He sobered, his brow firm. "I do not tease you now, lady. I will not depart until you have gone before me."

Jael looked at him for a moment, decided he was very serious, and began to move carefully toward the edge of the rock. In so doing, she could not hide her shoeless feet.

He laughed at her as he reached to take her hand and help her climb down. "Here is the reason then, for your reticence. Neither you nor I am fully dressed."

Her feet on solid ground, Jael stood looking out to sea for a moment before turning back to him.

He watched her, with a knowing smile. "You are happy here?"

"I love the sea."

"Have you seen it at its worst? Fierce it is, when angry."

She grasped her wayward hair and pulled it forward, to cascade over her shoulder. "More so than the brutal waters of Verani narrows?"

"I cannot say. I have no real memory of that time."

"Pardon my curiosity, my lord, but what was your first memory?" She watched his face as he understood her words.

He spoke, his voice low, "Of an angel ... in the firelight," he lifted one hand to touch her hair, "which danced upon her hair and in her eyes, whose tender voice sang a gladdening song of strength and praise." The space between them narrowed as he spoke, so slowly, she barely noticed.

She blinked and in that moment, he touched her lips with his own then drew back and whispered, "My lady, you had best be away. Wait—" He took hold of her hand and drew it up to look at it. "Where is the ring I gave you?"

Jael stared back at him. He had broken the spell. The world returned to its place and her mind cleared. "The ring? Why, I put it away, my lord. I ... did not wish to offend ... anyone."

"Offend who?" He smiled and shook his head at her. "Ah. I would say rather that you were offended, my lady. I know my mother well, you see. But the time comes when you will have no need to worry over such things. Now go, dear lady. Go, before the day becomes night again."

She ran, her shoeless feet barely touching the ground and he laughed to see her thus. She glanced back at him and lifted her hand in farewell. Then set off again, happier than she'd been in a very long time. Unfettered, her hair flowed freely behind her. She felt as wild and free as a will o' the wisp.

After such a wonderful beginning, Jael felt as though nothing could go wrong. It was a day of bustle and excitement in the compound. The queen planned a victory celebration and everyone was invited. King George made the announcement from the terrace.

Elizabeth, who stood with Jael, told her the king loved celebrations, especially victory celebrations. "More so, of course, when they are his own, but this will do well enough."

Afterwards, Elizabeth was called upon to help her mother with the invitations. Lady Bethalyn had prepared a special guest list, and invitations must go out post haste. Three days only, they would have to prepare for the event.

The servants ran about, doing the queen's bidding, scrubbing and cleaning, and making up extra rooms for overnight guests. Jael feared lest they come and claim her herbal room for some guest, but they left it alone.

Jael returned to her quarters to find Abigail and Hazel, rifling through her things.

"May I be of assistance?" she asked.

Abigail turned to look at her. "Oh, my lady, ye have nothing fitting for the celebration."

Jael frowned. She had three dresses. What were they talking about? "Oh, but I thought to wear the dark blue gown."

Abigail gave a slight gasp. "Oh no, my lady, that one will never do. I must find something better. Ye are too little concerned with these things. Ye must learn to do better."

Jael looked back at Abigail. She had never spoken to her in this way. "Abigail, what is the matter?"

Abigail turned and laid her hand on Jael's arm. "Oh dear lady, I have heard the most wonderful news."

"Noo, Abigail," Hazel interrupted, staring at her with wide eyes, "ye mustn't."

Abigail took a deep breath then slowly released it. She let go Jael's arm and turned back to the shelves, humming a tune in a very strange way. She glanced back at Jael and her face brightened. "Well, 'tis a good thing we have still two days yet to prepare. Pardon me, my lady. I'll just go and … er … see to something."

Jael watched her go then turned to Hazel, her brows raised inquisitively. Hazel swung away and made a great show of straightening the clothing on the shelves.

Without turning back around, she asked, "Be ye needin' anything now, milady? May I do yer hair?"

Jael shook her head in disbelief. "Hazel, what is going on?"

Hazel turned her head to look at Jael. "Ye will know soon enough, and then ye will be glad. But don't go snoopin' around and spoil His Majesty's surprise."

Jael bit down on her lower lip. What surprise? She took a step forward. "Another? I already have one surprise." She waved toward the tapestry.

"Oh, and it is beautiful, milady. What a charmin' gift."

As if she had only this minute noticed it. Jael eyed Hazel and sniffed. "Isn't it though? It hung in my own home all my life—Oh!"

Hazel spun around. "What is it, milady?"

Jael hesitated. She'd spent nearly half an hour talking to Lord William and had completely forgotten to ask about the tapestry. But she couldn't tell Hazel that. What would the woman think of her, knowing she'd been alone on the beach with His Lordship? Of course, she'd spent time alone with him before, but she mustn't speak of that either.

"Oh, I was just wondering where I put my slippers last night. Have you seen them?"

Hazel frowned. "Oh, milady, they've been put away with your other shoes. Ye needn't worry over such things."

More Discoveries

$\mathfrak{Since}$ Elizabeth was busy with Lord Toldar and their son, Jael found herself with time on her hands. She checked on the few patients she had left then watched as the warriors practiced on the parade ground, keeping her eyes open for sight of Lord William, but he was nowhere to be seen. She'd not gone back to the beach since that day, because he'd warned her not to go alone, but she'd wandered about, hoping to run into him elsewhere.

Was he avoiding her? Did he regret the kiss? Was it done in a moment of weakness, and now he was sorry for it?

Her imagination ran this way and that and her heart bounced along behind it, suffering bumps and bruises along the way. How she wished to be done with all this. To know one way or the other, whether he loved her or not. Had she a chance with him? Gracious, how could she even entertain the thought?

She purposely kept away from the main building, because everyone was acting so strangely around her. She could easily have sorted it all out. They none of them knew of her gift of keen hearing. She could simply stand and listen and hear any number of voices, but she didn't feel quite right about it. It was an invasion of privacy and she would not be guilty of it. Not on purpose.

So she strolled about the grounds and as she approached the main gallery on the lower floor of the residence, she heard voices. The doors had been thrown open to the day, so she drew her attention there. She found Young Will and Abraham within. Abraham directed two servants in the hanging of a new tapestry.

Young Will saw her first. "Dear lady, how good of you to come just at this time. Master Abraham and I have been discussing the perfect placement of this tapestry. Come see what he has made for my aunt."

Jael drew near, a polite smile covering her overactive curiosity. She inclined her head to Abraham and Young Will. Then she looked up at the tapestry which was still being held in place by the two servants. It was beautifully done, a perfect replica of the house in which they now stood. The compound was filled with soldiers, completing training exercises, as they often did. "Tis amazing," she murmured. "The men and the horses are so very lifelike, and is that ... Lady Elizabeth upon the porch?"

"Aye, my lady," said Abraham. "And in the compound, you will notice the three young lords."

Young Will beamed proudly as he pointed them out. They sat upon horses at the head of the compound, overseeing the exercises. "By rights you should have Lady Jael standing upon the parapet, for she is often observed there."

Jael sent a glance to Young Will.

He smiled at her. "What think ye, Lady? I believe it should be hung a bit further up and nearer the window." Immediately, the servants made the adjustment.

Jael stepped back in order to see it better. "Yes, that does look better."

"Then I am outvoted," Abraham said with a wave of his hand. "There, it shall stay. Make it so, patient workers. They have stood our back and forth arguments long enough, I think." He turned then and looked at Jael. "Lady Jael, would you consent to join me for tea? I am famished and cannot wait until dinner."

Jael happily accepted. It would afford her an opportunity to pick his brain, and would also use up a bit of this relentlessly long day. "Will you stay too, Young Will?"

"If you don't mind my presence, I will stay gladly. I am not allowed to join the men in their preparations. My uncle wishes me to rest."

Jael wanted to ask him where his uncle was, but resisted the temptation. She moved to the bell pull. "Your uncle is very wise. I am glad of your company. I'll call for the tea."

Young Will made his way to the nearest chair and sat, looking up at the tapestry. "It is a marvelous piece of work, Master Abraham. You have the family talent in spades."

"I thank you, Young Will. I do love the work."

"I cannot fathom how it is done," Jael commented, as she watched the servants make the final adjustments.

"Oh, then you must come and visit when you are in Coldthwaite, my lady. I will show you how it is done."

"I thank you, kind sir, but I do not know if I will ever go to Coldthwaite." She noticed a furtive glance pass between Abraham and

Young Will, but decided not to pursue it at this time. She'd seen many such looks and glances in the past several days.

"You are pleased to have your tapestry returned to you?" Abraham asked her.

She smiled and perched on the edge of a chair opposite Young Will. "I am indeed. I never thought to see it again."

Abraham sat next to Young Will and leaned back in his chair. "It is truly a great prize. There were two, you know."

"Ah yes, the other did hang in the great hall at Cragmorton," Young Will said.

Jael gazed from one man to the other. "Is it like mine?"

Abraham nodded. "Twas a companion piece, commissioned by John, ruler of the northern kingdom, the twin brother of Joseph."

"Ah," Young Will said. "Do I hear a story coming?" He settled back in the chair.

Jael turned to Abraham. "Do tell us."

With a pleased look, Abraham drew a breath and began. "Both tapestries depict scenes from the story of Ruth, which was a favorite of the king's daughters. In the second tapestry, Ruth lay at the feet of Boaz, upon the threshing floor."

Abigail brought the tea, but kept her eyes averted, never looking directly at Jael. This was most curious and so unlike Abigail. When the servant had gone, Jael turned again to Abraham and asked the question, burning in her mind since that first night. "Master Abraham, how came the tapestry to Verani Haven?"

He smiled and sipped his tea slowly. Picking up a small cake and holding it carefully between thumb and forefinger, he bit into it, sighing with pleasure as he chewed. "This is wonderful. I do love cake." Then he turned his attention back to Jael. "That leads us to one of the questions I have for you, dear lady. Have you heard the name of Lura?"

Jael nodded and set her cup on a nearby table. "I have. Lura Abingdon was my great grandmother."

"Aye, my lady—Lura Abingdon—she married the original Rogan, did she not?" Abraham seemed almost to be directing a troupe of musicians as he spoke, his hands were so well involved.

Jael smiled and nestled her own hands in her lap. "Aye, she did—she told me she was his 'thank you.' I never knew quite what that meant."

"So you do remember her?"

Jael entertained the memory of Granny Lura for a moment then lifted a smile to Abraham. "Indeed I do. She died in my fifth summer, or perhaps it was my sixth. She was very dear to me."

Abraham nodded. "She was a lovely woman, they say."

"Aye she was, and so kind. I loved her stories." Jael's mind drifted back again. "She would sit and braid my hair and tell me stories over and over. Then one day after noon meal, she sat down in her favorite chair and went to sleep. She never woke again."

"Ah, tis a good way to go. So peaceful." Abraham took another bite of cake. "Ah, well—you were wondering how the tapestry came to be in Verani Haven—'twas a wedding gift."

"A wedding gift?"

Abraham nodded. "Aye, my lady. The tapestries hung side by side in the great hall at Cragmorton. After Rogan rescued the heir, King John came to Verani Haven. When they returned to Cragmorton, Rogan accompanied them, in order to see them safely home. As you can imagine, there was quite a celebration. The whole family was so impressed with Rogan, but none so much as John's second daughter, Lura Abingdon du Frain."

He spoke the name slowly, pausing to let it sink in.

Jael sucked in a breath that seemed to echo through the quiet hall.

Young Will sat forward, his eyes wide open, watching Jael. "My lady," he managed to say, after moments had passed.

Jael could say nothing, only sit with her mouth agape. She did manage to remedy that by nudging her chin with the back of her hand.

Abraham seemed well pleased with himself. It was just the sort of reaction he dearly loved, from the look of him. He chuckled and his rounded belly shook. He sipped some tea then drew in a breath and continued with his story. "The great celebration ended with a wedding and when the couple returned to Verani Haven, they took the tapestry with them."

Jael sat back in her chair. "But how is it that I have never known this?"

"Few now know, my lady, for it was long ago, and the second daughter of a king is little celebrated. It is often only the sons who are remembered."

She forced herself to snatch a quick breath as she tried to work it all out. "But this means…"

"You and I are cousins," King George announced from the doorway, where he had apparently been standing for several minutes.

Abraham nodded and smiled. "Yes, yes."

Jael had risen when she heard King George's voice.

He motioned for her to be seated. A page rushed to provide another chair, so the king might sit beside Jael.

"As wonderful as that is," he continued, "there is greater honor, dear

Jael, for I have just heard of your great faith. Ere you believed in the Son, you were a steadfast follower of the Father. This, my dear, is a far greater legacy." He sat back and looked from one face to the other, ending with Jael. "So, what do you think of my gift to you?"

She blinked her eyes as a fleeting disappointment touched her soul. "*Your* gift ... do you mean ... the return of the tapestry?"

"Nay, my lady, the opening of the book—the revelation of your heritage—this is my gift. I do believe it will be of importance to you sometime soon." He glanced around again, his eyes merry. "Sometime very soon."

Ah. She settled back again. So it was William who'd brought her cherished wall-hanging. She smiled.

King George continued his speech. "Though, you have not changed. You are no different from the young girl I knew so many years ago, except that your beauty has increased." He leaned forward and smiled into her eyes, but addressed his grandson. "What think ye, Young Will? Is this news not diverting?"

"I am near to speechlessness, Grandfather. I was completely taken in," Young Will said, rubbing his thigh.

King George gave a hearty chuckle. "Now, I would thank you both to keep your new knowledge safely for just a bit." He waved his hand around the room. "Only these several pairs of ears know the truth."

Jael looked from one to the other, wondering what the man had up his sleeve. So this must be the surprise Abigail and Hazel knew of. Evidently, he was saving his discovery for another time. But why? And when did he plan to share it with the others?

Young Will pushed up from his chair. "If I may be excused, Grandfather. My leg is bothering me somewhat."

King George nodded to Young Will. "Aye, go, young one. Rest up for the big event. I must have you in good shape for that."

Jael rose and bid them farewell also, intent on seeing Young Will safely to his quarters. One last glance at the two remaining in the room told her they would enjoy their time alone. In fact, she'd not gone very far before she heard loud laughter from the gallery. She glanced at Young Will, but he was preoccupied with pain. She would make him some tea so he could rest and recover from his outing.

Long after Jael left the room with Young Will, King George was still chuckling. He was quite proud of his accomplishments. Bending forward, he slapped Abraham on the knee. "There, you see? I know how to make a woman happy."

Abraham cackled. "Aye, you do, and we never even told her about King Solomon."

"Och! I forgot all about it. Well, that would have been overdoing it a bit, don't you think?"

"Aye, old friend, I suppose it would. It is enough she's cousin of the great king that sits at Coldthwaite, she don't need to know she's descended from the really greats."

The two erupted into gales of laughter then, quite overcome.

The following day proved another very long day for Jael, but she managed to fill it by harvesting herbs. She found a good rich supply of Lastingweed just within the boundaries of the forest. This was an energizing herb she'd long wished for. Some of the men were slow to recover and could very well use its addition to their diets.

When her basket was full of the fragrant plants, she stood and wiped her brow on the hem of her apron. The heat of summer had fully come and in among the trees, it was very close. She stepped carefully along the narrow path to the edge of the forest. Here, she followed a well worn footpath to the base of the cliff which led down to the sea.

In the shelter of that great rock, she set down her basket and stood looking out at the water. Along the road near the shore, another carriage approached. There had been many this day, guests arriving for the celebration. This one was covered with much dirt, and Jael supposed it had made a long journey.

She turned her eyes to the deepening blue sky then closed them, to better hear her surroundings. The air was filled with voices. Something was building, but she could not place her finger on it, only sensed it in her spirit. Everyone was still being so secretive, though she was certain she already knew what it was.

How long had she stood there? She didn't know, but when she opened her eyes, was surprised to find Lord William standing just below her. He stood at first with his back to her. When he turned, his eyes widened. A strong breeze off the water blew in, lifting his hair, causing it to dance about his shoulders as he approached. A slight furrow creasing his brows, he looked at her. "How do you do that?"

"Do what, my lord?"

His eyes narrowed to slits as he watched her. "The other morn upon the beach, I passed you by, and did not see you, though you were there. Just now, you were not here, and then you were. What magic is this, my lady? Have you found another disappearing trail?"

He jested, she knew. She looked off into the distance for a moment before bringing her gaze back to his.

He'd turned solemn. "Or perhaps the disappearing trail has found you? Does it follow you?"

She found a spot on the ground and stared at it. What answer should she make? In truth, she wanted to be able to tell someone what she had discovered. But what would he think of her? Perhaps it was best to have it out in the open.

"You owe me an answer, lady."

He'd said that before, when he was with her in Verani Haven. The memory stirred her as she continued to gaze at the ground.

He lifted her chin with his fingertips to bring her attention to him.

As Jael plumbed the depths of his deep blue eyes, her will slipped away. She must tell him everything. "I hardly know what has happened, my lord." She told him all, beginning with Shinder's attack.

Perplexed, he reached for her hand and cradled it in his palm. "Shinder stood directly in front of you, yet never saw you?"

How perfectly at home her hand felt in his. She blinked to clear her mind. "He would not have seen me at all, except ... I was distracted." Like now. She swallowed hard. "When I saw Ferdinand running toward him ... I lost my concentration. I ... was no longer hidden."

His eyes flashed with emotion, his voice deepened. "I hate to think of you in such a dangerous situation. Where were your guards?"

"The past is past, Lord William, and dealt with."

He huffed out a breath. As he did, his eyes softened. "You are right. I am off subject. Are you able to control this ... this fading?"

"Yes, well ... sometimes. I do not always plan it. I seem to ... lose myself ..."

That deep line between his brows made another appearance as he concentrated. "Lose yourself? Can you disappear at will?"

"I believe so. It often happens when I ..." she looked away for a moment, ill at ease. "When I worship God. It's almost as if I ... blend into the rock, or whatever happens to be behind me. I can sense so many things ... and yet I do not always hear what is without."

He smiled down at her, thoughtful. "Can you do it now—blend into the rock?" He reached out and touched the dark surface of the cliff behind them.

Jael swallowed hard. Not with his eyes upon her thus, his hand holding hers. A tremor shook her. "Nay, my lord, I think I cannot."

He set his jaw, but this time, not in anger. A smile lit his eyes. "And why is that?"

Jael hesitated. From the look of him, he knew exactly why. "I ... it is difficult to ..." She shifted her weight from one foot to the other. "I must be able to concentrate, my lord."

He took a step nearer, still hiding a smile. "What hinders your concentration?"

She continued to gaze into his eyes. At the very moment she opened her mouth to speak, another voice called out from behind them.

William had neither seen nor heard the servant's approach. He was far too captivated by present company. He turned about quickly, shielding her for the moment, as he answered the servant who stood beyond the shadows.

"I am here. What message have you?"

The servant bowed. "My lord, Her Majesty has sent me for you."

Lord William glanced over his shoulder, but Jael was not there. He grinned and shook his head then moved farther out, nearer the servant. "What troubles the Queen this day?"

"New arrivals, milord—she says as they were wishin' to see you—as soon as may be."

Once more, he glanced over his shoulder, seeing only the rock face of the cliff. His gaze moved to the basket still in its place, so he knew she was there. He turned back to the servant. "Tell her I will come directly."

The servant sprinted away, carrying his very important message to the harried queen. After the man had gone, William turned back to address Jael. "Are you still here, my lady?"

She moved, seemingly out of the rock. He shook his head in disbelief. He had a number of questions, yet unanswered. He smiled into her eyes. "I was the distraction, I presume?"

In answer, Jael lowered her head.

He stepped back within the shadow of the rock, reached out and took her hand. "I regret I must answer my mother's call. I hope to see you at dinner this evening. You will be there?"

"Aye, my lord." She remembered the tapestry. "Wait, pray tell me, sir—was it you returned my tapestry to me?"

"Do you not already know?" He quirked a smile. "Who else would know twas yours?" He wanted very much to kiss her again, but did not dare do so. He knew not who may be watching. Instead, he pressed his lips against her hand and gazed into her lovely eyes.

As he made his way back to the compound, he thought about what she had shown him. What a powerful gift, but oh, how dangerous it would be in the wrong hands.

A Rose by Any Other Name

Lord William entered the house and was immediately directed to the main parlor. Who among his mother's visitors could be so important that she would summon him to come to her? His steps slowed as he entered the room and found not one, but three very unwelcome guests. He'd a good mind to turn on his heel and walk back out again.

He barely hid his anger when his gaze met with Mother's stern expression. In a twinkling, she graced him with a dazzling smile that belied the look in her eyes. "Here is my son. William, look who has come to join us for the celebration of your great victory—our dearest cousins."

Lord and Lady Fulcrom stepped near. Lord Fulcrom bowed, while Lady Fulcrom sank into a deep curtsey. Behind them their daughter curtseyed, her eyes seeking William's. He inclined his head and gave them a proper greeting. "Lord Fulcrom, Lady Fulcrom ... Miss Fulcrom, welcome to Corwinder. I trust you had a safe journey."

"Long and dirty it was," Lord Fulcrom said, and immediately launched into a drawn out narrative of the entire trip.

Lord Fulcrom was a tall man with a large, drooping moustache and dark, beady eyes. His wife was only slightly shorter than he, with dark, graying hair and eyes of a nondescript green color. She was always immaculately dressed and coiffed, but today seemed a bit off.

Lady Bethalyn ordered tea. Her behavior puzzled William. After everyone had been seated, he sat, but not because he wanted to. Euthagenia Fulcrom sat near him, hanging upon his every word. Near the end of his patience, he wished to disappear as Jael did. His gaze flitted to Euthagenia's. Wouldn't that be a handy thing right now?

They had only just received their tea when one of the royal pages entered. "Lord William's presence is required at once."

"What?" Lady Bethalyn set down her cup. "Who desires him?"

The page bowed again. "His Majesty, the King, Your Majesty."

William had already cleared the doorway. He'd no intention of letting her talk anyone out of anything. No doubt his good father had received word of the guests, and knew his son would need rescuing.

Hazel had done her job well, Jael decided as she walked to Elizabeth's door. Elizabeth pulled her into the room to look at her.

"What do you wear? Oh good, the blue. You look wonderful in the blue," said Elizabeth. "Here, let me add something. It needs a final touch." She draped a beautiful jewel about Jael's neck and tied the ribbon for her. Taking a step back, she admired her handiwork. "Yes, that will do very nicely."

Jael looked at her friend. "What is all this fuss, dear friend?"

"Oh, well ... you will see in a few moments. You and I must go in together. My husband will be rather late. He had some last minute things to attend."

Elizabeth threw a shawl about her shoulders and drew her door closed. "My son sleeps at last. Hazel's youngest daughter is a gift. She sits with him for me tonight."

Jael was amused, but curious. Every night, there were more guests added to dinner. Who were the special guests tonight? Why was Elizabeth so concerned about Jael's looks? As they started down the hall, Elizabeth reached for Jael's hand and looked at it. "Where is my brother's ring?"

"I have not worn it for some time, since your mother's reaction."

"Oh, but you must tonight—please, do go back and find it. I will wait for you here."

Now Jael was very curious indeed. She returned to her room, found the ring and placed it on her finger. Once again at Elizabeth's side, she held up her hand for inspection. "Are you happy now, dear Elizabeth?"

Elizabeth took her arm and they continued on their way, with no explanation of her odd behavior. Jael watched her as they descended to the main quarters. This was perplexing indeed. Elizabeth did not utter a word as they walked. Not a single word.

The seventh bell sounded as they entered the main hall, which by now teemed with people.

Jael made a quick scan of the room, missing one person besides Lord Toldar. Lord William was usually late, so she was not troubled by it. A tall young woman Jael had never seen rushed to Elizabeth's side.

"Lady Elizabeth, how I have missed you. It is so forlorn in Coldthwaite without my dear friend."

Elizabeth leveled a cool gaze at the woman. "I am flattered, but surely you don't mean it? What of Nevelyn and Grace? Are they not still in Coldthwaite?"

"Yes, but they are poor company without you. You were always the most congenial and good-humored. But where is that handsome husband of yours? I was certain he would accompany you." At this point, the lady looked at Jael, pausing but a moment. Elizabeth turned and took Jael's hand. "May I introduce you to a very good friend of mine, Miss Euthagenia? This is Lady Jael of Verani Haven."

Euthagenia bowed her head in lieu of a curtsey. "I am ... pleased to make your acquaintance."

Jael doubted that, very much.

When Euthagenia turned back to Elizabeth, her eyebrows arched inquisitively. "Is this not the *healer* of whom Young Will has spoken?"

Jael was more convinced than ever, as the young woman spoke the word *healer* as though it was a curse word. But she managed to keep her smile in place.

Elizabeth maintained her grace as well. "She is indeed. You have also heard my brother speak her praises. She, it was, who pulled him from the river."

Jael wanted to burst out laughing as Euthagenia's eyes raked over her, taking in every possible shortcoming before dismissing her again.

More communication at this point was thwarted by the call to dinner. The seating arrangements had been changed a bit to accommodate the newcomers. Not at all pleased, Elizabeth made her feelings known to Jael as soon as they entered. "Someone other than me has arranged these chairs, Jael. Do not think I did this."

Jael was amused to see Miss Euthagenia seated next to the end chair, which stood empty. This was Lord William's seat. Opposite Miss Euthagenia, Young Will's card was positioned, and next to his, Lady Elizabeth's, Toldar's and Jael's on Toldar's other side. This did seem a bit unusual, to Jael, but she wouldn't have given it a thought except for Elizabeth's objection.

With only a few moments to spare, Elizabeth orchestrated a small change. She moved a couple of cards so that Young Will would sit in Toldar's seat. This left two chairs open on the end.

Jael noticed Lady Bethalyn's sharp eyes taking in the scene. No doubt, she had been the culprit, and had noticed Elizabeth's transfer of cards. Jael prayed she would not make a scene.

Lady Euthagenia was Lady Bethalyn's choice for her son. Jael could see this depicted plainly in her eyes. Jael could do nothing, but sit quietly throughout those first few minutes of the meal, feeling keenly the glances of those near her. For once, she doubted her friend's wisdom in advising her to wear the ring. She wished only to hide it, for its presence upon her finger had brought only curious stares from the Fulcroms and a painful searing one from Lady Bethalyn.

A full quarter of an hour into the meal, Lord William and Lord Toldar entered the room.

"Here are my fine sons," King George pronounced. "How went your errand?"

Lord William and Lord Toldar exchanged glances. Lord William nodded at his father. "Very well, sir."

In response to a discreet nod from his wife, Toldar moved into place at the end of the table before Lord William could take his chair. With only the slightest delay, Lord William sat beside his sister. "You know what ire you bring down upon yourself?" Jael heard him whisper to Elizabeth.

Elizabeth answered with, "It is enough that you sit across from her, all the better to see her."

He kept his head down. "You are wicked," he whispered.

"As well you know, and have always known," she returned.

William smiled as he took up his utensils. "The look in Mother's eye is worth it all."

This was one time, Jael exulted in her gift of hearing. Once the two left off their furtive teasing, Jael turned her attention to Master Abraham, who was telling a most diverting tale.

Throughout the meal, Jael quietly watched her rival. This young woman was nearly a head taller than she, which was not unusual, as most adults were taller than Jael. Euthagenia had dark hair and dull green eyes set a bit too close together to be really beautiful. Her complexion was clear and soft and she had every inclination toward beauty, including a full figure.

Euthagenia watched Lord William, sending silent messages that Jael could read quite plainly. If he detected them, he gave no sign, though Jael could not always see him clearly. As soon as the meal was finished, both Lords Toldar and William stood and excused themselves, claiming to have business to attend.

Lady Bethalyn objected to their departure. "But my dears, you have only just arrived. Surely someone else can attend to this business?"

"Nay mother," Lord William said, "I am sorry, but our presence is required at once amongst the men. I'm afraid you will see very little of us until after tomorrow's celebration."

Lady Bethalyn gave a sigh and looked to her husband, who was no help.

He encouraged the young men to depart. "Go then, and see what wonders you can accomplish in these remaining hours. Astonish us with a wonderful parade. How I do wish I were still riding."

Jael watched their leaving and was not disappointed, for near the end, Lord William's eyes held hers. The look lasted only a moment, but it was enough.

William sat in the planning room, polishing his sword when Solis entered and bowed before him.

"My Lord."

William paused in his work to glance up at the man. "Aye?"

"The men wants to know if they will be riding, as is the custom at Coldthwaite, sir."

William raised his sword up to the light, checked the blade, turning it this way and that. "It is a fine thing, is it not?"

"Aye, my lord … tis a fine thing." Solis shook his head, sucking at his cheek. "What is it, my lord? Ye are growing more and more distracted by the day. I blame this fal-de-ral. It's nothing but play-acting. I miss the road." He kicked at a bench that stood in his way. "What of the horses, my lord?"

William smiled at the captain. Solis always grew agitated in times of peace. The man actually preferred riding into battle. "Ah yes, of course, Solis. We will ride. It makes for such a grand display and Lodan loves the attention." His humor seemed lost on Solis. William pushed away from the bench and sleeved his weapon. "Have you spoken with Young Will? I do not know that he can sit a horse as yet, so we must make some other arrangements for him."

"He and several others my lord, whose injuries will not allow them to sit a horse. Perhaps they would consent to an open wagon."

William frowned. "I doubt it, but we will see. Go at once, and attend to their needs."

William strode to the doorway of the compound and leaned against the wall, his arms crossed over his chest. He watched the men prepare for the celebration. On one side, two young warriors sparred with wooden swords. On the other, Courin led a battalion through their paces.

Above the parade ground, movement caught his eye. He smiled, even as his heart warmed. Lady Jael stood on the parapet, gazing out to sea. A white scarf at her neck danced on the breeze. He longed to be there beside her, longed to claim her as his own.

"My son," The king's voice echoed from the corridor. "I see what you are about. You'd best come away from there."

William turned to face his father, allowing a smile. "You know me well."

His father joined him. "She is a rare beauty."

"I will not disagree on that point. Have you come to oversee the preparations?"

"Aye. Shall we go?"

With one last look of longing at Jael, William set off across the compound.

Jael spent the entire morning checking on her remaining patients. Afterwards, she had lunch with Elizabeth and the child, who was still nameless.

Elizabeth released an impatient sigh. "Toldar insists on naming him Dartok. He will hear of nothing else."

Jael smiled to herself. "It's not so very bad, my lady. And perhaps you can come up with a suitable pet name for him."

Elizabeth's expression softened. "Can you not call me simply, Elizabeth, dear friend? We know one another well enough now, I think."

"It seems so ... disrespectful."

"How so? It is my wish, how can that be disrespectful? Do you fear what others will think?"

After a moment's reflection, Jael answered, "I confess, I do, and I would not have ... others thinking I make myself too familiar among my betters."

Elizabeth glared at her. "Do not say that ever again. Not in my presence, nor anywhere else besides. I am not your better. If anything, you are better than I." When Jael started to object, Elizabeth waved a finger in the air. "Nay, I will not hear it. Say it no more."

Jael laughed aloud at her friend's candid response. Something definitely roiled the air this day.

They stood to their feet a moment later, as the door opened to Toldar. He grabbed Jael's hands and kissed her cheek. She blinked as fire crawled up her neck and into her face. Such a thing had never happened. She drew in a breath, but no words came to mind. She could not even bring her gaze to Toldar's face.

Elizabeth laughed, as did Toldar, so long and so loudly, the baby began to cry.

"See what you have done," Elizabeth said, a broad smile lighting her face.

"Beg pardon, Lady Jael," said Toldar. "I see my over-familiarity has taken you by surprise. You will grow used to my ways in time."

Jael still found speech difficult. She sought the nearest chair and sat.

Still giggling, Elizabeth approached, carrying the child. Toldar met her and pressed a kiss to the baby's forehead. "Perhaps you can intervene on my behalf, Jael. My wife respects your opinion. What think ye of the name Dartok?"

With great difficulty, Jael suppressed a smile, but her eyes most likely gave away her true feelings, for Toldar exhaled loudly. "I cannot win."

Jael held up her hand. "But you must let me give it a moment's consideration, Lord Toldar. You have taken me very much by surprise. I am unsettled."

Toldar gave another chuckle. "Aye, you may have a minute. But consider this, George William Dartok Sauren. Does it not roll well off the tongue?"

Elizabeth, set the child in Jael's lap. "Is it not too much?"

Jael's face contorted in silent laughter. The baby cooed up at her. As she gazed into his sweet face, she was overcome by love for him. "You are so blessed, little one. You will be strong and tall like your father, valiant in battle. A truer friend, will no man know. Roses grow …" She halted her words, wondering why she'd said that last part. She looked to her friends, who were watching her. Disbelief and awe shone in Elizabeth's eyes.

"Roses grow there," Jael repeated. She still wasn't sure why she'd said it.

Toldar dropped to one knee beside her. "Roses grow? Did you see the place?"

Jael looked at the child again, giving a slow nod. "It was lovely, with rock walls … roses grew upon them. Dark, red roses."

Elizabeth sat down beside her and took her hand. She looked from Jael to Toldar. Toldar met her glance and smiled. "Tis Wrenook, my lady—my mother's birthplace—high in the Touris. We will go there to live when my time as a warrior is finished."

Jael felt overcome by sadness. She'd lose her friend when that time came. "In the Touris? So far away?"

Elizabeth smiled at Jael. "Not so very far, my friend, and you will come and visit."

Toldar stood and stepped to the open window. His hands on the sill, he leaned forward, then turned about, facing Elizabeth and Jael. "Nathaniel."

Elizabeth looked at him. A slow smile spread over her face, and sparkled her eyes.

Jael bit her lip to still its trembling at the honor she felt to be here when the child received his name.

Toldar took hold of Elizabeth's hands and pulled her to him. "His name is Nathaniel."

"George Nathaniel Sauren," Elizabeth said.

Toldar smiled into her eyes. "Aye, my love, but we will call him Nathaniel."

Jael smiled down at the child. "Hello, Nathaniel."

Celebration

What was all the secrecy? Jael finally decided it was just another quirk of the du Frain family.

She rushed upstairs and found Hazel in the greatest anxiety. "There ye are, my lady. I have been watchin' and waiting. We must hurry." Her bath was ready, so it was not long before Jael was clean, her hair combed straight down her back, so it would dry quickly.

Hazel helped her into some very nicely made under things that were new to her. Jael fingered the material. "These are very fine. I do not believe I've seen them before."

"Ye have not, my lady. They are a gift from Lady Elizabeth." Without another word, Hazel brought out the dress. It was made of a very soft and shiny fabric, finely woven, of pale pink, the color of a wild rose. Hazel tied a darker pink sash at her waist, the ends of which fell to the floor. When her hair had dried, Hazel insisted she wear it as simply as possible, pulled back and tied with a ribbon that matched the color of the sash. She then wove Sweet Anabel flowers throughout. Their fragrance filled the room.

"Now, go quickly, my lady, they wait for you on the great porch."

Just as she was about to leave her room, Jael remembered the ring. She went to her bedside, retrieved it from the drawer, and slipped it on her finger.

When Jael entered the great porch, Elizabeth came forward and took her hands. "Oh Jael, you are beautiful."

Jael tried, but could not hold back a smile. "As are you, Elizabeth." Elizabeth wore a dress of forest green trimmed in gold, with gold slippers on her feet.

When the queen joined them, she found them standing arm in arm, waiting for the first sight of the warriors. Lady Bethalyn was unusually quiet.

Jael sensed anxiety in her look. Indeed, it had entered the porch with Lady Bethalyn. Jael tried not to think of it.

Soon they were joined by the other invited guests, the Fulcroms among them. Euthagenia wore a dress of dark blue velvet. Her hair was piled high upon her head, threaded with a matching ribbon. She came to stand on the opposite side of Elizabeth. Master Abraham, Pastor Stephen, and Elenor completed the scene.

Below them, on the parade ground's grassy boundary, townsfolk and servants stood shoulder to shoulder, ready to cheer their victorious army. A small band, made up of horns and stringed instruments began to play as soon as they saw the flag bearers ride into view.

Jael held her breath as the first battalion rode through. King George led the grand parade, his son riding beside him. Lord William was resplendent in the dark blue and gold of his royal tunic. They rode to the dais and there the king dismounted and took his seat. As the warriors passed, they raised their swords to him.

Elizabeth whispered a running commentary to Jael. "They raise their swords to signify that their victory belongs to their king. When they are all past, they will turn and bow their heads to him before they ride away."

Between the main force, which was led by Lord Toldar and the home force led by Captain Solis, there was a low cart, draped with a wide, dark ribbon. Upon it was a coffin.

"It is empty—a memorial only—for those who did not return," Elizabeth told Jael.

After the cart, the injured marched on foot. "I do not see Young Will," Jael whispered.

"He will come after," Elizabeth told her. "He is with the second battalion."

As the second tier of warriors rode into view, Jael saw Young Will sitting proudly upon his horse. She knew he did not ride without great pain. When they had all assembled at the other end, facing the King, Lord William rode out ahead and lifted his sword. The men all bowed low upon their horses. The crowd cheered them on with loud huzzahs and the blowing of horns. Then Lord William turned Lodan's head and rode quickly off, followed by the other riders.

The small group on the great porch began their journey down to the ballroom, which had been opened on all sides to allow everyone entry. The crowd parted for them and waited until they had passed. By the time they entered the ballroom, many of the warriors had already arrived. Jael could not keep her eyes from searching the room for Lord William.

He had not yet arrived, so she made her way carefully to Young Will, who sat in a large chair near a window. He smiled and stood carefully, still assisted by the cane. "You needn't get up, Young Will."

"Do not take away my pleasure in greeting you, Lady Jael," he said with a smile, which she returned.

"I could not help but think you must have suffered greatly to ride just now."

"Only you know the truth, for I never let on. It was not so very bad and I knew 'twould be a short ride." Here they were joined by Toldar and Elizabeth. Jael found no opportunity to say more. She smiled at the friendly banter between Lord Toldar and Young Will.

"One would think they were brothers," Elizabeth said. "How they do go on." She raised to her toes and looked about. "Speaking of brothers, where is mine? I have not seen him since we entered. I believe the music will start up soon, and he has not yet asked you to dance."

"Perhaps he does not mean to ask me." She was thinking he may dance first with his mother's choice for him, which was Euthagenia. Elizabeth frowned at Jael. "Do not even say that. Of course he means to ask you."

Having overheard that last, Toldar turned his head quickly. "What are you telling her?"

Elizabeth arched her brows at him. "Just that she may expect to dance with my brother—I hope he will arrive in time."

Jael watched Toldar as the thought crossed her mind that he had suspected Elizabeth of telling her something else. But what? There was no time for further thought however, since the musicians were starting up, and everyone scrambled for partners. When she saw Euthagenia move into place, her heart nearly stopped, until she spied the lady's partner—Courin.

Jael was just looking for a spot to stand out of the way, when she heard Lord William's voice behind her.

"I hope you mean to dance, My Lady."

She turned to look into Lord William's eyes and at once, she answered, "No, My Lord, for I have no partner."

"You do now," he said, offering his arm. She smiled up at him and allowed him to lead her into the set. She had not danced in a very long time, but it came back to her quickly.

The first dance was always very formal, not very intricate. She caught sight of Lady Bethalyn's scowling face once, and knew that the woman was not happy, but for once, she didn't care. She was having too much fun. Afterward, it seemed Lord William wanted to say more to her, but the press of the crowd made speaking impossible. He drew her to a window where they stood for a moment, catching their breath.

"These celebrations are always very popular and well attended," he said.

"Do you not enjoy them, my lord?"

"Mostly. But tonight, my mind is on other things."

She smiled up at him. "On to the next campaign? Have you another victory in the works?"

He grinned back at her. "You tease relentlessly, my lady. My thoughts are much more pleasantly occupied. There are many things in the works. Fortunately, battles are not among them, at least for a time."

She sobered at his look. "Shall we have peace then for a while? You have earned it, I think."

Lord William drew in a breath and eased it out again. "Peace usually exacts a high price, as you know very well."

"Aye, I do know." She noticed Lady Bethalyn bearing down on them. "Your mother comes."

Lord William smiled into her eyes. "Let us see what she has to say."

"My dear," Bethalyn said to her son. "Can you not come forward and speak to your father? He means to make a speech before dinner."

"I had heard of his plans, Mother. He has something of particular importance to say and wishes it said before anyone should leave."

"But do you not think," she grew quite impatient and tugged at his arm. "Oh, William, do come."

William turned back to Jael. "I shall return quickly."

Lady Bethalyn scowled at Jael before turning away.

Jael waited until her patience gave out. As seven bells tolled, she made her way out of doors. She was tired of the crowd already and the heat was most uncomfortable. She sat down upon a stone bench and leaned her head back against the wall. From within, she could hear the music playing and knew there would be dancing, but she had no desire to go back inside. She knew that if Lady Bethalyn had her way, William would be dancing with Miss Euthagenia and she could not witness that.

The music stopped. A single trumpet blasted, the signal that the King had won the right to proceed with his speech. She listened for the sound of his voice. She'd have no trouble hearing him from this place.

"My lady!"

Jael turned to look at Abigail, who stood just outside the door. "What be ye doin' out here? Do ye not know ye are wanted inside?" She beckoned with both hands, most impatiently. "Come at once, my lady."

Jael smiled and shook her head as she rose to follow Abigail. What could they possibly want with her? She heard the king's voice as she entered.

"I have been given the great honor of announcing that a name has been settled upon for the child born on Holy Day!" After an effective pause, he continued. "His name is to be ... George Nathaniel Sauren!"

This announcement was greeted with much noise and wonder as everyone asked the same question. "Who is Nathaniel?"

As she drew near, Jael saw King George standing on the platform from whence he was speaking. Behind him stood the queen, proud and tall, beside her very handsome son. Behind them, Elizabeth stood with Toldar and Young Will sat nearby, holding his cane. Abigail pulled her to the front and Jael stood, watching as the king looked over the crowd.

"I am very proud of the victories we have won, but as I told you earlier, it is not yet over. There is much to be done in order to assure our continued peace. We must work to instill order and bring prosperity over the kingdom in its entirety. At one time, we were one kingdom with the north. We were undivided and we were strong. But as times changed and the population increased, it became more difficult to enforce law and keep peace.

So the kingdom was divided and given into the rule of the twin kings. Most all of you know this history and how the northern kingdom languished after the death of King John. For many years, its people suffered. Since my rule, I have endeavored to improve their situation, though my efforts were thwarted constantly by first one, then another evil magistrate.

Now the north has fallen once again into our jurisdiction. They are in great need of leadership. We have searched, but have found only one who is left of the northern du Frain family."

This statement brought whispers and a few gasps as his audience wondered who he spoke of.

Jael swallowed hard as she realized what he was about to say. Her eyes moved to Lord William's and found him watching her. Did he now know the truth?

"That one is here among us tonight," King George was saying and at his words, there was more whispering and movement. He waited until they quieted then reached his hand to her and said, "Lady Jael of the House of Rogan, great granddaughter of Lura Abingdon du Frain, would you please step forward?"

Jael froze in place, her legs and feet seemed made of lead. Lord William stepped up and extended his hand. She set her hand in his and stepped up onto the platform, amid tumultuous cheers and shouts. Lord

William smiled down at her as he led her to stand next to his father.

"Dear Lady," the king whispered. "I hope you will indulge me this? I know I am taking a great liberty. All things will be made clear to you in time."

As the crowd calmed down, he began to speak again. "I am working on a solution to these problems, along with my ministers and my son. But stand assured, we will return to the north and there we will leave a contingent. We will build an army and make them strong again. We will help them defend themselves. We will send whatever they need to begin again. They have a great deal to overcome." He turned then to Jael and made a great show of saying, "I make this pledge to you, Lady Jael, as a representative of the Northern Kingdom and I hope you will consent to go as our emissary."

Jael raised her brows inquisitively. Why was he springing this on her now? Did he fear her refusal? Did he think she would feel compelled to agree if all of these people stood near?

"You will not go alone, my lady ..." she heard William whisper behind her. Was that hope she heard in his voice?

She looked at the king then inclined her head. "I am your humble servant, Your Majesty."

The room erupted again into applause. The king stepped back to the front and dismissed everyone to go in to dinner.

Jael stood very still, hardly daring to breathe.

Lord William offered her his arm. "We must go in to dinner, my lady. No one else is allowed to eat until the royal family is served."

The royal family ... he had said it so blithely. She was one of them now. Had his feelings changed toward her? Would he treat her differently now? She could not detect it, but she'd hardly had the time.

"When did you know?" she whispered, her heart fluttering wildly.

"Not an hour prior to this night's celebration my lady, but it made no difference in my thinking."

The Ties That Bind

The dining hall hummed with the voices of happy guests. Jael sat between Elizabeth and Young Will. Lord William was seated at the end again, opposite his father. William told her he'd rather have been seated near her, but he may be content with a view of her. She caught him looking at her often, which unsettled her stomach, somewhat. But not the kind of unsettlement that would benefit from Morningstar blossom tea. No, this was an anxiety not altogether unpleasant.

Euthagenia and her family had been relegated to another table. Jael was pleased to see Courin sat with them.

"Jael," Elizabeth whispered, "you only pick at your food. I'm disappointed, for I know you usually love this fancy stuff." She gripped Jael's hand. "My father has taken you by surprise, I fear. Do not fret. I know you will do wonderfully well, whatever you do. And if you stay in the North, we shall be neighbors."

Jael tried hard to smile at her and share her joy. All she could think about was William. Did he really mean to go with her into the North? Would Lady Bethalyn stand in their way? His mother seemed dead set against any sort of relationship between them.

These questions seemed intent upon keeping away any good feelings she might otherwise have had. She searched her heart for a psalm to sing or a scripture that would bring peace to her soul. She began to speak to herself in the ancient tongue, repeating a psalm she had often heard her grandmother say,

> *Hear, O Jehovah, righteousness, attend my cry, give ear unto my prayer ... I called Thee, for Thou dost answer me, O God, incline Thine ear to me and hear my speech.*"[ix]

William smiled when he noticed Jael's lips moving. She sang to herself. It was just the sort of thing she would do. His heart overflowed with love. He could not say when it had begun, but he believed it was that very first sight of her, ministering to him as he lay wounded. He cared not what anyone else thought. He meant to make her his own before this night was out.

On purpose, he kept his gaze from his mother's face. He had disappointed her. Aye, possibly even broken her heart. She'd seen the look in his eyes as he'd gazed at Jael. Of that, he was more than certain. She'd even tried, one last time, to dissuade him. Tried to convince him that his cousin was far more suited a match for him. She was certain that when he saw the two together—Euthagenia and Jael—he'd see how great were the differences between them. "You must note the superiority of rank and upbringing," she'd told him.

He'd quieted her, once again, though he hated wounding her. "Yes, Mother, I do notice the difference, and I must say, I love the Lady Jael even more for it."

There was one consolation, however. He had a champion in his father, who was very much in favor of an alliance with the House of Rogan.

He pushed at his food, now and again, taking a bite. He answered politely when someone spoke to him, but through most of the meal, William fought distraction.

Young Will broke what had been a long silence, when an especially difficult piece of meat escaped from his knife and flew straight into Jael's lap.

Along with several of his neighbors, William waited for her reaction. Her eyes had opened wide as the morsel flew past her line of vision. She looked up to find Young Will's face contorting in silent laughter.

William hid his own smile behind his fist.

Then Elizabeth began to giggle, which set off Jael's bubbling laughter. Soon the entire table had erupted. Even his mother found it difficult to suppress a smile.

As soon as everyone settled back down, William sent a silent signal to his sister.

Elizabeth leaned close to Jael. "Take a walk with me, Jael."

Jael's head came up, a surprised look on her face. "Are you quite finished eating then?"

With a glance at her brother, Elizabeth nodded. "I have been eating all this time, while you have only been pretending to do so. Come, it is too close in here. I would like a walk."

William watched them go then motioned to a servant and had his cup refilled. He lifted it to his lips and drank. His stomach a mass of twisted nerves, he waited through the last course. At a nod from his father, he rose and excused himself, only to be detained once again, by his mother.

She reached out and took hold of his hand. "Dear, you are with us so little. Do stay a while and talk."

His father placed his hand over hers. "My love, do not delay our son. He has business to attend."

"But dear," she began, only to be interrupted again by her husband, in a quiet, but insistent tone.

"You speak not to a child any longer. He is a man, well able to make his own decisions. You must leave him to it."

William bent near to kiss his mother's cheek and whisper, "I do love you, Mother, and will always appreciate what you've tried to do for me. I ask only that you trust in God. I assure you, 'tis His direction I follow."

She withdrew her hand, lifted her chin, and smiled proudly. She made no audible answer, only nodded her assent.

Jael puzzled over Elizabeth's sudden need to leave the dining hall. There was fully another two courses left of dinner. Curious behavior, indeed.

Outside, Elizabeth began to chatter at such a rate, Jael had difficulty keeping up. They left by way of the main dining room doors, which opened out onto a large terrace. From there, they strolled toward the outer edge, where the terrace joined the formal gardens. Here they were greeted by the heady smell of roses in full bloom.

Jael would have liked to linger there, but Elizabeth seemed intent on some other path. Around the corner of the building they passed into the light of many torches, spilling out of the great ballroom. From within, came the sounds of revelry as the men continued to celebrate their victory.

"The warriors are frolicking," Elizabeth told Jael. "By the sound, I would say they're doing the sword dance. Have you ever seen it?"

"No, I think not."

"Then you must come inside. The sword dance is a sight to behold, and it's long since I've seen it—do come." Jael tried to turn away, tried to make some excuse, but Elizabeth caught hold of her arm. "You need to have some fun, Jael. You're far too serious this evening."

Jael could not explain her feelings. She'd been excited enough as the evening began. In fact, she was happy until William had been called away. Then there was the speech and her night had not gone well since. Perhaps she just needed more time to process all the information she'd received in the past few days. It was all very exhausting, but she couldn't expect Elizabeth to understand.

The warriors did seem very happy, and their dance really was exciting. No doubt the ale flowed freely here. She and Elizabeth joined the other women who shouted and clapped, urging the men to continue.

They were not there long before Elizabeth leaned close. "I must speak to my husband's cousin just over there. I'll be right back."

Left on her own, Jael considered a quick retreat. She could go back to the rose garden and enjoy the quiet. When she went to turn away however, she saw Lord William entering the room, so stayed where she was, for he had sighted her.

At his approach, she smiled, but saw no answering smile on his face. Instead, his eyes held a look she could not discern, though his gaze fully captured hers. She hardly knew what to think. Had she in some way offended him?

The music and revelry faded into the distance as she centered her attention on him.

He stood before her, looking down at her with that unnerving expression in his eyes. Slowly, as if in a dream, he moved. With his right hand, he removed his sword from its scabbard. Balancing it carefully with the palm of his left hand, he knelt upon one knee before her and laid it on the floor at her feet.

Jael drew in a quick breath. This was a custom she had only heard tell of in stories. She'd never seen it and could hardly believe it was happening now to her. The noise in the room came to a complete halt as all eyes turned to look.

When he had lain his sword down, Lord William stood and gazed into her eyes as he offered her his hand. According to custom, no word was spoken. She prayed silently, for her heart beat so strong within her breast, she found breathing difficult. The very air seemed filled with a strange kind of energy that flashed and popped. It had only been moments, but to Jael, much more time had passed. Her decision was an easy one. She laid her hand in his. He closed his fingers around them. With her other hand, she grasped her skirt, lifted it slightly, and stepped over the sword to join him on the other side.

He brought her close to his side, never taking his eyes from hers. There had been only silence in the great ballroom. Then a murmur went forth. "Who will stand with them?" It was repeated over and over as the crowd watched in great expectation.

After several long moments passed, Young Will stepped forward. Supported by his cane, he lowered himself with care on his good knee, to the floor. He laid his cane to the side and retrieved his uncle's sword, balanced it carefully upon open palms, and offered it to William. William smiled, took up the sword, placed it in the scabbard at his side then turned back to Jael.

The love in his eyes pierced her heart as sure as any arrow.

Young Will pushed himself into a standing position then bowed low before the couple. When he stood again, he leaned forward to kiss Jael's cheek. The crowd erupted into cheers and loud huzzahs.

William bowed to his men, never letting go of Jael's hand.

She stood in utter amazement, still unable to believe what had just occurred. For in the space of only a few moments, she had gone from great sadness to great joy. While William smiled and accepted congratulations from his fellow warriors, Jael replayed the scene in her mind, savoring every moment. In the way of the warrior, she was now a married woman. By laying down his sword before her, William had offered her his protection. By taking his hand and stepping over that sword, she had accepted him. It was simple, but straightforward and quite binding.

A broad smile on his face, Toldar strode forward with Elizabeth. Her face reflected joy as she kissed Jael. "I have so wanted to call you my sister." Then she moved to her brother and embraced him.

Once again, the room grew silent, for the king and queen stood at the door. They were followed closely by the invited guests.

William leaned down to whisper in Jael's ear, "I asked my father to keep the other guests in his custody until he heard the loud cheering and knew the deed was done."

Still trembling, Jael covered a smile behind her hand. She was reminded of a peacock as King George strode in.

He took Jael into a firm embrace. "I meant to bring the two kingdoms back together again and so I have done it."

"Once again, my father claims my victory," William said. Those standing close enough to hear chuckled at his levity.

"You are my progeny. Of course, the victory is mine," the king said. He waved his hands in the air, inviting more congratulatory shouts.

Lady Bethalyn stood before her son and her new daughter-in-law for a moment, holding tightly to William's hand. Jael could see she sought to draw strength from deep within. "God be with you," she said.

"Thank you, Your Majesty," Jael answered, for she knew the queen's heart.

The music started up again, in a traditional wedding song. William bowed before her then led her out to join with all of the other married couples upon the dance floor. Once, Jael's eyes were drawn to Euthagenia. The lady's pain was evident, but Jael knew she would recover. There would be other suitors. None so praiseworthy as the son of a king, perhaps.

There were many more well wishes to receive and they began at once when the wedding dance ended. At one point, William bent near to whisper, "Can you disappear now, my love?"

"I could perhaps, but where would that leave you?"

He feigned a frown. "What? You could not take me with you?"

There was not time for an answer since the men were intent upon exercising one more rite. They stood at attention with their swords uplifted, forming an arch. Through this narrow passage, William led Jael. From here, they left the room, amid showers of blossoms thrown by the ladies.

As the evening drew to a close, Toldar approached William. "All is ready, brother. Pastor Stephen awaits you."

At once, the family departed and together made their way across the compound and up the steps to the main house. Here they were met on the great porch by Pastor Stephen and Elenor. Pastor Stephen held a candle aloft and led the way down the long hall to the door of a room on the opposite end of the house. Here he stopped, and by the light of many candles, held aloft by their closest family members, pronounced a traditional marriage blessing. *"...therefore doth a man leave his father and mother, and hath cleaved unto his wife, and they have become one flesh."*[X]

"Insomuch as these two have performed the traditional Warrior banns, and as their spiritual pastor and guide, I do concur and pronounce that they are now and forevermore, man and wife. Let everyone here give witness..."

Everyone present, save Lady Jael and Lord William, answered with a loud "Aye!"

Pastor Stephen lifted his hand and said, "Then I shall offer a short prayer. Our Father, we give you glory for these two who will now become one, according to your Word. Bless their union and may they have a long and happy life together."

"And many sons and daughters," everyone said. This concluded the formal wedding rite. Pastor Stephen stood aside for William and Jael to enter the room. As they passed, Pastor Stephen handed his candle to William then closed the door.

The light from the single candle fluttered as William moved around the room, setting the lamps alight. When there was light enough to see, Jael drew a breath. Two tapestries hung on the wall of the spacious room. The one from her own room and the companion piece, Ruth lying at the feet of Boaz.

Finished lighting the lamps, William set the candle on the table and turned to her. "Welcome to my room, my lady," he said, pulling her into his arms.

Across the compound, the music began again in the great hall, as the festivities continued. But in this quiet corner of the main residence, only the hiss of the burning oil could be heard above the beat of Jael's heart.

William dropped a kiss on her forehead then her nose then full on the lips. A kiss she felt all the way down to her toes. Her mind reeled as she lifted her arms to encircle his neck. She moved into his embrace, losing herself in his presence.

He drew back for a moment, capturing her gaze. "You aren't going to disappear on me, are you?"

"Oh no, William. I shall be far too distracted for that."

The End

Translation Key

O tre mis corinor – Be settled (still) my friend

se din à domior – all is well

Se lunior le amistar – Watch over him: Se (Is) lunior (to watch) le (him) amistar (over)

mis corinor – my friend

Se dun mis corinor, se dun – It is good my friend, it is good

Lune de amistar à stordor – I have longed to see you: (to see over you with longing)

O tre mis corinor, se din à domior. Se din todor ànjes. – Be still my friend, all is well. You are in good company here.

Mis adone se lunior le amistar – Watch over my love: (My love, watch over him)

Se lunior se spare ... quon se din à domior ... aberono. – Watch; wait ... when it is all well ... open

Se abo se spare ... quon se din à domior ... veni – move, walk, go: (Listen; wait ... when it is all well, travel)

Se aberono hesperado ë porsè – Believing opens the door

Reader's Guide

This book, *The Lady of the Haven* is a work of fiction meant to inspire real belief. I pray the story blessed you and touched you. Perhaps you know a William or a Jael in your real life. Perhaps, like them, you have faced adversity and struggles of your own and relied upon your faith to see you through.

As an author, my hope is to challenge readers to understand that anything is possible with a very real God. Following are some suggested discussion questions that may be appropriate for personal meditation or a small group discussion.

In the story, Jael's character has Godly roots. She believes in and serves the God of Abraham, Isaac, and Jacob. Her forebears sang the Psalms to pass them forward from one generation to the next. Their purpose? To instill in their children respect for The Almighty God.

1. As a person of faith, how are you passing the message along?

Jael goes about her daily work singing one of her favorite songs, derived from Psalm 29:1-4. Read these verses in your preferred translation of the Bible and prayerfully consider the message.

2. How could this passage help you discern the voice of God?

3. What do you think it means to give glory and strength to the Lord?

Sometimes, it seems God drops our destiny into our laps. There's no question whether it's right or wrong, we just follow the path set before us. This is what happened when Jael rescued William. Jael's life was never easy, but she had learned to trust in God for her very existence. Read and prayerfully consider Psalm 17:1-6.

4. Are you so assured of your salvation, that you would challenge God to test you and try you?

5. How can we know God hears our prayers?

In Psalm 18:1-6, we meet God, the Mighty Deliverer. If you read this passage in The Message Bible, you can experience again Jael's early journey through the towering Touri Mountains.

6. What does this passage encourage us to do when faced with life's challenges?

Though some of the disasters that befell our heroine seemed unfair and undeserved, she later realized that even in the hardest places, God watched over her.

7. In what way did Jael's capture by the Brogies save her life? What scripture does this bring to your mind?

After her rescue, Jael watches in silent desperation as her destiny moves farther away. But God has a plan for her life that she does not understand at first. In John 1:1-5, Jael is introduced to the Son of God, someone she never knew existed.

8. Do you remember the first time you were introduced to the Son of God?

Sometimes we meet "the one," but the timing is off. As a follower of *The Way*, William could never allow himself to be yoked with an unbeliever.

Sometimes God orchestrates a pause in our lives and, during that interval, an opportunity comes. A door opens. With the help of friends, Jael overcomes a crisis and is fully persuaded to believe in the Son of God. As she opens her heart to Him, the door opens to her destiny.

Read John 14:1-6 and prayerfully consider the following questions.

9. Have you ever experienced "a pause" in your life when a decision was necessary to move forward?

10. One thing is required of us. What is that one thing?

Acknowledgments

This book is dedicated to my dad, who died before its first publication. He was proud of my writing and shared my stories with anyone who would listen. He always introduced me as his "favorite daughter." Of course, I was his only daughter. I miss him and appreciate all he gave throughout his life. He helped me become who I am.

To my husband, my best friend and greatest fan, I love you and appreciate you. Thanks for your help and encouragement. You are and always will be my "King George."

Many thanks to Gregg and Hallee Bridgeman at Olivia Kimbrell Press for your many hours of labor. I thank God for you. May He bless you many times over for all you have given.

I am most grateful for my precious Heavenly Father, Who has taught me to trust Him beyond the boundaries of my own understanding. He will always exceed my expectations.

About the Author

Born in the Pacific Northwest, Betty grew up in such exotic places as West Tennessee and San Diego, California. Today, she lives in Kentucky with her husband of nearly forty years. Now semiretired, Betty spends most of her time writing, studying about writing, and critiquing other people's writing. She's served as a deaconess at her church, sung in the choir for many years, sang, danced, acted in, and helped direct a very popular Christmas play for the last nine years. She loves to travel, watch movies, read, crochet, and spend time with her family.

They have three grown and married sons living in the area, along with three daughters-in-law, four beautiful granddaughters, two handsome grandsons, one very spoiled granddog, and a semi-famous grandcat named Smith Wigglesworth.

Besides her ACFW membership where she leads a critique loop, she writes on her own blog at www.bettythomasonowens.com and is a co-writer at www.writingpromptsthoughtsideas.wordpress.com. She remains active with Bluegrass Christian Writers.

Betty contributed to the collaborative romantic comedy novella, *A Dozen Apologies*, released on Valentine's Day, 2014. Watch for the first novel in her three-book Legacy Series, *Amelia's Legacy*, late 2014 with another publisher. The second novel in the Jael of Rogan series, *A Gathering of Eagles*, is also available from Sign of the Whale Books™.

Personal Note

When I finished writing *The Lady of the Haven,* Lady Jael's spirit stuck with me. She visited my dreams and inhabited my waking hours. She whispered in my ear as I worked at my day job. What lay ahead for the healer-turned-royal princess? And so I began to write again.

I was pleasantly surprised by her progression as she fulfilled her destiny and then some. I hope you will also enjoy the second part of Jael's story told in the book, *A Gathering of Eagles.*

EXCERPT – A GATHERING OF EAGLES

A Gathering of Eagles

Enjoy this exciting excerpt from *A Gathering of Eagles*, the second novel in the Jael of Rogan series.

An icy wind pummeled Jael as she crossed the frozen tundra of the upper Touri plateau. Every few feet, she stopped and angled her head to hear whatever sounds rode upon the wind. Voices came from far away, further than her vision could take her, but she could not make them out.

As the sun cleared the mountain peaks, she stood in silent meditation, her eyes lifted to the heavens where they were greeted by a sky bowl of the purest blue. Above her an eagle soared. She lifted a fur-bound hand as if to touch the great bird and spoke in the ancient tongue, *"Mis adone se lunior le amistar."* Watch over my love. She followed its progress until it disappeared below the horizon.

In the next moment, she was caught away to the base of a watchtower. Though she had experienced this before, it still took her breath away. Briefly, she leaned against the stone structure to steady herself.

Upon the heights, a purple and gold standard fluttered in the wind. The sound carried far. It was the only sound. A door at the base of the watchtower stood ajar, and she entered. There she paused a moment, until her eyes adjusted to the deep shadow within. She found the dusty stair and began a climb which ended at the top level, where a narrow ladder of hammered iron led to the roof. On the roof, she stood at the parapet and looked out over the vastness of the northern valley. The Touris where they stood against the horizon on all sides glowed purple in the early sun. The great, wide lake was frozen solid till spring rains washed away the ice.

As she waited, her spirit cried out to God and she prayed for her beloved and the brave warriors who rode with him.

"Six full moons have risen since William and his warriors rode out upon the heels of a dark enemy. How long, Oh Lord, must I wait, without even a word of his whereabouts?"

By now, William would have been joined by his brother-in-law Lord Toldar, leader of the southern forces at Corwinder. Toldar and Lady Elizabeth had arrived in the fall along with their son, Nathaniel. He'd spent only a few days at Wrenook, his ancestral home, before leaving again to join William.

Jael descended the ladder and then the narrow dusty stairs that wound down the height of the watchtower. She pushed the door open and slipped through, drawing the hood of her cloak down over her eyes to shield them from the brightness of the sun glancing off the snow.

She ran swift and light over the frozen surface of the lake to the foot of the castle, where an age-old doorway opened to a lower level. Here, another ancient stone stair twisted its way up into the underbelly of the castle to a dark wooden door. From there she entered into a vast corridor and padded quietly toward another flight of stairs and the one room on that level where a fire burned brightly, in expectation of her arrival.

Part-way up the staircase, she heard footsteps. She paused and smiled for she recognized them as Crispus'.

"Lady Jael." His voice echoed down the long corridor.

When she turned to face him, he bowed.

"Yes, Crispus?"

"A messenger has come my lady. In your absence, he was sent up to me." He held out a small scroll. Jael descended the steps and took it from him.

"Thank you, Crispus," she said. "Pray, tell me if you knew who rode?"

He touched his fingertips together. "Aye, twas Andor son of Ruda. He sits even now at her fireside in yon kitchen. She meant to feed him well ere he returns."

She looked down at the rolled parchment and then toward the lower end of the corridor from whence came the pleasant smell of baking bread.

Crispus held out the candle he carried. "Here is a lighted candle, dear lady." She drew near and broke the seal upon the parchment, unrolled it carefully and ran her fingertips over the tidy script she recognized as her husband's own hand. She looked up into Crispus' waiting eyes.

"They are forestalled. The enemy has taken refuge in the South, away from the brutal snows of the northern Touris."

"No doubt anticipated by your honored husband."

She glanced up. "It was indeed. The hearty northerners shall give pursuit. They shall find them out and conquer them. We shall see it, Crispus. I only wish it would be sooner, rather than later."

"I too, my lady for your sake as well as my own." His lips quirked. "There are too few ears to hear the great messages I receive."

She gazed at him, saw the mischief in his eyes. "Will you accompany me to Ruda's fireside?"

"Nay my lady, I value the hair on my head too well for that."

She gave him a one-sided smile as she rolled the scroll and set off down the dark corridor. Ruda was not known for her hospitality. She barely tolerated Jael's presence in her kitchen. Jael was not offended since Ruda was so accomplished a cook, but she often wondered what Abigail would think. Jael had never met another who compared to Abigail, housekeeper at Corwinder-by-the-Sea. Dear Abigail, what a good friend you were to me.

The passageway curved around and opened out into a large room where oak beams were hung with an assortment of iron utensils, dried herbs and smoked carcasses. Goatskin bags of wine hung in the cold dark recesses near the outer wall, and kegs of grain stood one upon another in the corner. A huge fireplace glowed at one end, where a small round woman knelt. As Jael entered, a young man stood and bowed from the waist.

"My lady," he said rather loudly, apparently for his mother's sake. Ruda shot a look over her shoulder, but did not immediately rise. She wrestled with a baking pan among the coals. After another moment she pulled it free and stood, holding it carefully with leather grips. A slight curtsy and nod were all she allowed before she ran to the table.

Jael addressed the young man. "I trust you had a good journey, Andor?"

He bowed again. "Aye milady, for the deep, it were a good journey."

Midwinter, the translation immediately popped into her head. She was improving. "Very good," she said to Andor.

Ruda cut off a slab of the hot loaf for her son and ladled up a bowl of stew. She poured out a flagon of strong, dark tea and set these down with a loud clatter on the table before him. Without looking up at Jael, she turned back to the fire to finish her tasks. Andor seemed embarrassed by his mother's flagrant disregard. He glanced at the meal set before him and then back at Jael.

"Do not mind me, Andor," she said. "Please, sit down and eat whilst the food is hot. I will away to my room, but only tell me if all is well at the front."

Andor bowed a third time. "Aye, milady, 'is Majesty, Prince William fares well and afore my leave-taking, 'e did welcome the southern forces." His face brightened. "That Lord Toldar is a sight to be'old."

Jael nodded. The natives were proud of Toldar, claiming him as one of their own.

"He is indeed," she said. "You have lightened my darkness a bit Andor, and I thank you. Come to my door ere you leave and I will send an answer back with you."

"Aye milady, I will do."

She rushed to her room, but a short message was all she had time to set down, as Andor was eager to be on his way. He was at her door before she could finish the first page.

"Weather won't hold, them high passes is a stickery mess in the blains."

She handed him the sealed parchment and pressed a coin into his palm. "For a hot drink on your journey."

A deep blush colored Andor's face as he bowed before her. "Yer kindness is greatly appreciated, milady." His steps were lively and quick as he left her door. At the landing, he paused to push the coin deep into the pack he carried.

Jael shook her head and smiled. He would never spend that money.

It was some time later, a soft knock on Jael's door roused her from a fireside nap. At her answering call, Elayna pushed the door open.

"Tis time fer tea, milady."

"Is it so late already?"

The young servant smiled and placed a carved wooden tray on the table. She poured hot water into a stoneware jug and left it to steep while she stirred the fire.

"Ye was oot so very early this morn, milady. Tis no wonder ye dinna know the lateness of the hour."

Jael smiled as she stirred from her chair and tugged her shawl close around her. She watched Elayna, who was one of the first of the locals to agree to work in the castle. Ruda's eldest daughter Tamara had worked as lady's maid until her marriage. She had managed to persuade her cousin Elayna to take her place. Elayna was tall and angular, a bit too plain to attract an early proposal, but she suited Jael. The girl was fond of sewing and loved nothing better than braiding her ladyship's golden locks.

When the tea was ready, Jael poured herself a cup and sliced off a chunk of Ruda's famous stonebread, a round loaf shaped like a stone and nearly as hard outside, but light and feathery inside. Spread with a generous portion of clotted cheese, Jael thought it was delicious.

Elayna rearranged the logs in the fireplace with the help of a poker and piled on more wood. "Ye did see my cousin return, I ken? What word had he of the warriors?"

Jael touched her lips with the soft towel that had covered the bread. "They fare well for now. The deep cold has stalled the attacks from the enemy. It seems Din Glun's men are not winter-hardy."

Elayna's quick intake of air at the mention of the name caught Jael's attention. These mountain folk were so superstitious. She watched with interest as the girl hurriedly cast ashes about the hearth in an attempt to assuage the evil powers induced by the utterance of the name.

What Jael knew of him, William had written in a letter.

His people call him Din Glun, which means of the sun. Descended of a great family of nomads who made their way slowly across the deepest desert and into the North by way of the Santouri River, it seemed to make no difference to them whether he was good or evil. They worship the sun, so in their opinion, anyone with such strength and power must have descended from there.

"Din Glun has amassed an army of bandits and outlaws; outcasts in their own land. They strike whatever targets promise the greatest return – ships at sea, caravans or entire villages. There seems to be no way to stop him. Even an army pursuing him from the southern cape could not catch him. His army would disband into the foothills and rejoin in the river valley. It seems impossible to follow their trail.

She had been especially interested in the personal description of the man. William knew she would be, so he provided great detail.

Din Glun stands just over five feet tall. He is thin and wiry, but very strong, with long dark hair and a filthy beard that covers most of his swarthy face. He chews a dark leafy substance that blackens his lips and gives his eyes a wild look. Survivors of his onslaughts are few, but those who manage it call him a devil. In those places, the name of Din Glun has become synonymous with the word for "evil one."

She sipped her tea and stared into the flames. The people of Cragmorton never laid eyes upon the man, nor even any of his footmen, but they had heard the tales told and their "livers were full," *worrisome* fears. She returned her cup to the tray and moved to the table where the note lay open. She touched the paper and whispered a prayer. She would not give in to fear. Her liver would not be full.

Betty Thomason Owens blog

www.bettythomasonowens.com

The Writing Prompts blog

www.writingpromptsthoughtsideas.wordpress.com

i. Psalms 29:1-4, Young's Literal Translation (paraphrased)

ii. Psalms 29:1-11, Young's Literal Translation (paraphrased)

iii. Psalms 30:1-5, Young's Literal Translation (paraphrased)

iv. John 14:1, Young's Literal Translation

v. John 1:1-5, Young's Literal Translation

vi. Psalms 18:1-6, Young's Literal Translation (paraphrased)

vii. John 14:1-4, 6, Young's Literal Translation, (paraphrased)

viii. Psalms 30:1-5, Young's Literal Translation, (paraphrased)

ix. Psalms 17:1-6, Young's Literal Translation, (paraphrased)

www.ingramcontent.com/pod-product-compliance
Lightning Source LLC
Chambersburg PA
CBHW060404180626
46817CB00007B/2515